THE
JACKAL

**Center Point
Large Print**

**This Large Print Book carries the
Seal of Approval of N.A.V.H.**

THE JACKAL

THE BLACK DAGGER BROTHERHOOD
— PRISON CAMP —

J. R. WARD

CENTER POINT LARGE PRINT
THORNDIKE, MAINE

This book is dedicated to all of the essential workers who have kept us going during the COVID-19 pandemic, especially those in the healthcare sector who have endangered their own lives to help others.
We are so grateful to you.

GLOSSARY OF TERMS AND PROPER NOUNS

ahstrux nohtrum (n.) Private guard with license to kill who is granted his or her position by the King.

ahvenge (v.) Act of mortal retribution, carried out typically by a male loved one.

Black Dagger Brotherhood (pr. n.) Highly trained vampire warriors who protect their species against the Lessening Society. As a result of selective breeding within the race, Brothers possess immense physical and mental strength, as well as rapid healing capabilities. They are not siblings for the most part, and are inducted into the Brotherhood upon nomination by the Brothers. Aggressive, self-reliant, and secretive by nature, they are the subjects of legend and objects of reverence within the vampire world. They may be killed only by the most serious of wounds, e.g., a gunshot or stab to the heart, etc.

blood slave (n.) Male or female vampire who has been subjugated to serve the blood needs of another. The practice of keeping blood slaves has been outlawed.

the Chosen (pr. n.) Female vampires who had

7

been bred to serve the Scribe Virgin. In the past, they were spiritually rather than temporally focused, but that changed with the ascendance of the final Primale, who freed them from the Sanctuary. With the Scribe Virgin removing herself from her role, they are completely autonomous and learning to live on earth. They do continue to meet the blood needs of unmated members of the Brotherhood, as well as Brothers who cannot feed from their *shellans* and injured fighters.

chrih (n.) Symbol of honorable death in the Old Language.

cohntehst (n.) Conflict between two males competing for the right to be a female's mate.

Dhunhd (pr. n.) Hell.

doggen (n.) Member of the servant class within the vampire world. *Doggen* have old, conservative traditions about service to their superiors, following a formal code of dress and behavior. They are able to go out during the day, but they age relatively quickly. Life expectancy is approximately five hundred years.

ehros (n.) A Chosen trained in the matter of sexual arts.

exhile dhoble (n.) The evil or cursed twin, the one born second.

the Fade (pr. n.) Nontemporal realm where the

dead reunite with their loved ones and pass eternity.

First Family (pr. n.) The King and Queen of the vampires, and any children they may have.

ghardian (n.) Custodian of an individual. There are varying degrees of *ghardians*, with the most powerful being that of a *sehcluded* female.

glymera (n.) The social core of the aristocracy, roughly equivalent to Regency England's *ton*.

hellren (n.) Male vampire who has been mated to a female. Males may take more than one female as mate.

hyslop (n. or v.) Term referring to a lapse in judgment, typically resulting in the compromise of the mechanical operations of a vehicle or otherwise motorized conveyance of some kind. For example, leaving one's keys in one's car as it is parked outside the family home overnight, whereupon said vehicle is stolen.

leahdyre (n.) A person of power and influence.

leelan (adj. or n.) A term of endearment loosely translated as "dearest one."

Lessening Society (pr. n.) Order of slayers convened by the Omega for the purpose of eradicating the vampire species.

lesser (n.) De-souled human who targets vampires for extermination as a member of the Lessening Society. *Lessers* must be stabbed through the chest in order to be killed; otherwise they are ageless. They do not eat or drink and are impotent. Over time, their hair, skin, and irises lose pigmentation until they are blond, blushless, and pale-eyed. They smell like baby powder. Inducted into the society by the Omega, they retain a ceramic jar thereafter into which their heart was placed after it was removed.

lewlhen (n.) Gift.

lheage (n.) A term of respect used by a sexual submissive to refer to their dominant.

Lhenihan (pr. n.) A mythic beast renowned for its sexual prowess. In modern slang, refers to a male of preternatural size and sexual stamina.

lys (n.) Torture tool used to remove the eyes.

mahmen (n.) Mother. Used both as an identifier and a term of affection.

mhis (n.) The masking of a given physical environment; the creation of a field of illusion.

nalla (n., f.) or **nallum** (n., m.) Beloved.

needing period (n.) Female vampire's time of fertility, generally lasting for two days and accompanied by intense sexual cravings. Occurs approximately five years after a female's transition and then once a decade thereafter. All males respond to some degree if they are around a female in her need. It can be a dangerous time, with conflicts and fights breaking out between competing males, particularly if the female is not mated.

newling (n.) A virgin.

the Omega (pr. n.) Malevolent, mystical figure who has targeted the vampires for extinction out of resentment directed toward the Scribe Virgin. Exists in a nontemporal realm and has extensive powers, though not the power of creation.

phearsom (adj.) Term referring to the potency of a male's sexual organs. Literal translation something close to "worthy of entering a female."

Princeps (pr. n.) Highest level of the vampire aristocracy, second only to members of the First Family or the Scribe Virgin's Chosen. Must be born to the title; it may not be conferred.

pyrocant (n.) Refers to a critical weakness in an individual. The weakness can be internal, such as an addiction, or external, such as a lover.

rahlman (n.) Savior.

rythe (n.) Ritual manner of asserting honor granted by one who has offended another. If accepted, the offended chooses a weapon and strikes the offender, who presents him- or herself without defenses.

the Scribe Virgin (pr. n.) Mystical force who previously was counselor to the King as

11

well as the keeper of vampire archives and the dispenser of privileges. Existed in a nontemporal realm and had extensive powers, but has recently stepped down and given her station to another. Capable of a single act of creation, which she expended to bring the vampires into existence.

sehclusion (n.) Status conferred by the King upon a female of the aristocracy as a result of a petition by the female's family. Places the female under the sole direction of her *ghardian*, typically the eldest male in her household. Her *ghardian* then has the legal right to determine all manner of her life, restricting at will any and all interactions she has with the world.

shellan (n.) Female vampire who has been mated to a male. Females generally do not take more than one mate due to the highly territorial nature of bonded males.

symphath (n.) Subspecies within the vampire race characterized by the ability and desire to manipulate emotions in others (for the purposes of an energy exchange), among other traits. Historically, they have been discriminated against and, during certain eras, hunted by vampires. They are near extinction.

talhman (n.) The evil side of an individual. A dark stain on the soul that requires expression if it is not properly expunged.

the Tomb (pr. n.) Sacred vault of the Black Dagger Brotherhood. Used as a ceremonial site as well as a storage facility for the jars of *lessers*. Ceremonies performed there include inductions, funerals, and disciplinary actions against Brothers. No one may enter except for members of the Brotherhood, the Scribe Virgin, or candidates for induction.

trahyner (n.) Word used between males of mutual respect and affection. Translated loosely as "beloved friend."

transition (n.) Critical moment in a vampire's life when he or she transforms into an adult. Thereafter, he or she must drink the blood of the opposite sex to survive and is unable to withstand sunlight. Occurs generally in the mid-twenties. Some vampires do not survive their transitions, males in particular. Prior to their transitions, vampires are physically weak, sexually unaware and unresponsive, and unable to dematerialize.

vampire (n.) Member of a species separate from that of Homo sapiens. Vampires must drink the blood of the opposite sex to survive. Human blood will keep them alive, though the strength does not last long. Following their transitions, which occur in their mid-twenties, they are unable to go out into sunlight and must feed from the vein regularly. Vampires cannot "convert" humans through a bite or transfer of blood, though they are in rare cases able to breed with the other species. Vampires can dematerialize at will, though they must be able to calm themselves and concentrate to do so and may not carry anything heavy with them. They are able to strip the memories of humans, provided such memories are short-term. Some vampires are able to read minds. Life expectancy is upward of a thousand years, or in some cases, even longer.

wahlker (n.) An individual who has died and returned to the living from the Fade. They are accorded great respect and are revered for their travails.

whard (n.) Equivalent of a godfather or god-mother to an individual.

CHAPTER ONE

Western New York State, Present Day

The whole "life is a highway" metaphor was so ubiquitous, so overused, so threadbare and torn-patched, that as Nyx sat in the passenger side of a ten-year-old station wagon, and stared at the moonlit asphalt trail cutting through brush and bramble in western New York State, she wasn't thinking a damn thing about how similar the course of roads and lives could be: You could get sweet-sailing easy declines of coasting. Bad, bumpy, rough patches that rattled your teeth. Uphill hauls that you thought would never end. Bored stretches between far-apart exits.

And then there were the obstacles, the ones that came from out of nowhere and carried you so far off your planned trip that you ended up in a completely different place.

Some of these, both in the analogy and in fact, had four legs and a kid named Bambi.

"Watch out!" she yelled as she clapped a hand on the steering wheel and took control.

Too late. Over the screeching of tires, the impact was sickeningly soft, the kind of thing that happened when steel hit flesh, and her

15

sister's response was to cover her eyes and tuck in her knees.

Not helpful considering Posie was the one with the access to the brake pedal. But also completely in character.

The station wagon, being an inanimate object set into motion, had no brain of its own, but plenty of motivation from the sixty-two miles an hour they'd been going. As such, the old Volvo went bucking bronco as they left the rural byway, its stiff, cumbersome body heaving into a series of hill-and-dale dance moves that had Nyx hitting her head on the padded roof even though she was belted in.

The headlights strobed what was in front of the car, the beams point-and-shooting in whatever direction and angle the front grille happened to be thrown in. For the most part, there was just a leafy morass of bushes, the green, spongy territory a far better outcome than she would have predicted.

That all changed.

Like a creature rising out of the depths of a lake, something brown, thick, and vertical was teased in the verdant light show, disappearing and reappearing as the shafts of illumination willy'd-their-nilly around.

Oh, shit. It was a tree. And not only was the arboreal hard-stop an immovable object, it was as if a steel crank-chain ran between its thick trunk and the undercarriage of the station wagon.

If you'd steered for a collision course, you couldn't have done a better job.

Inevitable covered it.

Nyx's only thought was for her sister. Posie was braced in the driver's seat, her arms straight out, fingers splayed, like she was going to try to push the tree away—

The impact was like being punched all over the body, and there must have been a crunch of metal meeting wood, but with the airbags deploying and the ringing in Nyx's ears, she couldn't hear much. Couldn't breathe well. Couldn't seem to see.

Hissing. Dripping. Burned rubber and something chemical.

Someone was coughing. Her? She couldn't be sure.

"Posie?"

"I'm okay, I'm okay . . ."

Nyx rubbed her stinging eyes and coughed. Fumbling for the door, she popped the release and shoved hard against some kind of resistance. "I'm coming around to help you."

Assuming she could get out of the damn car.

Putting her shoulder into the effort, she forced the door through something fluffy and green, and the payback was that the bush barged in, expanding into the car like a dog that wanted to sniff around.

She fell out of her seat and rolled onto the scruff. All-four'ing it for a spell, she managed to get up onto her feet and steady herself on the roof as she went around to the driver's side. Peeling open Posie's door, she released the seat belt.

"I got you," she grunted as she dragged her sister out.

Propping Posie against the car, she cleared the blond hair back from those soft features. No blood. No glass in the perfect skin. Nose was still straight as a pin.

"You're okay," Nyx announced.

"What about the deer?"

Nyx kept the curses to herself. They were about ten miles from home, and what mattered was whether the car was drivable. No offense to Mother Nature and animal-lovers anywhere, but that four-legged scourge of the interstate was low on her list of priorities.

Stumbling to the front, she shook her head at the damage. A good two feet of the hood—and, therefore, engine—was compressed around a trunk that had all the flexibility of an I beam, and she was hardly an automotive expert, but that had to be incompatible with vroom-vroom, home safe.

"Shit," she breathed.

"What about the deer?"

Closing her eyes, she reminded herself about the birth order. She was the older, responsible one, black-haired and brusque like their father had been. Posie was the blond, good-hearted youngest, who had all the warmth and sunny nature that their *mahmen* had possessed.

And the middle?

She couldn't go down the Janelle rabbit hole right now.

Back over at her open door, Nyx leaned in and moved the deflated airbag out of the way. Where was her phone? She'd put it in a cupholder after she'd texted their grandfather as they'd left Hannaford. Great. Nowhere to be found—

"Thank God."

Bracing her hand on the seat, she went down into the wheel well. And got a palm full of bad news.

The screen was cracked and the unit dark. When she tried to fire the thing up, it was a no go. Straightening, she looked over the ruined hood. "Posie, where is your—"

"What?" Her sister was focused on the road that was a good fifty yards away, her stick-straight hair tangled down her back. "Huh?"

"Your phone. Where is it?"

Posie glanced over her shoulder. "I left it at home. You had yours, so I just, you know."

"You need to dematerialize back to the farm-house. Tell grandfather to bring the tow truck and—"

"I'm not leaving here until we take care of that deer."

"Posie, there are too many humans around here and—"

"It's suffering!" Tears glistened. "And just because it's an animal doesn't mean its life doesn't matter."

"Fuck the deer." Nyx glared across the steaming mess. "We need to solve this problem now—"

"I'm not leaving until—"

"—because we have two hundred dollars of groceries melting in the back. We can't afford to lose a week's worth of—"

"—we take care of that poor animal."

Nyx swung her eyes away from her sister, the crash, the crap she had to fix so goddamn Posie could continue to give her heart out to the world and worry about things other than how to pay the rent, keep food on the table, and make sure they had such exotic luxuries as electricity and running water.

When she trusted herself to look back without hurling a bunch of be-practical f-bombs at her fricking sister, she saw absolutely no change in Posie's resolve. And this was the problem. A sweet nature, yes. That annoying, bleeding-heart, emphatic bullcrap, yes. Iron will? When it came it down to it, boatloads.

That female was not budging on the deer thing.

Nyx threw up her hands and cursed—loudly.

Back in the car. Opening the glove box. Taking out the nine millimeter handgun she kept there for emergencies.

As she came around the rear of the station

wagon, she eyed the reusable grocery bags. They were crammed up against the bench seat as a result of the crash, and it was a good news/bad news situation. Anything breakable was done for, but at least the cold items were cloistered together, united in a fight against the eighty-degree August night.

"Oh, thank you, Nyx." Posie clasped her hands under her chin like she was doing a devotional. "We'll help the—wait, what are you doing with the gun?"

Nyx didn't stop as she passed by, so Posie grabbed her arm. "Why do you have the gun?"

"What do you think I'm going to do to the damn thing? Give it CPR?"

"No! We need to help it—"

Nyx put her face into her sister's and spoke in a dead tone. "If it's suffering, I'm going to put it down. It's the right thing to do. That *is* the way I will help that animal."

Posie's hands went to her face, pressing into cheeks that had gone pale. "It's my fault. I hit the deer."

"It was an accident." Nyx turned her sister around to face the station wagon. "Stay here and don't look. I'll take care of it."

"I didn't mean to hurt the—"

"You're the last person on the planet who'd intentionally hurt anything. Now stay the hell here."

The sound of Posie softly crying escorted Nyx back toward the road. Following the tire gouges in the dirt and the ruined foliage, she found the deer about fifteen feet away from where they'd veered off—

Nyx stopped dead in her tracks. Blinked a couple of times.

Considered vomiting.

It wasn't a deer.

Those were arms. And legs. Thin ones, granted, and covered with mud-colored clothes that were in rags. But nothing about what had been struck was animal in nature. Worse? The scent of the blood that had been spilled was not human.

It was a vampire.

They'd hit one of their own.

Nyx ran over to the body, put the gun away, and knelt down. "Are you okay?"

Dumbass question. But the sound of her voice roused the injured, a horrific and horrified face turning up to her.

It was a male. A pretrans male. And oh, God, the whites of both his eyes had gone red, although she couldn't tell whether it was because of the blood running down his face or some kind of internal brain injury. What was clear? He was dying.

"Help . . . me . . ." The thin reedy voice was interrupted by weak coughing. "Out of . . . prison . . . hide me . . ."

"Nyx?" Posie called out. "What's happening?"

For a split second, Nyx couldn't think. No, that was a lie. She was thinking, just not about the car, the groceries, the kid who was dying, or her hysterical sister.

"Where," Nyx said urgently. "Where's the camp?"

Maybe after all these years . . . she could find out where Janelle had been taken.

This had to be Fate.

According to the history that had been explained to the Jackal, "Hungry Like the Wolf" was a musical "single" released in 1982 in the US by the British "new wave" sensation Duran Duran. The video, evidently working off an Indiana Jones theme—whatever that was—was put into heavy rotation on "MTV," and that "television airplay" shot the song onto the *Billboard* charts and kept it there for months.

As he whispered through one of the prison camp's countless subterranean tunnels, he heard the song and revisited its identifying tidbits like he was rereading a book he had memorized. But that was the nature of information down here. The mind yearned and churned for input, yet there was rarely anything new. Thus one had to replay things, just as his fellow inmate had to replay the song on that "cassette" tape player.

Moving along, the Jackal was of the shadows as he tracked the tinny refrain echoing off the damp stone walls. He recalled that he had been told of the "video." Simon Le Bon, evidently the lead singer, had been garbed in a pale linen suit and had gone through many crowded streets in a tropical locale. After which he had proceeded into the jungle, and into a river . . . all the while being pursued by a beautiful woman—or was it the other way around?

'Lo, the drama and intrigue.

And how he missed the outside world.

One hundred years after his incarceration, the world above, the freedom, the fresh air . . . were like the garbled sound of that song: dulled by time's passing and a lack of real-time refresh.

The Jackal made a turn and entered the block of cells he had long been assigned to. The barred cages they were relegated to dwell in were set at intervals into the rock, although the gates to each remained open. With the guards prowling around, monsters in the dark, there was no need to lock anything. No one dared to leave.

Death would be a blessing compared to what the Command would do to you if you tried to escape.

The source of the ghostly song, now nearing the end of its run, was three cells down, and he stopped in the archway of the prisoner in question. "You get caught with that, they're going to—"

"Do what? Throw my ass in jail?"

The male who spoke was reclining on his pallet, his huge body in a relaxed sprawl, nothing but a cloth tied around his hips hiding his sex. Unblinking, yellow eyes stared upward from the horizontal, and the sly smile showed long, sharp fangs.

Lucan was a laconic sonofabitch, slightly evil and maybe untrustworthy. But compared to so many of the others, he was a prince of a guy.

"Just watching out for you." The Jackal nodded at the silver-and-black cassette player that was tucked into the male's side. "And your little machine."

"Everyone's at the Hive, including the guards."

"You roll the dice too much, my friend."

"And you, Jackal, are too much of a rule abider."

As the song came to the end, Lucan hit the rewind button, and there was a whirring sound. Then the soft music started up again.

"What are you going to do when that tape breaks?"

The male with the alter ego shrugged. "I have it now. That's all that matters."

Wolven were a tricky, dangerous subspecies, and that was true whether they were loose to roam the night up above or stuck down here in prison. But the Command had a solution for keeping the male's other side in check—and it happened to be the same thing used for all prisoners. A heavy collar of steel was locked around the male's thick throat, preventing him from dematerializing or changing.

"Better run along, Jackal." One of those yellow eyes winked. "Don't want to get in trouble."

"Just turn that thing down. I don't want to have to rescue you."

"Who's asking you to."

"Burdens of conscience."

"I wouldn't know about that."

"Lucky you. Life is a lot more complicated with them."

Leaving his comrade behind, he continued on, passing by his own cell and hooking up with the main thoroughfare. As he closed in on the Hive, the density of the air increased, the scents of the prison population thick in his sinuses, the murmuring of hushed voices registering in his ears—

The first of the screams sizzled through the hush, pricking the hairs at the nape of his neck, tightening the powerful muscles of his shoulders.

As he arrived at the great open area, his eyes peered over the thousand scruffy heads, to the three bloodstained tree trunks that had been cemented into the raised stone ledge down in front. The prisoner who was strapped to the center post was writhing against the chains that held him in place, his bloodshot eyes wide with terror at the woven basket at his feet.

Something inside the basket was moving.

A pair of guards in clean black uniforms stood on either side of the accused, their faces set with the kind of deadly calm that a person should truly fear. It meant they didn't value life in the slightest. Whether a prisoner lived or died was of no concern to them. They did their jobs, and went to their quarters at the end of their shifts secure in the knowledge that, whatever pain they'd caused, whatever destruction, whatever harm, had been done in the line of duty.

No matter the depravity, their consciences were clear.

Something that stupid wolf needed to consider as he flouted the fucking rules like he did.

The ragged, grungy crowd was abuzz with adrenaline, bodies banging into each other as heads turned and talked and then refocused, eager for the show. These little "corrections" were given out by the Command on a regular basis, part bloodthirsty exhibition, part behavioral modification.

If you'd asked any of the prisoners, male or female, they would have said they hated these regular public tortures, but they'd be lying—at least partially so. In the crushing boredom and soul-numbing hopelessness down here, they were breaks in the monotony.

A theatrical show that was everyone's favorite program.

Then again, it wasn't like there was much else on Broadway.

Unlike the rest of the prisoners, the Jackal

shifted his eyes to one side of the ledge. He sensed that the Command was attending in person tonight—or perhaps it was today. He didn't know whether it was light or dark outside.

The presence of their leader was unusual and he wondered if anyone else noticed. Probably not. The Command was keeping themselves hidden, but they liked these displays of their power.

As the lid on the basket was lifted by one of the guards, the Jackal closed his eyes. The piercing scream that echoed around the Hive made the marrow of his bones ache. And then came the scent of fresh blood.

He had to get the fuck out of here. He was dying on the inside: He had no faith left. No love. No hope that anything would ever change.

But it would take a miracle to free him, and if his life had taught him anything, those never happened on earth. And rarely, if ever, up in the Fade, either.

As the crowd began to chant, and all he could smell was that blood, he wheeled away from the spectacle and stumbled back into the main tunnel. Even in his despair, and in spite of the countless males and females packed into the cave, he could feel the eyes that followed his departure.

The Command watched him and him alone.

Always.

CHAPTER TWO

Caldwell, New York

R hage was living his best frickin' life as he made the most important decision of the night.

"Rocky Road," he announced. "Definitely Rocky Road."

As he got out the two bowls and the two spoons that were Designated For Special Use, his daughter, Bitty, leaned into the old school trunk freezer and snagged the half gallon he'd picked. Then she narrowed her eyes on the thirty or so other choices.

"And what're you feeling tonight?" he asked as he braced a hip on the counter and settled in to wait.

You did not interfere in another's ice cream decision. No matter how long it took, no matter what the outcome, this was a sacred moment, a melding of mood and palate, whim and whimsy. It was not to be rushed or influenced unduly by third-party outsiders, even if said hangers-on were parental in nature.

"What are we watching tonight?" his daughter asked.

For a moment, he got lost staring at her wavy

brown hair and slender shoulders. She was wearing one of his black button-downs, and the thing was a full-length dress on her, the hem of the shirt reaching her ankles, the folds enveloping her like ceremonial robes. She'd rolled up the sleeves, and there was so much excess material around her thin upper arms that she looked like she was sporting bat-winged baby waders for the pool. But she loved his shirts and he loved that she wanted to wear them.

He loved every part of his daughter, especially the way she looked up to him—and not because he was three feet taller than her in his shitkickers. In her eyes, he was a superhero. A protector of the race. A fighter who took care of the innocent, the infirm, the less capable.

All of which was true given his role in the Black Dagger Brotherhood. He was on the front line of defense between the species and any and all who would hurt them. But he felt stronger thanks to her. More powerful. Better prepared.

He did not feel invincible, however. Oh, fuck no on the invincibility. As with all things good, there was a balance, and when it came to Bitty, in spite of the purpose and strength she gave him, his daughter made him realize his mortality to a painful degree.

He was more afraid of dying than ever before.

"Dad?"

Rhage shook himself. "Huh? Oh, the movie. I'm thinking *Zombieland: Double Tap*."

"Then mint chocolate chip." The decisiveness made Rhage smile. "And Ben & Jerry's Minter Wonderland, not the Breyers."

As Bitty palmed her choice and straightened, the glass door slid back into place with a bump, closing off the cold. "I'm not sure I need a bowl, though. This is just a pint."

Rhage looked down at what he was holding. He was surprisingly disappointed. They always used their bowls and spoons, which was why Fritz, the butler, kept the two pairs right here, in this far corner of the kitchen. It was part of the ritual.

"Well, then I won't use one, either." He put their normal bowls aside, opened a drawer, and got out two dish towels. "Let's wrap 'em up in this."

He tossed one to his daughter, traded her a spoon for his half gallon, and they were off, walking through the hotel-sized kitchen, outing via the pantry. As they emerged at the base of the foyer's grand staircase, he put a hand on Bits's shoulder.

"I'm glad I'm off tonight."

"Me, too, dad. How's your foot? Are you okay?"

"Oh, yeah. No worries." He kept the pain and the limp to himself. "Bone's going to heal just fine. Manny took care of it."

31

"He's a good human."

"He is."

They walked up the red-carpeted steps together. In spite of the Your Majesty decor, all that gold leafing and the crystal, those marble columns and the painted ceiling high above, this was home. This was where the Black Dagger Brotherhood lived with their families and took care of Wrath, Beth, and L.W. This was where the best lives for all of them transpired, here under this heavy roof, here within these stout stone walls, here protected by the *mhis* that Vishous threw.

A fortress.

A fucking vault, which was where precious things belonged, safe from theft or destruction.

The movie theater was way down on the second floor, past the Hall of Statues, out into the staff wing. Given that it was after twelve, on a work night, no one was around. The fighters on rotation were out in the field. The injured who needed treatment or rehab were in the training center. And the staff were on break to eat after having cooked, served, and cleaned up First Meal. Meanwhile, Mary was in session with Zsadist down in the basement. Wrath and Beth were playing with L.W. up on the third floor. And the other *shellans* and kiddos were in the bouncy castle out by the pool.

So it was nice and quiet.

The movie theater was a professional gig:

Stadium seating with padded leather ass-palaces. A candy counter and popcorn machine maintained, as everything was, by Fritz. A huge screen, framed by red velvet drapes, that had just been updated. Dolby surround sound and then some, with the kind of woofers that made you feel the T. rex's footfalls in *Jurassic Park* all the way through your marrow.

Rhage and Bitty took the two seats right in the middle, halfway up the rows. It was where they'd sat the night before, so the remotes to the computer system were in the drink cupholder between them.

Work of a moment to rent the movie on Amazon and get things rolling.

As they popped their lids and settled in, Rhage exhaled long and slow.

Perfect. This was just—

"Cheers, dad."

Bitty was holding out her spoon, and Rhage clinked his against it. "Cheers, daughter."

In the dark, as the adventure in the movie began, Rhage smiled so wide that he forgot about the ice cream. Everything was right in the world. All circles completed. Nothing gray in any area of his life.

He had his daughter.

He had his beloved *shellan*.

He had his brothers and his buddies.

Yes, there was stress, and the threat to the

species continued, and the fucking humans were always up to shit. But he felt like his life was similar to this fortress of a house.

Solid against the storms and assaults of Fate.

Capable of withstanding anything that was thrown at it.

It was the first and only time he had ever felt like this, and it made him believe, deep in his bones, that no matter what, nothing was going to change. His Mary was his heart and soul. His Bitty, his future and his hope. His brothers and friends, the limbs on his body.

And what a wonderful thing that all was.

Digging into his Rocky Road . . . he had no idea what was coming his way. If he had, he would have chosen a much different ice cream.

Like motherfucking vanilla.

Caldwell, New York, 1913

"Oh, but she was a lovely one, she was. And her sister. Right?"

As Jabon the Younger went on about things that had been already forgotten by the party being addressed by him, a sense of restless boredom crept up Rhage's body sure as if it was sewage seeping through the floorboards of the pub. Indeed, he had to relieve himself not just of this tedious company, but the place he was in. The air here was thick with the sour sweat of raucous

34

patrons and the cloying mead from the tankards that abounded in every meaty fist.

Jabon leaned in. "Tell me what you did to them."

Rhage focused on two drunkards seated upon stools across the crowded cramp of the establishment. They were humans with beards thick as dog fur and clothing the color of manure. Unsteady from their imbibing, their shoulders bumped and separated by turns, the contacts a metronome counting down until the inevitable fight erupted.

"Wouldnae you speak, then." Jabon moved his chair closer and put his smooth, pampered hand upon Rhage's forearm—but he reconsidered this impulse as Rhage shifted his gaze over. Immediately, he retracted the feather weight. "But you conquested them both. At the same time, presently. You must tell me what it was like."

Rhage returned to the two laborers over there on the stools. Things were coming to a boil, and he was concerned one or both were armed.

"Are you coming on this next eve, at least? Unto my home? You will find further conquests, I promise you."

The laborer on the left, the one with the darker hair, whipped his face toward his compatriot. Brows furrowed, chin extended, face red as a barn door, he sputtered what couldnae be aught but curses. And then he shoved up to his feet, steady as a two-legged table. Called unto confrontation, his compatriot promptly lurched off onto his own boots.

A push. A shove. And then the hand of the one who had started it went inside his sloppily made coat.

"—you must come on the morrow. I have told many you will be in attendance. And I promise, there will be females of availability—"

Rhage clamped a grip on the back of Jabon's finely constructed high-collar jacket. Shoving the male down under the table, Rhage ducked as well as the first lead shot rang out. With the discharge of the gun, the drunken joviality of the establishment lost its ebullience. There was no shouting in alarm, however. This was not the first time such had happened and humans commenced to take cover as if they had been well-drilled in the response.

Beneath the table, Jabon's pale eyes widened and he clutched his fine coating tightly, pulling the lapels up close to the front of his throat as a fragile chain mail of wool and silk and cotton.

There was an ensuing rustle of bodies and shuffling of feet, the crowd scrambling to duck under oak tables and chairs, beside the stone hearth, behind the bar—although that latter was stopped by a barman with his own gun who held his turf with greater interest than whatever was occurring within his pub. 'Twas a good businessman, that one.

"What shall we do?" Jabon put his face all the way down on the rough, stained floorboards. "What shall we do, what shall we do . . ."

Rhage rolled his eyes. The danger would not last long and he was right. Three shots off and it was done.

Through the sturdy table legs and the twisted bramble patches of upended chairs, Rhage assessed the damage with little interest. Both combatants were down and unmoving so he sat up and stretched, rotating his bad arm. Jabon stayed down as if he had taken up a new pursuit of becoming a carpet. Most of the others did the same.

The door to the pub opened and closed as someone entered. Rhage did not pay that any mind. This human establishment was known only for trouble of their variety. The enemy did not come upon this theater of human depravity often, as lessers did not court with them if they could avoid it. The same was true for vampires, although members of the species could pass far easier among the rats without tails. And one did wish for adventure.

Adventure was all one had, really.

The human mat formed by all those who had sought to avoid the bullets began to break apart as heads were lifted and torsos tentatively rose.

The curling impatience as characteristic to

Rhage's corporeal confines as his blond hair and his blue-green eyes took its cue and weaved through his muscles and his bones. Ever on the move, he turned to take his leave not only of the humans and their silliness, but of Jabon's incessant nagging—

The strike came from the left and it was a full-body one, something large and heavy taking Rhage back down to the floor. It was whilst he hung for the briefest of moments in midair that he noted two things: One, as his vision swung 'round, he witnessed a bullet passing through the space from which his flesh and blood had been forcefully vacated, the lead slug burrowing into the oak paneling of the pub's homely wall, creating a circled coffin for its honed metal body.

The second realization was that Rhage knew who had come upon him.

His savior was not a surprise, either.

The landing was hard as he bore both his own heft and another's of similar tonnage, but he cared not about the bruising. Looking through the forest of table and leg anew, he eyed the resumed skirmish whereby the initiating combatant, briefly resurrected, had raised his gun once more and attempted to ensure death had indeed arrived upon his fellow drunkard.

The threat he represented was currently being addressed by the other patrons, however. Several jumped on him and disarmed him.

Rhage was able to take a deeper breath as the boulder upon him was removed. And then a hand extended toward him to help him up.

He laughed and accepted the lift. "That was rather fun!"

Darius, son of Marklon, did not, evidently, feel the same. The brother's blue eyes were the color of slate from disapproval. "Your definition of that word and mine are not the same—"

"You must come as well!"

Rhage and his brother in service both looked down at Jabon, who had popped up from under the table like a gopher from a hole.

The cloying aristocrat clapped his hands. "Yes, yes, you as well. On the morrow's eve at my home. You know where it is, do you not?"

"We shall be working, I'm afraid," Darius announced.

"Aye," Rhage said, though he had no particular plans.

"There will be females of noble blood."

"Of noble complication, you mean." Rhage shook his head. "They are a bore in too many regards to consider."

Darius hitched a hand under Rhage's arm and led the way to the pub's door. When Jabon sought to join, all that was required was a stern stare over the shoulder and the male was cured of the impulse to exit à trois.

Outside, the moon draped the village landscape

in a shimmering illumination, the contours of the brick and timber buildings of commerce glowing in a saintly way, as if they had converted their purpose away from the base, temporal concern of money. Summer was in its early bloom of June, the leaves on the trees in the square fully unfurled, yet of a pale green. Jade, as opposed to the deep emerald of August.

"Whate'er you doing in such a place," Darius demanded as they walked off over the cobblestones.

"The same question could be asked of thee."

Rhage's counter had no censure in it. Not only did he not bother himself with the concerns of others, he well knew of Darius's reputation for decency of thought and action. The paragon of virtue would no sooner partake of debauchery than he would cut off his own dagger hand.

"I am in search of workmen," the brother stated.

"For what purpose?"

"I have in mind to construct a house of great safety and security."

Rhage frowned. "Is not your current abode sufficient?"

"It will be for another purpose."

"And you would use humans to construct such a place? You'd have to dispose of your workforce when it was finished, one grave at a time."

"I search for workmen of our kind."

"No such luck in that pub, then."

"I knew not where else to go. Our species is too scattered. One cannot find oneself in this morass of humans."

"Sometimes it is best to remain unseen."

As a series of bells began to ring out across the flower-scented night, Rhage looked to the clock tower of Caldwell's square. Stopping, he started to smile as he recalled a rather comely female of obliging countenance who lived three blocks over.

"Forgive me, my brother, I have somewhere I need to be."

Darius halted as well. " 'Tis not out to hunt, I presume."

"There is time on the morrow." Rhage shrugged. "This war will ne'er be over."

"With your commitment to the conflict, you are correct."

As Darius turned away, Rhage caught the male's elbow. "I shall have you know, I took down two lessers this midnight, or do you think this ink stain is indeed ink?"

Rhage presented the sleeve of his calfskin coat for regard. But Darius's stare did not drop thereto.

"Well done, my brother," the male said in a level tone. "I am so proud of you."

At that, Darius reclaimed his arm and stalked off, heading down to the river's shore. Left to

41

his own, Rhage glared at the space the brother had taken up. Then he departed in the opposite direction.

It was some distance before he could calm himself sufficiently to dematerialize unto the female who had never turned away his carnal inclinations. He told himself the emotion that plagued and delayed him was anger at the self-righteousness of that brother.

'Twas a lie he nearly believed.

CHAPTER THREE

The following evening, after the sun had set and it was safely dark enough, Nyx opened the front door of her family's farmhouse. The creaking screen was next, and as she stepped out onto the porch, its frame banged back into place with a clap and bounce.

She'd heard that sound all her life, and as it registered in her ear, every age she had ever been was strung along the percussive cadence. The child. The pretrans. The young adult. Where she was now . . . wherever that was.

Janelle had left over fifty years ago—

The screen door opened and closed again, and she knew who it was. She'd been hoping for some alone time because the day's hours had been very long. But the silent presence of her grandfather was a second-best option. Besides, he wouldn't stay long.

"Off to the barn?" she asked without looking back at him. "You're a little early tonight."

His reply was a grunt as he sat in one of the wicker chairs he had made himself.

Now she frowned and glanced over her shoulder. "You're not going to work, then?"

Her grandfather took his pipe out of the loose pocket of his work shirt. The tobacco pouch was already in his hand. The filling of the chamber was a ritual that felt too intimate to witness, so Nyx lowered herself down on the top step of the stairs and stared out over the lawn toward the barn. The *shcht* of him initiating his old-fashioned lighter was followed by the sweet smell of the smoke, another familiar.

"When do you leave?" he asked.

Nyx twisted around. Unlike the screen door's frame strike or the pipe's aroma, her grandfather's voice was not something that frequently registered. And it was such a surprise that the soft syllables didn't immediately translate into words with meaning.

When they did, she shook her head.

But that was not her answer.

Her grandfather got to his feet and came forward, the puffs of sweet smoke released from his mouth rising over his head and lingering in his wake. She thought he was coming to address her, but he didn't stop as he passed by. He continued down the steps and onto the fresh green lawn.

"Walk with me," he said.

Nyx jumped up and scrambled to his side. She couldn't recall the last time he'd asked her for anything, much less to be in his company.

They were silent as they progressed over to the barn, and he opened the side door, leaving the big bay panels locked in place. As she entered the cool darkness and smelled the wood shavings, Nyx was aware of her heart pounding. This was their grandfather's sacred space. No one came in here.

Illumination flared overhead and all around, and Nyx tried not to gasp in wonder. Strings of little lights had been strung around the rafters, a galaxy of stars, and the other old-fashioned fixtures glowed golden yellow. As she breathed in deep, she couldn't stop herself from going forward to the two sawhorses in the center of the bay.

A work of art was being constructed upon them.

Adirondack guide boats were a thing of the gracious past, first built in the mid-1800s to serve the sporting needs of the wealthy who came north to enjoy upstate New York's lakes and mountains. Designed to accommodate two passengers and their gear, they were lower-gunwale'd and of broader beam than canoes, and they were rowed cross-handed from the center seat by a guide who had a set of oars.

Although so much had changed in the last hundred and seventy years, there were still those who valued the antiquated, beautiful glide of the handmade creations, and her grandfather made and serviced them for a small list of loyal customers.

Nyx ran her fingertips over the long, raw cedar laps that ran horizontally along the cedar ribs.

"You're almost done with this one." She touched the rows of tiny copper nails. "It's beautiful."

There were four other guide boats on sawhorses in the barn: two that had received their first coats of varnish, the honey color of the wood and graining coming through. Another one was just a skeleton. Another was being repaired.

Nyx pivoted around. Her grandfather was standing by his display of tools, the gleaming array of chisels, hammers, handheld sanders, and clamps mounted down the wall of the barn over a long work counter. Everything had its place, and there was no power anything. Her grandfather made the boats in the old way . . . because that was how he'd done it since he'd begun making them in the Victorian era. Same process. Same discipline.

"When do you leave?" her grandfather said.

As she focused on him, she realized she often dropped her eyes when he was around. Part of it was his preternatural self-containment, and her sense that he preferred not being looked at. Most of it was because she felt as though he could read her mind, and she preferred her thoughts to be private.

Maybe he could see into her thoughts, maybe he couldn't.

She'd rather not know either way.

God, he'd aged. His hair was all white now, and

his cheeks were hollowed more than she remembered, but his shoulders were straight and so was his spine. Surely they had more time with him. In vampires, you had to worry as soon as the first physical changes of aging started to manifest. The decline was usually lightning fast thereafter.

"Grandfather," she hedged.

"Do not lie to me, young. There are others who must be considered here."

He didn't mean himself, of course. Posie was the problem, the thing that was holding everything up. As usual.

"At midnight," Nyx said. "I want to leave at midnight."

"I heard you speaking with that pretrans. He told you where the camp was?"

"It's hard to know exactly what he was saying. But I think I know where to go."

"He's stopped speaking the now."

"He'll be dead by dawn's arrival." Nyx rubbed her eyes. "Posie's going to lose it. She needs to stop rescuing things. Not everything is a puppy to keep."

"Your sister gives her heart freely. It is her way."

"She should snap out of it." To keep from cursing, Nyx paced around the guide boats, her boots loud over the well-swept bare floor. "And I have to at least try."

"Janelle is who she is as well. You accuse Posie

of trying to rescue things. You may well heed your own counsel with regard to your departure this night."

"How can you say that?" Nyx looked across at her grandfather. "Janelle is stuck in that prison—"

"She earned her place there."

"No, she did *not*—" Nyx forced herself to calm down. "She did *not* kill that male."

Her grandfather puffed on his pipe, the smoke he released in the still air blooming and then dissipating. His face was so calm and composed, she had to look away from the contrast to her anger.

"I won't be gone long," she said.

"It's more likely you will not come back," he countered. "You need to stay out of this, Nyxanlis. It's too dangerous."

At eleven fifty-three, Nyx shoved the last thing in her backpack. She had two water bottles, six protein bars, a flashlight, a fleece, a fresh pair of socks, and her toothbrush. That last one had been an afterthought and stupid. Like she needed to worry about dental health or bad breath?

As she tested the weight by strapping it on, she picked a baseball cap off her bed. Then she looked at her thin pillow. Of course she was going to put her head there again. She was going to be back—

"He's doing so much better."

Nyx closed her eyes before she turned around to her sister. And she made damn sure none of her the-hell-he's-getting-better showed in her expression.

Posie was leaning into the bedroom, her eyes bright and shiny, her hair damp and flat as a board, fresh from a fragrant washing. Her dress was buttercup yellow and had small blue and pink flowers all over it, the lace hem at the bottom brushing the tops of her bare feet.

"Come, see—" Posie frowned as she noticed the boots, the pack and the hat. "Where are you going?"

"Nowhere. Just out for a hike."

"Oh, okay." She motioned furiously. "See for yourself how well he is!"

Nyx followed her sister into the guest room next door. Across the dim interior, a slight form under heavy blankets lay without motion.

Posie lifted her long skirt and tiptoed across the throw rug. "I'm here, Peter. I'm right here."

Her sister knelt down and took a hand in both of hers. As her thumbs rubbed a palm that was gray, and fingers that did not move in response, Posie put her face close to the pillow. There were too many quilts to see anything, but the desperate murmurs coming out of her mouth were entreaties that Nyx knew would not be answered.

"Posie—"

Her sister looked up with expectation. "See? He's so much better."

Nyx took a deep breath. "When was the last time he spoke?"

Posie looked down at the blankets. "He's sleeping. He needs his rest. So he can heal."

Before Nyx said something she'd regret, she nodded, strapped on her pack, and went into the kitchen to exit through the back door. She looked at the dishes that were stacked in the rack, drying. The windows that had had their heavy daylight curtains opened. The messy bouquet of meadow flowers that Posie had picked before they'd made that fateful trip for groceries.

"Nyx?" Posie came in, her brows lifted like she was worried. "Don't you think he's getting better?"

Nyx pictured a shovel in her sister's tender hand. Dirt from a freshly dug grave on her bare feet. Tears running down that soft face.

"No, Posie. I don't."

"But he ate something last night." Her sister padded forward, clutching her skirting in desperate, straining hands. "And he drank something this afternoon."

Nyx looked out of the window over the sink. The barn seemed far away, by a factor of miles. Their grandfather was going to be out there all night long.

"He's going to recover, right?" Posie's voice

grew reedy. "I mean, I didn't kill him, did I?"

With a curse, Nyx unstrapped her pack and let it dangle from her hand.

"Aren't you going for a hike?" Posie asked.

Nyx let that pack fall to the floor, and then she bent down and unzipped it. Taking out one of her waters, she took a deep drink.

"Posie, listen to me. Accidents happen. You never meant to—"

Their grandfather entered the kitchen through the back door, unexpected and quiet as a ghost in the house. He didn't look at either of them as he passed by with a nod and went down into the basement. The fact that he left the door open behind him was weird, and his footsteps grew softer as he descended the stairs he had built with his own hands. Maybe he needed something from down there? All of his tools and wood and boat-making supplies were out in the barn, but there were plans for canoes and fisher skiffs. And other schematics, too.

The male could make almost anything out of wood.

When no sounds drifted up and he didn't return, Nyx looked at Posie. Refocused on the open door.

"What's he doing down there," she muttered as she put her water bottle on the table.

She approached the cellar stairs and listened. Then she put a foot on the top step.

51

From down below, her grandfather said softly, "Tell your sister to wait up there."

Nyx tightened her hand on the door knob. "Posie, you go sit with Peter. We'll be back up in a sec."

"Okay. You'll come say goodbye before you leave?"

"Yeah."

Nyx waited until that yellow dress flowed out of sight. Then she stepped down and shut the door behind herself. At the bottom of the stairs, she frowned as she looked around at the washer and dryer. The closed entrance to the underground rooms and the escape tunnel. The orderly shelves of paint cans, hardware, and supplies.

"Where are you—"

"Over here."

Nyx followed the sound of the voice around the base of the stairs and found her grandfather standing in front of a narrow passage in the concrete walling that she'd never seen before. And as she approached, he ducked down and shuffled out of sight. Bending low, she proceeded along a cramped tunnel in the pitch darkness. Some distance in, there was the sound of a heavy lock being released, and then light flared from a single source.

"What is this . . ."

Nyx lost her voice as she entered a metal-walled space that was ten feet square with an eight-foot ceiling. Mounted on brackets from floor to ceiling was an arsenal of weapons, ammunition, and tactical gear.

As she grappled with shock, her grandfather went over and picked up an empty duffel bag. Putting it on a low table, he began picking off guns and clips of bullets from the display. A length of chain. A knife. A spike that looked like something out of a Dracula movie.

"What are you doing?"

"I cannot change your nature, either," he said with quiet resignation. "So I send you off prepared. I know you've trained yourself how to shoot. I know you've trained yourself how to fight. You will take this and go. I will see to Posie."

With that, he zipped up the bag, turned to her, and held the collection of weapons out.

"How have I lived here my whole life and not known about this?" When her grandfather did not reply, she shook her head. "I don't know who you are."

"You know enough from my having kept your sister and you safe all these years."

"Against what threats?"

"No part of this world—or any other—is safe. You and I know this. We are similar in this regard, though I have tried over the years to ignore the parity. I would rather you enjoy the life Posie lives."

"That will never be me."

"And yet you go after Janelle because your heart refuses to let it rest." Her grandfather jogged the duffel. "You will need what is in here if you have any hope of returning. I will watch over Posie."

Abruptly, Nyx stumbled forward toward a dagger with a vicious . . . black blade. "Is this what I think it is?" She sent a glare over her shoulder. "Where did you get that."

Her grandfather stared back at her, the bag of weapons he had chosen for her hanging in the air between them.

There was a long period of silence. And then Nyx took a step forward and accepted the arsenal.

"You have forty-eight hours," he said.

"And then what? You're coming in after me?" When there was no reply, she wanted to curse. Except . . . "Wait a minute. You know where the prison entrance is, don't you." When he said nothing, she raised her voice. "You know where Janelle is. Don't you."

"You have forty-eight hours."

"How you can let her suffer? For fifty years." She looked at the weapons. "Goddamn you, you know where Janelle is, and you've done nothing to help her get out even though she's inno-cent—"

"You believe what you must."

"What I must? She didn't kill that male!"

"Yes, she did. And I was the one who turned her in."

Nyx stopped breathing. Leaned forward. Put her head to the side like her hearing wasn't working. "What did you just say."

"I turned your sister in for the murder."

Nyx started to shake her head, but it made her dizzy. "Why would you do that? *How* could you do that? How could you send her into that terrible place? I've heard the rumors—I know you have, too. She's a female!"

Her grandfather's eyes stared back at her with that calm of his, and in response, a fury she had never known raced through her veins.

Jabbing a forefinger at the old male, she spoke in a low, grim voice. "When I get back with her, I'm taking Posie, and we're all getting away from you and this house. Blood does not make people family, and I disavow you from this moment forward."

Nyx wheeled around for the tunnel.

Just before she ducked down into the low over-hang, her grandfather repeated, "You have forty-eight hours."

Glaring over her shoulder, Nyx wished she could leave the weapons behind, but now she was even more determined to come back in one piece.

"Or what," she said bitterly. "You're going to turn me in, too?"

CHAPTER FOUR

Nyx re-formed about five miles away from the farmhouse and fifty yards off the shoulder of the highway. For a moment, she just stood where she came to in the low-brush, flat terrain of the valley. Her head was a damn mess, and she got lost in making up further exchanges with her grandfather, dubbing in his side of things and moving her lips as she ran through her comebacks. She wished her parting shot had been more along the lines of her being absolutely *nothing* like him.

How could he betray his own granddaughter like that?

How could he sleep every day knowing that not only was Janelle in that horrible prison, but that he had put her there for a crime she didn't commit? It was unfathomable. Fifty years Janelle had been gone. Fifty years she had been alone in a terrifying, dangerous place with no one to help her, no one to care for her if she went hungry, got sick, was injured—and only by a stroke of luck, a random confluence of chance and highway circumstance, had Nyx finally learned how to get to their missing family member.

Now she knew why her grandfather had tried to talk her out of going.

And thank God she had forgotten that sleeve of bagels at the grocery. If she hadn't had to double back to the bakery department when she and Posie had been checking out, they would have missed that pretrans crossing the road when he did.

"Focus," she said out loud. "You need to focus."

The truth about what her grandfather had done was ugly, and greater scrutiny wasn't going to change the pockmarked face of it. Also, the countdown to daylight was on.

Shifting her pack into place on her shoulders, she noted how much heavier it was now that she'd added the pair of guns, the bullets, and the knife he'd given her. She'd left the chain and the spike behind. And that duffel of her grandfather's.

She was looking forward to giving his weapons back to him. And leaving that house with both her sisters. Christ, what a traitor they'd been living with.

Off in the distance, something howled at the moon, and she told herself it was a farm dog. Her adrenaline gland, on the other hand, ascribed the sound to something far more deadly. The good news was that she had three-sixty visibility from where she was standing between the two big hills.

On that note, she measured the way into town. The ribbon of pavement undulated over low rises and soft falls, the highway visible for quite some distance in both directions thanks to the hard winters that stunted the growth of anything green. A car—no, it was a truck, a boxy, non-descript delivery truck—passed her by, its head-lights trained on the road ahead. As it approached the exact place where Posie had struck that pretrans, Nyx turned away and started walking in the opposite direction.

In her head, she replayed the dying pretrans's babbling.

Back when he'd still been talking, he'd spoken of God, over and over again.

At first, it had made no sense. Vampires had a different spiritual tradition from humans. If the pretrans had been of the other species? Fine. Go on about a heavenly Father and a savior named Jesus and the steeple and cross stuff when you knew you were on the verge of death. But the fixation made no sense given his biology.

Except then Nyx had realized it wasn't about religion or eternal salvation. It was where he had come from.

Where he had escaped from.

As Nyx strode over the ground cover, weaving left or right whenever there was something too large and fluffy to easily step over, she looped her thumbs into the straps of her pack. Back when she and Posie had had horses, like fifteen or twenty years ago, she'd ridden all over this valley, sometimes with her sister, sometimes on her own. Posie had enjoyed the scenery. Nyx had been looking for anything out of place, anything that didn't make sense.

Specifically, an entrance to the underground prison that everyone knew was out here, somewhere in the valley.

Going back to those midnight rides, she let her memories inform her choices in direction, the decaying structures and unkempt tree lines of farms no longer used like stars in a map of the constellations. The farther she went, the more she began to worry she'd gotten it all wrong. Maybe what she was in search of was more to the west? Or—

She stopped as she came around a short-stop rise. "There you are."

The abandoned church was partially collapsed now, its spire and roof caved in, its stained glass windows missing, the stone steps up to its faded red door chipped and discolored. On the approach, she took note of the paint that had peeled off its whitewashed clapboard exterior, and she compared the state of its decay to what she had last seen from horseback, maybe a decade ago?

Time had not been kind.

This seat of God, built, sustained, and ultimately abandoned by humans, had once serviced the spiritual needs of the farmers who had tilled the valley's good earth. That era was over now, and the nearest house of worship that was functioning was a hundred miles away in the suburbs of Rochester. Then again, the nearest town of any note was thirty miles away. Thus the infrequency of grocery trips.

This had to be what the pretrans had been talking about in his delirium. God on earth. For humans.

And maybe used for something else.

When she came up to the main entrance, she tried the double doors. Locked. Not a problem. Willing them open with her mind, she—

Got nowhere with the dead bolt.

She tried again, sending a command for the steel components to shift their positions. Nothing.

Bending down, she felt a surge of triumph. "Copper."

Looking up to where the pointed spire should have been, she felt a tingling at her nape and across her shoulders. Humans wouldn't use a copper lock. Vampires would, though. If they wanted to keep members of the species out of a place.

Mental manipulation didn't work on the stuff that made pennies.

She had to get inside, but dematerializing into a space where you didn't know the layout or the debris field was too dangerous. Good job the windows were Swiss cheese'd. Heading around,

61

she picked one of the high-set empty frames, jumped up, and grabbed onto the lip.

With a grunt, she pulled herself high and propped the front of her pelvis on the sill like it was a pair of uneven bars in the Olympics. Tilting forward, she checked out the interior. Yup. Nothing but a salad of broken beams, busted pews, and cracked slate tiles for croutons. Swinging her legs up and over, she hung for a moment and then dropped down from the sash, her hiking boots making a thunderous noise that made her wince—

Doves fluttered into flight from hidey-holes in the tangle, and ducking down, she covered her head as wisps of feathers floated down in the moonlight. When the coast was clear, she straightened and looked around. The collapse of the roof had created an impassable terrain in the congregational area.

"Shit," she said to herself.

Assuming "Peter" had emerged from some kind of secret whatever-the-hell, he couldn't possibly have come through the mess. The splintered lumber and raw nails were an obstacle course and a half. Plus, if someone, anyone, had tried to get out of it or come up from under it, their path would show. There would be a disruption in the pattern of snapped boards and broken beams, and some blood, too, thanks to all the shards and sharpies—and pretrans couldn't dematerialize.

The exit would have had to be done on foot because he was too short to jump up to the empty window jambs.

Oh, and then there was that copper lock.

No, he hadn't come through here.

Maybe she was nuts. Maybe . . . he'd converted to human religion in the prison? Although it was only for vampires so how the hell would that work?

Before she left, she looked to the altar, which was strewn with red, blue, and gold chips of stained glass. Then she glanced to where the steeple had fallen from its great height, the brass cross somehow landing faceup on top of one of the few flat boards that was not tilted or smashed. The dusty gold face of the symbol of faith caught the moonlight, flashing with a warmth that, inexplicably, made her eyes water.

She wished she had something to believe in.

Dematerializing out of the window hole she'd come in through, she re-formed back on the scruff around the church and checked the building's foundation, looking for transom windows into a basement . . . or a storm door entrance . . . or a crack large enough for a one-hundred-and-ten-pound pretrans to slide out of.

"Damn it."

This was going nowhere.

The idea of heading back to the farmhouse with her tail between her legs, because she'd taken the ramblings of a dying boy, conflated them with her emotions around Janelle, and given herself a wild-goose chase, made her feel smaller in her clothes and made the pack with those weapons of her grandfather's feel heavier.

Nyx walked around again, looking for prints in the ground cover. Nothing—

Later, she wouldn't be able to pinpoint what made her turn her head. It wasn't a sound or a flash of light or a voice, but something commanded her to look behind herself.

At first, the congestion of overgrowth seemed like just another vine-draped knot of trees. But the more she stared at it, the more she recognized that there were contours . . . corners.

There was an old iron fence under all that ivy, four-cornered by some big maple trees. And inside of it, also covered with weeds . . . was a graveyard.

Walking over, she discovered that the gate of cockeyed iron points had been forced open. Someone had come through it recently, leaving the vines freshly broken, the leaves just beginning to wilt. And given the thin wedge? It had been someone who was small.

Nyx had to push things much wider to fit her grown-up body through, and in the moonlight, the pathway that had been traveled through the graves was visible, but barely so. The ground cover of weeds and grasses had been trampled by feet that had passed through only once. Another week? A good rainstorm? The distance traveled would disappear completely.

Nyx followed the winding way through the moss-covered markers and imagined Peter, confused and scared, maybe fleeing from somebody, tripping and falling, orientating himself in the moonlight by the stone stanchions and that gate. The fear that kid must have felt? She couldn't imagine, and had he known where to go? Had he had a safe destination?

She was pretty sure he had just been running scared.

Right into a hit-and-killed accident with a Volvo station wagon.

The trail of disturbance ended at a stone crypt that was choked by vines thick as tree branches. Its marble entry was open a crack, the departure from its interior one that, like the gate, had had to be forced through the braided tentacles of the flora that had claimed the human monument of mourning.

Gripping the thick stone panel, she had to put her back into it, and she knew, as she groaned against the resistance, that Peter must have been riding pure adrenaline as he had shoved his way out. Terror was a true source of strength, the only saving grace you could really count on when things went tits up.

She got her flashlight out and clicked the beam

on. There was a short set of stairs that led down to a stained marble floor and a sarcophagus set in the center of the space. As she moved the spear of illumination around, something scampered out of the way—

With a quick jerk, she looked over her shoulder at the graveyard.

Her eyes double-checked the greenery, the gate she'd forced open, the headstones and the trail the pretrans had forged.

Nothing moved. No scents, either.

The pounding of her heart was loud in her ears, and a flush of sweat broke out across her chest. "You're fine," she whispered.

Turning back to the crypt, she rechecked the interior and then sideways'd in past the heavy panel. Descending three stone steps, she got a load of the dust. The cobwebs. And especially the footprints across the floor.

Small footprints, with a high arch and tiny toes.

She thought of newborn young and the way parents checked the fingers. Checked the toes.

Closing her eyes, she wondered how Peter had been born in the prison camp. What that must have been like—

"You shouldn't be here, bitch."

The click right next to her ear was soft, but she knew what it was.

The safety of a gun being taken off.

CHAPTER FIVE

*T*he following evening, Rhage ran fast, ran strong, ran . . . too fast, in truth. Too strong.

Later, after the first of the night's surprises came upon him, he would reflect that he should have known by his sprinting gait what was inevitable. But such portents were not on his mind as he chased after a pale-eyed, pale-haired lesser.

He and his enemy were far from where their footrace had started, back at the blacksmith's shop behind the Village Arms rooming house. Up on the second floor of that dubious establishment of hospitality, Rhage had come out of a vigorous private session with a woman of questionable repute. Driven there by a desire to even himself out, as opposed to any true sexual need, he had done what he could to release some of his energy overload, and having exercised himself thus, his intention had been to eat and drink, and then set out in search of slayers to further take his edge off. As he'd proceeded down the stairwell, dissatisfied with his lot and itchy under his skin, he had regarded the night out of a window, hoping there was no rain.

Through bubbly glass, he had seen clearly what he now chased.

There was only one thing that had hair like corn silk and the flour-colored visage to match.

The slayer had been speaking with the horse minder, and money had changed hands. For animals to travel upon? Or fresh shoes for those already owned? Though motor carriages were being purchased by humans of late in some number, the Lessening Society had not embraced the newfangled conveyances.

Rhage had had a thought that he needed to let it go. But an image of Darius's eyes sent him down those stairs two at a time.

That condemning stare had been what had kept him up during the day as well. And what was currently the nettle under the saddle of his mood.

As Rhage had emerged from the flophouse's rear door, recognition had passed in an instant between enemies, and reaction was swift. Quickly departing itself of the blacksmith, the lesser *had taken off at a fast walk down a narrow alley that smelled of horse dung and spoiled food. That the undead had limped suggested this would be over before it started, and Rhage had followed at a leisurely pace, keeping up without o'ertaking— for as long as they were in range of so many humans, there could be no conflict.*

It was the one thing that vampires and the Lessening Society agreed upon. Neither side desired meddling from Homo sapiens.

After some number of blocks, the pace of the footrace had picked up some, and in any event, took them away from the settled part of the village's core. Away from the stragglers idled by the search for sex and the imbibing of beer. Away from potential eyes behind the windows of the abodes.

As Rhage continued in the vile-smelling wake of the slayer, he was aware of a bad vibration in his head and his body, and he'd wondered if mayhap he should have stayed longer with the woman. Then again, the problem had been kindling even whilst he had been with her. Indeed, he had slept naught during the daylight hours in his underground lair. Haunted by a familiar ghost garbed in the tattered threads of self-loathing, he had tossed and turned upon his pallet and then given up altogether on finding repose.

His brother Darius had been a plague upon his mind, and he had found much to say unto the other male. The fantasized arguments had passed the time until sunset, even though it was difficult to argue with a person who was not in the same physical space as you were. The benefit to that, however, was that when it came to the point/ counterpoint, he had won every round against Darius and taken a hollow satisfaction in his victories.

And now he and his enemy were upon this

field by the shores of the river. So he had further opportunity to improve his lot.

Palming both his black daggers, Rhage dematerialized and re-formed in the path of the *lesser*. As he raised his blades, he planned his next hour. This. Then food. Then he was going to have to find Darius and speak unto him—

In the periphery of Rhage's vision, he saw the other slayers emerge from the tree line, six wraiths glowing with menace, pale shadows of the humans they had been before their inductions into the Omega's league of vampire murderers.

Instant frustration came upon him. He should have known. He had heard about this encampment down by the Hudson, and should have been more aware of the course he had been led upon. But there was no time for self-admonishment. Slashing the daggers back into their chest holster, he went to his hips and the pair of guns awaiting his grip there.

He was not the first to shoot, however. The popping of bullets discharged from enemy weapons ricocheted through the night, lead slugs entering his thigh. His side. His shoulder.

Without warning, this little excursion had gone the way of deadly complication, and he had only himself to blame. Closing his eyes, he started shooting in a circle at the same time he forced himself to concentrate so he could dematerialize. He had to calm himself in order to—

Another shot went into his shoulder, kicking his torso back.

Opening his lids, he witnessed that he'd made a dent in the picket fence of lessers *that had surrounded him. There were holes in the vertical uprights, at least two down, and the others were ducking back behind the tree trunks. Unfortunately, they were shooting while they went. And they would continue to shoot after they were protected—*

Beneath his skin, his curse awoke.

Rhage crouched down and continued to reload and discharge his own weapons, aware that he was very much alone in this skirmish—and tragically, that was about to change. Trying to find his breath, he did not dare to pause to try one last time to dematerialize, although he hoped he could perhaps avoid—

An unholy roar came out of him, rising up his throat and erupting from his mouth, and the sound was so unexpected and alarming to the enemy, there was a respite in all the shooting. And then everything receded for Rhage, his senses, his mind, his inner self, submerging under a great and terrible transformation.

As his bones flew apart and his joints exploded, as his body morphed and expanded, as his vision left him and he was forced to cede control of everything he was, and all that he was capable of, unto his curse, he panicked.

There was no fighting the tide, and his last thought was that his beast might well be saving his life.

At least in the short term.

But the problem was not these six slayers—well, four now—and their limping comrade. What he was concerned about was what happened after he woke up. If there were more lessers *in those woods? An entire camp of them?*

Then he was a sitting duck for the enemy when he resumed unto his true form and had no more strength or presence of mind than a newly born young.

And if there was no lesser *presence? There were humans around and the sun rising in six hours. Worse, his brothers might show up to defend him, and risk getting eaten in the process, for his beast did not discriminate between friend and foe.*

This was bad. All of it was so bad.

And he feared it was going to get much worse.

CHAPTER SIX

As Nyx froze, her awareness of reality bifurcated. One side of her brain focused on the very immediate present: The scent of the male standing beside her. The smell of gunmetal. The sound of his steady breathing.

Which suggested he was very familiar with pulling guns on females.

The other part of her thought back to her self-defense teacher. He had been a human, and she'd found him through a gym. The combat lessons had started as a thing to do, another way to exercise, but the more she had learned, the more she had liked being able to handle herself. She'd gotten a lot from her teacher, and the basis of it all had been something he had stressed over and over again: If you ever need to defend yourself, there will be no time and no conscious thought to do so. The only thing that will save you is your training and your practice because adrenaline will overwhelm the frontal lobe and your rational faculties, leaving you only with rote memory.

Nyx drew in a long, slow breath.

And then she moved faster than she would have believed possible.

Up with the flashlight, pegging her aggressor in the eyes with the beam and blinding him. Down with the torso, getting her head out of range if he discharged his weapon. Around with her body, taking control of the hand and wrist governing the gun. Punching out with her boot, nailing him in the kneecap.

As he pitched forward, Nyx almost dropped the gun as she transferred her hold from the base of the muzzle to the grip proper. And then the male got over his surprise at her quick response, going for her braid and yanking her off balance.

And that was when the gun discharged.

The sound was cracking loud in the echo chamber of the crypt, the kind of thing she felt in her skull rather than heard. Ducked on a reflex—

The hold on her hair instantly released, and the freedom from the torque was so unexpected, she flipped forward, her momentum pitching her into a headlong fall. Catching herself on the sarcophagus, she spun around—and gasped.

Her flashlight had fallen free during the scuffle and rolled off to one side.

So its shaft of illumination was trained on the face of her attacker.

Or what was left of it.

The bullet had hit him at the base of the jaw, and the angle of its trajectory had carried the lead slug through the interior structures of the front of his face. Its exit had been through the outside corner of the left eye, and it had taken extensive tissue and bone along with its departure.

Hollow-point bullet, she thought as her stomach rolled.

Clicking noises rose up from what remained of the mouth, and glossy red blood oozed out of the ruined anatomy, a puddle gathering width and depth on the dusty stone floor. There was twitching at the extremities, but even without medical training, she knew he wasn't getting up anytime soon.

Nyx shuddered and leaned back against the sarcophagus, her lungs pumping too fast with draws that were too shallow. As her body went numb, her head grew fuzzy and her vision went bad bulb on her, flickering in between sight and blindness.

Control the breathing, she told herself. *Slow and easy. Rebalance the carbon dioxide in the blood.*

It was only through what she had practiced with her self-defense teacher that she was able to resist the urge to keep panting, and her eyes were the first function to stabilize. Then the trembling and strange paralysis that came with panic attacks eased up—as long as she didn't look at the body. Hard to do. The male's remains were slowly losing their autonomic jerks, death claiming what had been alive like a meal consumed—in bites.

Pushing her hair out of her face, even though there were no strands in her eyes, nose or mouth, she looked around. No backup coming into the space. No explosions. Nothing from outside of the crypt.

When she leaned down to pick up her flashlight, she realized she had a gun in her right hand. Duh.

God, she hated that fresh-copper smell of blood, and a part of her, way down inside her core, wanted to cry even though it had been a his-or-her-life situation. She needed to get over that. Forcing herself to go over, she frisked the body and came up with a bounty worth the trouble of overriding her gag reflex. Keys. A communicator. A pass card with no photo or name, just a magnetic strip. Three ammo clips that went with the gun.

This was the guard of a professionally maintained facility. She had to be close to the prison.

She pocketed or packed all of it, and stood up with her flashlight. Sending her instincts out, she listened for soft sounds and breathed deep, searching for any scents over and above the male she had . . .

Killed.

She debated hiding the body. Humans weren't going to come this way, but maybe there would be others like him? Had she tripped an alarm of some kind? Or had he been on a regular security check? He'd come out from the side, but that wasn't much of an indicator because he'd clearly dematerialized—

The trail of those little footsteps led her eyes

to a vent down on the floor. The iron grating was about two feet high and three feet long, and given the pattern of scuffs in front of it, that was where the pretrans had gotten out of wherever he'd been. To hide his tracks, he must have put the grate back in place, even though the disruption in the dust layer was a flashing neon sign.

Going over, Nyx squatted down, put the gun and the flashlight off to the side, and squeezed her fingers in through the slats. When she pulled, the frame came out with a high-pitched screech, and she froze. When no one with a weapon appeared around her, she started breathing again, grabbed the flashlight, and trained the beam inside.

There was a shallow area about five feet down, but she wasn't sure she wanted to dematerialize into it because she had no sense of what could be waiting for her down there. Big blind spot. Huge.

Leaning in even farther, she worried that it was her only choice—

A subtle beeping sound went off and then there was a *whirrrrrrrr.*

Wheeling around, she palmed the guard's gun and pointed it at the panel that was sliding back on the far side of the sarcophagus. In her light, the corridor that was revealed was gray, narrow . . . and empty.

For the moment.

Putting the grating back into place, she stood up and looked across at the guard. A split second later, she went over to the male's feet and tucked his nine millimeter in her waistband.

"Sorry . . . sir." Sir? Like she needed to be polite to a guy who'd been ready to kill her? And who, P.S., was frickin' dead? "Just, ah, relax."

Okay, she was losing it.

Bending down, she took the body by the ankles and pulled the dead weight—natch—across the floor. The stairs were tough. As she dragged him up the steps, the sound of the back of the skull bumping along had her wincing.

"Ouch, ouch, ouch," she whispered.

Out in the hot air of the night, she took a deep breath. Then she pulled the male over between a pair of lichen-covered markers and let his feet drop into the tangle of grass and ivy. Checking on the sky, she tried to remember what the weather forecast was. Sunny. Wasn't it supposed to be sunny tomorrow?

One ray of sunshine and the body would disappear, nothing but a scorch mark in the greenery.

Nyx gunned up again and rushed back to the crypt, thinking of that scene from *The Sopranos* where Tony killed Ralphie Cifaretto. In the movies, on TV—for the most part—murders were slick. People were killed in a coordinated set of moves. In real life? Someone like Tony gets wasp spray in the face while he's offing someone for hurting an animal.

Or, in her situation, she leaves a hidden

entrance wide-spanking-open while she drags her first murder victim out of a crypt.

Back inside, she made sure there was no one around and then penetrated the opening in the wall. A tiny red light blinked to the side of the doorway, and when she leaned in to look at it, there was a beep and the panel slid back into place.

Frowning, she took the guard's pass card out of the pocket of her windbreaker. As she moved it over the red light, the panel slid open once more, and then she closed it with the same motion. There must have been another reader down by that vent? Whatever, she had bigger issues. A few self-defense classes and one lucky takedown were nothing compared to a professionally trained and outfitted police force in a facility with some level of sophisticated security.

Picturing Janelle's face, she turned to the left and started walking. As she went along, motion-activated lights set into the tunnel's ceiling flared to life, and she could have done without the help. But like her flashlight wouldn't have given her away?

Walking toe-heel helped her keep the sound of her footsteps down, but it did absolutely nothing for the beating of her heart. The sense that she was in way over her head made her feel like someone was choking her, but at least the stalking thing was an easy monitor.

She looked behind herself every three feet.

And then she came up to a solid metal wall. Taking out the pass card, she swiped it by another blinking red light and shifted to the side, trying to take some cover as the panel slid back.

The scent of the earth made her recoil.

What was on the other side was bare rock.

I should not do this, she thought. *I need to turn around, right now.*

Over the course of the century he'd been down below, the Jackal had made a study of the guards. Their ranks and shifts. Their pairings and solo trips. Their territories within the prison complex. He knew their eye and hair colors, and which ones were distractible, and who was cruel. He was aware of who had let their physical conditioning go and who was lean and muscled. He tracked them from where they entered the common halls from the Command's private area to the furthest reaches of their responsibilities.

He witnessed them dealing drugs to prisoners. Having sex with the incarcerated. Throwing punches that were deserved and tormenting people who were following the rules. He knew their secrets and their vices, their blind spots and their fields of vision.

He was careful never to get noticed. It was not hard. There were so many prisoners.

One thing, among many, that was not readily

available in the down-below were clocks, but the guards helped with that. With their regular schedules and routes, they were a metronome, a way of marking the passage of time. Provided he kept his stride at the same distance and at the same cadence, he could track and anticipate the shifts and their responsibilities and, thereby, the cycles of night and day. Or something close to night and day.

The Command made sure that people stuck to their duties.

And that was how he knew something was wrong.

Dropping his eyes, he looked down at the handmade leather slips on his feet. His stride was correct, an easy extension of his thigh out of his hip socket, and his speed was on point. He was in the right tunnel, too. Wait . . . was he?

The Jackal stopped and looked over his shoulder. Retracing his left and rights mentally, he thought . . . no, this was the correct location. He'd run his D, E, and F routes in the last three nights/days. This was G. He was supposed to be doing G.

So this was right.

Where was the damn guard?

Narrowing his eyes, he regarded the tunnel ahead of him. And waited.

Warning bells started to sound out in his head. The guard should have been passing by now, transitioning to being off shift. Had they changed their schedule?

That would be a problem. Their predictability was critical.

Pressing on, he made a turn, hit a straightaway, and then came up to a branch that was marked with a white paint spot on the rough-cut archway of the tunnel head. Before he penetrated the area, he made sure he was not followed. Then he strode forth, staying close to the left-hand side of the walling. His black and gray clothes, loose garments that allowed him to move freely and fast, were the color of the walling, but the bald lights strung every twenty feet overhead on wire meant that he was a sitting duck—

The Jackal stopped dead.

Lifting his nose to the air, he breathed in deep.

The scent that came down to him was tantalizing on a level he had never known before— and it was utterly foreign. For all the years, the decades, the century, he had spent here underground, he had never come upon it before, and it was a sad commentary on his life that he had to reach so far back in his memory to put a definition on it.

Fresh flowers.

Closing his eyes, he drew in another breath, greedy for more of the fragrance. Yes, fresh flowers, and not the sickly sweet kind that had proliferated in the grand houses he had once visited and lived in. This was lush and lovely in an honest way, not a cultivated one.

And it was getting stronger.

The Jackal willed off three of the loose light bulbs, creating a sixty-foot-long stretch of darkness.

The sounds of footsteps were faint, and on the approach, there was one and only one explanation for them.

Somebody who shouldn't be in the prison had found a way in.

CHAPTER SEVEN

*T*he taste in Rhage's mouth was a scourge upon the tongue, spoiled meat and crushed, molded strawberries in concert. But that was the lesser of the ills that plagued him. As he lay upon the grass, his eyes were sightless, everything dark around him such that he could not orientate himself unto the hour by the constellations. He had no concept of time's passing, no clue how close he was to dawn—and with the pain in his arms and legs, his torso and head, he couldn't tell whether his skin was sending him messages of warning as to the approach of sunlight or whether the agony was his beast's parting salvo.

Rolling onto his side, Rhage retched as his stomach roiled and revolted. He had consumed many slayers. He knew by the nausea in his gut and that taste in his mouth. But how messy was the scene? Human attention would be especially bad the now, and dead bodies—or rather pieces of them—were something that garnered notice.

His ears were the only thing he could rely upon, and they provided him with nothing good. A dripping sound was close by. Something was leaking. His own blood? Or was it a slayer's? Or had he punctured a container of mead? His nose was too clogged with the stench of the undead to provide him with any clues. For that matter, was he as yet in the clearing down by the river or had he roamed—

"My brother."

At the familiar voice, Rhage exhaled in relief. Darius was the last male he would have sought out, but the very perfect aide in this situation. Further, it meant there was still darkness, still time to get unto cover.

"You must move me." His voice was but a weak rasp. "I must be moved."

This, though again, he knew not where he was. The beast could take him far from where it first commandeered him.

"Yes." In the pause that followed, Rhage imagined the brother looking around. "Indeed."

"Where am I?" Rhage asked.

"I have a horse. Allow me to lift you upon it."

"I am feeling rather ill."

On that note, he became sick, and it was a while before the expulsions passed sufficiently for him to speak again.

"Help me, please."

"I have you, my brother."

As arms came around him, Rhage groaned in response, and then things got so much worse. The movement was awful, his sore limbs and aching, bloated torso screaming as Darius picked him up under the knees and at the waist, and shifted him onto a horse that stamped and whinnied *in protest. Because of the smell? The weight?*

"Dearest Virgin Scribe," Rhage grunted as he was draped facedown like a sack over the saddle.

The pressure on his swollen stomach was untenable, and he fumbled to push his palms against something, anything, to relieve the constriction.

"No, no, no—" And then he was sick anew.

After that round was over, Darius cursed and lifted him off. Back upon the ground. More retching.

"I'm going to hide you," the brother said. "And then I shall return—"

Rhage lost consciousness behind his unseeing eyes, his awareness disappearing not on a gradual fade, but in the sharp manner of a gaslight being extinguished.

There was no way to ascertain the further amount of time that passed, but the next thing he was aware of was a levitation that roused him. Throwing out his arms, he fought against air in the event this was not one of his own.

"No, no, be of ease, my brother." The sound of Darius's voice instantly calmed him. "Tohrment and I are removing you upon a pallet."

"Thank you. Both of you." At least that was what he was trying to say. He wasn't sure what was coming from his mouth. "Return me unto my abode—"

"You need tending to."

"This is merely my recovery—"

"You have been shot at least four times."

" 'Tis not the first—"

Tohrment, son of Hharm, spoke up from the compass point of Rhage's feet. "Be of silence and save your strength. We have some travel ahead unto Havers."

Rhage wanted to fight the tide that was carrying him forth, but he lacked the energy—and mayhap that was the point. It was hard for him to discern which pain was from what source, and therefore, how much of his weakness was due to blood loss from bullets.

Mayhap it was best to take the word of those who could see the damage done.

Similar to when the beast came out, he now had no choice but to release dominion over himself and his body, and he tracked the trip he was taken upon by its sounds and sensations: A breeze over bare skin as he was carried over onto something hard. Movement up, and then a swaying as he was transferred by pallet. Creaking as he was settled into a coach of some kind. Stomping hooves and a whinny, as if he made the horses uneasy. Jostling with a sway as they set on their course at a steady clip.

By the time they halted, sometime later, more of his senses were upon him and he was aware of a ringing pain in his side. There were three other focal points of similar nature, but it was the one under his ribs that made him think his brothers had been correct in taking him unto the species' healer.

Another transfer upon the pallet. A door opening and closing.

Voices now. A number of them.

Along with the scents of roasted beef and lamb. And . . . quite distantly . . . the sound of a string quartet?

This made no sense.

He turned his head back and forth, the movement doing nothing to aid his sight.

"Is this the healer's abode?" he mumbled.

And then a voice he recognized, but that further confused him.

"Of course, he will have a room. The very best room my home has to offer."

What the hell was he doing at Jabon's estate?

CHAPTER EIGHT

Every step forward Nyx took was a fight. Even though the tunnel she was going through was empty, no barriers in front of her and no stalkers behind, she had to force herself to keep going on the gradual descent. She had her flashlight in one hand, the guard's gun in the other, and her anxiety riding her back like it had thrown a saddle over her spine and put on spurs. As she approached another turn and things flattened out underfoot, she couldn't believe how far she had gone, and to make sure she didn't get lost, she took only lefts. At any of the branches she came to, she went to the—

Coming out of a corner, she stopped.

Up ahead, there was a stretch of darkness, the lights strung along on the ceiling extinguished.

Nyx jumped back out of sight of that which she could not see. Putting her shoulder blades against the damp wall of the cave-like cutout in the earth, she willed the light above her off—

The hands that grabbed her and pushed her face-first into the wall were hard, biting into her upper arms. And before she could react, the gun was taken. Her flashlight, too. Then her pack was ripped off and a palm clamped on the back of her neck to hold her in place.

Not a word was spoken, and the speed was such that it seemed to all happen between one heartbeat and the next.

As Nyx was pinned to the walling, she grunted and fought against the male. The punishment for the attempt to get free was an even greater pressure on her nape—and the muzzle of that gun pressed to her temple.

"You do not belong here."

The voice was whisper-quiet and very, very deep. There was an accent to it as well, but she didn't waste time trying to place it.

"Let me go," she said tightly.

"How did you get in here?" There was the draw of an inhale. "And you killed one of them, didn't you. I can smell the blood on you."

Before she could calibrate a response, a soft, rhythmic sound registered in her ears.

"Damn it," the male hissed.

And that was when her chaotic brain put a definition to that noise. Marching. There were a number of people marching in unison. And going by how the sound was getting louder, they were on the approach.

"Don't make a sound," the male voice ordered.

As the pressure eased up on her neck, Nyx did some quick math. Whoever this was had her weapons and considerable control over her—for the moment. But she didn't think he was a guard. Which meant he was a better bet than those boots that were heading her way. Like she had a choice, though?

She looked over her shoulder at the male—

In the dim shadows, she couldn't believe his eyes. Blue-green. They were brilliant, glowing blue-green eyes that reminded her of pictures she'd seen on TV of the tropical sea.

The rest of her first impression came in fast: Black hair pulled back. Big shoulders, tall body.

Lips that shouldn't have even been on her notice list.

As he pulled her arm, she tripped, but regained her balance quick. He took her back the way she had come, the lights hanging from the ceiling going out as they approached and coming back on as they went by. And then he stopped short.

"Here," he said softly.

There was a whirring sound, and then a different smell came to her nose. Before she could place it, she was pushed forward into a pitch-black space and the whirring came again.

"They're going to kill you if they find you," he whispered as they were closed in together. "Especially with the blood of one of their own on you."

In the sensory void, his disembodied voice made everything feel like a dreamscape, and Nyx's eyes strained against the darkness, even though there was no point. Meanwhile, outside wherever the hell they were, the sound of those multiple sets of boots hitting the hard ground in coordination grew louder.

"I want my gun back," she said as the guards seemed to pass by.

After the marching sounds faded, a candle flared.

Nyx blinked in the warm glow, and was glad she'd gotten a look at his peepers out in the tunnel. Otherwise, she might have shown surprise. Or . . . something else that would have been really stupid to share.

Still, she was captivated. His stare seemed to be backlit from inside his skull, unlike anything she had ever seen before. Jewels. Paraíba tourmalines. Only more beautiful than that.

She could not look away.

In her peripheral vision, other details of him registered. He had a freckle under the eye on the left, and its contours were unusual. Like a heart. His clothing was dark gray and loose, but not rags. He was clean and relatively well-fed. His scent was . . .

She refused to let herself think about his scent. Nope. That was not going to help things.

"We need to get you out of here," he said grimly.

As his words sank in, she had a thought that she wanted just a little more time to stare at him so she could memorize all the details of his face. But that was ridiculous.

"I'm not leaving," she countered.

• • •

The Jackal closed his eyes briefly. In spite of the reality of his own situation, and the overriding focus it mandated, he had a thought that he must get this female out of the prison. With her strange-looking clothes, her provisions, and the flashlight he'd stripped from her, it was clear she didn't belong here. And with what she had done to one of the Command's guards? If they got a hold of her with those bloodstains on her jacket, she was going to learn things about pain that would make death look like a gift.

She was not his responsibility, however, and he was not in a position to take on any further ones. And it wasn't like she was fragile or weak.

On the contrary. The female was meeting him right in the eye, and even though she'd been disarmed, she was ready to fight. The resolve was in her braced stance, her unwavering stare, the fists that were up in front of her chest. Her hair, which was black, was pulled back, the tail of it long enough to curl over her shoulder and extend below her collarbones. Her eyes were the color of brandy in good lighting.

By the weight of her pack, and the way it moved, he knew she had more weapons with her. Probably ammunition, too.

"Give me my shit back," she demanded.

The Jackal frowned. "I beg your pardon."

"You heard me, asshole." When he didn't reply, she snapped, "I already know you speak English, so don't pretend you're confused."

"I understand every word you've spoken. I'm simply not used to hearing females curse as readily as you seem to."

She blinked. Leaned in a little, like maybe he was stupid. "Exactly where do you think we are? A gourmet restaurant?"

"I just believe that the fairer sex has better ways of expressing themselves."

The female put her hands on her hips. "Just my luck. I get mugged by Emily Post."

"Emily who?" He narrowed his eyes. "And I did not mug you."

"Then why do you have all my *shit*."

As she drew out the enunciation on that last word, something unfamiliar woke up in the back of his brain. To cover up the thoughts and feelings, he forced himself to focus.

"Where do you think you're going," he said.

"You don't have to worry about that."

"I'm asking the wrong question," he muttered. "Why are you here."

"Also none of your business."

Heat went through him, and he studiously ignored the area between his thighs where it pooled. "You don't seem to understand your situation. You are going to die if you don't get out of here, and unless you have some help getting free of this hellhole, your grave is a sooner-not-later situation."

"I'm not leaving."

"What is worth more than your own life?"

"It's not about me."

When she simply stared at him, the Jackal looked away. It felt odd to hide his eyes from a stranger, but it seemed vitally important that she guess nothing about him. Especially not what was happening to his body.

Although something told him she wouldn't be shocked. The female was brazen, and not just with her vocabulary.

"Who are you looking for?" When she crossed her arms and narrowed her stare, he smiled. "Ah, it would seem I got it right, and spare me the games. You're not in a position to play them. You have no idea where you are, where you're going, or how to find someone in the maze down here."

"I will figure it out."

"No, you won't. I've spent a hundred years in this prison. I know more about the tunnel system than anybody else still alive in it. You have no idea where you are. Now tell me, who are you here to find."

The female broke off from him and walked around. As he gave her the space to come to the inevitable, he was acutely aware of what was going on outside the secret passageway. A squad had gone down to where she had gained entrance.

And the guard whose presence had not been accounted for, who had not been where he should have been, was the one she had killed.

"Where did you put the body?" he asked. When she stopped short and glanced over with feigned regard, he rolled his eyes. "Stop the acting. After you killed him, where did you leave him?"

Silence. And then she started to pace again.

As he thought about his own prime directive, he lost interest in the art of persuasion. She was stubborn and she was arrogant, and life had corrections for that. Especially here, underground.

He had too much to lose himself to spare her the evolution.

The Jackal went back over to the sliding panel. Listening carefully, which was easy because the female sure as hell wasn't saying anything, he heard nothing out in the tunnel. Triggering the panel to retract, he was aware of a tightness in his chest as he off-shouldered her pack and tossed it back across to her. Her gun and flashlight followed, and she caught each with a suspicious surprise.

"Good luck," he said as he turned away. "The panel will close in three seconds on its own. Whether you're in or out is up to you—and where you go next is the same. Good luck unto your quest."

Stepping out into the tunnel, he walked off in

the direction of the Hive. He had to hurry to catch up to where he should have been on his route G, although with the disruption the female had caused, there was a chance that all guards would be out of sync for the rest of the night.

And it had to be night, or as a vampire, she wouldn't have been out and about in the above. It was probably earlier rather than later in the evening as well, assuming she'd wanted to provide herself with the maximum amount of travel time. No doubt she was stupid enough to think she could free whoever she had come to liberate before dawn's inevitable arrival.

As he made note of the time frame reference, and integrated it into his knowledge of the guard shifts, he didn't like the sense of anticipation as he waited for her to call him back.

When she didn't, he wasn't surprised, although the grim pall that darkened his emotions was a surprise. Why should he care about her? If prison had taught him anything, it was that one had to take care of oneself.

It was the only way to survive.

CHAPTER NINE

*R*hage's eyes returned unto their service in the
midst of the tending to his wounds. It was
early for his vision to come back upon him, but
the combination of an unfamiliar environment
and the fact that someone was cutting into him
seemed to cultivate an urgency with regard to
that particular of his senses.

'Twas all rather blurry, but he could see enough
to ascertain the race's healer, Havers, dressed in
a tuxedo and bending over with a scalpel. Further,
Rhage could make out his two brothers on either
side of the bed he had been laid upon, both in
ballroom togs. And there, across the opulent
bedroom by a door, was Jabon. The master of the
estate was likewise in formal evening attire, and
his expression was one of great satisfaction, as if
the fact that there were multiple members of the
Black Dagger Brotherhood under his roof was a
reward brought unto him by providence's good
nature.

Somewhere on a level down below, stringed
instruments played on, and Rhage imagined
members of the glymera, gentlemales and gentle
females, linked by delicate touch, the fine figures
moving smoothly through carefully dictated
dance positions on the black-and-white marble

floor of a ballroom. Colorful gowns would twirl and toss their skirting, and the diamonds and colored stones upon slender throats and wrists would flash and sparkle. No one would be smiling, and there would be a hierarchy within the hierarchy about when, and in what fashion, and by whom/to whom, eye contact could be made.

The rules of the glymera *were legion and dispositive, and the consequences of violating them were dire and potentially generational in nature. More than their money and their land, their possessions and their position in the race, the aristocracy's strictures on conduct were their most precious resource. Whether it was the purity of an unmated female or the seating chart of a dining table or the manner in which an individual responded to an invitation, they had long ago created a battlefield of their own, land mines of propriety due to combust at any moment.*

Rhage had never understood it. If he were going to be on such alert? It was going to be to keep from being stabbed. Beheaded. Shot. It was not going to be worrying about which fork he used—

He groaned as a streak of agony at his ribs stole his breath. Were they taking out his lungs?

"Forgive me," Havers said in a gentle tone. "The bullet is removed."

There was a clank! *as something metal hit*

something metal. And then there was a momentary relief before the next sharp pain, this time lower down, by his hip. The sequence of a spike of pain followed by that clank! was repeated two more times.

"Thank you, healer," Rhage mumbled.

"It is my honor to be of service."

There were stitches to follow, but they were a mere inconvenience rather than anything uncomfortable. And then everyone seemed to take a step back and regard him as if they were looking for further injury. Or perhaps his expiration.

"Will you take no pain relief?" the healer asked.

"No, none."

Time to go, Rhage thought.

With that resolve, he went to sit up, fully invested in the intention of getting upon his feet, but every hand that was around him landed upon him. As a chorus of "No, stay down" rippled through the bedroom, he was prepared to argue— and yet his tongue seemed sluggish in his mouth and his brain couldn't quite get the wording right.

"You need to feed," Havers said. "Is there a . . . would there be . . ."

"A female of whom to avail myself?" Rhage prompted as he collapsed back against pillows that he must have stained. "I am sure I could find one."

"*That is a difficulty he has never suffered from,*" Darius muttered.

"*No, no, allow me to bring you a fitting vein,*" Jabon spoke up. "*I will be certain that you will be revitalized by her. I have one presently in mind and she is downstairs.*"

"*All right.*" Rhage glared at them all, even though they were little more than a fog around him. "*But then I will be off.*"

Havers cleared his throat. "*I'm afraid, sire, that you must rest the day herein. And perhaps stay longer. You have much to recover from.*"

"*You have to stay here,*" the aristocrat rushed in. "*We shall attend all of your needs with promptness and precision, ensuring your speedy recovery.*"

Just what he was looking for. A debt owed to a sycophant. The infernal repayment of such an obligation was going to be more than he could endure cheerfully.

"*You overestimate my injuries.*" To prove his point, Rhage pushed their palms off of himself, sat up and swung his legs off the edge of the bedding. "*I do not need to feed and I am—*"

As he put weight upon his soles, he had a brief moment of triumph.

The collapse that followed was a total repudiation of his purported strength and independence. And but for Darius's quick hold upon his biceps, he would have hit the floor—and likely shattered as glass dropped upon stone.

The other brother did not address him. "Yes, Jabon, we shall avail ourselves of your hospitality, and if there is indeed a willing female with a vein, we would be most grateful for her service. Further, please reassure her that the feeding will be witnessed."

"Right away," the happy host said.

As a door opened and closed, the sounds and smells of the gathering below flared briefly. And then all was quiet.

"I have done what I can thus far," Havers said. "Send a doggen unto me if he requires aught during the day. My home is across the street, as you know, so I will be able to get to him in a covered conveyance if I must. I believe he will be well enough provided he feeds, however."

"Thank you, healer," Tohrment intoned.

When Rhage was alone with his brothers, he grimaced. "Mayhap we should clean me if there is a female to be present?"

"Aye," Tohrment said. "I shall start the bath. Jabon took all pains to inform me that his tubs have gas burners underneath, so you will be warm."

Thank the Virgin Scribe, Rhage thought as the male went into the bathroom.

When the sound of rushing water drifted over, he turned his head to Darius and frowned. "You are in formal dress as well."

"I was attending the ball when you were found

down by the river. I was summoned unto you."

"Who found me?"

There was a pause. "Zsadist."

Now Rhage lifted his head, in spite of his sore neck. "You lie."

"Whyever for? 'Tis the truth. To keep you safe, he slaughtered the population of that lesser encampment in the forest there. He fought them all off after you collapsed, and the stragglers he hunted down and killed after he came and found me here at the celebration. You should be grateful unto him."

Rhage pictured the brother with the scarred face and the dead, black eyes. "That male kills because he likes to, not to protect anyone. He cares not even for his blooded brother."

"Whatever his motivation, you are alive only because of him."

"Where is he the now?"

"Who knows."

After a moment, Rhage frowned. "So he sent word unto you somehow?"

"Oh, no. He walked right into the ballroom, lesser blood dripping from him and a black dagger in his grip. His entrance was a scene to remember, I assure you."

Rhage chuckled. "I can only imagine."

"The announcement of his presence was the virtuoso violinist's bow screeching across his strings. All stopped. Two females fainted, and at

106

least three males ducked out of the ballroom and ran. As a public service, I went readily unto him and rerouted him out of the gathering."

"He has the stare of a demon."

"And the cold heart of one as well. He is as dangerous as your beast in many ways."

As they fell into silence, Rhage considered his wakeful hours during the previous day. "My brother, I must explain something unto you."

"What of it, then?"

"I know you do not respect me—"

Dimly, Rhage was aware of the brother putting both his palms up and leaning away. "Now, Rhage, let us not set upon this—"

" 'Tis true. And you are not the only one." He cleared his throat. "I know there are others in the Brotherhood who feel as you do. You believe me frivolous and distracted by females, unfocused and uncommitted."

"My brother, again, now is not the time—"

"Now or later, the truth is what it is."

Rhage wished he could read the nuances of Darius's expression. Except then he realized it might be best to have them blurry. Disdain and distaste were not going to help him farther unto his speech.

"You are well aware of the curse I live with," he said, *"and this night, when you went unto the shores of the river, you saw anew what it is capable of. I do my best to keep it in check, and*

the way I manage the beast is by laying with women and females and fighting. If I do not burn my energy off, then it can come out, perhaps at an inopportune time. Perhaps around you all."

"Truly, my brother, there is a better circumstance for this conversation—"

"Is there? Or will you avoid the awkwardness again? I am unsure that you comprehend the extent of my weakness of will and command when the beast is expressed. I do not know what it does. I cannot see or hear or temper its strength and fury in any fashion. But I must live with the aftermath. If one of you were hurt by it? Then it is my fault and I would have to carry that burden for the rest of my nights. Which would be unbearable. I would never recover."

He pushed himself upward upon the pillows, and in the back of his mind, he wondered if he had stained all the bedding, not just what was against the headboard.

Of course he had.

"You believe," he continued, "that I am more committed to the hunt for females than the war. This is not false. I am compelled unto them because I must manage the energy that seethes within me every waking moment and all the ones whilst I sleep as well. I hate the sex. It is a meal I am not hungry for in the slightest. The alternative, however, is something I cannot abide.

So please know, I am as focused as ever upon the war. But when I fight our enemy, I am at times with you and the other brothers, or imminently to be in your company. My primary concern is, and always will be, the safety of the Brotherhood. It was a blessing of luck I was alone this eve. However, that is not, and will not, always be the case."

There was a moment of dense quiet. And then Rhage felt his dagger hand clasped by Darius.

"I did not know," the other brother murmured. "I had no idea."

Embarrassed by his revelations, Rhage shrugged. "As I said, it is what it is."

"Why have you not spoken of this before the now?"

"Let us change the subject—"

"Your honor has been unfairly maligned."

"I'd rather be known as a whoremonger than a coward."

"How are you a coward?"

Rhage closed his eyes. "I fear that which is inside me. It terrifies me, for I cannot ensure the safety of those I care most about, and it is mine own self whom I cannot trust. But enough of this. It is done."

The water rushing in the bathroom beyond seemed to grow louder in the silence.

"I am sorry, my brother," Darius whispered.

"I should not have said aught." Yet there was

something about Darius that made a male want to have his respect.

Clearing his throat, Rhage tried to consider what else they could discuss as that tub, which was evidently deep as a pond, filled at a snail's pace.

"I must confess, I am surprised that you attended Jabon's fête," Rhage forced himself to comment. "Not readily for his company you have ever been."

"This is true." Darius cleared his throat, as if he were changing the course of his thoughts. "As it turns out, our host has an acquaintance who may be of aid to me."

"You need a vein as well, my brother?"

"No, a master of the works for my house upon the great hill. I have had no success finding workmen within the species, and moreover, I believe I have gotten ahead of myself. I need plans and supplies first . . . as well as a person who can conduct a crew. All I have is the mountaintop. Yet there is a male here this eve who has built several constructions in Caldwell and also in New York City and Philadelphia. I met him. He seems a fine sort, although he has an odd name."

"What does he go by?"

"The Jackal."

CHAPTER TEN

I can't pay you much!"

Nyx shouted the words as she jumped out of the hidden space, just before the panel slid back into place. Then she cursed at how loud she was.

Up ahead, the male with the broad back and the long braid stopped. When he didn't turn around and look at her, she had no idea what the hell he was going to do. What she was clear on? It was good to have her weapons back on her body. And in her hand.

The male slowly pivoted on his heel. As their eyes met, her breath caught, but damned if she was going to show it.

"Pay me," he said. "As in give me cash?"

"I have five hundred dollars. That's all I've got."

The male looked past her and then behind himself. "And just what do you think I shall do with money down here?"

"Isn't there, like, a black market or something?"

"A black market?"

"You know, bribing guards. Or other prisoners."

Yeah, like she was such an expert after all those *Lockdown* episodes she'd watched from her living room armchair.

For a moment, he just stared at her. And as a scent like dark spices entered her nose, she frowned—and so did he.

When he walked back over to her, it was easy to stand her ground considering she was armed and he was not. What was difficult was the way she tracked his movements. With every step he took, there was a powerful shifting from left to right, his shoulders and his hips counterbalancing his muscular weight.

It was the kind of thing that made a female wonder what exactly he could do with his body. If he happened to be naked.

His eyes scanned her face. "You will have to tell me who you're looking for."

Nyx's heart skipped a beat. But not because of what he'd demanded. It was that scent that seemed to come out of every single one of his pores. God, it smelled good, wiping out all the damp earth and mold in her nose.

"It's my sister," she said. "I'm going to get her out of this nightmare. She should never have ended up here in the first place."

"What's her name."

Not a question. Then again, they were solidly in rhetorical land, weren't they.

"Janelle. She was incarcerated fifty years ago."

"I don't recognize the name. But that doesn't mean anything."

"So you'll help me. For five hundred dollars."

His eyes, those incredible, glowing, blue-green eyes, narrowed. "Maybe."

Oh, for fuck's sake. "What's with the maybe. You're in or you're out."

The smile that curled his lips was calculating. And sensual. "Curious choice of words, female."

This isn't happening, Nyx thought. *This is* not *happening.*

And yet she focused on his mouth. And thought of where he could put it on her body.

"No," she said as she caught his drift. Because it was where her dumbass mind had gone, too.

"I would have helped you for free before," he drawled. "But now that you've brought up payment, I find myself with a change of heart."

"Five hundred. And we keep this professional. That's what I'm offering."

The male inhaled deeply, his nostrils flaring. Then he laughed, the rumble low in his throat. Like a purr. "I think you're offering quite a bit more, my dear."

Nyx reached out and grabbed the front of his shirt, yanking him forward. "Don't. Call. Me. 'Dear.' And I'm *never* going to be yours."

Later, she would reflect that manhandling the male was a mistake. Later . . . she would wish she could take that back. But not because she felt physically threatened.

"I will call you anything I want," he said as he focused on her lips.

"Oh, so it's like that, huh. I drop two curse words and you figure you don't need to show me any respect at all. Classy."

There was an electric pause. "On the contrary. I am more than prepared to show you something."

"Yeah, you can keep that to yourself." She punched at his chest and stepped back sharply. "Now do we have a deal."

"I don't want your money."

Nyx laughed with a hard edge. "Well, it's the only thing of mine I'm offering."

"I haven't told you what my price is."

"I know what you want."

"Do you," he drawled.

Yes, she thought, *because I want it, too.*

But now was not the time for her sex drive to finally get out of neutral. Nor did she want to start something with a criminal, for godsakes. Not only did she not know this male, she had no idea how he'd ended up down here. Although . . . well, Janelle didn't belong here, either, and—

Wait, was she really making excuses for this guy? What the hell was wrong with her.

Crap. He smelled really good.

As if he were reading her mind, the male's eyes dropped lower on her, to the front of her windbreaker, to her legs. When they rose back up to meet her stare, he was clearly laying out his position at their negotiating table without words.

"Five hundred dollars," she repeated.

114

"Tell me what I want."

"Excuse me?"

"You said you knew what I want. What is it."

He went back to looking at her mouth, like he wanted to watch it move, and she had a thought that he was thinking of places she could put her lips on him. Hard places. Places that, with a certain amount of attention, got things very, very messy.

And not just in an "it's complicated" kind of way.

"You want to have sex," she said. "But it's not going to be with me. So I'd suggest you take the five hundred and pay someone to put up with your grunting and groaning."

"How do you know what I sound like when I come." His voice was like velvet, his words running together. "Hmm?"

"Fine. Maybe you sing the Kit Kat song. Maybe it's your grocery list. Hell, it could be the Star fucking Banner. Whatever it is, it's none of my business."

"Oh, I'm afraid it is. If you want to find your sister."

Nyx glanced over her shoulder. There were no other noises coming from behind her, but that was not going to last. Sooner or later those guards were going to return and she couldn't believe this male was just standing here calmly, negotiating for sex, like they were on the sidewalk of a city street in a good zip code at one in the afternoon.

Right. Because that was where these kind of deals went down.

"I'm not fucking you," she said. "So either you get over this or—"

He moved so fast that she didn't have any time to react. One second there was space between them, the next, he was back in her face. And turning his head to the side. And dropping his mouth so that it was a thin inch from her own.

As she gasped, she smelled those dark spices.

"I'm afraid that's what I want from you," he whispered. "And I dare say, it is what you want as well." He breathed in deep again. "Fates, you smell like something I want to taste."

"No, I do not," she said roughly.

She went to slap him but he caught her hand, his reflexes faster than her own. And then he forced her arm back, his grip so tight she didn't even try to yank away.

He just stared at her with those mesmerizing eyes, and the next thing she knew, she wasn't thinking of pulling back. She only thought about getting closer to him.

It was the stress, she told herself. It was this strange, dangerous, knife-edge-of-adrenaline situation. That's why she was getting . . . turned on.

The male dropped her arm and regarded her with triumph.

"Let's find your Janelle then," he said. "Shall we?"

The Jackal didn't return the female to the hidden passageway. He was tempted, but he'd always had a sixth sense about the guards, and something was telling him that backtracking even a couple hundred yards in that direction was a bad idea.

But they had to get moving.

Fates, it had been so long since he had wanted a female. And after everything he had been through, he needed to feel that spark of attraction again.

It meant he wasn't as dead as he thought he was.

"Take your jacket off and put it on over that pack," he said as they headed off and he forced himself to snap out of the sexual spell. "And keep your eyes down and your hands in your pockets. I want you right behind me, and stay close. My reputation precedes me and that will be of benefit to us, but you do not want to be noticed. We don't want to push it."

The female complied so fast with the reorientation of her supplies and outerwear that he upgraded his opinion of her. Mayhap she could survive this. Yet as he sensed her falling lockstep into his wake, he wished he were leading her out of the hellhole instead of deeper into it.

117

She would try it on her own, though. She was just that reckless.

The prison's tunnels had been carved out of the earth with no rhyme or reason to their layout, which was what resulted when you had a system that had evolved rather than been designed for a given function. He was confident that a lot of prisoners didn't know half of the prison's confines, and he wondered about the guards.

The Command knew, however. He'd learned that the hard way.

For at least a quarter mile, they ran into no one, but as they got within range of the Hive, other prisoners were encountered. He kept her well away from the common area, skirting the high-traffic passages on a just-in-case. And it was strange how her presence changed things for him. Ordinarily, other prisoners were not on his radar; he worried about the guards. Now, anything that approached them was a threat to be assessed.

The closer he got to his cell, the faster he went, as if the lack of complication they'd had thus far was the kind of thing that could run out over distance.

The cells for the incarcerated were set in blocks in the oldest part of the prison, and you were lucky if you had one. The males and females who didn't were forced to bunk up in one of the common sleeping areas.

Which were rife with corruption. And worse.

His carved-out compartment in the rock was the last in the row of the oldest ones, and as he proceeded down the lineup of berths, he deliberately looked into each and every one. None of the other prisoners paid him attention. Most were lying on their pallets, sleeping off work shifts. One was reading a *Life* magazine that had a picture of a male human with the name "Richard Nixon" under the black-and-white portrait. Another had a tattered book with no jacket upon it cracked open.

When he got to his cell, he stood to one side and nodded for the female to go inside. Verily, he wished he had something better to offer her than these harsh, barely inhabitable accommodations. The days of luxury were long past him, however.

Staying put, he stared in the direction they'd come from. No guards. No prisoners. Nothing.

So her scent hadn't been noticed.

As he ducked into the ten-by-ten-foot space, he cleared his throat. The female looked over from checking out the rock-hard wooden platform he slept on.

"Where are the bars?" she asked as she nodded at the open archway.

The Jackal leaned to the side and pulled the set of iron slats and steel mesh out from the rock walling. "Here."

"So wait, you can leave anytime?"

"Was it easy for you to get down here?" As

she closed her mouth, he nodded. "The escape problem is not the cells, it's the prison itself."

"But how is order maintained?"

The laugh that came out of him was low, and even to his own ears, mean. "The Command has its ways."

"Is that the warden, you mean? The head of the prison?"

"Yes."

"Who does he report to?" She motioned around. "And who's in charge over him? Is this run by the King or—"

"The prison has always been under the ultimate rule of the *glymera* and the Council."

The female frowned. "Are you sure about that? Because the Council has been disbanded by the King, and the raids killed most of the aristocracy off."

"What raids?"

"The Lessening Society attacked the Founding Families in their homes about three years ago. No one has any idea how they found them. They slaughtered almost the entirety of those blood-lines." As the shock he felt must have shown on his face, the female tilted toward him, but didn't touch him. Dropping the volume of her voice, she said, "Exactly how long have you been down here?"

"What precise year is it?"

"You don't know?"

"I wouldn't have asked if I did." He shrugged. "And it doesn't matter. I was incarcerated in nineteen fourteen, and since then, time has had little meaning to me."

The female blinked. "You've been here for over a hundred years."

"Yes."

"You have had no contact with the outside world since then?" She shook her head. "I mean, no visitors?"

"Do you think a place like this has visiting hours? As if we are a hospital ward down here?"

She started to say something else at that point, but he found himself distracted by the movement of her lips, paying more attention to their pursing than the syllables they released.

"You stay here," he said, cutting her off. "And get under the bedding platform."

"What?"

"I'll be gone for not more than five minutes." Not that he had a watch. Not that he knew that for a fact. "Get under the bed. Unless you want to run the risk of some of my fellow prisoners making your acquaintance—and I can assure you, they won't do it by shaking your hand."

"Take me with you."

"No. I'm going to the Hive. I can't protect you there if it's only me on my own." He pointed to the bedding platform. "Get under there and don't make a sound."

CHAPTER ELEVEN

Nyx had never been good at following directions, but survival instinct made her uncharacteristically compliant. So, sure, fine, she all-four'd it and planked her way into the crawl space under the roughly constructed "bed." Staring out at ground level, she watched as the male left and then listened to the sounds of the prison: the voices off in the distance, the footfalls . . . someone singing a Duran Duran song?

Jesus, when was the last time she'd heard that? It had to have been when Ronald Reagan was in office and folks were watching *Family Ties*— and as she considered the lag in culture and progress, she couldn't fathom how much things had changed up above as those incarcerated down here had stayed the same. For godsakes, back when Simon Le Bon had been singing about how hungry he was, the Internet hadn't been invented yet, Amazon had only been a jungle, and electricity had been for vacuum cleaners, not cars.

Janelle had missed out on so much—

Through the open archway of the cell, she saw a draped figure walk by slowly, its head lowered, nothing of the hands or feet showing out of the hems of the asphalt-gray robing. It was too small to be a male.

It had to be female.

"Janelle?" she whispered.

Nyx shuffled out from under like she was saving someone from a fire, and as her pack got caught on something, she shucked it off quick, leaving it and her windbreaker behind. Popping to her feet, she broke free of the cell and hung a right. There wasn't much running involved on the catch-up, and as soon as she was in range, she reached out and touched the sleeve of the robe.

"Janelle?"

The figure stopped. Pivoted around.

"It's me, Nyx—"

As the female looked up, the hood lifted and the light from the bulbs overhead penetrated the shadows obscuring the face. Nyx gasped and jumped back.

The female had lost an eye at some point, and the injury had been badly treated, the socket stitched closed with black thread that remained in place even though the skin had healed. The mouth had been likewise ruined, part of the upper lip missing so that the long shanks of rotten teeth and the gray pads of discolored gums showed.

The snarl that came out from under the robe was as vicious as a rabid dog's, and what was left of the mouth curled back—

Something pink was wedged in between those chipped teeth. Pieces of . . . meat?

"Now, now," a male voice drawled, "you just keep going. I know you can't be hungry. I just saw you eat."

Nyx didn't bother looking at whoever was putting his two cents in. She was too busy worrying about whether she'd be tackled so her face could be chewed off as dessert.

After a tense moment—during which a spool of drool dripped off that chin as the eye went back and forth between Nyx and the male who was standing behind her—the female lowered her stare and shuffled away.

As a wave of relief replaced the panic, Nyx turned to thank—

The prisoner who had interceded on her behalf was enormous, which explained why that scarred female had done the math and left. But he was no savior. As he leaned casually against the rock wall, his glittering yellow eyes were heavy-lidded and calculating, his muscled body clearly capable of getting him whatever he wanted.

And that warning about making acquaintances had been right. This predator was not looking to shake her hand.

"I don't think I've seen you around here, have I," he said.

Nyx looked back toward the cell she'd left.

Thought of her backpack. Thought of the relative safety she'd left on a desperate whim.

"If you're new here"—he crossed his arms over the heft of his chest—"I'll give you a quick orientation. First rule is, don't approach anyone who's not looking for your company."

As her heart pounded, she glanced in the other direction. That female was making a turn, moving out of sight.

"Just so you know," the male said with deceptive softness, "I am very open to meeting you."

Nyx refocused on the prisoner in front of her. She hadn't wasted time taking note of his hair or his features, but she tracked every nuance of him now, from the long, wavy hair that was streaked with gray to the arch of his brows and the hard cut of his jawline. In other circumstances, she might have considered him attractive, but not down here. And not with that look in his eye.

He was a killer.

And he was . . . something else, too.

There was something different about him.

"You can run if you want to," he murmured as his eyes traveled down her body. "It'll make it more fun."

The Jackal hoped he did not have to go all the way to the Hive to find who he was looking for. And this wasn't the only thing on his mind as he entered the main concourse tunnel. Going along, he found himself making assessments as to the other prisoners: How tall they were. How strong. How weak. How fast. How slow. Almost all of them were wearing the same kind of loose, grungy-colored clothing he was, but there was a lot of variety in all the other physical characteristics displayed. Different hair colors. Eye colors. Ages and weights. He had some thought that he had done this back when he had first found himself in the underground.

Then, it had been a case of wanting to survive.

Now, it was through the eyes of that female that he took the measure of those with whom he was familiar. There were at least fifteen hundred prisoners down here, which sounded like a lot until you spent a hundred years with the same set of faces—and it wasn't like there were new people coming in anymore. In fact, he couldn't think of a fresh arrival in the last ten years.

Then again, what had the female said? The raids. The Council gone. Most of the Founding Families dead.

Seventy-five years ago, if that disruption in authority had occurred? Fifty years ago? Perhaps the population down here would have revolted and escaped. But not now. In spite of what he'd told his guest, the *glymera* was no longer in charge of the prison they had created—and they hadn't been for at least two decades.

The Command had been gathering the reins of control for quite some time—

Up ahead, a figure among the others stood out. Taller than most, with what the Jackal's grandfather would have called "a regal carriage," the male somehow turned his common clothes into tailor-made masterpieces just by the controlled swing of his proper gait.

Speak of the aristocrat.

The Jackal jumped ahead, falling into the wake of his target. In a low voice, he said, "I need a favor."

It was a testament to the kind of vampire he was dealing with that nothing changed about the male. Not the stride, not the straight-ahead of the focus, not the swing in those arms.

But there was a quiet reply, low and soft. "What do you need, my friend."

"Come to my cell."

"When."

"Now."

There was the briefest of nods, and then, at the next branching-off, the male deviated from the flow of bodies headed to the Hive, and penetrated a tunnel with narrower walls and no foot traffic. The Jackal stuck with the prisoner, and they went quite some distance before stopping.

Nothing was said as they waited.

When there was no trail and no guards, the Jackal walked forward a couple of yards and paused with his back to the stone wall. The other male played lookout as the hidden switch was hit and a soft clicking sound was released as the panel slid back.

A moment later, the pair of them were in the other end of the hidden passageway that the Jackal had brought the female into in the first place.

"Tell me," Kane said as candles flared, and they started walking.

Kane had been the biggest surprise when the Jackal was first learning the ropes of the prison. Another aristocrat who was both educated and smart—not always the same thing—the male had, no doubt as a throwback social courtesy, extended a hand in mentorship. The two of them had much in common, and not only when it came to their backgrounds and fall from status.

"I'm going to let her explain it," the Jackal murmured.

"Her?"

The Jackal let that stand and went along faster, covering the distance to the nearest of the three exits with alacrity. Emerging from the passage was always a risk, and he was forced to stop and listen. When there was nothing on the other side, he released the hold and the panel slid back without a sound.

Extraction was faster than a blink, and then he and Kane were almost to his cell—

The Jackal jerked to a halt. Even though that was the wrong instinct. But he couldn't understand what he was looking at.

The civilian female, who he had witnessed hiding herself well and properly under his bed, appeared to be out and about, and she had managed to cross paths with the ultimate bad penny in the prison. She was standing within swiping distance of that wolven—and Lucan was looking like he'd found Little Red Riding Hood alone in the forest. The huge hybrid was staring down at her with hunger in his face and in his powerful body, the sexual intent rolling off of him in waves.

The Jackal would have shouted, except he didn't want to draw any notice from anybody. Instead, he lunged forward, prepared to tackle the other male—

The female moved so fast, no one saw it coming.

Not even the wolf.

In a single, decisive surge, she outed a sharp knife, planted a palm on the hybrid's sternum, and jabbed the blade's tip right up into his crotch.

In a calm voice, she said, "I'll castrate you right here, right now. Or you can back up off me. What's it going to be, big guy? Doesn't matter to me which way we go, but I have a feeling you're going to want to keep what's down here or your swagger's out the window."

To emphasize her point, she put some muscle into the weapon.

The wolven let out a squeak that was wholly at odds with his size and his—what had the female called it? Swagger?

Behind the Jackal, Kane let out a soft laugh. "Well," the aristocrat said, "at least I know what we're dealing with."

CHAPTER TWELVE

Following Nyx's bladed face-off with that golden-eyed male's most delicate of areas, things were a little tense. Then again, guys did tend to do a groupthink wince when anybody with their anatomy got their hey-nannies threatened by something sharp and shiny. After the situation de-escalated, and the others were able to stand without covering themselves with both palms, she followed all three of them into a hidden tunnel and down to a low-ceilinged open area that everyone but she had to duck to get into. Candles, not light bulbs, lit the way and lit the talk spot, the circle of flat stone "seats" that surrounded a fire pit making her wonder just how cold it got down here in the winter.

She sat when the others did, and she cracked a smile as she noted that the big male with those yellow eyes and the big ideas sat waaaaaaay across from her.

And closed his knees together like he wasn't sure exactly how put away her knife was.

"This is Kane," the male with brilliant blue eyes said. Then he tacked on dryly, "And you've met Lucan."

There was a silence, during which she stared at her paid guide to the prison. He had stayed close to her when they'd been going through the passageway, and he sat on the stone next to hers. Given the glower on his face, she could guess that he was talking to her in his head, no doubt berating her for the impulse that had taken her out from under his bed and provided her with the opportunity to meet all kinds of new friends.

God, that female with the ruined face.

Nyx glanced over at the one who'd been introduced as Kane. His silver eyes were steady, his body was giving off no signs of aggression or sexual charge, and he had the kind of open, handsome face that made you think no matter what was going on, things were going to be okay.

This situation could use about fifteen more of him, she thought.

"How can I help you?" he asked in a calm, level tone.

In contrast to his speech, hers was rushed. Rough.

"I'm looking for my sister. Her name is Janelle. She was falsely accused of murder and got two hundred and fifty years." By their grandfather, for godsakes. "She's been down here since nineteen sixty-seven. June second, nineteen sixty-seven. I'll tell you anything you need to know about her."

"Everyone's falsely accused of something in this prison," Lucan, the one she'd almost turned into a Lynette, muttered.

Kane lowered his eyes for a brief moment. "May I ask, what do you think you will do if you find her?"

"*When* I find her. And I'm going to get her out."

"How will you do that?"

"I know how I came in. I'll backtrack there and take her home."

"And you think they will not come after you?" He lifted a hand and gestured around. "The guards here have a job and they are accountable for it. The head count must register properly for the work shifts. If it does not, those males are beaten—or worse. They will choose themselves over you and your family, I assure you."

"I'll be gone before they know I'm here."

As the other males looked at each other and shook their heads, Kane said, "Do you live with anyone you care about? Because they'll slaughter everything around them if they must reclaim a prisoner from hiding, and they will bring the bodies back here to show their duty is done. Life and death is not only for the prisoners herein. It is for everybody the Command administers and all who seek to disorder the order. In this, the guards are no different than we prisoners."

"My sister is innocent."

"In your mind, perhaps. But that is not a defense if you help her escape."

Part of Nyx wanted to argue that her situation was different, that however many people here needed to be imprisoned, Janelle was not one of them. But then she thought about that guard in the crypt. She'd never killed before, yet it was the work of a moment to choose her own survival over a threat to it.

"I'll take Janelle far away," she said. "No one will find us."

Kane reached up and pulled open the front of his loose shirting. Around the base of his throat was an inch-thick band that he had evidently worn for so long, it had discolored and dug into his skin.

"Yes, they will." He shifted the thing around so that a subtle blinking dot showed. "They will absolutely find you. And her. These track collars are our leashes."

"I could take it off her—"

"No, you can't."

Her male with the brilliant blue eyes spoke up. "They're explosive collars. If the connection is broken at the back, the charge instantly detonates. There's no surviving it. They're also rimmed with steel on the inside so there is no dematerializing."

Okay, first of all, this male was not "hers," she reminded herself. *And secondly . . .*

"So that's why the cell doors are all open." She glanced at the three prisoners. "That's why no one leaves. But don't the batteries eventually wear out?"

"When the light changes to orange," Kane said,

"you have twenty-four hours to replace them. If the power gets lower than that, it explodes."

Lucan spoke up. "It's a hell of an incentive to check in, lemme tell you."

"That's how they register the count for the shifts." The male beside her rubbed his face like his head hurt. "There's a radio receiver in each one that confirms the location of the band."

"But this passageway is hidden, right?" she said. "Why don't they know where you are now?"

Kane closed his shirt collar as if he were hiding nakedness, as if he were ashamed. "It's not that precise. But the system is more than sufficient when it comes to the boundaries of the prison. If we try to go above-ground, it will notify instantly our location and track us."

Nyx slowly shook her head. "There has to be a way to beat it. There just has to be."

"Kane, why don't you tell the nice female how long you've been down here," the male beside her said.

Kane's eyes drifted to the fire pit, with its cold ashes and sooted remnants of logs. "What is the precise date."

When Nyx told him, his shoulders slumped, and there was very little pause on the math. "Two hundred seventy-three years, eleven months, six days."

Nyx's breath left her lungs. "I can't imagine."

It was a moment before Kane seemed to

137

refocus. "Neither can I. And the point is, there are many people down here trying to figure a way out. Determination and a fresh set of eyes on this problem are not going to change our reality, and I am sorry to have to tell you this. Getting your sister free is impossible."

That steady stare was full of compassion, and Nyx's heart answered the call to unburden her struggles. As tears came to her eyes, she hid them by looking at her hands.

"There has to be a way," she said with a voice that cracked. "There just has to be."

The female was so strong, the Jackal thought as he watched her fight to maintain composure. And the fact that he was moved by her, that he wanted to reach out and offer her support, was an unfamiliar impulse.

Then again, it seemed like she was the key to many of his locks.

I can still close those doors, he reminded himself.

As she sat there in silence, no one interrupted her internal thought processes. Then again, down here, one didn't waste one's energy on things that were inevitable and outside of your control.

"Let me take you back to where you came from," the Jackal offered. "When it's safe. Let's get you out of here—"

"I want to see her." The female looked up

sharply. "I want to find my sister and see her."

"There are almost two thousand people down here," he countered. "It would take a month or more to go through all those faces, and it's more likely the guards will notice you before you cross her path."

"I don't care. I'm not leaving until I see her."

"Even if it kills you."

"It won't."

The Jackal let out a hard laugh as he rubbed his aching head. "For truth, I cannot decide whether you're courageous or crazy."

"I'm neither. I'm just someone's sister. If you knew you had a sibling out in the world who needed you, wouldn't you go after them?"

"How do you even know she's alive?" The way the female snapped to attention made him regret his choice of words. But had she never considered that possibility? "I'm sorry, but death is prevalent here. Disease, malnutrition, natural causes. You're assuming she lives, and again, forgive me for being blunt."

"We could take her to the Wall," Kane suggested. "If the three of us—"

"No." The Jackal burst up to his feet. "We're not going into the Command's sector with her."

"What's the Wall?" she demanded.

The other two males deferred to the Jackal on that. So he answered. "It's a tally of those who have died herein."

The female glanced around. "We have to go there."

"No," the Jackal said. "I shall go myself, and see if her name is listed—"

"I don't trust you." She got to her feet and stared at him. "You want me to leave here. How do I know you won't lie and tell me you saw her name just to get me to go."

"I give you my word."

"I don't know you well enough to judge whether your 'word' is worth anything more than the breath you use to speak the syllable. I want to go and see her name myself, and if it was your blood, you'd feel the same way."

The Jackal crossed his arms over his chest. "You keep talking like we have these family ties in common. We don't. So you're not going to motivate me with that kind of argument."

"Fine." She kicked her chin up. "I'm either going to that Wall or heading to the Hub to see if I can find her face in the crowd."

"The Hive, you mean."

"Whatever."

As their eyes clashed, the Jackal felt his blood stir. "You don't want to go there."

"I don't want to *be* here. For a lot of reasons. But I am where I am."

After a tense moment, Kane spoke up. "We can wait until the shifts change. There is time during check-out and check-in. We could sneak her through and get back out before anyone notices."

"Great plan." The female went over to Kane. "How long until the shifts are over?"

"It has been over a century and a half since I've been able to measure anything passing by an hour hand. But it would be a work night."

"Twelve hours?"

"Or eight. Or ten. But the changeover just occurred, so it will be a full shift."

"Then I wait. Where do I find you all again?"

The Jackal considered the merits of arguing, but given the grit of that female's molars and the bow-of-a-tanker thrust of her chin, he was going to get nowhere trying to talk sense into her.

"We will reconvene here," he said grimly. "And you will stay with me."

The other males did not fight that, and he wasn't surprised. Kane was too much of a gentle-male, and as for Lucan? Well, apparently he preferred his courting tackle right where it was.

So the wolven seemed very happy to take his leave with the aristocrat.

The Jackal waited until he heard the whisper-soft sound of the passageway's exit opening and reclosing. Then he looked over at the female.

She was staring at the unlit fire, and he had a feeling if she knew how much exhaustion was showing on her face, she would have hidden it quick.

She seemed to shake herself back to attention. "I want to get my weapons from your cell. And I'll stay here alone until you come get me."

When he didn't respond, she shook her head. "No, you're not talking me out of anything."

"Something tells me there are few who can do that."

"Try none."

He considered her for a moment. "What is your name. It seems like I should at least know it by now."

"Nyx." She stuck her hand out. "You?"

Leaning in, he slid his palm into hers and took note of the feel of her warm, slightly callused skin. He approved of the latter and wasn't surprised by it. The warmth? He could have done without noticing that.

"The Jackal." He bowed a little, as if they were making acquaintance in a drawing room. "And yes, that is my name."

No, it wasn't. But he didn't use his real one. Hadn't for . . . well, since after his transition.

"Your first name is 'the'?" she said dryly.

"It was a nickname that stuck."

"Down here?"

"And up there." He shrugged. "It doesn't matter."

There was a long silence, and as she broke off and walked around the fire pit, he studied her movements.

"How would you care for a hot bath," he asked.

"Like this place has running water?"

"In a manner of speaking, yes, it does. But more than that, the bathing pool is in an even more secure place. I'd suggest you allow me to get your pack and show you the way."

"I'll get it myself. Which way do I go."

The Jackal put his hands on his hips and stared at the stone floor. Then he strode over and got right in the female's face.

In Nyx's face.

"Enough." He loomed over her. "I have had enough. You're going to stay here. I'm going to get your pack. And then we're going to the bathing pool."

"No, I'm going to—"

"Your desperation to find your sister is making you reckless. If that gets only you killed, fine. You deserve it. But Lucan and Kane are now involved and I will *not* let you endanger their lives."

"How does me going back to get my stuff have anything to do with them?"

"Because I'm going to be obligated to save you and what do you think they're going to do? They're going to come help me. Or are you saying that they don't matter. That they're just prisoners who are expendable. Hmm? Is that how you feel?"

"Of course not," she spat.

"Then for once in your life, do what you're told and stay here."

Nyx crossed her arms over her chest and glared at him. Going by the way her jaw moved, it was obvious she was grinding her molars, and her eyes were spitting fire.

Except then she muttered, "Fine."

The Jackal threw up his hands and turned away. "Finally. A fucking breakthrough."

"FYI, you just cussed. And it was a big one."

"See what you drive males to?"

As he stalked off, she called out, "I get along with most people, you know."

"If you believe that, you're delusional as well as obstinate," he tossed over his shoulder as he kept on going.

Before he did something stupid.

Like kiss her.

Although that was their deal, wasn't it. He got her to her sister. She gave him what he wanted.

Fates, that was a tricky bargain, he thought as he left her in the dust. Because it had to just be about the sex. He had to remain emotionless and apart from her, only the physical side of things connecting.

"Not a problem," he told himself.

Things kept up as they were, and he couldn't *wait* to get rid of her.

CHAPTER THIRTEEN

As Nyx waited by the fire pit, she kept the knife she had almost used on that big Lucan guy against the palm of her dominant hand. Left on her own, her heart beat fast and her eyes skimmed around the secret gathering place, tracking shadows that did not move and contours that remained the same. Underground water easing out of fissures in the walls slicked the stone, and in the candlelight, she could pick out the carving marks that were testament to the effort that had gone into creating the space.

Had the Jackal made this with the others? Over a period of years? Decades? She couldn't fathom the time lost.

She took out a burner cell phone and looked at the time. Four hours had passed since she had left the farmhouse. It felt like four years. Naturally, there was no signal down here—and she hadn't expected there to be one—but she had plenty of battery life. And with the lack of notifications, she wondered if Posie had sent anything that hadn't gone through. Her sister must have noticed her too-long absence by now. Unless . . . maybe Peter was in crisis. Had he died yet?

Probably.

The idea that she'd had to choose between sisters sucked.

Nyx checked the screen on her phone one last time, focusing on her wallpaper. It was a photograph she'd taken back in June, of the front of the farmhouse. Its lights were aglow, the cheerful yellow illumination spilling out onto the lawn and flowing over the peony beds that were in full bloom.

In her mind, she told Posie she would be back soon. But she didn't say the words out loud because she feared they were a lie.

Then she turned off the unit to save the battery life and zipped it into an inside pocket.

Glancing over her shoulder, she thought she heard footsteps. No. It wasn't the Jackal coming back, and it wasn't anybody else, either.

That male drove her nuts. Especially because he was right. She was being reckless, and if she kept rolling the crazy dice, snake eyes was going to come up and get her.

God, she hoped he was being honest with her.

Unable to stay still, she walked around the fire pit three or four times. Stopped and looked again to the tunnel where her host had gone. When he'd suggested he be the one to go get her pack, she'd agreed. Had that been a mistake? Was he even now selling her grandfather's weapons and ammo on the prison's black market, or whatever they called it?

She should have gone with him—

The sound of heavy footfalls brought her head up, and when she recognized the scent, she wasn't sure whether to be relieved or not.

The Jackal emerged from the darkness, and he had something in his arms.

"I got some food," he said as he headed by her. "I figured you must be hungry."

When he kept right on going, she didn't immediately follow, and he glanced over the provisions at her. "Are you coming?"

"We're not staying here?"

"Does it look like there's a bath where you're standing."

Falling into step with him, she peeled her pack from his shoulders and strapped it on. "So where's this bath place?"

"Close."

Some distance along, he stopped short. Looked both ways. Triggered something. "We're here."

As a section of the rock walling slid back, Nyx recoiled. But not because things smelled bad.

On the contrary, the scent of clean water was as obvious as it was a surprise.

Nyx walked forward, called by the relief from the cloying aroma of earth. As she entered a narrow passageway, she rushed forward, her way lit by candles that flared one by one down at the floor. In the back of her mind, she had the sense that he was lighting her path, willing the wicks to life.

Then she made a corner and faltered as she confronted a dense black space. The sound, though . . . oh, that was gently falling water. And there was humidity in the air—and warmth.

The Jackal stepped into the darkness behind her. "This is where I go when I need . . ."

He didn't finish the sentence. Then again, as candles flared in a broad circle around a natural spring, he didn't have to.

"Oh . . . my God," she whispered.

From somewhere in the ceiling, a natural flow of water dropped into a ten-foot-wide pool, some kind of heat vent down in the natural basin bubbling the clear water and causing steam to rise up.

"I thought you might like it here." He put the bundle down. "So, yes. At any rate."

He sat on the smooth back of an enormous boulder, unpacking bread and what looked like cheese. There was also an old-fashioned milk bottle filled with something the color of a red poker chip.

"This is not fancy," he said, "but you can have it all."

Nyx approached him and lowered herself onto the granite "sofa." "What about you?"

"I can find more for me. It's more important for you to be strong."

He leaned to the side and took something out of a hip pocket. Flipping the cloth free of its folds, he made a little table and then laid out the picnic.

"I wish I had something better to offer." He opened the glass bottle. "This tastes wretched, but it has singlehandedly kept me from getting scurvy."

He took a deep drink and swallowed. As he closed his eyes, she thought it was a little odd that he was savoring the stuff as if it were wine—

His lids flipped up. "It's safe."

"Safe?"

"Untampered with." He offered the drink to her. "I didn't make it, so I have to be sure it's okay for you."

Nyx took the glass container, her fingers brushing his. "Thank you."

He nodded and then tore off a piece from the loaf. As he chewed, he closed his eyes again. Then he did the same with the cheese.

"This is all safe as well."

Putting her lips to the open neck of the container, she had a thought that his mouth had been where hers was now—and that really shouldn't have mattered.

As she took a test taste, she frowned and looked at the red liquid. "This is Kool-Aid. Or at least that's what it tastes like."

"What is that?"

"I'm not sure whether this has any vitamins

in it." She drank some more. "But it's good."

Funny how everything was relative. Back home, she would have given the swill a solid pass. Down here? It was strangely comforting.

"I haven't had this since back in the seventies," she murmured. "I used to make it for Posie before her transition."

"Another sister?"

"Yes, the youngest in the family. Do you want some more of this?"

"No, it's all for you."

"I'm willing to share."

When he just leaned back on the rock wall and extended his long legs, she shrugged and finished what was there. Then she hit the bread, which had been baked fresh and tasted pretty damn good, and the cheese, which had almost no taste but was definitely not spoiled. She ate fast, her hunger much sharper than she'd thought.

Then again, the sense of imminent danger made her feel like she could be interrupted, in a bad way, at any second.

And then the food was gone.

Nyx shifted her eyes to the swirling water because things got too intense when she was looking at him. But as the silence went on, she had to glance over at the male.

His eyes were closed, his breathing even. But he wasn't asleep.

"Finished?" he said softly.

"Yes."

His lids opened, but not very far, that vivid blue stare glowing.

"How many people know about this place?" she heard herself ask.

Why does that matter, she thought. Even though she knew exactly why she was making the inquiry.

"Kane and Lucan. Two others. But they won't come here. I told them to stay out."

"Why did you do that?"

"Why do you think."

The female—Nyx—looked to the falling water again, and as the Jackal recognized where her eyes were, he also knew where her thoughts had gone. She didn't want to speak them out loud, and he respected that, but her scent was giving her away.

"No one will come here. You're safe," he said.

"I don't feel safe."

"You have your weapons." He thought of Lucan. "And I've seen you use them."

"I didn't cut that male."

"You would have if he'd moved."

"True." Her eyes returned to his own. "What is he?"

The Jackal debated playing dumb, but just shook his head instead. "That's his story to tell, not mine."

"So he's not just a vampire."

"Not my story." He let his stare drift down to her lips. "Do you want to get into the water?"

"Are you going to stay here?"

"I'll give you my back. If you want it."

As he waited for her response, he reminded himself what this was all about. They were using each other, and it was a relief to set those boundaries. Meanwhile, inside his body, down to his very marrow, things stirred, things he had not felt in so long that he had come to believe and accept that they had been killed, casualties of his prison experience. This female had proved otherwise, and he was not losing the opportunity. But more than that, there was the satisfaction that in laying with her, he would hurt another, hurt the one who had done such damage to him. Even if he was the only one who knew it—and he was going to have to keep it that way—the rebalance of power, the reclamation of his autonomy, was nourishment to his blackened soul.

Before he could act upon his instincts, however, something occurred to him.

"Why did your family send you on this suicidal mission?" he asked abruptly. "Have you no brothers? No sire?"

Her brows arched. "Males aren't the only people who are capable of things."

"No. This should have been carried out by a

male relation of your bloodline. Have they no shame?"

Nyx seemed to need a moment to gather herself. "Wow. You know, in the hundred years since you ended up down here, a lot has changed. They let us girls drive cars and hold jobs—oh, and we can vote. Or, well, if I was a human, I could vote. But still."

"I have offended you," he said levelly. "For that I am sorry."

Nyx tilted her head. "But wait, lemme guess. You're sticking with your dated and sexist position."

"You expect me to apologize for wanting to protect females? You will not get that, now or ever."

" 'Protection' is another word for subjugate."

"It is? You must explain."

"You think you need to protect me because I'm weaker than you are."

"I can most certainly lift more than you can."

"And that's everything? Please. Spare me the caveman routine." She jabbed a finger at him. "Your problem is that you think being able to bench-press a car gives you the right to dictate things that are none of your business."

"You'll have to remind me of this when I ensure your safety against the guards."

"I'll save myself, thank you very much—"

"It must be nice to know everything about

everything. And you accuse me of being an overlord? All you need is a castle and a moat and you're a medieval knight. At least in your own mind."

"That's where it counts most, buddy—"

"Fates, you can't ever concede a point—"

The two of them were speaking faster and louder, and in the back of his mind, he knew what was happening. Both of them were uneasy with the sexual attraction, unsure of how far to take things, but dearest Virgin Scribe, he was hungry. For her.

And she was the same. Her scent had changed, and everything that was male in him recognized her arousal—and was driven to do something about it.

"—males like you boxing us in, making us feel less than—" She stopped. "What."

"Do go on." He crossed his arms over his chest. "I enjoy watching you argue with yourself."

"FYI, you were tossing a few sentences back there yourself, Judgy McJudgerson."

He shook his head and frowned. "I'm sorry? I am not a magistrate?"

Nyx opened her mouth. Closed it. "Have you ever heard of a meme?"

"Of course. A performer in black and white who doesn't speak."

"That's a mime. A meme is . . ." As she seemed to let her thought recede, her temper appeared to deflate. "You don't know anything about the Internet, do you. Social media. Microsoft. Apple."

"Small and supple, you mean? And the latter is a fruit I have long missed the acquaintance of. As for the rest, I'm afraid you have me at a loss." As they stared at each other, he knew she was tallying his deficiencies with regard to the modern world. "You can stop that right now. Don't you *dare* feel sorry for me. I don't need or desire your sympathy."

She looked to the swirling water again. "I just can't imagine being down here for so long, that's all."

As she struggled, the Jackal cursed under his breath. "I have missed much then?"

"In a hundred years, yes." She cleared her throat. Looked back at him. "By the way, is it okay if I just call you Jack? The 'the' thing is a little weird."

He had to smile. "You may call me whatever you wish."

"Even if it's a curse word?"

"Rest assured you would not be the first."

"That I can believe."

He found himself wanting to smile. "Tell me, what would you pick?"

"Out of the full catalogue of bad words?" She regarded him with grave seriousness. "I think I would go with . . . 'boneheaded chauvinistic throwback boomer.' "

The Jackal blinked a number of times. "I don't recognize those words as curses. And I'm not sure what this backwards-pitched boomer is?"

Ducking her head, she hid a smile he was desperate to see. "I guess I'm more of a lady than I thought. 'Twat-waffle' and 'fucktard' just seemed below the belt and inappropriate."

"Twat-waffle? What is that?"

"I don't know, but it's not good."

They fell silent again, but the tension was gone—although not the heat. Therefore, he felt compelled to say, "I would kiss you the now, if it would not offend."

CHAPTER FOURTEEN

It was out of an obligation to all that was rational that Nyx tried on a bunch of responses to the kiss question in her head, making a deep cognitive dive. Into Netflix and Spotify.

Emma Thompson, ca. *Sense and Sensibility*: *You must cease and desist all such lustful thoughts, you beast.*

Emma Stone, ca. *Zombieland*: *Over your dead body.*

Julia Roberts, ca. *Pretty Woman*: *Big mistake. Huge.*

Cardi B, in any situation: *Bitch, please.*

All of those worked. Unfortunately, what was more likely to come out of her mouth was straight-up Jennifer Lawrence: *I volunteer as tribute.*

Eight hours, Nyx thought. Wasn't that what the gentlemale in the prison clothes had said? Maybe ten.

So it was going to be a very long time until she and Jack could get going to the Wall.

And talking was overrated, wasn't it.

"I'll do the kissing," she muttered. "Thank you very much."

With that, she crossed the space between them with her lips, putting them on his. And as the

157

softness of his mouth registered, she was surprised, but that made no sense. All mouths were soft, even if they came attached to big, strong bodies. And what do you know. In spite of his obvious arousal, he didn't jump her. Instead, Jack stayed where he was, reclining against the smooth rock, letting her set the pace as she explored and . . . enjoyed.

Tilting her head, she deepened things, running her tongue along his lower lip. Then she licked inside of him.

The shaking that rose up from his body was erotic. The way his breath caught was hotter than hell. The taste of him and the scent of him and—

He pulled back sharply, his glittering blue eyes finding hers. There was a flush on his face and the cords in his neck were straining, like he was forcing himself to stay put.

"You do not disappoint," he said roughly. "Not in the slightest."

That was when he grabbed her and pulled her onto his chest. His kiss was nothing like hers. It was not tentative. It wasn't a caress of lips. It wasn't soft, lilting, a polite exploration that was a prelude to passion.

He was a full-blooded, fully aroused male and he took what he wanted, his hands biting into her upper arms, his mouth hard on hers, catching . . . owning. And she told herself that she felt it all so acutely because her senses were alive in this dangerous, strange prison.

But that was bullshit. She would have felt the same up above, in the real world, if they were out on a date and he was kissing her up against a car in a restaurant's parking lot. Her body was alive because of him, not where they were.

"Will you let me inside," he asked against her mouth.

"Yes," she breathed. Even as she told herself to stay quiet.

Her need for him was something she felt like she should hide. It gave him power over her, the kind that had nothing to do with the dead lift thing or the bullcrap that came with his antiquated view of females.

But like her response was a secret? Especially as she split her legs and sat on his hard, muscled thigh, her core rubbing against him, creating delicious friction. And as if he knew what she was doing, he purred, deep in his throat, one of his hands coming up to cup the back of her neck. When her hair tie was pulled out, she knew that was the prelude to him taking her clothes off, and she was ready for the naked, starved for the next level to all this—

Just as Jack had overtaken her when she'd first entered the prison's labyrinth, he again moved so fast, she couldn't track him. One moment, he was underneath her and their mouths were fused. The next, he was all the way on the far side of the pool.

As he began to pace back and forth, he put one of his hands to his forehead. Meanwhile, she was stuck on the stone sofa, wondering what the hell had happened.

What the hell had gone wrong.

But he'd been feeling her. She knew it.

Hell, she could see it, in that bulge in the front of his loose pants.

"Are you okay?" she asked.

"Yes," he snapped. "I am perfectly well."

"Well, that's good. You know, you look fine. You look totally, completely fine. I mean, honestly, the poster child for fine."

"Will you please stop talking," he muttered.

"You could make me. If you kissed me again."

At that, he stopped and looked over at her. She braced herself to be called a hussy, or some other old-fashioned word. Instead, the full force of his sexual arousal sizzled across the warm, humid space.

"You're afraid of me," she said. "Aren't you."

"I am not."

"Yes, you are. You started a game and now you're afraid of finishing it." She crossed her arms over her breasts. "Why is that."

"I am not afraid of anything." His tone was dead. "This place has taught me to know no fear."

Nyx opened her mouth to argue with him,

but she didn't follow through on the knee-jerk impulse as all of the life drained out of him. No more light behind those beautiful blue eyes. No more arousal in his magnificent body. No more connection to anything around him, even her.

"What did they do to you," she said through a tight throat.

He looked away, and she studied his handsome face in the candlelight. When she wasn't busy being irritated with him, his male beauty captivated her. He had perfect bone structure, and sensuous lips that she now knew all too well, and that torso of his, so strong and wide at the shoulders, so narrow at the hips, was the kind of thing males up above went to the gym to try to get.

"It doesn't matter." He shook his head. "After the damage is done, the cause of it is no longer relevant. All you have is what has been broken."

"I'm sorry—"

"Your commiseration is unnecessary and unwelcome—"

"—that I haven't taken this as seriously as I should." She lowered her eyes from him. "You're right. I don't think I have any idea how bad this place is."

After all, if they could break a male like him?

And that was what had happened. She didn't need the details, like he said, the loss of spirit was enough, and the center of her chest ached for him—and for Janelle. Dear God, what had they done to Janelle?

"Would you like to take a bath?" he said roughly.

"Yes." Anything to stop thinking.

He turned his back to her and sat down on the ground in a random place—and she was willing to bet he had no clue where he was in the cave. He was like a star in a strange orbit, outside of the galaxy. Outside of reality.

"I can give you more privacy," he said. As if he were offering her something tangible, something he could hold in his palm and put out toward her. "I can leave."

"Stay," she replied. "So I know I have backup."

His head nodded. "All right."

She waited a moment, although she wasn't sure what she expected to happen or change in the pause, and she spent the time looking at the ponytail that ran down his spine. It was very long. Then again, he'd been growing hair for a hundred years.

What would it look like, free of that tie, spilling over his naked chest?

On that Fabio note, she turned her back to his back and quickly got out of her clothes. Covering her breasts with one of her arms, she went to the water, her skin goose bumping both from an awareness of how naked she was and also from the temperature drop. Fortunately, as

162

she stood over the pool, the rising heat eased the chill, although it did nothing for her sense of vulnerability—which, to be fair, wasn't that big a deal.

Somehow, she knew she could trust him about that.

"Ohhhhh . . ."

As Nyx stepped down into the pool, the sensation of perfectly warm, gently moving water against her body was a revelation sure as if she'd never been in a bath before. It was all just so unexpected, though. The depth. The temperature—which she wouldn't have adjusted up or down. The movement of the currents.

The fact that this was happening at all.

"Feel good?" Jack commented in a low voice.

"Yes."

His head nodded. "It has saved me. Many a time."

Splaying out her arms, Nyx cupped and released undulations within the pool.

Don't do it, she thought. *Don't ask.*

"From what," she said.

The Jackal tried to imagine what she looked like submerged in what he thought of as his property, his domain. There were other pools in the prison, common-use ones that the confined dropped themselves into from time to time—or were thrown into—but this one was his. If his cohorts, such as Kane or the others, partook on occasion? He always regarded it as a courtesy extended by himself to them.

Her dark hair would be loose, the ends drifting over the gentle, churning surface of the pool, and he imagined that tendrils would begin to curl up around her face. Her cheeks would flush, although they'd already been colored by arousal. Her skin would become dew'd and dreamy.

Not that it wasn't like that all by itself.

How much explanation do I owe a stranger? he thought as he contemplated her question.

"This prison is a dirty place." He rubbed his face as he answered her inquiry not at all. "Very dirty. It's hard to stay clean."

"You don't have to talk about it."

"I have no idea what you refer to."

To give his words some credibility, he glanced over his shoulder at her. She was focused on him, and he'd been right about the curls that were forming around her face. Also about the blush. But her expression was not as relaxed as he'd pictured in his mind. She was intense, and he had the sense that he had opened a door before he had properly assessed whether he actually wanted to go through it.

Then again, that had happened way before now with her, hadn't it.

"You will let me fuck you," he asked in a low voice. "Really."

Her eyes narrowed, but not because she was offended. And her lack of anticipated reaction made him realize he had phrased the question in a crude way because he had hoped that would be the case.

"The question is more whether you'll let yourself fuck me," she said. "Tell me, who is she."

He whipped his head away from her. "There is no one for me."

"Liar." She laughed a little. "And you can be honest. It's not like whatever you tell me is going anywhere. I don't know anyone here and I'm not staying. Besides, we're strangers."

When he said nothing further, she cursed softly. "Come on, what else do we have to do but talk for the next eight hours? Or is it ten? Of course, I'd had other plans for how to spend the time."

"Oh, really. And what were they?"

"Having sex with you seemed like a good way to pass the time."

"Just some casual exercise," he muttered. Then again, he should be used to that, right?

"Like it's anything else on your side?"

"And that doesn't bother you."

"Oh, so we're back to the virtuous female stuff, are we." She exhaled long and slow. "I believe in living in the moment. That's all I can say on that one."

"I did not lie," he said in the quiet between them. "There is no female for me."

He watched her play with the water, moving her hands through it. "Did she die? Did you have a *shellan* and she died?"

"I have never been mated, and I never will be."

"Why's that?"

"I believe that is self-evident." He motioned around. "We are in a prison, remember?"

"So how old were you when you came in. And how long until you—"

"It's a lifetime sentence. For now, at any rate."

"What did you do?"

"We don't ask those questions down here."

"Well, I'm a foreigner in these parts. As you like pointing out all the time."

When she lowered her eyes to the water, he waited for her to say something, to challenge him. Instead, she remained silent, and it occurred to him that she needed to answer her own question for him.

"And you?" he said. "Mated?"

"Hell, no." She threw her head back and laughed. "No."

That was good. It meant he didn't have to kill another male. Well, at least not because they were with her—

Groaning at his misplaced territoriality, he put a hand to his temple.

"If I ask you again if you're all right," she said,

"do I get to listen to another defensive monologue on how great you're feeling?"

"No. I think I'll spice it up and describe the pounding headache you give me."

"Oh, my God. You made a joke."

Dropping his hand, he sent a glare her way—and promptly lost the surge of anger. From over in the pool, she was smiling at him, her lips lifted at the corners, her eyes twinkling. His heart stopped. And then redoubled its beat. She was sexy when she was mad. And infuriating the rest of the time. But like this?

Her brows lowered and she pursed her mouth. "What."

When he didn't reply, she frowned. "Why the hell are you looking at me like that?"

Lowering his eyes, he said softly, "I have not seen the sun since before my transition. Can you blame me for staring."

CHAPTER FIFTEEN

*T*was an infection that ended up grounding *Rhage, and he was woefully disappointed in his body's failure of resolve when it came to the wound on his side. The other three places of lead invasion and operation had healed suitably well. The one under his ribs, however, insisted upon lingering, a houseguest with annoying habits and a pervasive lack of urgency about its departure.*

And thus he lay upon Jabon's guest bed, in the gentlemale's guest room, and was waited upon incessantly. All of his needs were looked after. Food, drink, ablutions, clothing. Sex and blood. He had the sense that had he required someone to breathe for him, that function would have been taken up readily by the staff. Indeed, it seemed churlish not to greet such attention with effusive gratitude, but dearest Virgin Scribe, he could not wait to return unto his humble abode and the resonant solitude therein.

How he craved an utter lack of company.

Plus it was not as if the staff had nothing else to do. There were plenty of opportunities for the household's doggen *to offer service unto other guests. There were quite a number of females and males tarrying under Jabon's roof. Rhage could hear them walking the halls and catch their* scents in the draft that came under his closed door. Further, there was much conversation on either side of his accommodations. The mansion seemed more hotel than home, and things were never quiet, never still. Not during daylight. Not during mealtime. Certainly, not during the parties that seemed to be held every eve.

One had to wonder the point of such a vacuous, consumptive existence. Then again, Jabon was unmated, and there had been some gossip, not that Rhage particularly cared, that the male's sire and mahmen were dead. Therefore, it appeared as though the aristocrat was buying his family, his hospitality the currency he used to secure his purchase of affection, constancy, and support—

The knock was soft and respectful. And Rhage gritted his teeth. In the beginning, he'd assumed the staff were just ascertaining whether he breathed or not. Now, he believed they were providing him greater attention over any reasonable standard because they'd been instructed of his affiliation. Members of the Black Dagger Brotherhood were of higher social standing than even Founding Families. Jabon, well versed in the exigencies of hosting, clearly saw the accommodation of such a warrior as an enhancement unto his social standing, and therefore, someone to whom he intended on providing every possible courtesy.

With the aid of every single doggen *on Earth.*

"Aye," Rhage said sharply. Because if he did not reply, they would return again and again.

The door cracked. And a face peered in that he did not expect.

"Darius, whate'er you do?" he said.

The brother stepped forth and closed himself in. 'Lo, what a sight for sore eyes. The brother's familiar face was like moonlight after a long period of clouds, a beacon. Unsurprisingly, he was not dressed for war, but had taken care to be in fine civilian garb. However, there would be weapons all over him, hidden beneath the fine blue wool of his perfectly cut evening suit.

Rhage could not wait to hold a dagger once again.

"How fare thee?" Darius asked.

"Would you be so kind as to remove me of these premises?"

"Are the accommodations not to your liking?" Darius glanced around the luxurious room. "I have heard you are quite well tended to. Jabon sends me a missive each night detailing your care. He provides me with details I could well do without."

"I would seek to free up this bed so that it may be promptly filled by another. Others should share this bounty."

"How considerate of you," Darius said with a chuckle. "But I have spoken with Havers."

"Oh." Rhage pulled the sheets higher on his bare chest. "However is he? Well, I hope."

"You believe I wasted inquiry upon his life? Truly."

"Fine. What did he say over my condition."

"You are as yet unhealed of a sufficiency to be released of your burdens herein. I am afraid you must continue to stay abed and be waited on hand and foot."

Rhage groaned as he sat up, but he did manage to take his torso higher upon the pillows. "I am finished with this, regardless of what the healer says—"

"Do you know what I most admire about you?"

"My absence in any given place?"

Darius frowned. "I do not have such a low view of your company."

As the fighter seemed honestly hurt, Rhage relented. "I jest, my brother."

"Well, allow me to say that what I admire most is your ability to follow cogent, sound advice. It's one of your most distinguishing characteristics. Truly impressive."

"I have never possessed that virtue and well you know it."

"Indeed? Because I have found it to be among your most chief and laudable qualities."

As Darius cocked a brow and regarded with steady expectation the naked, wounded, piece of meat before him who, even the now, was feeling *dizzy at having his head off a stack of pillows, it was rather hard to argue a contrary position.*

"You bore me with your character analysis," Rhage muttered.

"Yet you cannot disagree, brother." Darius smiled. "And see? Regard you being so utterly reasonable—"

"If you start to applaud me, I will get out of this bed to give you a very bad result."

Darius inclined his head. "Duly noted."

Allowing himself to recline once more, Rhage eyed his brother. "Did you just come here to mock the loss of my sense of peace and well-being?"

"I am doing no such thing. And staying here truly drains you so much?"

"Being attended to constantly does," Rhage said dryly. "I am not one for extended courtesy, evidently."

"Then you are working with the right sort of males in the Brotherhood." Darius removed from his waistcoat a gold pocket watch and consulted the time. "And in addition to assessing your health, I am meeting with that master of works of whom I spoke."

"About your house?"

"He is a guest here as well, as it turns out— wait, what are you doing?"

"I believe it is obvious." Rhage pushed himself off the pillows and swung his legs out from under the sheeting. "Bring me that robe, will you?"

173

Darius looked across at the silk fall that had been laid upon the chair by the writing desk. His stone-faced expression was as if he were unfamiliar with what sort of garment it was—and he was worried that perhaps it was poisonous in some manner.

"My brother," Rhage prompted. "Do bring me it, or would you prefer I join you naked?"

"If you are no well enough to procure your own dressing, you should not be upon your feet downstairs."

"Oh, I am plenty strong to retrieve the robe. I am just trying to spare you the inevitable comparisons between our malehoods. Your disappointment would be legion. I am quite phearsom.*"*

"You are full of it." But his brother smiled as he went over to the chair. "And I am only acquiescing to your demand because I fear you will attempt the stairs yourself in your naked-ness. It has naught to do with girth or length."

"As you believe." Rhage swallowed a groan as he pushed himself to his feet. To avoid toppling over, he planted a hand on the carved headboard—and attempted to look as if he did not in fact need the support to stay upright. "I should not wish to disabuse you of your delusions. Often, they are all we have—"

"My brother, you are unwell."

Rhage opened eyes that he was unaware of shutting. Darius had come to stand before him, and the brother seemed to be taking note of every weakness shown.

"I would beg to differ." Rhage looked the other male dead in the eye. "And I am coming downstairs, if only to be propped up on a sofa to listen in on your conversation."

Darius seemed sad. "You must be desperately lonely, my brother."

"No, I just don't want someone to ask me if I need another goddamn thing."

And that was the extent of it. Even though Darius had to help with the draping of the silk over Rhage's flesh, even as aid was required for full verticality to be enjoyed, even when the trip to the staircase was slow and arduous, nothing more was spoken on the issue of health and relative wellness.

Or the lack thereof.

To distract himself from his infirmity, Rhage looked around Jabon's home as he descended the stairs. He'd had no impression of the environs on his trip in, and he was not surprised that it was all very grand, with rich tapestries of ruby and sapphire and emerald on the walls and a full painting of cherubs and goddesses on the ceiling above the imperial stairway. However, in the very impressive front-hall receiving area, there were too many crystals twinkling off of fixtures and candelabra, and too closely set were the gilt-framed oil paintings and the sculpture.

In the end, the decor was like the host's guests, too many and too gaudy.

By the time Rhage made it onto the marble floor of the foyer, he decided that Jabon's need to prove himself had turned the mansion into a display case for both objects and people. And in a way, the proliferation of . . . everything . . . made Rhage feel better about his forced convalescence. He would certainly not have chosen Jabon for a host, and with so many others likewise availing themselves, it made it less personal.

"What is the male's name again?" he asked his brother as they entered a drawing room. "I find I cannot recall."

Before Darius could answer, a male across the overly appointed space rose to his feet. As Rhage looked unto the "master of works," he was struck by a flare of recognition. He could not place where he had seen the vampire before, however.

The male likewise did a double take. "Ah . . ."

But evidently his was for another reason. When the stranger's stare went down and then promptly traveled elsewhere, Rhage looked at himself. Well, this was something he had not considered. The robe was sufficient to provide a certain modesty, but it was wholly incapable of fulfilling its job when it came to arm and leg, and it struggled likewise as things pertained to the torso, the V created by the lapels so deep, most

176

of his chest was on display. Including the sacred star-shape scar of the Brotherhood.

But what of it, Rhage thought.

"It is so hot herein," he drawled as he did a little spin, "that I find this refreshing."

The male inclined his head, as if he were dealing with someone who struggled with reality. "But of course. It is rather warm out this eve."

"Yes." Rhage smiled. "You understand."

Darius provided introductions, and Rhage proffered his dagger hand unto "the Jackal." "A pleasure."

As their palms clasped, the male narrowed his eyes. "Forgive me, but you look unwell."

"He is in recovery from a wound," Darius murmured as he went over unto a broad table that was the only clear space in the room. "Dearest Virgin Scribe . . ."

With his brother's commentary drifting, Rhage's interest carried him forth. As he got within range, he recognized that with which he had little familiarity: Architectural renderings of building plans, the broad sheets of paper with lines of rooms and roof laid out in a stack of—

"How many chambers does this have?" Rhage said as he propped his palms on the table edges and leaned in to relieve the burden of his weight upon his legs. "And how many floors?"

The Jackal peeled the top sheeting up. "There

are three or more levels aboveground, depending upon what elevation one regards."

The pages were lifted one and another, and Rhage's eyes could not keep up with all of the facilities.

Looking over at his brother, he shook his head. "How many people do you intend to stay under that roof?"

"As many as we can fit."

"Then you endeavor to have the whole of the species in your residence. You will have to fight Jabon for guests."

"Not hardly." Darius reached out and traced the lines of something labeled "East Wing." "But perhaps, someday, there will be shellans. *Young. A community that is a family."*

"This is for the Brotherhood, then?"

"Aye."

Rhage opened his mouth to discount that frivolous fantasy. Wrath, the supposed King, had refused to lead for centuries, and the brothers were singular actors who, on rare occasions, came together—mostly because the paths of two lessers *being separately chased happened to intersect. What conception in Darius's mind could possibly conflate that solitary, transient landscape into any kind of a whole?*

For example, Zsadist? Mated?

Then again, that broken male would likely be dead in a few years anyway. Although . . .

178

people had been saying that for a while now.

" 'Tis a fine thing to have dreams," Rhage murmured remotely.

"Mayhap you will accept these renderings with my best regards," the Jackal said unto Darius as he lowered the broad pages back into place. "After you study them, you can come back here and we can discuss whether you want to use them and, if so, what you would like to change."

Darius's stare moved around the topmost sheet as if he were translating the depictions of rooms and hallways into three dimensions in his head. "Do you have time to go through this with me the now?"

"Of course, but there is no hurry if you wish to study at your leisure. I am staying here for two weeks."

"Are you a relation of Jabon's, then?"

"We do not share a bloodline. We have been of acquaintance for some while, however. When I was orphaned, his sire helped me on my way."

"Have you no living blood?"

"My mahmen *passed two years following my transition."*

"What of your sire?"

The Jackal tapped the plans. "Do you want to start at the top and work our way down? Or commence from the basement?"

Darius inclined his head, acknowledging the

179

firm change in subject. "The basement. Let us build from the ground up."

The Jackal carefully folded back the layers, at last exposing a sheet that had far fewer compartments. "First, allow me to explain the plumbing system and heating provisions. I have some new ideas—and I urge you to consider outfitting the structure for electricity. It is the standard for all buildings of the future."

"Yes, I see that it is becoming popular, the now."

As their heads tilted in, and the master of works began to describe all manner of things that were of little interest, Rhage dragged a chair over and lowered himself down into its silk confines. His side was talking to him—cursing him was more apt—but he did not want to return unto that bed. At the very least, if he stayed here and watched the pair of them discuss Darius's mountain house that would e'er remain empty, he would be distracted from the infernal pain—

Out in the receiving area, the front door unto the mansion opened and closed, a gust of fresh outside air rushing in as if it were yet another enthusiastic guest. But there was something else reaching his nose. Perfume.

Rhage glanced over his shoulder. And abruptly wished he had stayed upstairs upon his back.

The gracious, desperate host of the household, who had noticed who was in his drawing room, rushed forth, the wide smile on Jabon's face the kind of thing that made Rhage probe his infected wound for whether progress unto healing had been made in the previous ten minutes. As he winced, he feared he was going to be stuck for a considerably longer time.

Perhaps an eternity. Or at least it was going to feel as such.

"Come, come, you must meet my very special guests," Jabon said as he motioned to those who had entered with him. "Come!"

The gentlemale swept into the drawing room, dressed as if he were imminently going to be sitting for a formal portrait, his cravat of silk, his waistcoat bearing a pattern of peacocks, his well-tailored jacket and slacks perfectly fit. In his wake? Two females of obvious breeding, distinction, and relation, the mahmen *and daughter garbed in gowns and capes brightly colored and adorned with seed pearls and much decorative stitching.*

Rather as if Jabon's sense of decor had been translated into textiles.

Rhage turned away from the females, well aware that as soon as his display of comely thigh and calf registered, it would take care of the intrusion.

And sure enough, there was a twin screech and fast shuffle as the females went into a giggling retreat.

Shaking his head, Rhage awaited the censure of his host.

Instead, Jabon laughed. "Save yourselves, dear females. Avert thine eyes!"

There was further giggling out in the receiving area. "Our stares are well averted," one of the two of them replied.

Jabon's eyes sparkled with delight. "The Black Dagger Brother Rhage makes an impression, does he not. As does the Black Dagger Brother Darius."

Rhage ground his molars, and his brother seemed likewise annoyed. The response, meanwhile, from the females was immediate. From out of the corner of his eye, Rhage noted the way the pair leaned around the parlor's jambs and regarded him and his fellow fighter with burning interest.

Propriety was apparently relative. Depending upon the social status of that which was of offense.

Shaking his head, Rhage thought, Truly, I should have stayed abed.

CHAPTER SIXTEEN

Talk about sleeping with one eye open.

As Nyx sat propped up against the damp wall of the carved-out cave, her feet stretched toward the pool, her clothes back on, her hair still wet in the braid she'd put it in, she decided she'd never truly thought about the expression. Kind of like "life is a highway," the words were the sort of thing you heard from time to time. Read in a magazine article. Caught in the middle of the chapter of a book—or at the beginning of one. Like all other stock phrases, however, the combination of words was so overused that it ceased to really mean anything. Plus, if you dissected it, the whole clause fell apart. Unless someone propped your lid open with a toothpick, the fact pattern behind the saying couldn't get off the ground. And at any rate, if somebody *had* done that to you, you wouldn't be sleeping. You'd be taking out the toothpick and thanking them for the effort with a knuckle sandwich.

Okay, so there was another useless set of words that just didn't frickin' work: "Knuckle" and "sandwich."

Whatever. Her eyes—both of them—were closed, and she was aware of losing track of time's passing so she must have been getting a little sleep. Talk about interruptions, though. Her awareness, her senses, her prickling, adrenaline-fueled paranoia, was a Geiger counter going off constantly.

There were a lot of false positives.

Sounds, real or imagined. Smells, real. Shifts in temperature or draft, real but ultimately indicative of nothing.

Every time she was roused, her eyes shot over to Jack.

On the far side of the pool, he was in the same position she was, his body at a right angle to the wall's verticality, his thick and heavy legs out in front of him, his broad shoulders taking up a hell of a lot of space.

As her lids popped open for the hundred and seventy-fifth time, she wasn't sure what exactly had gotten her attention, but like tracing the vapor trails of ubiquitous vernacular sayings in her head, the "huh-what?" had turned into kind of a game. Fun, fun.

When there was nothing alarming—prisoners, guards—coming at her, and Jack wasn't reacting to anything, she closed her lids again.

But there was no slipping back into one-eyed sleep this time.

She uncrossed and recrossed her legs. Did the same with her arms. Cracked her neck.

Glancing around, she wanted to know exactly what had disturbed her, as if the answer would bring some kind of peace. Or at least unplug the adrenaline hose that was hooked up to her heart muscle.

The only thing that came back at her was the way Jack had answered her question.

What did you do?

We don't ask those questions down here.

After he'd spoken the words, he had headed over to where he was now to sit down. For a while thereafter, he'd reported on things relevant to their situation: Guard schedules. How much more time they had to wait. How he was going to check at given intervals to keep track of where they were with the shifts.

She hadn't followed much of it. And she'd had the sense that neither had he.

And now they were here, pretending to snooze. Or at least she was. He looked like he was actually asleep, although he had to be used to the catnap routine by now.

Jesus. A hundred years down here. She still couldn't comprehend it.

Unzipping the front pocket on her windbreaker, she took out her phone and turned it on. As the unit booted up, she braced herself for learning that only ten minutes had passed. And also if it was ten hours later and now they had to go.

When the time came up, it had been six hours since she'd checked last, and she was surprised that she had no real reaction at the news flash.

185

Then again, it didn't come with a call to action, did it. There was no jumping up and going to that place with the names. The Wall.

Turning the phone back off, she had never once, in fifty years, considered the idea that her sister was dead. Not once. She still refused to believe it was possible. In her mind, she saw herself going up to a flat plane of engraved names, checking down the list, and finding absolutely no Janelles. And when that happened? She knew what was up next.

Jack was going to press her to leave. She was going to stay. And they were going to have a blowup and a half.

In the meantime, all she could do was wait.

As she zipped her phone back in and reshuffled her body in its upright position—like the tray table on an airplane—she was too antsy to pretend to sleep. And her butt was so numb, she was pretty convinced it had turned into an inanimate object.

Confronting the reality that she couldn't go anywhere and she had nothing to distract her except the collection of stupid cat tricks and mental pushups in her head, she was reminded of the year after Janelle had been taken away. All those sleepless days had been just like this, the special torture tincture of exhaustion and buzzy, twitchy awareness battling it out under her skull, under her skin.

Was this what it was like for those serving out their sentences? She couldn't imagine suffering through—

The sound was sharp and unexpected, and as she tried to place whatever it was, her brain told her that this was not the first time she had heard it. In fact, the odd vocalization had woken her up.

Putting her hand down, her palm locked on the gun she'd set on the rock at her hip, and she flicked the safety off. Absently, she decided it was going to be ironic if she ended up shooting another guard with the nine she'd gotten off the first one she'd killed—and then her brain segued past that to another question: Had the sunlight claimed that dead male she'd dragged out between the graves? By now, there had to have been more than enough sunshine to do the ashing—

The sound repeated for a third time.

Frowning, she looked across the pool. Jack's face was all furrowed, his brows down, his lips pulled back in a snarl of aggression . . . or maybe it was pain. Hard to tell. And he was making noises in his throat that, when they reached a certain volume, were enough to travel over to her in spite of the falling water.

Grunts. Growls. His Adam's apple working up and down the front column of his throat.

In his lap, his hands were twitching. Then

curling into fists. And his feet at the ends of his legs were flexing and releasing as if he were rushing forward. Or rushing back?

"Jack?" she said.

His head jerked on his spine, but quickly resettled into its position. After which his mouth moved as if he were mumbling, and then he seemed to be reclaimed by whatever his subconscious was playing out.

"Jack."

Even though she put a little volume into his name, he stayed in his dream state and things grew more intense for him. Now he struggled, arms flopping, head kicking forward. Kicking back.

A single tear escaped his eye and traveled down his cheek—

Nyx jumped to her feet and went around the pool. "Jack!" she barked.

Nothing seemed to get through to him. Nothing verbal anyway.

As soon as she bent down and touched his arm, his eyes flew open and his head snapped toward her. *"What?"*

"You were dreaming."

He stared up at her as if he didn't recognize her. Then he blinked. In a hoarse voice, he said, "It was not a dream. It was done to me."

"What was done to you?"

Even as he looked at her, there was a strange

emptiness in his eyes, as if he were not seeing her. "All of it. All of it was done to me."

Before she could ask him anything further, he pulled her into him, her stiff body going off balance, his chest her landing pad.

"Is it you?" he said hoarsely. "Is this really you?"

His hand traveled over her hair and down onto her neck. "I need to know it's you."

Underneath her, he was fully aroused. She could feel him. But his eyes were tortured, and there was a begging to his tone.

"Yes, it's me," she whispered.

"Can you make it go away?" Before she could ask him what he was talking about, he stroked his thumb over her lower lip. "I don't want to use you, but I need . . . can you make it go away, even for just a little while."

Their faces were so close that she felt bathed in the light of his teal eyes—and captured by him, too, although not because he was holding on to her. The pain inside of him was what called to her.

"Who hurt you?" she breathed.

"It doesn't matter. Will you help me? That's all I need from you. No questions, no ties . . . just this."

As he tilted his head to the side and leaned in, she closed her eyes. The feel of his lips on her own went through her whole body, and though she didn't understand so much, the heat that thickened her blood and went to her core was all that mattered for now.

When he pulled back, as if he were giving her time to answer, she replied by sitting up on his pelvis, the hard ridge of his erection pressing into her. With steady hands, she took off her windbreaker, and then she lifted her shirt up and over her head.

The purr that came out of him rose up in the electric air between them, and then he was touching the sides of her ribs, following the curve of her torso up to the bottom of her bra.

"You're beautiful," he said softly. "In the candlelight. When I look at you, I'm somewhere else, somewhere far from here."

His hands cupped the weight of her breasts and she let her head fall back as she began to ride him, that rock-hard arousal moving against her sex.

"I just want to touch you." His thumbs brushed over her nipples. "Forever."

He leaned forward and kissed the side of her throat, one long fang traveling over her jugular as he pushed the bra up. Nyx gasped when she felt his skin on her own, his touch caressing and then teasing the tips that were so ready for his mouth.

"That's right, ride me, female." More of that purr. "Fates, you feel good to me."

Her bra disappeared at that point, the fastening

released, the freedom making her feel wanton and hungry. Especially as his mouth traveled down . . . down . . . down . . .

It was a contortion trick to keep leaning back so he could cover the distance, and she had to pop her lower legs out from under her before her knees snapped. But then she was lying back against his thighs and she got to watch his dark head lower to her breast. His mouth was hot and slick as he sucked, and when he inched back, his eyes glowed as he looked up at her.

"It's you," he said. "This is all you."

His head went back down, his tongue leading the way as he licked at her. Sucked her in again. Nuzzled at her.

As her bones turned to liquid and her blood roared with need, her hips started working again, her core rubbing against his lower belly, their clothes cumbersome, annoying. She gripped his thighs, wishing she could touch him, but he didn't seem to be in any big hurry, and what do you know, she was really good right where he was.

When he finally lifted his head, he stared down at her breasts as they strained, swollen and tight, after his attention. Running one big palm down the center of her, he stroked her body as if he were memorizing every detail.

"Take my pants off," she said.

"I thought you'd never ask."

He worked fast on the loose track bottoms she'd worn, pulling the nylon bow free, helping her peel them off her backside. Things got uncoordinated at that point, her legs requiring a shuffle, nothing working right.

So she stood up off of him and pulled them down herself.

As he growled deep in his throat, she realized she was buck-ass naked in front of someone who was all but a stranger. Except . . . Jack didn't feel like a stranger. He felt like a lover, even though the sex had yet to happen.

It was coming, though.

Especially as one of his big hands went to that bulge of his and rearranged the erection that was pushing at the front of his pants.

"Turn around for me," he said. "I need to see all of you."

Raising her arms over her head, she went up on her tiptoes and did a slow pivot for him. She had no idea where the brazenness was coming from, but she didn't waste any time trying to figure it out.

"Come here, female." He held his arms out. "Let me be where I need to be?"

Nyx was nodding as she went back to him. Putting one foot on either side of his legs, she walked her way up the length of him and then knelt down.

He kissed her again, his tongue penetrating into

her, his hands gentle even though she could tell by the twitching in his shoulders and the way he started to pant that he was starved for her. And then he dropped his arms and undid the laces at his fly. She had a quick impression of something very long and very thick, but then he was touching her between her thighs.

"You're so ready," he groaned as he stroked at her. "Dearest Virgin Scribe . . ."

She rode against his touch, her breasts tingling as her bare nipples rubbed against his rough shirt. How this all felt so natural she had no idea, but like her newfound confidence in her body, she just accepted the way it was. Accepted it . . . and needed things to go further.

As if he read her mind, his fingertips, now slick from her, disappeared and she felt something blunt and hot probing the hypersensitive flesh he had been stroking. She was the one who lowered herself down, and they both gasped as he slid inside, the friction, the stretching, the depth he went to lighting up all the receptors in her body.

Her head fell back again and she would have cried out if she'd been sure they were safe. She knew they weren't, though.

And that was what made this all so much more urgent.

She started to move, her thighs doing the work of lifting her off him and impaling herself once again. And up . . . and back down . . . the penetration making her grind her teeth. Wrapping her arms around the back of his neck, she held on as he tightened his hold on her backside.

Nyx cried out as her release came fast, and he did not last long, either. As his hips jerked and then he locked her down on his erection, her eyes flew open wide and she focused on the rock ceiling above as he ejaculated, filling her up. Beneath her nails, his shirt wadded up, and she had to bite her lip to keep from making any more sounds other than desperate gasping.

"Female," he said into her throat. "You undo me . . ."

And then they started moving again.

She was everything he had hoped.

As the Jackal came so hard that he had to close his eyes or risk things popping out of his skull, he breathed through clenched teeth and relished the fact that he was inside Nyx's sex, buried deep and ejaculating some more.

He was leaving his scent behind, marking her, so that all would know she was his—

Stop it, he told himself. There was no room for that.

Forcing his eyes open, he angled his head back and looked at her. Her cheeks were flushed and her mouth, that incredible mouth, was open. The tips of her fangs, white and sharp, were just barely showing, and he wanted them in his vein.

He wanted her drinking of him as he fucked her.

Or the other way around, him drinking and her doing the fucking.

To choose this. To feel this. To be here . . . doing this . . . it was what he had needed, the bargain they had struck fulfilled on his side. And yet he found himself not wanting this to be the only time.

Moving his hands to her waist, he eased her up off his cock and back down, and up again, and back down. She was right there with him, falling into the rhythm. Looking between them, he watched as he penetrated her and came out glossy and thick. The sight of her thighs splayed wide and the sex happening kicked off another orgasm, and he fought to keep his lids open. He didn't want to miss a thing, especially not about her body. Her breasts, full and pink tipped, swayed, and her head was thrown back, and her beautiful torso was so naked, so powerful, arched against his hands.

In the back of his mind, he thought . . . Fates, she was the most beautiful thing he had ever seen.

This was what he had been searching for from her.

This was exactly what he had needed.

She joined him in the next release, and he felt the rhythmic contractions all along his shaft. He just kept going. He never wanted to stop. She was the pleasure that cleansed him in a way the pool never could, the first time in so long when he could choose someone, and be with them honestly and purely.

Yet eventually, it had to end.

When he finally stilled, her eyes opened, and meeting her stare, he wished he could paint her, though he had no hand at all with a brush. He wanted to remember this for the rest of his life, though—and he would. Still, like all memories, she would fade after she left him behind down here, and that was why it all should be more permanent.

This was going to have to last way after she was gone. Forever, after she was gone.

And now, especially with this gift she had given him, he was going to have to make sure she made it out of here alive. He wouldn't be able to live with himself otherwise.

How in the hell was he going to keep her safe.

How in the hell was he going to let her go.

"It's all right," she whispered.

A thousand deflections went through his mind. His reply was honest, however.

"No," he croaked. "It's not."

The compassion in her face ruined him in ways he couldn't have begun to guess at. And for one treacherous moment, he considered unburdening the whole truth to her. But no. That would just put her at risk.

"I'm sorry," he said.

"For what?"

"I don't know."

"Well, don't be."

"I should . . ."

Pull out, he finished in his head. Except in spite of all the chaos that suddenly sprang back into his mind—or maybe because of the chaos—he found that he did not want to remove himself from her. Meanwhile, Nyx smoothed his hair, the stroking easing him under his skin. And as she continued to meet his eyes, he had the sense that she expected nothing from him. Neither explanation nor more of the sex. She just . . . accepted him.

The Jackal put his lips back to hers—

The instant the contact was made, he felt as though he had kissed her for years, and more than that, his hunger resurged. He welcomed the mating instinct. Embraced it. Held on to it as if it were precious.

Because it was.

Instinctively, he closed his eyes—

And immediately reopened them. The darkness behind his lids took him back into the dream—or threatened to—and he wasn't risking that kind of confusion.

Looking into Nyx's face was the cure. He had to stop kissing her to do that, but as he rolled his hips and penetrated her core, the way she gasped . . . the way her head kicked back once more . . .

the way one of her long canines locked down on her lower lip . . . gave him plenty to make up for the relative loss of contact.

He watched her orgasm. Felt it again, too, down below, in that part of his body that he had become separated from. She brought him back together, though, reuniting his soul with what had once been a necessary and defining part of him, but which had become nothing more than a vestigial appendage.

The alchemy she created should not have surprised him. From the moment their paths had crossed, her presence had stirred him unexpectedly. But he had never seen this deeper level coming.

He had never anticipated she would . . . heal him.

And that made her dangerous.

CHAPTER SEVENTEEN

"Are you sure I can't get you something to eat?"

As Jack asked the question, Nyx looked over at him. They were both standing—fully clothed.

Okay, he had always been fully clothed, except where it really counted. She was the one who'd had to get dressed again.

It was almost like the sex they'd shared had never happened. Well, provided she didn't move. Whenever she did, the internal ache reminded her of what they'd done together. Not that she needed the refresher. She remembered every kiss. Every arch. Every gasp, each grab, and all the orgasms in between. When they'd finally stopped, she had continued to lie on his chest, and that period of holding him close had struck her as risky. Then came the awkward questions about rebathing, and she'd ended up back in the pool.

After he'd given her a bar of harsh prison soap, he'd walked off down one of the tunnels.

As she'd washed her hair properly, the subtle scent of tobacco had wafted down to her, cutting into the spruce-tinted spice of the lye. Had he been smoking? Who else could it have been.

Immediately after he'd left, she'd waited for him to return and maybe join her in the warm, churning water. But after a while, she'd gotten the sense that he was waiting for her to step out and get clothed, so she had. As soon as she was back in her pants and her tops, he'd emerged from the shadows as if he'd been watching her.

And then he'd resettled on the far side of the pool once again, propped up with his legs straight out. Like maybe, in his mind, none of what had happened between them . . . had happened.

As she'd followed his lead and returned to where she'd started, she'd been of a mind to demand they talk it out. But that was a relationship move, and hello, she'd known him for less than twenty-four hours. In a hostile environment.

At least it was time to head out now. She was tired of worrying about what had been done to him and what he'd been dreaming of.

And what the hell had happened to end him up here.

"Nyx? Would you like food?"

Refocusing, she shook her head. "I'm fine. Do you want to go and get something for yourself?"

"I'm not leaving you—"

Both of them turned at the same time in the same direction, toward the tunnel on the left. Going by the scents, four males were approaching, but damned if she could hear anything over the falling water.

As she went for the gun she had tucked in her

waistband, Jack said sharply, "It's just Kane and the others."

"Others? Plural?"

From out of the shadows, the males came one by one. She relaxed as she recognized Kane, the aristocrat, and Lucan, the one with the yellow eyes.

The next male was taller than the others, with a body that was slightly leaner, but no less hard. He had white hair that was streaked with black, although not because he was in the latter part of his life, and the stuff had been pulled back and braided as seemed to be the custom. What was odd about him, though, was that his irises had the same lack of color that that braid had. As a result, his pupils were pits that were somehow unreadable. Sure, he was smiling— nice surprise, there. But there were depths there that she couldn't guess at, and that meant he was unnerving.

"Hello!" he announced to Nyx as he jumped into some kind of surfing position. Moving his hands back and forth between them, he said, "It's you. It's me. We're here together!"

Then he threw his arms around her, wrapping her in a hug that was surprisingly un-creepy: There was nothing sexual in the contact, he smelled good, and he didn't hold on for more than a split second. As he leaped back and clapped his hands, like it was game time and he was more

201

than ready to face the opposing team, he revealed a set of fangs that had already descended.

"Let's get on with this, motherfuckers."

As Nyx glanced at Jack, Jack rolled his eyes. "We do what we can with him—which is not much."

"Oh, shit, sorry—Mayhem." The male shoved his hand forward. "Sorry, I shoulda introduced myself before I hugged you."

Nyx clasped what was offered. "Nice to meet you."

"Nyx, I know." As he smiled widely, she was once again struck by the fact that she had absolutely no clue what was behind that expression. "Great name, by the way."

"Has anyone ever told you you remind them of a yellow Lab?" she asked. At least on the surface.

"I get that all the time."

"You haven't gotten that even *once,*" Jack muttered.

Mayhem leaned to the side and dropped his voice. "I'm trying to make her feel more comfortable. I read it in a self-help book."

"You did not. You can't read, and there are no volumes like that here. And speaking of which, she's in a prison. How much more comfortable do you expect her to be?"

"For one, my eyes are bad, okay. It's not like I'm illiterate. Two, there could, theoretically, be self-help books somewhere around here. And three, I concede your second point, as I believe her comfort is your territory, if ya know what I mean. Wink, wink."

Nyx started to smile as Jack looked like he was going to pound the male into a throw rug.

"Relax, Jack, he's good," she said. "It's all good."

"Oh, nicknames." Mayhem elbowed Jack. "Moving fast. We're into nicknames."

"I swear to Fate, I will kill you with my bare hands."

"Jack," she cut in. "Seriously, it's fine—"

Her voice dried up as the fourth presence registered. Whoever it was had stayed in the shadows, outside of the glow of the candles around the pool, but she had a sense of the bulk of him. The evil, too.

Menace rolled out of the darkness, curling across the rock floor as tangible as a black magic fog that threatened to crawl up a person's legs and body and choke them with ghostly hands. Nyx took an involuntary step back—and had the thought that unlike the others, where she wondered how they'd found themselves in this hellish place, she knew exactly why that one was here.

Not the particular details, no. But he was a killer because he liked it.

"That's Apex," Jack said softly. "Don't mind him."

Yeah, right. That was like suggesting she ignore a predator who'd gotten out of a zoo cage before lunch. And she was tempted to ask if they could leave him behind, but she had a gun, and no matter how fierce he was, he wasn't going to beat a bullet shot into his brain.

"It's time." Jack went over to a stack of folded prison garb. "I'm going to ask you to put this on over your backpack."

"Good idea." She strapped her things on and then pulled the loose, grungy-colored shirt over her head. "Which way are we headed?"

"Into the main concourse. You're going to be in the middle of all of us. Keep your head down—"

"And don't make eye contact. You've told me the drill. But what's the plan? What do I do—"

"You stay in the middle of all of us. We'll take care of everything else—"

"Which is what, exactly."

"Keeping you alive."

Frowning, she stepped up to him and leveled a hard stare. "FYI, I'm in on that job."

Lucan spoke up. "It's true. I've been there with her."

When Jack didn't respond, she thought he was going to blow her off. Or stomp away. But then he rubbed his eyes.

"We're going to walk you through to the Hive, and we're timing it so that we get there when the guard shift happens. The Command has private quarters and that's where the Wall is. These males will help you and me get in there, and once we're inside, we'll have only a matter of minutes, so you'll have to keep up."

"That's not going to be a problem," she said dryly.

As he turned away, she grabbed for his hand. When he pivoted back to her and broke the contact, he had a stern expression on his face, like he didn't want her getting too personal in front of the others. Or maybe it was more of an "at all" situation.

Whatever. She wasn't wasting time with lovey-dovey girlfriend crap in this situation.

"Here." She put the guard's gun in his palm. "You take this. I've got another."

As they departed the pool, the Jackal instructed Kane to take the front position in the lineup because of all of them, he was the least controversial, the least likely to be noticed by the guards. Mayhem was on the left flank. Lucan on the right.

Nyx was in between the two of them.

The Jackal was right behind her. With the weapon she'd given him in his hand.

Finally, in the wake of their little squadron, quite a bit in the rear, the caboose to their train was Apex. The male would lag at quite a distance, something that was a tactical advantage as well as the kind of thing he would have done anyway. He didn't get close to anybody, and one might have assumed that that loner habit would have been incompatible with this kind of concerted effort. But Apex loved killing guards. It was his favorite pastime. He wasn't here for Nyx, or even the Jackal, who he did owe a debt to.

No, he was looking forward to drawing blood—and he often did. If a guard disappeared and no body was found? Chances were Apex had done the deed, and then cooked up the remains and ate them to cut down on the conversation. His success and privacy around these clandestine murders were assured by the prisoner's code. As vicious and self-serving as most of the people incarcerated were, they never stepped across the aisle to share information like that—plus there was the reality that they were more scared of Apex than the Command's henchmales. And as for the Command? Had it noticed that it had missing guards? Given the complex schedule, it must have, but it hadn't retaliated against Apex. Not yet, at any rate.

Including that male in their plan was a gamble. The last thing the Jackal needed was a rogue aggressor on their team. In the end, though, he'd decided that the value the violent fighter brought in a knock-down/drag-out was worth the risk, and in any event, it was too late to change things up now. Apex was already on the hunt.

As they cautiously emerged out of the hidden passage, and walked in a loose configuration deeper into the prison, they came upon a few prisoners shuffling along. And soon, many others. There was always a flow of people going in and out of the Hive. Then again, that was where the black market trading took place. Where many of the hookups started—and some actually occurred. Where people connected for whatever reason, whether it was arguing, fighting, even laughing and card-playing. Or all that sex.

Given what work was like for so many of them, and the bleak existence they groaned through during their off-hours, one could not blame the congregation of the damned. But with all those fallow attention spans, he was worried about attracting notice—and not just from the guards.

Fortunately, Kane, Lucan, and Mayhem were often seen around him. And he had to believe if they kept tight, and Nyx dropped that head of hers, the assumption would be there was Nothing Here, Nothing Here at All.

And no one messed with Apex. So he was a nonstarter in that regard—

As the first waft of the telltale stench hit the Jackal's nostrils, he assessed it as if for the first time, as Nyx would take it in. The combination of sweat and dirt, sex and corporeal decay, was a stain in the sinuses, the kind of thing you smelled long after you had left the vicinity.

He wanted to take her hand. Just reach forward and touch her in some way so she knew he was right with her.

Instead, he tightened the grip on the gun she had put against his palm.

The noise of the Hive was the next harbinger to register. The low-level, resonant humming was the genesis of the nomenclature, and he thought the reference to bees was apt on another level. The guards were not stupid. A concentration that thick of prisoners was a wasp nest waiting to explode, and they took no chances with any roiling or agitation.

But shifts had to change. Even the Command couldn't keep those guards working around the clock forever. The Jackal and Nyx had only a sliver of opportunity, the duration of which was not much longer than the blink of an eye. He'd studied the patterns for decades. He knew exactly when it was going to come, and how long it would last, and where they had to go.

Focusing on the female in front of him, he thought of what they'd shared by the pool. What she had given him. Ironic, that the very thing he had demanded of her had created a debt in her favor from him. He would do right by her and honor her need to know the fate of her blood.

And then he was going to get her the hell out of here.

CHAPTER EIGHTEEN

*T*hree nights later, close unto the dawn, Rhage sat back upon Jabon's guest bed, the covers rolled down to just above his sex, the banding of gauze that covered the wound on his side peeled back. As he studied the contours of the fierce red ring around the surgical slice, he tried to ascertain any minute change to the landscape of infection. Bigger? Smaller? Improved over on the left edge? A little worse upon the right?

Cursing, he re-covered the ugly, angry patch of skin. The damn thing was like another appendage, a third arm that had sprouted and promptly been sprained so that it required constant accommodation. In addition to his infernal monitoring of the snail's pace of healing, he had to watch how he sat, how he stood, how he walked, how he slept, to avoid upsetting its precious little sensibilities. Indeed, the whinging was rather constant, and he was beyond annoyed by its persistence.

Verily, he had come to feel as though he were in a prison in this mansion, and the key to his cell door was the wound. The warden was Jabon, and his guards were the relentless stream of obsequious doggen. Catered and comfortable did not matter when one could not voluntarily *leave a place, and the walls closed in upon him regularly, no matter that they were covered with silk and hung with oil paintings of pastoral sheep and running streams.*

Yet surely the tide would soon turn in his favor—and he would have left against the advice of Havers, et al. The trouble was, his legs were loose, his balance unreliable, and in fact, he did feel unwell, even though he was not upon death's door. No, he was in that purgatory between overwhelming illness and relative health, just infirm enough to have his activities curtailed, but not delirious and flat upon his back such that he was unaware of time's languorous passing.

He would almost have preferred the latter. For him, the hours crawled, and he was painfully aware of their pernicious laziness.

Returning the sheeting over his abdominals, he grunted as he twisted and reached for the oil lamp on the bedside table. As he extinguished the low-seated flame, he fully reclined and held his limbs in strict stillness to avoid any conversation from his wound. Whilst he became as a statue, frozen save for his breathing, he tried not to dwell on the fact that one night, perhaps sooner or maybe much later, he would be thus for eternity, dead and gone, his soul unto the Fade.

As he contemplated the afterlife, he wondered if it would be thus. An eternal lie-in, every need met, no future to worry about because there was a forever too vast to comprehend ahead of oneself, and that meant one had the present and nothing else. After all, it was the rarity of time that led the mortal to be concerned with things like fate and destiny, and perhaps the relief of that worry and angst was the point of the Fade, the reward for the struggle upon the earth. But after this experience herein? Rhage was not sure how much of a boon would be granted upon one's last breath. Timelessness struck him as a bore.

If he'd had a shellan, though . . .

Well, if he had found a true love, someone who alit his heart and not just his sex, a female of strength and intelligence to complement him, then the prospect of eternity would have been wholly different. Who wouldn't wish to be with their beloved forever?

But love for him was like Darius's communal fantasy.

Never a reality, ever a dream.

That male of worth could build a hundred houses on a hundred hills—the Brotherhood was never going to show up and fill those rooms. Just as Rhage could ever imagine a love that went deeper than sex, but that didn't mean it was going to come and find him—

The door to the guest room opened, and the slice of light that pierced through the darkness got him right in the aching head.

With a curse, he lifted his forearm to shield his eyes.

"No," he snapped, "I require naught. Please leave me thus."

When the doggen *did not readily accept the relief of their duties, he lowered his arm and glared into the illumination. "If I must get up to close that door myself, I will not thank you for forcing me unto the effort of rising from this bed."*

There was a pause. And then a female voice, a young female voice, made a reedy inquiry. "Are you unwell then?"

As he recognized who it was, the scent affirming his identification of the voice, he wanted to curse. 'Twas the unmated daughter of fine breeding, the one who had come in with her mahmen *and Jabon when Darius had been reviewing the renderings of that mansion.*

The one who had curved herself around the archway into the parlor and regarded him with open curiosity.

The one who had taken it upon herself to sit at his elbow at each meal he attended.

Indeed, he had been making an effort to descend unto the dining table for at least First and Last Meal. He had some thought that the activity would speed his healing, and up until this moment, he'd felt as though it was right to force himself to go.

But he had neither the interest nor the energy to deal with what had breached his doorway.

"You are in the wrong bedroom," he said. "Go now."

The female took a step forward, the light streaming in from behind her illuminating the outline of her body as it was draped in some diaphanous dressing gown. "But you are ill."

"I am well enough."

"Mayhap I can help you." Her voice was soft. "Mayhap . . . I can make it better."

As she turned to shut the door—to ensure a privacy that was the very last thing Rhage wanted—he sat up sharply and let out a groan. And then the room was plunged into darkness once more, and he had the sense she was walking over to him.

"No," he snapped as he willed the door back open.

She froze as illumination flooded in once more. "But, sire . . . do you not find me . . . acceptable?"

"As a meal companion, certainly." He held the sheets tightly over his chest, a classic pose of virtue that was laughable given his proclivities. "Nothing more than that—"

Oh, dearest Virgin Scribe. Tears.

Even though he could not see her face because of the orientation of the hall lighting, he was well aware of her escalating state of agitation and hurt: The acrid scent of tears emanated from her,

213

much like the delicate fragrance of her arousal, and he truly, utterly wished to be absent of both.

"Forgive me for speaking so rashly," he muttered. "You are of much virtue and beauty. But I am not what you are looking for."

The female glanced back at the door, as if she were contemplating another closing attempt—no doubt because she had been ordered to complete this mission or not return to whatever wing she and her mahmen had been put in. Yes, she may desire him, but no female of any breeding would come thus into any male's room—unless the suggestion had been placed there by an elder relation who saw much benefit to a forced mating ceremony.

"That door is staying open," he said firmly, "and you are going back to the bedroom you share with your mahmen."

"But . . . but . . ."

"Return unto your mahmen." He did his best to keep his exhaustion from making his tone too cutting. "This is not about you, and there is nothing wrong with you. But it is never happening between you and me. Ever. I only like females who are experienced and free of complications. You, my dear, fulfill neither of those requirements."

Talk about shutting doors—well, certain doors. But he had to make sure she understood there was no future in this.

"You deserve more than what I can give you,"

he said, tempering his voice. "So you go and find yourself a nice male from a good bloodline, yes? And leave the likes of me alone."

At this point, he had no clue what he was telling her. He just wanted her out.

"You are a hero." She sniffled and wiped her eyes. "You fight for the race. You keep us safe. Who could e'er be more worthy than you—"

"I am a soldier and a killer." And cursed by the Scribe Virgin. "I am not what you're looking for. You have a wonderful life awaiting you, and you must endeavor to go find it. Elsewhere."

Out in the hall, a figure passed by, and Rhage whistled.

The Jackal, as the male turned out to be, pivoted and presented his form unto the open doorway. In a dry voice, he murmured, "Somehow I cannot believe this is a situation that requires an audience."

How wrong you are, *Rhage thought.* And not because he was an exhibitionist.

"Ellany was just leaving," he said. "Perhaps you will be kind enough to hold the door open for her."

Across the tense air, the female lowered her head and sniffled. Then she gathered her gossamer robing unto her breasts and scooted out past the other male.

"Shit," Rhage muttered as he collapsed back into the pillows. "I cannot wait to get out of here."

"I must confess," the Jackal said, "I am unsure how to respond to that. Given the opportunity you just turned down."

"That is not an opportunity, that is another kind of prison, the warden of which is her virtue, or rather, the loss thereof. And there is no response necessary from you—no, wait. That is incorrect. I bid you, breathe deeply the now."

The other male glanced down the hallway. Then he looked across to the bed once more. After a long, slow inhale, he nodded.

"There is no evidence of your arousal. If that is what you seek for me to attest."

"Yes. And I may need you to share this impotence with others, should the need arise."

"But of course." The Jackal laughed softly. "A honey trap averted, then."

"Poor little female. She has been thrown into depths in which to drown thanks to that mahmen of hers."

"Assets are to be used by the glymera in whatever form they come, be they houses, horses, or daughters. It is their most reliable trait, other than censure."

"Are you not one among them, though? Your accent belies your status. As do your clothes, and the fact that Jabon has welcomed you herein."

"That male does cultivate quite a crowd of swells, doesn't he. And as for the mahmen of your

216

half-clothed visitor? She is well-connected unto our host. She has been here before many a time and she does not sleep alone, if you understand my inference."

Rhage had to smile. He could respect anyone who wished to keep their own details private.

Not that such reticence would prevent him from inquiry.

"You have been here very much often yourself or you would not know this."

"The mahmen took pains to tell me how often she stayed. However, I learned from another that she is rather hard on her luck, I'm afraid. Hellren passed unexpectedly with gambling debts. I believe she sees the comely nature of that daughter as a lifeboat for the both of them. Jabon accommodates them with some regularity on account of certain . . . preferences, shall we say . . . lavished upon him by the mahmen. I think she will be ultimately disappointed in him, though. However generous he is with his guest bedrooms, I gather he is tightfisted when it comes to cash dispersals."

"How convoluted it all is."

"Not really."

Rhage thought of the daughter. "The sad thing is . . . I cannot recall even her hair color. Nor that of her eyes."

"She is fair of both. And rather attractive."

"Ah." Rhage cocked an eyebrow. "What of

217

you, then? Perhaps you could avail yourself of the opportunity."

"Never."

As Rhage just continued to stare across the room, the Jackal once more glanced behind himself to the empty hallway. "Is there something awry?"

"Nothing awry." Rhage smiled anew. "But I do feel compelled to comment on something."

"I believe you've covered the young female and her first-blooded relation nicely."

"There are two kinds of people who keep things from others—"

"Well, I must continue on to my own room—"

"Those who have something to hide and those who wish to hide how little they possess." When the male went to turn away, Rhage put some real volume into his voice. "I want you to know that in either case, I do not judge."

The Jackal stopped and lowered his brows. "You do not know anything about me."

"I am not so certain about that. I recognized you the first moment I saw you."

"Our paths have never crossed."

"I know you from somewhere and you had the same feeling. I saw your expression when first we met." Rhage wagged his forefinger back and forth. "And nothing you say or do will change my mind—"

"I hail from the South. I was born there and

was raised there. I told you Jabon's sire aided me when I was first orphaned, and so of course, I have stayed in contact with the son. That is all, I am afraid. So uninteresting."

"Your parents are from the South, then." As the male closed his mouth with a clap, Rhage winked. "Careful there, your impervious wall of secrecy has a small crumble in it."

"I have divulged nothing. You know nothing."

"My dear fellow, even if you revealed all, I would still know nothing. Do not underestimate my capacity for silence."

"It's more your inquiries I have difficulties with."

They stared across at each other for a moment. And then Rhage was entirely unsurprised when the male bowed in respect and took his leave.

The door shut silently in the Jackal's wake, the room going dark.

As Rhage closed his eyes, he tried to get comfortable in the perfectly soft bed against the perfectly soft pillows. Out in the street, on the other side of the thick drapes and the interior black-out shutters that covered the glass windows, he heard the activity of the daylight hours begin to come forth, the sun calling the humans onto the road the grand house sat upon. Horses clopping. Carriages creaking. A motor carriage now. Soon there would be people.

Busy, busy. The humans always so busy—

The door to the guest room opened once again, and Rhage did not bother to lift his head. "I am dead. Leave me thus—"

A soft voice, but this time not female. "I am not supposed to be here."

Rhage tilted his heavy skull up. The Jackal had leaned into the room, most of his body still out in the hall, as if he would have wished to avoid the whole thing.

"Are you hunted?" Rhage demanded. "Because I can take care of that."

There was that dry laugh once again. "You cannae stand unaided."

"Wait for it."

"Thank you, but I do not need protecting. I am not pursued."

The gravity with which Rhage spoke next made no sense to him: "If you are e'er in need of such, I will come unto you."

"You don't know me."

"I do. Somehow, I do."

The male looked around. Or at least Rhage assumed he did, given the circle the black cut of his head made. "Why . . . would you offer such a vow unto me?"

In truth, Rhage was not sure, and he felt compelled to fabricate one. "Because you have been of aid to my brother Darius."

"You are very close then?"

"Not at all. We are opposites. He is a male of

great worth. Great courage, great strength." As he considered Darius, he realized he was not lying anymore. "For a brother such as him? Anyone who aids him, I shall take care of."

Yet that was not the only reason when it came to this male, whom he could not place.

Abruptly, the Jackal's head lowered. It was a while before he said aught. "I promised my mahmen *I would never come to Caldwell, right before she passed unto the Fade. It has taken me ten years to get over the vow that I should never have made to her, and I confess that the violation of my word continues to sting."*

"Who do you seek to avoid here in this village?"

"My father." There was a short laugh. "Of course, he is the very one I am in search of. Rather ironic, is it not."

At that, the male ducked out and disappeared, the door closing with a click.

CHAPTER NINETEEN

Nyx was hidden behind a fortress made of shoulders. Front, back. Side to side. She was surrounded by broad, heavy torsos.

In a totally different set of circumstances, she could have been at a bachelorette party.

As she moved with the males through what had to be the prison's main tunnel, given its width, she kept her head down, but she did not avert her eyes. She tracked everything. Each person they passed. The turns that were made. The height of the ceiling, the feel of the packed dirt floor under her boots, the change in temperature.

Things were getting warmer.

The fact that they were approaching some kind of fulcrum made the back of her neck prickle and her palms sweat. There were many more prisoners around now, going in various directions. Nearly all of them were on their own, walking alone, and she wondered whether this grouping thing was going to be a red flag. But there was no time to worry about that. No other option, really.

The entrance to the Hive presented itself with little fanfare. The effect of the place, however, was disproportionate to its lack of demarcation.

One last turn and then the tunnel opened into

a space so vast, her first thought was how the hell did the curved roof to it all stay aloft—but then she saw the supports, the rough concrete stands thick as cars and unevenly spaced, like the architects who'd designed the prison didn't give a crap about aesthetics and barely cared about structural integrity. Holy hell, the interior space was cavernous, easily a couple hundred feet wide and just as long. And way down in front, there was a focal point to it all. Across the distance, there was a raised dais, with three tree trunks stripped of their bark and branches standing straight up like their roots were driven deep into the rock.

The dark brown stains on them made her stomach churn.

Don't think about that, she told herself. *Worry instead about the . . .*

Nyx's feet faltered when the number of prisoners registered in the dim overhead light. There were hundreds of them, all dressed in dark, loose clothing, moving like wraiths in the same kind of shambling gait—which she couldn't tell was affect or affliction. Maybe it depended on the individual.

The smell was horrible. Like a barn stall that had not been cleaned out for two weeks.

And she had little hope of finding Janelle in the crowd. It was too dark to track faces, and the stench meant her sister's scent wouldn't carry.

Nyx wanted to ask Jack how much farther. And how he would let her know when it was time to run—or was it better to walk? They should have talked this out beforehand—

The first guard she saw was standing with his back against the wall, by the dais. A matte-black, long-nosed gun was across his chest, and he had his finger on the trigger and the muzzle up by his shoulder. His head was moving back and forth as he scanned the crowd, and his expression was a mask of deadly composure. And there was another opposite him. Armed in the same way with that same professional calm about him. And still others, ones she'd missed because their black uniforms blended in to the rock, those powerful guns capable of ripping bullets through the crowd of males and females in the blink of an eye.

It was a testament to their effectiveness that they hadn't been the first thing she'd seen.

The route Jack took down to the dais was circular and slow and diverted. The six of them continued to move as a unit, but she was aware of the males creating space, then closing it, then creating it again. She had no idea why they bothered—until she realized that it was to make things seem like they were just sort of together, instead of definitively so. In fact, the coordination was so subtle and randomly unrandom that they had to have done this before, and she wondered when. Under what circumstances. But like that mattered?

When they reached the dais, her eyes locked on those posts. Down at the bases, there were bundles of chains, the blackened links piled up.

There was fresh blood on one of the trunks.

Her eyes went to the nearest guard. He wasn't looking at her. His stare was behind her and tracking something.

It had to be that male, Apex—

Lucan looked at her. "What did you say me? What the *fuck* did you say to me?"

Nyx stopped short. "Wait, what—"

Mayhem leaned in. "I said you're ugly and impotent. And when you're changed, you're hairy as an afghan."

Lucan bared his fangs. "You mother—"

The two of them went for each other, their big bodies lunging around her and slamming hard, fists curled, faces flushed with aggression—and as soon as the fight started, a flank of guards poured in from the right-hand side of the dais, jogging out of some darkened place. Were they always on backup? Or was this the changing of the guard—

Jack's hand grabbed her own and gave her a sharp pull backward.

As the other prisoners surged forward toward the fight, crumpled paper money coming out and being wagered as Mayhem and Lucan went at it, the guards circled around—and she and Jack hustled to the edge of the tremendous and growing knot of bodies, going against the flow of other prisoners who headed toward the commotion.

Pulling her along, Jack skirted the disturbance and led her into a thin fissure in the rock wall about twenty-five feet off from the dais, the fight, the guards. The pitch-black split in the cave was so narrow, they single-filed it at first, and then had to pivot and shuffle sideways when not even her shoulders could fit. The smell was moldy and stale, and she came face-to-face with an unexpected shot of claustrophobia thanks to the overwhelming stink, the prevailing darkness, and the close touch of the cramped space.

With no other orientation, she clung to the soft sounds of Jack's movements like they were light to orientate herself with. The shifts of his clothing, the whisper of his feet, the occasional grunt as he obviously tried to squeeze his bigger size through the ever-narrowing passage, were the only reasons she could keep going.

Jack didn't slow down. Until he had to. As the fissure became so cramped she had rock in her face, on her back, on her butt, she bumped into him.

"It's not much farther," he whispered. "You can do it."

He must have scented her fear. "It's not me I'm worried about."

Liar, she thought.

Just when she was about to lose it, when she was opening her mouth to tell him she couldn't go another foot, the smell changed.

Is that fresh air? she wondered.

Jack stopped and had to force his head around. Or at least she assumed that was what he did, given that his voice suddenly reached her ears more directly.

"We're heading to the left, and we're going to have to move very fast. I don't need to tell you how dangerous this is."

"I got it."

"Nyx, I'm serious—"

"Shut up. If this fails, it will not be because of me," she vowed.

For a brief moment, the Jackal closed his eyes in the black void of the fissure. Courage was as basic a need as air in life. Like oxygen, it kept a person alive, and in the darkest of hours, in the worst of circumstances, at the most dire of cliffs, one needed more of it than ever.

He was not surprised at Nyx's iron resolve.

More than that, he was inspired by her. And it had been a very, very long time since that pilot light in the center of his chest had flared to life with any kind of engagement for the opposite sex. Yet here he was the now, buoyed by her steady resolve, propelled farther by her example.

If he could have dropped his lips to hers, he would have. Instead, he did what he could.

He took her where she had to go.

The last fifteen yards were the hardest, the tightest. But finally there was a glow he could focus on, and he made sure there were no sounds or smells outside before he shoved himself from the constriction. As he popped free into a shallow open area that was stacked with canned food in crates, his eyes stung in the light. Wheeling around, he caught Nyx as she fell forward, pulling her up against his body and holding her tight for the briefest of moments. As he took a deep breath, her scent replaced everything.

When he stepped back and nodded, she nodded back. Ready. Set. Go—

He kissed her quick, even though he probably shouldn't have, and then he took off, ducking out of the pantry area and shooting forward down a twenty-foot passageway. Nyx was right with him, sticking close by.

When he put up his hand and halted, she stopped along with him.

No sounds up ahead. No smells. No alarms, either.

On his signal, they slipped out into the Command's compound proper—which was nothing like the prison at large. Here, all the passageways and rooms were finished, the rock walls and ceilings hidden behind proper plaster, the lights set into panels, the floor tiled. There was no mold anywhere and no damp, earthy smell, due to a heating system that ran constantly, pumping fresh, warm air into the cold subterranean lair. There were other creature comforts, too, such as running water, and the light boxes with the moving pictures, and other technological things the purpose of which were tied to the prison's business endeavors.

"There are different sectors herein," he said in a low voice. "The guard bunks, the work area, and the private quarters."

"Which one do we go to?"

"The private quarters."

They moved in concert, him in front, her in back, their bodies sleek and silent on the balls of their feet, guns down by their thighs. On one level, he was surprised at how easily they formed a working alliance of function. On another, given the way they'd had sex, he should have known. Their bodies moved well together in any and all situations.

As they closed in on the private quarters, he became utterly paranoid that they were being followed. While that appeared to be untrue, he braced for a guard to jump out into their paths up ahead. However, if he was right about the time—and given the guards' shift change, he had to be—the Command would be in the work area, for it checked in on productivity personally at the beginning and end of each work cycle. The Command took the product far more seriously than the prisoners, and one might have wondered why the business end of the prison wasn't taken somewhere else, somewhere safer and less complicated. A workforce was needed, however, so the prisoners were necessary, and they were free, after all, no wages to worry about. Indeed, he was well aware that the only reason the incarcerated were fed and given even rudimentary medical care was because of the shift requirements of the product stations. What was more, based on Nyx's report of the year they were in, he had a feeling that many prisoners had exceeded their sentences. Workers were required, however, and so they stayed trapped in this timeless, dim nether land.

It was unconscionable. All of it.

As he came up to a bifurcation in the hallway, he held up his palm again and they both stopped. Pause. Pause . . . pause.

Nothing. No sounds, no scents.

On his nod, they continued on. The private quarters were well guarded when the Command was *in situ*. When it was not, the place was a ghost town. Even still, as he led Nyx with efficiency and silence toward their destination, passing by all manner of doors and offshoot halls, his heart pounded in a disproportionate fashion to the amount of exercise he was experiencing.

And it was not only because he was preparing to run into the guards or an off-schedule Command. As he closed in on the Wall, he realized that there was another reason he had insisted on coming with Nyx on this mission. Another reason he wanted to get back here.

As they went around one of their last corners, he faltered.

Tripped.

Caught himself on the plastered wall by throwing out a hand.

"What is it?" Nyx whispered. "Are you ill?"

Up ahead, the cell that had been constructed some twenty years before, that had been kitted out with things from the world above, presented itself like a diorama. A stage set. An exhibit illustrating life the way it had been lived.

The Jackal approached the bars with shaking hands and a pounding heart. As his mouth went dry, he tried to swallow so he could offer some reply to Nyx. None came, especially as he peered in through the iron bars and the steel mesh.

There was no one in there. Not on the soft bed with its clean sheeting and blankets. Not at the writing desk with the books and the notation pads and the pens. Not in the porcelain bathtub nor dressing area behind the screen.

Breathing in through his nose, he caught the

familiar scent, and tried to reassure himself that there was still time—but in truth, time had not been what hindered him in this ultimate duty he must fulfill.

Abruptly, he thought of Nyx's determination and courage.

"Who lives in here?" she asked softly.

CHAPTER TWENTY

As Nyx spoke, she felt like Jack wasn't hearing her. Standing in front of a cell that was kitted out like a nice hotel room, he seemed utterly unplugged: His huge body was still, and except for one deep breath, it was like he'd turned to stone.

This was where his female stayed, she thought as he placed his palm reverently against the steel mesh that ran across the front of the space. The yearning, the sadness, the mourning, that permeated not just his face and eyes but his entire body, changed the air around him, charging it with an uncomfortable, dark aura.

The stab of jealousy that went through her was unacceptable on a lot of levels, but there was no stopping the red tide of aggression that was directed at a female she didn't know, couldn't see, wasn't even around. Before she could stop herself, she also inhaled deep, curious as to what his mate smelled like, but all she got in her sinuses was a revisit to the stench of the Hive.

Probably for the best.

This was not her business.

"We should go," she said. "We need to go—"

Jack's shoulders jerked and his eyes swung

around. For a split second, as he looked at her, his face was utterly blank.

Nyx shook her head. "Not right now. We can't do this now. I need you back here."

As she pointed to the concrete floor between them, he glanced down. And then he came back online.

"This way," he said in a low voice.

As they continued on, he didn't look back at the cell, and she took that as a good sign. Distraction in the only one who knew where the hell they were and where they needed to go was like a car without a steering wheel. In a life-or-death chase. Just before things were about to hurl off a cliff.

Her hand tightened on the butt of the gun her grandfather had given her, and she checked behind them again. No one. Yet.

Up ahead, there seemed to be nothing but more of what they were going through, the finished hallway reminding her of some kind of institution in a Stephen King novel. But eventually, they came up to a fork in the tunnel. She knew which way they were going to go even before he pointed to the right, to where things reverted back to raw stone and torches that spit and hissed fire from their mountings. Now, they were back around what they'd left behind: Bare black rock, everywhere. The smell of the earth. A dampness that was no longer overridden by an HVAC system.

Some hundred feet on, Nyx stopped without having to be told. Then again, there was nowhere else to go.

They'd arrived at the Wall.

In the flickering candlelight, the inscriptions of hundreds and hundreds of names seemed to move across the rock they had been carved into. And it wasn't until she stepped in close that she realized the listings were made up of symbols from the Old Language rather than letters. The lines of the inscriptions were uneven, some sloping up, some down, and there were a number of people who had done the carving, the names executed in various and inconsistent styles. There were no dates, no decades or years, much less months and days. But she gathered that it had started over on the upper left because the first name was right at the ceiling . . . and then all the way across, there was a column that was halfway done, with plenty of rock beneath ready for more memorials when the time came.

Given that Janelle's incarceration was relatively recent, Nyx went to that last name in the lineup. At first, her eyes refused to focus on the slick, reflective stone, the strobing effect of the candlelight making things a challenge even for vision unaffected by heightened emotion.

And meanwhile, her heart was pounding.

Running her forefinger across the name at the bottom, she sounded the syllables of the symbols out in her head. *Peiters*. And then she did the same to the one above it. *Aidenn*. And then the next. *Obsterx*.

She repeated the process over and over again, one more up, and one more up, and one more up . . .

She went slowly, and discovered that a lot of the names were misspelled. Accordingly, she didn't jump the gun on whatever was coming next for fear of inadvertently missing something. There was one shot to do this. They were not coming back. And if she got it wrong, she might well endanger her own life searching for a sister who was—

J. A. N. N. E. L.

With a gasp, she traced the symbols one by one. Then retraced them.

As she weaved on her feet, her eyes flooded with tears—which seemed a little strange given that she felt nothing whatsoever. She was instantly numb, her body cold, her lungs freezing in her ribs, her blood seeming to stop in her veins.

"Jannel," she whispered aloud. As if maybe the syllables added up to something different if they were uttered instead of just translated from the inscription inside her brain.

Janelle. Her sister's name was Janelle. So this had to be another prisoner, with a name close, but not exactly—

Closing her eyes, she sagged. She had gotten it right. The name was just spelled wrong, like a lot of them were. Maybe the carvers didn't know the Old Language any better than she did. Or maybe they were just careless fuckers who didn't seem to get that they were disrespecting the dead when they didn't get it correct.

As she stood there, the soft breath of the lit wicks all around her, the dropping of wax from the three-foot-tall black candles loud as an off-key chorus in her ear, she was tempted to fall apart—but mostly she wanted to scream. Janelle. Jannel. For fuck's sake, at least the guy with the chisel could have spelled the name right.

"Is it her?" Jack asked roughly.

The sound of his voice was a reminder of where they were. "Yes."

But before she turned around, walked away, started the process of getting herself out of the prison, she went to touch the inscription with her fingertips one last time—

What the—?

Her cell phone was not only in her hand, she'd turned it on, and all she could do was stare down at the thing and wonder how the hell that had happened and what in the hell the thing was for.

Oh . . . right. Picture. She needed to get a picture.

She lifted the unit up and snapped a photograph

239

of her sister's name. Then she turned around and—

Froze where she was. Jack had a guard up against the wall, a hand locked on the front of the other male's throat. Before Nyx could react, two shots went off, and she lunged forward, prepared to engage—except Jack was the shooter, not the other way around. And there was no loud, ringing echo of the discharges around all the stone. The bullets were muffled, sure as if the gun she'd given him had a suppressor on the end of the muzzle—except it did not. The guard's own flesh, the body that the lead slugs had been driven into, was what had dampened the noise.

As Jack dropped his hold, the body fell in a slump. Then he looked over at her.

His fangs were bared and long as daggers, and his expression was nothing like anything she had seen on his face before.

"We've got to get out of here," he hissed. *"Now."*

CHAPTER TWENTY-ONE

*T*he following eve, as Rhage stepped out of his accommodations in Jabon's very busy house, he was in a rather chipper mood. Closing the door, he smoothed the suit coat that adorned his chest, and regarded with a jaundiced eye the slacks that had been fitted to his enormous measurements. Jabon's tailor had delivered the fine wool togs the hour before, and had insisted upon putting the set onto him—not something Rhage would have volunteered for under any other circumstance. However, given that all of his clothing had disappeared when the beast had come out of him in that meadow down by the river, he had indulged the textile intervention.

And it had perked him up some. Yet the true elevation of his mood had come from the elevation of his corporeal form, one that was occurring without dizziness or the need for aid.

Good news had finally presented itself, that which he had been anxiously awaiting at long last turning up upon his doorstep, the parcel materializing, the calling card obtained, the audience granted: For the first time since his infection had presented itself with red-rimmed fanfare about that bullet's entry site, he had witnessed this nightfall a true turn in its course for the better. Indeed, when he had peeked under the bandage upon his awakening, he had seen a verifiable reduction in footprint and intensity. And that was not all. He could move so much better the now, the pain markers that had flared with every minute reorientation of his limbs or redistribution of his weight quieting down, even silencing, for a spell.

So, yes, there was a spring in his step as he descended the staircase unto the receiving area. On time. For First Meal.

The dining room was to the left, and there were guests already milling around the seats at the carved table, high-style hogs at the proverbial trough, but he did not proceed thereto. A familiar voice in the parlor drew his notice, and immediately thereafter, his footfalls.

Entering the room, he smiled. "Regard the two of you, still a-work, I see."

His brother Darius and the Jackal looked up from their joint perusal of the plans spread yet again upon that cleared table. The pair of them were both perfectly attired, as usual, and the males smiled readily. It appeared that all were of good cheer this warm June eve.

"And look at you," Darius said as he straightened, pencil in hand. "So upright and mobile, so very much better. I was going to come unto you, but you have come to me. Well done."

"Thank you, my brother." Rhage took a wee

bow, and as he righted himself, he braced for a light-headedness that did not claim him. "I feel quite well. A corner has been realized."

"I shall call Havers unto you as soon as we are done here." Darius's smile stayed broad, whilst his eyes became serious. "We will be sure he agrees with your self-assessment, prior to your imminent departure, which I sense, given those clothes, is more immediate than the meal about to be served across the foyer."

"Bring on the healer." As Rhage lifted his arms, he ignored the squeak of pain from beneath his ribs. Still, it was so much improved. "I am ready for him to conclude my convalescence."

"Good." Darius beckoned. "In the meantime, see here now our final product. I am very proud of our outcome."

The Jackal nodded. "He has much improved my ideas. This is going to be quite a palace, constructed for a long viability by master crafts-men."

Rhage indulged them both, moving across to stand over the plans, nodding and exclaiming excellence at their every turn of the broadsheet and point of an index finger—even though, for truth, he had no idea what he was looking at or of what they spoke. For these males, the translation of two dimensions into three was a ready accomplishment. For him? Such endeavor was but a logjam of cognition. The nonsensical *bunches of lines on those architectural renderings went absolutely nowhere under his skull.*

He could certainly appreciate their enthusiasm and sincerity, however, and besides, in his current mood, he was o'erflowing with fine humor, so such temperate well-wishes were easy to extend. In fact, he was even prepared to thank Jabon on his way out of the mansion—and not just in a polite, obligatory fashion. As trying as this ordeal had been, he did appreciate all of the hospitality. Though he most certainly was not going to miss the doggen.

"So it is set to be constructed?" he asked when there was a pause in the discussion of rafters and buttresses and "load-bearing" things.

The Jackal nodded in deference to Darius, and the future owner was the one who answered. "It is indeed ready for building. Thanks to this male here, who has pulled yeoman's duty. How many hours did you spend upon this, these last three nights?"

"It matters not. I do not sleep." As Darius focused on the male, the Jackal made a show of replacing the renderings' proper order. "And it is easy effort when the owner is such a decisive and incisive client."

After a moment, Darius returned his eyes unto the plans. "And you have gotten for me all of the workmales, too. However did you accomplish such a thing?"

"You may credit our mutual acquaintance Jabon. He was forthcoming with a reference, who in turn proved a fount of labor provision."

"But you will stay on and see the project through, yes?"

The Jackal inclined his head. "I intend to carry it from cornerstone to finishing touch, and to center my thoughts on the proper sequencing of it all, I have outlined the orders herein." He tapped a stack of more reasonably sized white pages. "This is a copy for you to keep and comment upon. I am looking forward to this project like no other."

"I am glad that you will be in charge. Such a relief unto me—"

Later, when Rhage replayed the ensuing series of catastrophes within his head, he would recollect that the footfalls coming down the stairs, those urgent yet delicate footfalls, were harbingers of the downfall. Of many downfalls. Yet, as with so many prescient signs, he did not, at first, recognize their significance.

The shout from the second floor was a different story.

As he turned about to see what of the commotion, Ellany flew off the last of the staircase's steps, her silken dressing gown not at all appropriate for the public areas of the house. And the instant she saw him, she stumbled to a halt, the peach silk that covered her swirling around in a perfumed furl. If he hadn't been standing in the parlor, he was quite sure she would have escaped the house entirely and run out into the street.

Her mahmen's *voice was sharp as it repeated her name. Twice more. And when Ellany did not even glance to the head of the stairs, another set of footfalls came down.*

Ellany as yet paid no heed. Her gaze was fixated on Rhage, her eyes glazed with tears.

"I did it for you," she whispered. "I did it . . . for you."

That was when he noticed the blood on the silk. Down upon the skirting portion.

Warning bells rang loud and insistent in his head. "Whate'er do you speak of, female?"

Ellany finally looked unto her mahmen *as the older female descended to the marble flooring and shot across over to her progeny. The* mahmen, *who was properly dressed, grabbed onto a thin arm and shook the poor girl.*

"What did you do?" the female blurted.

Ellany's desperate eyes returned unto Rhage.

Across the receiving foyer, in the archway of the dining room, Jabon appeared, a linen napkin in one hand, an expression of pleasant inquiry on his face.

When he saw what was transpiring in his foyer, that all changed. He put a sharp hand behind himself, as if ordering the others in the dining room to sit and stay. And then he stepped forward and pulled a set of double doors shut behind himself.

With a stern look that seemed wholly out of his character, he addressed the two females. "This is neither the time nor the place."

Both sought him with their eyes, and there was a long moment of silent communication. But Rhage cared not for whate'er transpired betwixt the three. He spoke loud and clear to all who could hear.

"I disavow any carnal knowledge of this female under your roof," he said. "I have had no attentions thereupon her, and the Jackal can attest as such."

As he stepped aside and indicated the other male, Ellany recoiled as if she had been unaware there were any others with Rhage in the parlor.

Gathering her silken gown such that the stains were covered, she looked around at all of her elders, a swimmer of little skill and even less strength about to sink into a watery grave.

"He was the one who deflowered me," she announced. "It was him."

Rhage opened his mouth to recant the slanderous accusation . . . until he realized she did not point at him.

She was indicating the Jackal with trembling hand and red-rimmed, tragic eyes. "He deflowered me."

CHAPTER TWENTY-TWO

The Jackal grabbed Nyx's hand, but there was no need to pull her along into an escape. She raced right for the run he set them on, and they pounded back to the finished parts of the Command's quarters.

Had he been wrong about the timing? Had he gotten the shifts incorrect? When that guard had come up to the Wall, he had been surprised— but so had the other male, and that moment of confusion had provided him with an opportunity he had taken immediate advantage of. Now, though, he was concerned that duties had changed. And worse, that backup had been called before he had killed the guard.

Rounding the corner, he—

The flank of four guards were in two-by-two formation, marching along in a coordination that was quickly interrupted. The first pair immediately dropped to their knees as guns were taken out of holsters, and four muzzles were pointed forward.

The Jackal jumped in front and spread his arms wide. "You know you cannot shoot me."

"What?" Nyx hissed behind him.

"You cannot shoot me." Lowering his voice, he said softly unto her. "Do it."

He had no idea whether she would understand what he meant. But then he felt her hand braced on his back, between his shoulder blades, and her gun appeared under his right arm.

She pulled her trigger. Over and over again.

As the weapon went off, he wondered just how far the moratorium on physical aggression by the guards toward him went. And then he stopped thinking altogether while he ducked and protected as many internal organs as he could without sacrificing the cover he offered Nyx. Who turned out to be a very good shot.

One guard dropped to the ground. A second slumped from his kneeling position.

The third was blown back as something red exploded out of the back of his skull.

And the last of the quartet turned and ran.

The Jackal tore after the male. If a communication went out to the guard center, Nyx was as good as dead. They'd drop the incremental barriers to prevent escape, and the place would flood with guards. When they caught her—and they would—she'd end up on that dais.

And females were made an example of prior to death in the most degrading and violent fashion imaginable. He'd seen it before.

Spurred by the threat to her, he threw himself into a chase that did not last long. Leaping forth, he took the male down onto the rock floor, and as his weight landed on the guard's back, something snapped deep within him. Baring his fangs, he palmed the skull and slammed the face forward, a sharp crack ringing out as the face was driven into the unforgiving ground.

The scent of blood bloomed.

And then everything became dim.

The Jackal had no conscious thought of rolling the guard over. Was not aware of his hand forcing the chin high. Was barely cognizant of lowering his own head down.

But he knew when the taste in his mouth changed. Everything went copper—

Now he was spitting out something. Something that tasted of fresh, uncooked meat.

As his head went down once more, he had a passing thought that he needed to stop what he was doing. He had a feeling that he had removed at least a portion of the male's larynx. No more vocalization was going to occur, so the purpose of silencing the guard had been served, and the next imperative was to get Nyx back to the hidden pool.

Except he couldn't cease and desist. The inner core of him was activated to the point of breaking free, a monster called out from the cave of his self-control, and once unleashed, it refused any and all calls to heel.

He continued to bite, and was certain he swallowed some of the anatomy. And he should have cared about the visuals he was subjecting Nyx to—moreover, he should have cared about the increased risk to her life as he savaged his victim. But all of those rational, reasonable thoughts were submerged beneath the tidal wave of his aggression—

His name was being called, repeatedly. He was fairly certain of this. However, he heard the syllables as if they were far, far off.

And then someone touched him.

The Jackal snapped at the hand. Then returned to his prey—

All at once, the guard was taken from him, dragged off by some unknown, unseen force.

No, that was wrong. He was the one removed, his vision swinging up and around as he was lifted bodily from the guard. The next thing he knew, he was thrown face-first into the tunnel wall and pinned in place.

He fought against the hold, snapping with his teeth, thrashing his legs and arms, bucking his hips.

He only stilled when he heard a low, threatening voice in his ear.

"He's dead. There is no more for you to do to him."

The Jackal stopped fighting against his captor. "Apex?"

It was bizarre how, in times of acute crisis, your brain could kick something random over your transom of awareness.

252

As Jack had viscerally destroyed the front of a guard's throat and most of the male's face, Nyx's brain decided to take her back to one year before Janelle was taken away to prison. There had been a horrible, howling ruckus in the woods outside the farmhouse. She and her grandfather had gone to see what it was, while Posie had put herself in the basement with a blanket over her head. Janelle had been out of the house. She'd always been out of the house.

Both Nyx and her grandfather had been armed, a pair of shotguns up on their shoulders. The concern had been something attacking one of the goats in the pen.

But it hadn't been coyotes.

Two massive timber wolves had been going at it, the animals up on their hind legs, teeth gnashing, claws slashing. Their powerful bodies had seemed so large, too large, but then savagery had a way of increasing mass. Both had been bleeding from various wounds, though the black and brown and gray fur had masked the specifics of the injuries.

The pair had been so locked into their aggression that the presence of a pair of vampires hadn't registered. Not until her grandfather discharged his shotgun into the moonlight did the four-legged combatants separate and scatter.

Jack had had the same degree of savagery just now. And if that killer, Apex, hadn't come and pried him off the guard? He'd be at it still.

And now, they had a new problem, didn't they. With shaking hands, she kicked the empty clip out of her gun, and brought her backpack around under the loose tunic, grabbing a fully loaded replacement and slamming it into place with the heel of her palm.

Her eyes went back to the guard.

His boots were twitching, but not because the male was going to stand up anytime soon. Apex, that killer, was right—and hey, he would know about death, right?

Oh . . . dear God . . . that face. Not that there was much of it left. Blood glistened and dripped free of the anatomy, flashes of white bone showing through the meat. The tongue was clicking—or maybe it was the teeth—and that jaw was working up and down, as if some part of the guard's consciousness was still sending signals to call for help.

Snapping out of it, Nyx pointed her gun at Apex's shaved head. "Let him go."

That head—or that skull, was more like it— slowly moved in her direction. The eyes that stared back at her were dead, no animation or character behind the black pits as the male focused on her.

"Shoot if you're going to," he said with boredom. As he did not release Jack.

"Let him go."

254

"Where are my hands, female."

It was then that she realized he had already dropped his hold. "Step back then. If you're not going to hurt him, step the fuck back."

"If I wanted to kill him," Apex drawled, "I'd have done so a decade ago. You're late to this party, female."

"Step back."

Apex's upper lip twitched, and she had a thought that she was going to need to watch her back after this. But instead of snapping his fangs at her, he smiled in an evil way, revealing two solid gold canines.

Jack solved the issue by sliding out from between the wall and the other male. Wiping his bloody mouth on his sleeve, he did not meet her stare. His loose, dark clothes were stained and out of joint, the tunic twisted around, not that he appeared to notice. Not that it mattered.

"We need to get rid of these bodies, but there's no time," he said hoarsely.

"I'll take care of them. Go. Now."

Jack glanced at the other prisoner. "Are we even, then."

"Yes." Apex nodded toward the tunnel. "Go. There will be more coming."

The killer didn't have to ask twice. Nyx was so ready to leave all of this behind. Intent on getting to Jack, she went to step over the bloody, dead guard—

As she transferred her weight, the dead body came to life. With a rasp and a gasp, wild, white-rimmed eyes flared, and the male reached for her ankle. The grab was strong enough to throw her off balance, and as she went into a free fall, the guard brought up a gun from out of nowhere.

Pointing the muzzle directly at her, he pulled the trigger—

Jack lunged across the distance as the gun went off, except he was too late—and so were Nyx's reflexes. Before she could shift in midair, the bullet ripped into her with a blaze of pain, but she didn't have time to track where the entrance was or if there was an exit. She landed hard, half on the guard, half on the floor, the side of her face taking some of the impact.

She was stunned as she lay where she landed, and when there was a *clunk!* sound by her head, she realized that her grandfather's gun had slipped out of her hand.

Shit, she thought as she grabbed the weapon again.

"Nyx!"

Jack's eyes entered her vision as he knelt down. His bloodstained face was pale as snow, his pupils dilated, his expression of horror the kind of thing that made her think about old-school *Friday the 13th* movies. Which made no damned sense. Then again, hello, shock.

"I'm shoot." She closed her eyes in frustration. "Shot. I'm shot."

"Your shoulder. I know."

"Not my chest then?"

Had there been one bullet? Or two? Why wasn't she in pain?

Beneath her, the guard started moving again, and a sudden jolt of adrenaline gave her a burst of strength. Shoving Jack back, she put the muzzle of her gun into the oozing open wound of that face—

And pulled the motherfucking trigger.

She wasn't even horrified as the body jumped under her, the extremities bouncing on the floor, a horrible gurgle rising up as the popping sound disseminated.

Where had she gone, she thought as she lifted her eyes to Jack.

He was staring back at her with a remote expression, and meanwhile, Apex loomed over them both, not a threat so much as a condemnation of her and her actions. Sometime between her entering that crypt and finding her way down here into the prison, a part of her had gotten lost. Or perhaps been ruined.

And she knew it wasn't coming back.

Apex laughed dryly. "Nice shot. Then again, point-blank improves accuracy."

"Shut up," Jack snapped.

Putting her hand out to him, he read her

mind. He helped her up onto her feet, and as she steadied herself on his arm, he looked her over as if searching for arterial bleeds. With uncharacteristic deference, she waited for his conclusion even though it was her body and he wasn't a physician. Then again, she felt like she couldn't trust her read on anything.

"We've got to move fast," he said.

Before she could start running again, he bent down and scooped her into his arms.

"No arguments," he barked. "You need to shoot if we get into trouble. Let my legs do the work for the both of us."

Just before they took off, Apex smiled again, flashing those gold fangs. "Quite a honeymoon you two are enjoying."

"Fuck off, Apex," Jack said over his shoulder as he took off at a jog.

CHAPTER TWENTY-THREE

All the Jackal could smell was Nyx's blood. All he could feel was the warm flush of it soaking through the clothes she had on and the sleeve of his prison tunic as he carried her. All he knew was the distance he had to cover if he was going to get her to safety.

Make that relative safety.

He ran as fast as he could without bouncing her around too much, but going by the way she grunted and stiffened in his arms, he knew he was hurting her. She wasn't lowering that gun, though. As he backtracked through the Command's compound, she had that muzzle up and ready, and she was alert, leaning into the corners he took and staying steady on the straightaways he bolted down.

Damn it, he'd lost the weapon she'd given him when he'd gone after that guard. There had been no time to look for it, though. At least she had more in her backpack, going by the metallic shifting it always made.

When they came up to the prison cell with the closed mesh panels, he couldn't stop himself from glancing inside—

Nyx's shout brought him back to attention.

Shit, he thought as he skidded to a halt.

Four guards were lined up in front of them, a uniformed wall of thou-shall-not-pass with plenty of gunmetal in their hands.

The Jackal considered a turn-and-bolt, but there was nowhere to go. Worse, the Command would be returning to these quarters soon, either because the review of the work area was over, or, more likely, because an alarm had been sounded. More backups for these guards were also surely on the way, and Nyx did not have the strength for another protracted battle.

"Gun to the temple," he whispered. As Nyx's eyes flared, he bared his fangs. "Put your gun on my temple. *Now.*"

As she did what he told her to, he addressed the guards. "I want you all to throw your weapons at my feet and go facedown or she'll shoot me. She'll fucking do it, and then you're going to have to explain how you let me get killed right in front of you. Do you want to be the bearers of that news?"

To prove his point, the muzzle of Nyx's gun, which was still warm and smelling distinctly of discharge, pressed into the side of his skull, right by the corner of his eye.

"No, no," he warned as the fair-haired guard on the left bent his mouth down to his shoulder, where his communicator was mounted by his epaulet. "None of that. Facedown, right now. Or this is going to get very, very ugly—and not just because my brains are blown out all over the wall."

As the guards tossed their weapons and lowered themselves, a figure entered the corridor from the fissure that led to the Hive. Whoever it was was draped in black folds from head to foot, and their face was hidden under a hood. They had covered their scent well, too, masking their identity with smells from the prison's kitchen. Bread. And garlic.

Thank the Virgin Scribe, the Jackal thought as he motioned the wraith down with the hand that was under Nyx's knees. Kane came quickly.

What a wise, wise male to hide his identity. And as always, the well-bred was on time.

"Hands behind your backs," the Jackal ordered the guards.

There was shifting on the floor, wrists presented at the small of backs, and Kane moved with the kind of grace only the aristocracy possessed, his lithe body under those folds smooth of stride and stretch—and yet he had a soldier's practicality and efficiency. Picking up one of the discarded guns from where they'd been thrown, he handcuffed each of the guards with their own equipment in the work of a moment. And in the course of his confining duties, the male also stripped them of their ammo and communicators, as well as a number of knives, creating a pile of equipment by their feet.

261

When Kane nodded, the Jackal took off once more, holding his precious load as gingerly as he could while he ripped past his dear friend as well as all the incapacitated guards.

"I had the safety on the whole time," Nyx said as they rushed forth. "Just so you know."

The Jackal could only shake his head. His emotions were too chaotic to put into proper order, but he suspected, even if he could have parceled them out, he wouldn't want her to know how much or of what he was feeling.

The fact that he couldn't have asked for a better partner seemed like something best kept to himself.

As did the reality that he was going to relive her getting shot for the rest of his life.

When Jack brought them up to the fissure, Nyx was ready to get down and hustle on her own. Good thing, because there was no way he could carry her through the tight squeeze. There was barely room for one person to fit through, much less an on-the-chest carry of a gunshot victim.

Not that she was a victim.

Pushing against his shoulder, she peeled herself free of his hold, and she could tell by the way his hands lingered on her waist that he didn't want to let her go even as her legs accepted her weight. No time to talk. She went directly into the darkness, pressing her body into the narrow, earthen embrace of the fissure—and she did not look back. No reason to. Jack would be behind her. He would back her up. And as she shuffled along, the damp rock scraping over her backpack under the tunic, she was curiously unafraid.

Which made no sense. Then again, at least no one was shooting at her inside this super-dark, super-cramped little hole.

Although when they reached the end, maybe that was going to change.

A soft glow marked the terminal of the crack in the cave's core, and Jack's hand on her shoulder slowed her as she reached their exit. For a moment, they waited. Breathing in, she got a refresher on the stench of the Hive, but she recognized that it was less intense somehow. Things were quieter as well. Maybe after the fight Jack's buddies had play-started, the place had been emptied out?

More likely, some alarm had been sounded as a result of the video game's worth of bodies they'd left behind in the Command's quarters.

"I don't hear anything," she whispered. "Is it safe?"

"Keep your gun ready, but hidden."

As Nyx had been the first in, she had to be the first out, and in retrospect, she maybe should have let him go ahead of her. Too late. No trading places.

Turning her head, she wished she could see

263

him, if only to take some strength from the sight of his face. It was too dark, though.

"I'm okay," she said softly. "Just so you know."

"You're in shock."

"I am not—"

"Of course you are—"

"Don't tell me what I am—"

They both stopped at the same time. And she had to smile—although the expression didn't last long.

"Under different circumstances," she said, "I really could have fallen for you."

She didn't expect a reply from him. But then his voice, so deep and low, weaved its way through the darkness to her.

"Under different circumstances, I would have fallen even harder for you. And not regretted my heart's tumble for a moment."

Closing her eyes, she felt a pain that had nothing to do with her bullet wound lance through the center of her chest. To hell with that better-to-have-loved-and-lost-than-never-loved-at-all bullshit. She would much rather have never met Jack.

Now, she was going to have to live with everything she would never have.

Assuming she made it out of the prison alive.

Tilting forward, she peered out into the Hive. "It's completely empty. Is this normal?"

"No. Not at all."

"What do we do?"

"We can't stay here, and we can't go back. We need to return to the hidden passageway. Head to the left and move fast, but don't run. Just walk like you know where you're going."

Taking a deep breath, she said a quick prayer, and when she slipped out of the fissure's cover, she did not look around. She stuck close to the Hive's outer rim, so close that her wounded shoulder bumped along against the stone walling, each impact making her grit her teeth. Head down. Eyes down. Shoulder on the wall. Head down. Eyes down. Shoulder on the—

Jack jumped ahead and she was relieved. In the lee of his huge body, she felt safer—until she realized the gun was in her right hand. Under the loose cover, she switched the weapon to the left so that it was on the wall side. The last thing she needed was some flash of the metal giving things away.

It wasn't until they were back in the main tunnel, the wide one that had been crowded with prisoners, that she realized they'd left the Hive behind. She hadn't even noticed. Where was the turn . . . where was the turn . . . that would take them back to the hidden place. To the waterfall. To the pool.

She craved that cloistered space as if it were something from her childhood, a destination she had visited many times, an enclave of security from any storms outside the family home.

Oh, emotions. Nonexistent if you were looking for something to touch or hold in your palm, but still so very corporeal given their capacity for great feats of transformation. Sure as if they had hands to build, to paint over, to wallpaper and carpet, they could turn a carved-out cave in the middle of a prison into a dreamscape home.

That was what was on her mind as Jack tugged her sleeve and took her around a corner to pull her to a stop. As he checked to see if they were being followed or about to be jumped, she studied him. The lower part of his face was still stained by the blood of the guard he'd all but eaten, and strands of his long dark hair had come loose from its braid. Fresh red blood stained his tunic in a couple of places, and every time she breathed through her nose, she caught her own scent. Meanwhile, Jack was panting hard and very flushed, but he was not scattered. His eyes were sharp and decisive. So were his movements as he reached around her and flipped something on the wall.

As the hidden panel slid back, she all but threw herself inside the protected passageway. Still, she didn't relax until they were closed in together safely.

Candles flared down at the ground level. But Nyx knew which way to go.

She led them once again—not that there were any decisions of direction to make—and as the sound of falling water and the fresh scent of clean air reached her senses, she started to tremble.

Her legs gave out as she came around the last bend and saw the pool.

Jack caught her. As always, or so it seemed.

When he eased her down onto one of the smooth sofa rocks, she gave into gravity's greedy hold and stared up at the glossy ceiling. Their movements had disturbed the flames at the heads of the wicks all around, and she watched the shadows on the rough rock ceiling dance above her.

God, her back hurt—no, wait. She was laying on her pack.

With a grunt, she shucked the tunic and then the nylon bundle of weapons, and as the latter flopped onto the floor, she relaxed into exhaustion. Or maybe she was passing out. Hard to tell.

When Jack's face appeared over her own, she wanted to kiss him. Just because he was still alive and so was she.

For the time being.

"Let me take your windbreaker off," he said. "We need to see how bad your shoulder is."

She nodded, and did what she could to help him remove the layers that covered her. When she was down to her short-sleeved shirt, they both inspected her shoulder.

"It's only a flesh wound," he said as he closed his eyes and sat back. Rubbing his face, he muttered, "Blessed Virgin Scribe."

As she prodded the red streak on the outside of her upper arm, the bleeding started up again, so she left things well enough alone. Thanks to the way vampires healed, the wound, which was not so deep as to reach the underlying musculature, was already knitting itself back together. If she played her cards right and didn't get too physical in the next couple of hours, it would soon be fully closed.

But did they have that much time?

Letting her head fall back onto the stone, she closed her eyes and tried to remember the last time she had felt this tired. And then she heard Jack's voice in her head, repeating the pronouncement about flesh and wound and only . . .

Monty Python.

From out of her bone-marrow-deep weariness, she saw that scene from *The Holy Grail*, where the knight on the losing end of the sword fight, while he was gushing blood from every leg and arm socket he had, exclaimed the same in a haughty British accent.

It's only a flesh wound.

"You are much relieved then?" Jack said.

Nyx opened her eyes. "I'm sorry?"

"You're smiling."

"Oh, it's not because of . . . it's this movie,

you've definitely seen it—" She stopped herself. "I mean, it's nothing."

He hadn't seen that movie. Or any other.

She focused on him again. And when she reached out to him, he scrubbed his jaw and chin with his palm, as if he were embarrassed by the stain of the male they had killed together—as if he wished she hadn't seen what she had.

"Come here," she said.

"We need a plan."

"I know. But come here first."

When he finally moved into range, she pushed his hand out of the way of his lower face. Going to the top of his tunic, she freed the buttons on the high neck and spread open the lapels.

His eyes grew remote. Like he knew what she was staring at.

"You don't have a lock collar like the others do," she said. "And the guards can't hurt you. Who are you really and why do you choose to be here."

"I am just like any other prisoner."

Nyx shook her head. "You're lying to me."

CHAPTER TWENTY-FOUR

*S*tanding in Jabon's drawing room, Rhage absorbed the details of the diorama of catastrophe as if the triangulation of figures would somehow reveal the truth beneath the surface of the allegation: Ellany, with her stained peach dressing gown and pale, heartbroken face. Her mahmen, poised for flight in her finery, gown skirting lifted—although given the fury on her face, it seemed as if she intended to engage rather than run.

With her daughter? *Rhage wondered.* Or with the male who had been accused?

The Jackal, meanwhile, was looking aghast, his shock so deep and honestly held, it was clear he could not respond.

And finally, there was Jabon, standing before the closed doors of his dining hall, his remote, masklike expression concealing what had to be the alarm going through his mind: A member of the glymera *might entertain countless guests— including some who may have been of less than perfect repute—in a manner that was, at times, questionable, but provided the "questionable" activities with the less-than-"reputable" visitors occurred behind closed doors, and with no undue attention upon the comings and goings from*

271

bedrooms, there would be little social fallout. True, there were invitations unto Jabon that might be, and no doubt had been, revoked, and there would be certain high-bred females who would refuse to be seated beside him at festivals, but largely he would be left to his own devices, free to open his mansion up to whomever he chose.

However, all of that leeway would be rescinded in the work of a moment if a well-bred female of mateable age was dishonorably stripped of her virginity under his roof.

The downfall Jabon would experience would be swift, epic and lasting through countless future generations of his loins.

"I did it for you," Ellany repeated unto Rhage.

He shook his head at the young female. "You did no such thing as I have never asked anything of you. Even when you sought me out."

"Ellany!" her mahmen exclaimed. "Whatever did you—"

"Enough," Jabon snapped with surprising strength.

Gone was the bon vivant. In its place was an utterly serious head of household who enjoyed his social station—and apparently wanted to retain it.

"You have disgraced my home," he said to the Jackal. "You have mistreated an innocent of fine breeding under my roof—"

"I did no such thing!" The Jackal stepped

272

forth, a strong figure, also of fine breeding, who knew exactly what would transpire upon him if the accusation stuck. "I have not put a hand upon her, and she knows it—"

"So ruining her body was not enough, now you must befoul her character?" Jabon slashed a hand through the air. "How dare you! You will take your leave of mine property at once, and there will be consequences to this."

"She is lying." The Jackal's eyes bored into Ellany's, who could not bear the scrutiny. As she ducked her stare, he cursed. "But yes, I shall depart at once, and ne'er return. My honor has been offended for the convenience of a social ploy that does not involve me, and I resent the implication into whatever scheme is being played out here. It has nothing to do with me."

The gentlemale stalked out of the parlor, and as he came abreast of the mahmen *and the daughter, he spoke in a low tone. "My scent is not upon her flesh, nor is it in her bed. Well you know this and so does she."*

As he inhaled, his nostrils flaring, his expression grew grimmer and his stare shifted to his host. "Did you coach the girl unto this before or after you left her garden so well plowed?"

"Get out," Jabon said as he flushed with fury. "Get out!"

The Jackal jogged up the stairs, his back straight, his chin high.

273

In his absence, Rhage cursed and shook his head. "I do not believe for one moment that male did aught—"

"A word," Jabon interjected, "if I may."

As their host strode across the receiving area, he commanded something in a low tone unto the two females, and whatever it was, their compliance was prompt. And suspicious. In spite of the fact that a male who had supposedly done a terrible thing to them both had ascended unto the second floor, they returned upstairs as well in the wake of the apparent offender.

When Ellany looked over her shoulder, Rhage shook his head. But not at her. At the whole situation.

Jabon came forth into the parlor and shut the doors, pulling varnished panels closed. His fine clothes and natty style seemed a stage set, but then was that not what this all was about. This house, these guests, this social station of his.

"I bid you," he said. "Listen unto the truth before you render judgment."

Rhage scented the air around the male. All he got back was the choking bouquet of fancy oils that Jabon regularly applied unto himself. What mattered was what was upon the female, however Rhage was not going to traumatize her further by chasing after her just to smell her.

"Did you take that newling." Rhage crossed his arms over his chest. "And do not lie unto me."

"No, of course not." Jabon placed his right hand upon his chest. "On my honor."

"The Jackal's protestation was quite clear. So was his accusation unto you."

Darius spoke up. "And the male has been quite honorable in all my dealings with him."

"You do not know him as I do." Jabon walked over to the fireplace, and stared down at the white-barked birch logs that were stacked and unlit. "He is a liar. He's lied about everything. Who he is, where he's from, what he does."

"And his story is what," Rhage intoned.

"That he hails from an aristocratic line, and is here in Caldwell with all the rights and privileges thereto. But he has always refused to divulge his family colors. He is nothing but a drifter and a con male that seduced my sire into patronage—"

"Then why have him under your roof."

"I just kicked him out," Jabon countered with an edge.

"Because he was accused of an unthinkable violation of an innocent," Rhage shot back. "Somehow I believe, if it had not happened the now, I would be sitting across from him at First Meal as we speak."

"He is guilty! Am I supposed to tolerate such social disobedience and all the harms it exposes me to then?"

"Not the point." Rhage tilted forward onto his hips. "And I am not worried about propriety. I am worried over that poor female. Fuck the social rules, are they truly all that bothers you in this?"

"Of course not." Jabon waved his arms around. "And as for that male's baseless accusation unto me, her scent is not upon me. Inhale well and know my truth."

Rhage shook his head. Jabon had immediately stepped out of the dining room when the females had come down, so it was impossible to tell whether his scent was upon the air because of his presence in the foyer or because of what he'd left upon the dressing gown and flesh of the young female.

Their host clasped the front of his silk evening jacket. "I should never have invited the Jackal under my roof, and moreover, when his story began to be cast in doubt in my mind, I should have relieved his dubious presence of this house immediately. I regret not acting as such, and moreover, I regret that one who should never have suffered has been hurt by my failure of judgment. I will make this right. I swear upon my deceased sire's soul."

On the far side of the closed panels, Rhage's ears picked up on a muffled rhythm descending the stairs. And then the front door opened and shut soundly.

Through the glass panes that faced out the front of the mansion, he witnessed a dark figure with

276

a suitcase in hand stride down the walkway and take a right to progress away from the property.

The Jackal had departed with his possessions.

Abruptly, Rhage looked down at the suit coat that had been prepared for him. The slacks. The leather shoes.

Peeling off the formal jacket, he draped it over the back of a silk chair. Then he yanked off the cravat, loosened the waistband of the slacks, and kicked off the shoes.

As he disrobed, Jabon blinked in confusion, as if he had neither performed nor ever seen such actions before. Darius, on the other hand, rolled his eyes.

All the way to naked.

Rhage took it all off, and then itched his back and rolled his shoulders. "Thank you for the hospitality. You can keep these clothes. I'm leaving as I came in."

Jabon stuttered. "You—you—you cannot depart thus! What will—"

"Do not ever ask me for anything, especially not unto this house," Rhage announced. "And if you see me out upon the town, look away, walk away. I do not wish to be associated with any-thing under this roof, and I do not believe your story of that male who just took his leave of us. I have no proof, however. So do as you wish, but do not seek to entangle me—or I might just feel the need to share my opinions of you and this

household and this situation with others of ready ear."

"You are wrong about me, and wrong about him!" Jabon shook his head as he launched into much pleading. "And you shall see. I will ensure that this is redressed the proper way. Punishment will be levied and served for what he has done. Please do not shun the hospitality that shall always be available herein for any member of the Black Dagger Brotherhood!"

"I do not believe you." Rhage shrugged. "About anything."

With that, he nodded unto his brother and took his own leave, dematerializing through the glass panes of the windows through which he had regarded the Jackal's own departure. As he spirited out into the night, heading at long last for the isolated home he had set for himself far from the center of town, he resolved to avoid all persons unless absolutely necessary.

Nothing good ever came out of interacting. And that was before one contemplated the roaring complication of his beast.

As well as the utter unreliability of others.

Best that he continued as he was meant to go on.

Alone.

CHAPTER TWENTY-FIVE

I am a prisoner just the same as any."
As the Jackal spoke the words again, he pulled the top of his tunic closed and held the two halves in place. "My story is no different than any of the others, and my sentence is what it is."

"It isn't." Nyx shook her head. "You could leave here. If the guards can't touch you and you have no collar, you can just dematerialize out. You're choosing to stay—"

"No," he said sharply. "I do *not* choose to stay. I would leave here if I could, just like all the others."

When she shook her head again, he got to his feet and went over to the stack of neatly folded tunics and pants. Yanking his stained top off, he wadded the thing up and threw it into the shadows. As he pulled on a fresh one, he wanted to take a full bath. Instead, he settled for going over and kneeling by the burbling pool. His hands were not steady as he cupped them and splashed his face, over and over again. The water was warm. He wished it was cold enough to ice over.

Fates, he could still taste the blood of that guard, yet found it bizarre that he could remember nothing of the male's features. Not his eye color or hair color. Not whether he was handsome or ugly.

Sitting back on his heels, he dried his face with the bottom of the tunic.

Meanwhile, Nyx simply stared at him, and he knew without asking what the silence meant. She would go nowhere with him, do nothing to ensure her safety, until he explained himself.

The Jackal cleared his throat. "I was accused of bedding an innocent. Taking her without a commitment, and worse, without her consent. In truth, I had no carnal knowledge of her. The closest I ever came was sitting at a dining table three seats down from her. Upon my honor, I was never even alone with the female. I was sacrificed to save her and her *mahmen*'s reputation when a mating ploy failed."

Nyx's eyes narrowed. "You didn't have sex with her and yet you ended up here. For a century. On a false accusation."

"There was no objective court for me to go to, no impartial body weighing the truth and the falsehoods. I was called unto the Council, and evidence was presented against me by a male who lied to protect himself, a *mahmen* who needed to have her daughter be a victim rather than an unmated consort, and a young female who was in over her head with no virtue to give a future *hellren*. I didn't have a chance."

"But that's not fair." Nyx sat up, propping herself on her elbow. "Surely truth is the ultimate defense.

"Don't be naive. How did you think this place got so full?" He rolled his eyes. "This prison was established and run by the Council to serve the needs of the *glymera*. I was an easy sacrifice, given the others who were involved. And of course I went unto the Council intending to prove my innocence, but I never had the chance to speak. I was sentenced on the spot and dragged off by guards, my civil liberties dashed, my life, my pursuits, my future, gone. I died that night in all the ways that mattered." With a harsh laugh, he rose to stand. "Little did I know there were even worse moments ahead, nightmares that, at the time, and as horrified and shocked as I was, I couldn't have even begun to guess at."

She fell quiet for a moment. "But you could leave."

"No."

"I don't understand—" Nyx stopped. Then cursed under her breath. "Of course. That cell that was furnished properly. That's where your female is. She's the reason you don't leave. She's what keeps you here."

The Jackal crossed his arms over his chest. "It is not a simple situation."

"Enlighten me."

"I can't. But I swear, it does not affect . . ." He motioned between them. "It has nothing to do with us."

"*Us?*" She sat up properly, dangling her arms off her knees. "Like we're dating? Like this is the monogamous/nonmonogamous conversation of two people about to decide whether to be exclusive or not? Don't be ridiculous."

"But it doesn't affect us." He had no idea what else to say. "It's not about . . . you and me."

"There is *no* you and me." She smoothed the errant strands that had come out of her banded hair. "I'm leaving here as soon as I can, and I'm never coming back. You'll never see me again. Instead, you'll sit down here, under the ground, and rot until you die and your name is inscribed on that wall. But the difference between you and the others who are listed there, like my sister? You are choosing that kind of death—just like you're choosing this kind of life."

"You don't understand."

"You're right. I don't. The good news is that I don't have to. You're either a fucking coward and avoiding what's up above, or you're feeding me a line of bullshit and dumb enough to think I'll believe you because we had sex. Either way, it's not any of my business—and more to the point, I'm bored by your games."

The Jackal eyed the passageway he could use to take his leave of her. And he willed himself to initiate the steps that would carry him off. His feet did not move, however.

Instead, he looked back at the female.

"You have your conclusions about me," he said in a harsh voice. "And I must confess, I am confounded that they are so low. Then again, I should be used to this considering the actions of others that ended me thus—"

"Ended you thus? What the fuck. You can leave! And spare me the justifications—"

"I will *not* spare you a defense of your accusation," he snapped. "I was denied that right once, and believe me when I say that will never happen again. You have accused, and you will now listen to my side."

Nyx's brows flared. And when she went silent, he spoke on. "I do not owe you an explanation— something that strikes me as a convenience as it is clear that you will afford me no impartiality. This in spite of the fact that I have done nothing but ensure your safety and the success of your mission to ascertain the fate of your sister. This in spite of you not knowing anything of me but what I have shown you, which I think we can both agree has been nothing but courtesy and protection."

As she exhaled, she spoke in a low voice. "When is the next change of shift. That's all that I care about."

The Jackal opened his mouth. Then closed it.

After a moment, he spoke quietly. "You are worried about yourself. But of course."

"I just want to get out of here."

"And strangely, or perhaps not, I find myself in utter agreement with this goal of yours." He rubbed his eyes. "We are past being able to concern ourselves with shifts. There are dead guards now, in a place that only a limited number of people have access to. The prison is on lockdown as we speak, in which case I have to go back to my cell for mandatory count. Assuming I have not missed it already."

"How do we find that out?" she said. "Whether we're on lockdown, I mean."

"I will go—"

"No." She got to her feet. "We go together."

The Jackal stared across at the female he had seemed to be in such concert with when they had been fleeing the guards. All of that communion and partnership was gone. He was dealing the now with somebody who was a total stranger, one who was, moreover, incompatible with him.

"As you wish," he muttered. "Far be it from me to get in your way."

This was all over, Nyx thought as she put on her windbreaker, strapped on her backpack, and walked around the pool. This whole bizarre, too-dangerous, heartbreaking interlude was over. She was going to go back the way she'd come in, and then she was returning to the farmhouse and her family—

As she thought of her home, and her remaining sister, she cursed, remembering the picture she'd taken of Janelle's name in the Old Language.

There had been plenty of very worthwhile distractions since she'd stood in front of the Wall, but grief surged now: Janelle was dead. And she had likely died alone. Had her body even been buried? Or had it been thrown out like trash.

And it was all their grandfather's fault.

"Put a new tunic on," Jack said.

"I don't want to."

He went over to the stack, picked one up and threw the thing at her. "Put this on now."

Yanking the garment over her head, she promised herself she was going to burn the damn thing as soon as she could find a fireplace.

As Jack stalked off down the passageway, and the candles extinguished in his wake, she fell into step behind him and kept focused on the only thing that mattered. He might choose to stay here, but she was free to go—and she was not going to look back. Literally or figuratively. She was not going to ruin her future over a male she didn't know who was stuck in a situation she couldn't understand—and didn't believe anyway.

These were the resolutions that propelled her away from the pool, and kept her going as he led her out into one of the main arteries of the prison.

There was no else around. No sounds, either. Like rats fleeing from a subway system, all of the prisoners had taken cover.

The lockdown was definitely happening. In which case, fine. She didn't need him. If he took her to the way she'd come in, she would handle the rest of the way—and he could go back to his cell and waste the rest of his life down here.

Excellent choice on his part. Really, really great.

"Stop," she said.

He didn't. "What."

"I know the way from here."

Now he turned around. Staring down at her from his greater height, he lifted an eyebrow. "Do you."

"It's a left here, and then four rights, one after another." She shrugged. "It's not hard."

"Of course it isn't. Not for you."

"I took all lefts when I came in."

"What?"

Nyx repositioned the backpack under the tunic he'd made her wear. "When I came in here, so I didn't get lost, I took all lefts. This tunnel here"— she pointed to the one they were standing in front of—"will take me to the first of the corners I took. Three more and I'm there. So we're done. You can go back to your cell alone, which is what you wanted."

His brilliant aquamarine eyes narrowed on her. "You have all the answers, don't you."

286

"I know how to save myself. And I know the way out of here. Those are the only two answers I need."

"Well, then." With a gallant bow, he stepped aside and motioned forward with his hand. "Allow me to get out of your way."

"Thank you."

Nyx was tempted to offer him her palm, but there was no reason to be petty, and that did seem like a taunting move. So instead, she walked by him—

And kept going.

For the first fifty yards, she had one ear on what was behind her. She expected him to follow her or call her back. And when there were no footfalls and she didn't hear her name, she was relieved. She didn't like the prowling frustration he caused, and she sure as hell could take care of herself—

"Enough," she muttered. "Just stop with him."

The rights she needed to take came at the proper intervals, what she remembered for distances between turns the same as what she was finding. When she came to the last corner, with no scents in her nose or sounds in her ears, she felt triumphant. Rounding the final right, she—

Stopped dead in front of a massive steel wall.

Wrenching around, she recounted her turns in her head. Pivoted back around.

No, this was wrong. There was another fifty

yards, and then there were the locked steel panels across the entry she'd used coming in here. The ones she had the pass card to.

Putting her palms against the cold metal, she pushed at the barrier even though she knew that was going to get her nowhere. The damn panels had dropped down from the ceiling and were bolted together. Did she think she was going to punch a hole in them?

"Shit."

As sweat broke out under her arms and across her chest, she felt herself begin to panic. But then she turned her head and saw the blinking light on the wall.

"Pass card . . . pass card . . ."

With shaking hands, she went under the tunic and patted every pocket she had. Just as she was convinced she'd lost it along the way, she felt the stiff card. Ripping the thing out, she jabbed it at the reader pad that was bolted onto the rock wall.

Nothing.

She went up with it. She went down. Across. She tried both sides of the card. Twice.

"Shit."

As she considered her options, time was not her friend, and if she did the math right on the distances, then the barrier also blocked her from accessing the first hidden passage Jack had taken her into—because that one was closer to where she had entered the prison from the crypt. Her only shot at getting hidden and doing a proper reset on her plans was going back to the pool.

If she could make it—

Voices.

And the telltale marching. Of many, many boots.

Nyx began to tremble. Putting her shoulder blades against the steel panels, she closed her eyes for a brief moment. Popping her lids back open, she quickly went into her pack and palmed up not one but two guns.

Assuming the guards were coming her way, her only chance was to try to shoot her way out of this.

Not that that was going to get her far. She was trapped down below, a prisoner just like all the others.

CHAPTER TWENTY-SIX

The Jackal returned to his cell in the nick of time. Just as he shot into his private space, he heard the first of the guards enter the corridor down at the other end. There were shouts of names and replies from prisoners as the Command's detail walked the line, the sound of the boots getting louder as they came toward him.

Fuck, the scent of blood was all over him. Even though he'd changed tunics and rinsed his face off, that didn't go far enough.

In the rear of his cell, in the corner, there was a ready stream of water that flowed down the crease where the rock walls met, and he ripped off his tunic, lunged forward, and shoved his head into it. On a ledge, he kept a bar of that homemade prison soap, the rotgut combination of lye and herbs like sandpaper, and he massaged the pumice-like egg in his palms under the rush, calling up the anemic suds.

Face. Neck. Chest.

Under his arms.

There was nothing he could do about his braid, but he didn't think he had much blood in his hair—

"Lucan," the guards called out.

Three cells away.

"Yesssss," the wolven drawled. "Oh, I'm sorry, is this bothering you?"

Grabbing the fresh tunic, the Jackal dried himself and was about to hit his bed when he looked down at his pants.

"Fuck."

More blood than he'd thought on them.

As the mouthy wolven went back and forth with the guards over Fates only knew what, the Jackal dropped his loose pants, washed what he could of his lower body, and dried off on his way back under his bed. He hid the stained pants under the platform.

Even though lying down was the last thing he wanted to do, he stretched out on his pallet, propped his head against the stone wall, and pulled the rough blanket over his nakedness. Throwing his hand down to his stack of old books, he grabbed the first one that hit his palm, brought the thing onto his chest, and held it open in front of his face.

Upside down. Words were upside down.

With a curse, he swung the book around and was just focusing on a line of dialogue when two guards appeared in front of his cell.

Peering over the top of *Macbeth*, he cocked a casual brow. "You rang?"

The guards were related to each other, going by their identical dark-colored eyes, their similar heights, and the fact that both of them had a strange cowlick in the front of their hairlines. But they were not twins, and he did not recall having seen them before. Then again, going by their hesitancy, they had to be new hires.

"I'm here. You can reassure the Command." When they didn't move on, he inquired, "Would you like to come in and watch me read?"

Their eyes narrowed at the same time and in the same way. But as vocal as they had been with the others, they did not take his verbal bait, nor did they chastise or punish him. They just turned and continued on.

The Jackal waited, keeping his position even as one of his bare feet tapped the other, the kinetic energy flowing through all of his muscles impossible to contain for long.

The guards came back shortly thereafter. Whether it was a test to see if he'd moved or just a natural course of their duties, he didn't know. It didn't matter. And this time, they kept going all the way down the lineup of cells, their foot-falls growing fainter and then disappearing altogether.

The Jackal tossed the book off the bed and sat up. Over at his clothes stash, he got a fresh set of slacks and jerked them up his thighs. As he tied the waistband, the wolven appeared in his doorway.

For once, Lucan was not smiling. "Everything's

locked. All the peripheral tunnels. And they canceled the work shifts."

The Jackal looked up sharply. "They've never done that before."

"How many guards did you kill in the private sector?"

"Is that a rhetorical?" When the wolven just stared at him, he shrugged. "Four for sure. Then there were another four that were handcuffed together on the floor. Apex was on cleanup."

"Were the quartet still alive when he came to them?"

"He may not have been the one who found them."

"If he did, they're dead, too—"

The Jackal stiffened. Breathed deep. Dropping his voice, he whispered, "Go back to your cell. Now."

"Look, if your little girlfriend with the knife skills is loose in this place, she's in deep trouble—"

The Jackal punched his comrade's shoulder. "Go! You don't want to be here."

The wolven opened his mouth like he was going to argue, but then his head wrenched to the side as he clearly caught the scent as well.

"Fuck. Be careful."

Lucan disappeared as the Jackal lunged for his bedding platform. He was pulling the blanket over himself again when a tall figure, draped from head to toe in black, drifted into the archway of his cell.

But it wasn't Kane.

It smelled of sandalwood oil.

The Jackal's stomach turned so violently, he had to swallow the bile that rose into his throat. Not from the scent, specifically. From what the scent represented.

He looked over at the figure, pegging the dense mesh that covered the face with hard eyes. "Yes?"

The Command's voice was low and deep. "I understand that you were in the restricted area and you had a gun to your head. That an inmate threatened you. Is this true?"

Prison tunic. He'd made Nyx put that tunic on.

The guards didn't know she was from the outside. Except why the lockdown if they thought she was one of them?

"It was," he answered. "But it is over."

"Who was it. Where do I find her and that gun."

"I don't know."

There was a pause, and he knew damn well the Command was testing the air for scents other than his own. "Did you enjoy your bath just now?"

"Don't be jealous. It doesn't look good on you."

"Watch yourself, Jackal. I'm short-tempered tonight."

"Things not going to your liking? Such a pity—"

A guard rushed up to the Command. "There's a female in prison gear cornered by the western checkpoint. She is armed, but she is about to be subdued."

The Command's head swiveled back to the Jackal. "Well. It looks as if this little problem has solved itself. Any explanations you'd like to offer before I enjoy interrogating her?"

The Jackal reclined back against the wall, putting his hand down on his stack of books again. As *Macbeth* resumed its position front and center on his chest, he shrugged.

"I don't know her or where she came from." All true. "She had a gun. I did what she told me to do. Then she made me face the wall and count to ten before I turned back around. I went to fifteen, just to be sure, and I found that she was gone. She's your problem, not mine. You run this place, after all."

"What did she ask you to do?"

"Take her to the Wall."

There was a pause, and he imagined the frown on the Command's face. "Why?"

"She was looking for her dead. I don't know."

"So she's not a prisoner."

"Like I said, she had a gun, so I wasn't inclined to press for details. I did what she demanded. She left me unharmed. That's all I know."

One of the black sleeves lifted toward him, like the Grim Reaper was pointing. "I'll know if you're lying. Pain has a way of bringing out the truth, especially from females."

"Do with her what you will. It doesn't matter to me."

"Expect to be called on later."

"Don't rush on my account."

The Command shifted under those robes, that body changing positions. "Don't play hard to get. It doesn't suit you."

The Jackal shook his head grimly. "On the contrary, it's the only reason you want me."

"Oh, no." The laugh under the hood was low and sexual. "You are so very wrong about that."

As the Command turned away, the Jackal kept his eyes on the book and his body as still as he could.

Dearest Virgin Scribe, Nyx was worse than dead.

CHAPTER TWENTY-SEVEN

A s Nyx stared at the lineup of armed guards in front of her, she felt herself recede from reality. Considering the number of them, the mental lapse seemed like a perfectly reasonable response, even though it was totally unhelpful. Then again, there was no thinking her way out of this. No talking her way out. No shooting her way out, even with the two guns.

"Drop your weapons," one of the uniformed males ordered. "Or we're going to kill you here and now."

She was tempted to tell them she accepted what was behind door number two, even if it was the proverbial "Goodnight, Irene." She didn't want to die, but she knew that falling into their hands was going to be worse than taking her last breath here in this tunnel.

"Drop your weapons!" he repeated.

Too many guards. Too many weapons on them that they had been trained to use—

He will win who knows when to fight and when not to fight.

From out of nowhere, she heard her defense teacher's voice in her head, variations on the phrase repeating over and over again: *If you cannot win, do not fight. Evade.*

Sun Tzu. *The Art of War.*

Taking a deep breath, Nyx slowly lowered both her weapons. Then she closed her eyes and pictured the pool, with its waterfall and its clean scent and the candles down on the floor. She imagined herself sitting beside it, on the sofa rock, warm and safe.

Not enough. She wasn't calm enough—

"Drop your weapons on three! One, two—"

From out of nowhere, Jack appeared in the image, and he was as he had been the night before, watching her, his astonishingly blue eyes on her—

Nyx dematerialized out from under the guards.

One second she was before them, with their guns in her face. The next she was just a scatter of molecules, traveling past them through the air, invisible.

Untouchable.

Back when this had all started, when she'd come to that old, decaying church, she couldn't have dematerialized inside of it from where she'd been on the ground because she didn't know the interior. Now, at least she knew the tunnel system to some degree, although she prayed that more steel barriers hadn't dropped down from the ceiling. If they had? She was going to slam into all that steel and die a pancake.

Willing herself into a fast-track backtrack, she re-formed when she was about twenty yards from where she believed the entrance to the hidden pool's corridor was. Her heart was pounding and her brain scattered, and she had a thought that her being able to dematerialize had been a Hail Mary and a half. She couldn't do it again. The whole calm-and-concentrating thing was now out the window.

Left side. Hadn't the release been on the left side?

She put one of her guns away, and patted her palm down the carved rock. She wasn't sure what she was looking for, and wished she'd paid more attention to what the damn thing had looked like—

Nyx froze and glanced over her shoulder. Shouting.

Prisoners? Or guards? Probably guards looking for her. Her heart went haywire in her chest, and she frantically patted the rock—

Without warning, there was a click and part of the walling slid back soundlessly.

"Thank *God,*" she said as she jumped into the darkness.

But then it was a case of panicked waiting. Three seconds, right? Jack had said it took three seconds until the panel closed automatically.

More shouting. Rushing footfalls that were heavy getting nearer.

"Close . . . *close* . . ." She reached out and tried to pull the barrier into place. "Goddamn it!"

She felt like she was in a horror film, standing in an elevator, praying for the doors to shut before the monster skidded around the corner on clawed feet with jaws gnashing. But the urgency wasn't just her own survival. As pissed off as she had been at Jack, she didn't want to be the one who blew the cover on his secret place—

The panel finally started to close. And as the boots got ever nearer, the fricking thing took twenty-five million years to lock into place. Just as it did, and the hidden passageway plunged into darkness, the commotion got much louder.

Directly outside the panel.

Nyx stepped back and put her free hand over her mouth. As she panted in and out of her nose, she told herself they didn't know where she'd gone. They couldn't know about the release. They weren't going to find her.

In the choking sensory void, she screamed inside her skin.

"No, she must have gone this way!" one of the guards barked in a muffled voice. "The other tunnels are blocked—"

"She couldn't have made it this far—"

"For fuck's sake, stop yelling, I can't hear my earpiece—"

And then a fourth voice, low and sinister: "I will shoot her the second I see her."

"You can't kill her. The Command wants her. You'll get us all fucking killed."

Nyx took another step back. And another. The idea that she was not going to get out of the prison didn't just dawn on her. It submerged her, sinking her down into a terrible mental state.

Splaying her arms out, she moved to one side to orientate herself, and she connected with the wall when the muzzle of the gun in her hand hit the rock. As the clang of metal rang out, she froze, sweat beading on her forehead.

Her heart pounded so hard that she couldn't tell what was coming from her chest and what might have been more guards racing to find her. Stumbling, tripping, she retreated in the darkness, the sound of her windbreaker shifting against her body under the tunic, the soft rattle inside the backpack, the shuffle of her boots over the ground, loud as bombs going off. Desperation and exhaustion drove her past the point of breaking into a state of numb despair. She tripped on something. Kept going.

After what was a lifetime, her ears perked to the sound of falling water.

The sweet, soft chime of the pool's feed was such a relief, she worried she was imagining it. But as the water got louder, and the voices of the arguing guards disappeared, she was tempted to outright bolt for the sanctuary.

The possibility of tripping and falling was too great, and besides, there was no magic to the pool. It offered no special cover or protection.

When she finally stopped at the pool's edge, she didn't immediately will the candles on. She stood where she was, one hand going back to lock onto her mouth, the other keeping its death grip on her gun. Her lungs were burning even as she sucked in air through her nose, and she was aware of the cave spinning around her. Afraid she was going to pass out, she let her knees go loose and landed on her ass on the rock floor.

The ringing in her ears was not helping. She couldn't hear properly.

And her shoulder wound hurt.

After a while, after a long, long while, she dropped the hand clamp from her mouth. When her heavy breathing eased up, she listened hard, and when she could hear nothing but the waterfall, she willed one of the candles to life.

The fragile yellow light did not carry in the dense darkness. It was more like a star in the galaxy, a twinkle far off that revealed nothing about its immediate environment.

Lowering her head into her hands, she was acutely aware of the nine millimeter's metal across her forehead, cool and hard. With every breath she took, she smelled gunpowder residue, and it was hardly reassuring.

Prison on lockdown. Guards looking for her. No way out that she was aware of.

Jack was right. She'd been reckless and naive to come down here. Never once had she considered a mortal risk to herself. And now she was trapped—

Without warning, all of the candles lit and she jerked her head up, blinking in the glow. When her eyes adjusted, she couldn't understand what she was seeing.

"Is it you?" she whispered.

Jack—or what her mind was telling her was Jack—seemed to be standing in front of her, dressed in a fresh tunic that was free of blood, his face clean, the scent of herbs coming off him. Something was in his arms, a bundle.

"Is it you?" he countered softly.

Bread, she thought. She was smelling bread.

"You brought food?" she said in a voice that cracked.

"I didn't know . . . whether you made it. And I thought if you did . . ."

They stared at each other for a long moment, and she was aware of embracing him in her mind. She saw everything about the contact—from her jumping up and lunging forward, to his arms coming around her, to his chest, solid, strong and warm, up against her own.

But then she remembered what she had said to him.

It was clearly on his mind, too, as he stayed back.

Eventually, he cleared his throat and sat down on the sofa rock. Unfolding the fabric wrap, he took out a loaf of white bread, and as he bit into it, she thought his hand shook. Maybe it did. Maybe it didn't.

Leaning forward, he offered her the thing. "You better eat. You're going to need to be strong for what's coming."

In contrast, as she reached out, her hand trembled visibly, and when she took a bite of what he had brought for her, her mouth was so dry, she didn't think she could chew. She did, though. And she was hungry again—

"Your shoulder is bothering you?" he asked as he tried the cheese.

"What—oh, I don't know." She looked down at her arm. "It's fine."

"You need to feed." He held out some cheese. "Soon."

"I am eating—" Nyx stopped as she realized he was talking about her taking a vein. "Oh. Ah . . . I think I'm fine."

"We can talk about that later." He opened a container of Kool-Aid, or whatever that red-colored drink was. After he took a sip, he put the bottle forward. "Here."

Nyx set the bread in her lap, placed the cheese on the ground in its wrapper, and took the liquid. As she swallowed deeply from the bottle, she realized she was parched.

Lowering the container from her mouth, she stared across at Jack. His brilliant blue eyes were locked on the waterfall, but she had a feeling he wasn't seeing anything. The far-off look on his face suggested he was thinking of options for her.

For her safety and her escape.

Even after everything she'd said to him, he was still taking care of her.

"I'm sorry," she blurted. "You know, that I jumped down your throat earlier. "

"There's no reason to discuss any of that." He shook his head and seemed to refocus. "But how did you get away from the guards?"

To hide her emotions, Nyx took a bite of the cheese. Drank some more. Ate more bread.

Then she frowned. "How did you know about the guards?"

CHAPTER TWENTY-EIGHT

The Jackal still couldn't believe he was sitting across from his female—and thank God he had snagged those meal provisions. As he had rushed here from his cell, heart in throat, terror ripping through his body, he had passed an abandoned food-delivery cart and taken a serving on a lark.

The fuck it was on a lark. He had grabbed the bundle as a talisman, as if maybe the food he had for her would ensure her presence, her survival. Such bullshit.

The only thing he'd known for sure was that if she was alive, she would come here.

When he had seen the single lit candle, off in the distance, at the terminus of the passageway he had ducked into, he had felt a glimmer of hope. And then, as he had willed the candles on and she had been there . . . he had wanted to throw himself at her. Embrace her. Feel the warmth of her body.

Mindful of her low opinion of him, he had stayed back.

And he had taken her current apology for what it was: gratitude for the food.

What had she asked of him? Oh . . . right.

"The guards went through all the cells and

performed a bed check. During the process, one of them rushed up to the others and reported the disturbance." He was not going to speak about the Command around her. "But they said they had you at gunpoint. I don't understand how you made it back here."

"I dematerialized," she said in between bites of bread and cheese.

Fates, but the malest part of him—stupid as it was—was gratified to see her eat the sustenance he had brought to her, but he was worried about that shoulder. There was a fresh bloodstain on the tunic he'd forced her to put on—

"Wait, what?" Shaking his head to clear his thoughts, he leaned forward. "You *dematerialized?*"

Surely he had misheard that.

Nyx shrugged and took another drink from the glass bottle. There was a soft pop as she released the seal of her lips around the open neck. "The guards were in front of me and I was up against some kind of dropped-down steel wall. I couldn't retreat any farther, there was no going forward, and I wasn't going to win a shoot-out with them. So I did the only thing I could. I got the hell out of there."

The Jackal blinked. "I can't . . . how did you do that? How did you calm yourself?"

"I just made it happen. You do what you have to do in situations." She took another long drink, nearly finishing what was in the glass container. Then she tacked on dryly, "Which was how I ended up down here in the first place. Anyway, do you want any of this?"

"No, thank you. I brought everything for you." He found himself continuing to shake his head. "That is . . . remarkable. That you could have the presence of mind, the self-control, in that confrontation to save yourself."

"Like I said, it was just what I had to do." She picked at the bread, pulling free a soft wedge from the center. "And now I'm here."

"I have another way to get you out." When she looked up sharply, he told himself he felt nothing. At all. "The work shifts have been canceled, and as soon as they're reinstated, I'll take you out that way. They'll be behind in production, and there will be a scramble to catch up. I'll bet they double up on workers and the chaos will be in our favor."

There was a long silence, and he was confused. "What."

"You're helping me." She chewed slowly. "Again. Even though I owe you an apology."

The Jackal watched the candlelight play over her face. She had a scratch on her cheek. Dirt on her forehead. Hair that had frizzed up by her left ear.

She looked worn-out, and he preferred her full of piss and vinegar, even if she was yelling at him, even if her comments were unfair. It meant she could fight. And he knew, without asking or waiting to see if he was wrong, that the food was not going to revive her enough.

For what was ahead of her, she was going to need more physical strength and mental acuity than those prison rations could give her.

"You have to feed." As her brows rose, he put his palm out at her. "You're bleeding, again, and I bet you don't even know it."

The way she looked at her shoulder answered that one.

He cursed softly. "If we're going to get you through this, you need to be strong, and you've used up a lot of your energy. You know this, too."

She muttered something under her breath. "I don't want to . . ."

"You don't want it to be me? Fine. Use Kane. He's a gentlemale and will not take advantage of the . . . shall we say, situation—"

"I don't want to have anyone but you," she said sharply. And then the fight went out of her fast. "I just don't want to use you again."

"When have you used me up until now?"

"Really? You're asking that?"

"I volunteered." Besides, he had needed her for his own purposes—so they were even. "And I am volunteering my vein, if that's what you want."

"I can't believe you're still helping me." Her

eyes went back on the food, which she'd stopped eating. "You're a saint."

"Not even close," he said bitterly. "Remember how I ended up in this prison?"

"You said you didn't touch the female." Her eyes flashed up. "You said you were falsely accused."

"And you didn't believe me. So I'm merely dubbing in your thoughts."

"You don't know what's on my mind."

The Jackal stretched out, crossing his feet at the ankles. "Yes, I do. Now, finish the food and we can argue about you taking my vein—"

Nyx cut him off. "I was angry at you before because I don't understand why you wouldn't free yourself from this. Especially if you're here under false pretenses, because someone lied about you." She shook her head. "I was also pissed off because you know my reason for coming here, and I resent the fact that you didn't tell me yours for staying."

Before he could respond, she rubbed her eyes. "Look, I know that doesn't make any sense. And things don't need to be fair between us. But that's—well, that's why I said what I did, and I'm sorry. You're right. You've been nothing but good to me, and you owe me nothing. Not even explanations."

After a moment, the Jackal sat up. "It's safer for you not to know anything."

Nyx shook her head. "It's okay. You don't have to—"

"That's the truth, though. The less you know about me, the less danger you're in."

"Can you at least tell me why? Why you stay?"

As her eyes rose to his again, his heart skipped a beat in his chest. She was so beautiful to him, even in her disheveled state—or maybe especially because of it, given her unbelievable feat of self-preservation—and he entertained a brief, vivid fantasy of them on the outside, up above, back before Ellany had spread her lies and Jabon had done something about them and then so many other, more terrible things had happened.

"You're right," Nyx whispered in the candlelight. "There is a you and me. I didn't want to acknowledge it because I don't want to feel as crushed as I do—you know, when I think about me leaving . . . and you not. It kills me, even though it shouldn't. The reason I was so mad . . . is that I want you to come with me."

As Nyx spoke, she was aware of Jack's utter stillness. And going by his lack of movement, she guessed that she'd shocked him.

"I suppose I shouldn't really be saying any of this." She shrugged to downplay the very important things she'd given airtime to. "But something about almost getting shot full of holes—for the second time in twenty-four hours, or was

314

it the third or fourth?—makes me want to talk."

The joke fell flat, even to her own ears. "Sorry."

"Nyx . . ."

"I know. I'll stop." She forced herself to eat more even though she wasn't tasting anything. "So what's the new plan?"

Jack looked away to the wall. When he refocused on her, his expression was neutral. "I have to go find the others. We're going to need them again."

"Will Lucan and Mayhem get into another convenient 'fight'?" She put air quotes around the word. "Or is there another strategy this time. At this point, I'm open to anything."

As she waited for him to talk, she wanted to touch him. She wanted to hold him. But she stayed where she was and finished the food as he watched her eat.

"Let's check your shoulder," he said. "And then I'll go round them up."

"Okay."

As Nyx went to pull off the tunic, she winced. Her shoulder did hurt, as it turned out. Who knew?

She took off her windbreaker, too, and pulled the sleeve of her T-shirt up. "Oh . . . yeah, it is bleeding."

In spite of the fact that she had managed to save herself and had somehow gotten here, she felt like she was making a mess out of everything.

When there was a shifting sound, she glanced up. Jack had come over, and as he bent down to inspect the injury, a flush went through her body.

"It's reopened," he said grimly. "I wish I could stitch it up for you. And there's no way I can take you to the infirmary."

"It'll be fine."

"When you take my vein, yes, it will."

His stark statement made her recall another ubiquitous phrase, one that was used far and wide when not-so-hot ideas were brought up in whatever way they were: *Now is not the time, and here is not the place.*

It covered things nicely at this moment. The problem was not his vein. It was what was going to happen the instant she took it: Now was definitely not-time/not-place for her to get him good and naked. Not that she would take it for granted that he'd be down for that again.

Meanwhile, as he stared across at her, his astonishing blue eyes were level. Calm. Reasonable. "I promise it won't lead anywhere."

All she could do was shake her head at herself. "It's not you I'm worried about," she muttered.

"What?"

"Nothing." She rubbed her eyes. "No, actually, I don't want to lie to you. The truth is, I fear the taste of you."

"Why's that?"

One more thing to mourn, she thought.

"I'm going to want all of you," she replied roughly as she looked over at him.

His eyes flared, as if she'd surprised him. And then he lowered his lids to half-mast.

"I will never tell you no." His voice was a sexy rasp as he spoke. "Not ever."

Before she could respond, he pulled up the sleeve of his tunic and extended his arm. "Take my wrist."

Her eyes locked on the veins that ran from the base of his palm up the inside of his forearm. They were heavy compared to her own, and beneath the cover of his flesh, she could see the pulse.

Hunger surged and made her shake. From anticipation.

"Are you sure you want to do this?" she asked him, thinking of that cell he had stopped in front of. That female he was so tied to, regardless of what he'd said.

"You need me," he replied. As if that explained everything.

"When I came here in the dark," she said, "I had nothing to guide me, and that increased my fear until I was choking on my paranoia. As soon as I was sure that I had not been followed, I lit one single candle. It increased my risk, but it was a small thing, and it grounded me. It kept me from losing it. If I can understand just one piece of who you are, it'll be like that single candle. It will ground me."

317

Jack dropped his head. As the silence stretched out, she didn't try to persuade him. He had to make up his own mind—and still his vein lay exposed between them, the temptation so strong, she clenched her hands into fists. She knew, though, that these were going to be among her last moments with him.

"Or tell me why the female in that cell doesn't affect us," she prompted with a helpless shrug. "Just give me something to go on. Anything."

"There is no female for me." His voice was hoarse. "Nothing affects us . . . because you are the only one I have. The only one I want."

"Truly?" she whispered.

He took her clenched hand and put it to his heart. "On my honor, you are the only one who is held here. And I wish things were different for me, I truly do. They are not, however, and what I feel for you doesn't change my situation."

Closing her eyes briefly, she was aware of a crushing defeat. But she was glad for the honesty because it gave her even greater faith in what he had revealed.

She had her single, tiny flame. She had her orientating light. She had her grounding.

And it was the one that mattered the most.

"Take of me," Jack said roughly, as if he knew exactly what was going through her mind.

As he lifted his wrist to her mouth, his eyes were luminous, so bright and blue, that she felt as though she was falling into him. His big body was beautiful, and so was his face, but those eyes . . . it was the way they revealed his soul that called to her the most.

With a trembling hand, she reached up and drew his long braid over his shoulder. "May I see you with your hair down?"

There was a pause, and then Jack went to the leather tie that bound the thick end. He undid the strap, and then his fingers pierced through the bottom of the weave, starting to pull apart the lengths.

"Let me do that," she said.

When he dropped his hands, she took over—and she took her time. Piece by piece, she unwound the tight plaiting, the dark hair lengthening as it was released from its confinement, the waves shiny and lit with blue-black flashes. Long . . . thick . . . smelling of sandalwood, his hair was luxurious in the candlelight, the ends extending down past his chest, onto his heavy shoulders and thick arms.

Running her fingers through his hair, pulling it back from his face, her breath caught. He had been handsome before. Now . . . he was transformed into something otherworldly, some kind of fallen angel or tortured deity, expelled out of heaven to suffer here on earth.

"Yes," he whispered.

"What?"

By way of answer, he brought his fingertips to the high collar of his tunic. One by one, he freed the ties, revealing the strong column of his throat.

"You don't have to," she said softly.

"As I told you, I will never deny you."

"I didn't know I'd spoken out loud to ask."

And as for the never denying her, that was true . . . except for when it came to leaving with her. But enough thinking about that.

Jack pulled the tunic up and over his head, revealing himself to her naked from the waist up, his pectorals and ribbed stomach caressed by the firelight of the candles, his incredible hair spilling around everywhere, his stare alit with blue flame.

"You don't have to speak of it." He reached across the electrified air between them and brushed her cheek with the back of his knuckles. "What you want is in your eyes."

He moved his thumb to her lower lip, running it over her mouth before penetrating in and stroking first one, and then the other, of her fangs. With a moan, Nyx felt the contact down deep in her core, the licks of arousal tightening her nipples, making her pant.

Jack purred, as if he knew what he was doing to her. Or maybe he was looking forward to what her canines were going to do at his throat. Both were different sides of a very good coin.

"More," he said, as he repeated the ring around

her fang. "I want to hear more of that sound."

Giving in to the command, Nyx went limp, the blood hunger, the sexual starvation, overriding her senses. And as she lolled to the side, he gathered her to him, moving her into his lap, cradling her against his naked torso.

"Take from me," he said roughly.

"Jack, are you sure?"

"Never more so."

"I'll be careful."

"Don't be."

Nyx moaned again as her eyes closed, the sexual current shooting through her body like someone had poured honey mixed with accelerant into her—and then lit the cocktail on fire.

As he lifted her into position, holding her in his strong arms, she ran her hands under his hair, finding so much of his warm, smooth skin and very hard muscle. In the back of her mind, she heard him tell her she was his only female.

That whatever was in that cell had nothing to do with them.

And as she nuzzled into his neck, she thought to herself, *Not the place, not the time, was a meaningless expression.*

Especially when it came to a moment like this.

"Jack," she sighed as she bared her fangs with a hiss and ran one of the sharp tips up his jugular. "Oh, Jack . . ."

CHAPTER TWENTY-NINE

The Jackal palmed the back of Nyx's head and held her to the vein at his throat. Closing his eyes, he was aware of his body coming alive, a sense of curling, urgent anticipation thickening his blood . . . thickening another place on his body, too. As his cock hardened, it crammed itself into an awkward, uncomfortable angle, but he didn't care.

He was too busy wondering what it was going to feel like. Her bite. Her suck. Her taking him inside of herself—

Her strike was everything he had anticipated. Sharp. Decisive. Greedy.

Jack gasped and jerked. Then his head fell back and he groaned. "Fuck . . . yes, *fuck* . . ."

The cursing exploded out of him—and his erection kicked and bucked at his hips. But she had to get the nutrients she needed first. As much as he wanted her, this was about her survival.

This was his strength amplifying her own.

As she nursed against him, swallowing in a rhythmic fashion that made him think of his penetrations into her sex, he felt the urge to orgasm, to come inside of her, to fill her up as she drained him. There was also an overriding sense of very masculine satisfaction, that he was taking care of her.

What he did not feel? For even a moment? Even one single heartbeat?

Was any confusion about who he was with. There was no question that Nyx's lips were the ones at his throat, that her fangs were what had punctured his vein, that her mouth was drawing at his blood. He knew exactly who he was with, and even as he absorbed all of the sensations, his body taking in the pleasure and the purpose like dry earth under a warm spring rain, he thought about her single candle, her need for a grounding.

She was what shone through his darkness. She was the light that he had been drawn to, and now followed readily.

Sweeping his hand up Nyx's waist, he cupped her breast over her T-shirt and was rewarded with a moan from her that went straight into his arousal. As he caressed the rise, and focused his attention on the hard nipple, his hips began to roll, jerk, punch out.

His body was seeking hers.

And he worried he wasn't going to be able to deny the impulse even though he needed to focus on her feeding—

Nyx solved his internal debate by shifting herself about and straddling him. Then, without breaking the seal on his throat, she wriggled around, shucking her pants. How she managed to do it, he didn't know. He was not in a position to argue, though. He sprung his erection, and—

The sound that came out of his mouth as he slid into the hot, slick hold of her was like nothing he'd ever vocalized before. And as she continued to nurse at his vein, drinking deeply, he opened his mind and his soul to the feel of her as she rocked on top of his hips, his arousal penetrating and retreating, penetrating and retreating, all due to her movements. He wanted to help her somehow, but he couldn't risk getting in the way of her feeding. She was the one in control, her mouth and her sex milking him, taking from him, using him . . .

And he was consenting to all of it.

He was not trapped. He was not being forced. He was not tied down and taken against his will, used for the pleasure of another without regard to what he wanted.

This was his choice, and all the more sweeter, freer, better, for that. He was choosing her. He was choosing this.

Nyx was his beacon in the darkness and he would give her all he could.

No panic. No regrets. Nothing but . . . his female.

This was the unexpected blessing that he had unknowingly been waiting his whole life for. And even though he was going to give her up, he would at least know he'd had such a connection once.

He had known . . . love . . . once.

As the word came to his mind, as the definition of the warmth in the center of his chest was made manifest, it shocked him so much that his eyes flew open.

Love.

As he focused on the ceiling of the pool's cave, he was aware of his eyes getting watery, of his vision blurring. He was confused at first, and wondered whether water from up above had somehow dripped down onto his face.

But that was not it.

With his hands on her hips and Nyx riding him, with the pleasure overtaking him, so unexpected and so raw . . . what called the pain from him was not the now. It was the inevitable that he couldn't avoid:

When the Command came to take him once again.

The leverage they had over him, and the control it gave them, was such that he could not say no, and he would be called into service soon—and this beautiful moment, this cleansing, affirming passion, would be replaced by the very thing that was worse than the false accusation that had landed him in the prison, and the loss of ten decades of his life, and the darkness that he had lived in and would continue to do so.

The stain would return.

Closing his eyes, he could not bear it.

But Jack had no choice.

Nyx could have stayed at Jack's vein until he was dried out—and that was the problem. She had to force herself to stop drinking from him even though it was the very last thing she wanted to do. The taste of him, the dark wine down the back of her throat and in her body, the swell of power and strength from what he was providing her, were more intoxicating than any drug.

And that was before the sex, the incandescent sex, was added as a chaser.

She would gorge on him if she could.

She *was* gorging on him.

Then again, Jack was answering the call of her thirst unlike anything she could ever have dreamed of, and he was doing the same with her sex. He was filling her up, his massive erection kicking out releases in an unrelenting stream, and dimly, she wondered what it would be like to have him service her in her needing.

The thought should have shocked her. It didn't.

In a rush of hot, naked, wild images, she imagined him being the one to ease the pain of her fertile time, pleasuring her and keeping the burn at bay, their bodies melding together and staying there for hours and hours.

God, she wished they were both fully naked now.

And yes, she wanted to keep this going for six hours. Eight hours. Ten. She was pounding down hard on his hips, his sex going in and out of hers, tip to base, over and over again, and he was coming and she was coming and they were coming together while she was drinking from him. It was all too much and she only wanted more. She wanted to be covered in him, slick from him, loose and dizzy and on another planet from the exhaustion of making love all night and day long. She wanted him to take her in all positions, in all ways—

"Stop!"

As she cried out, she crashed back to reality. In spite of the fantasy and the sex and the rush, she ripped her fangs from his throat and focused on the cave wall, panting, blood-lusted, still hungry.

But she was terrified about taking too much from his vein.

"Jack—" she blurted in a panic.

"No, you haven't killed me." He smiled, even though there were puncture marks in his throat that were bleeding, twin trails tantalizing her, making her lick her lips. "Not even close."

As she stared down at him, she wanted to remember him like this forever: A slight smile on his beautiful lips, his hair flowing out all over his hard shoulders, a strange air of contentment surrounding him like a tangible aura in spite of how intense the sex was. He was beautiful as he penetrated her, as he so generously gave himself over to her.

"I need to seal you up," she said, mostly to herself—as a reminder that when she put her mouth back on him, it was *not* going to be to drink.

"I wish I could tell you not to worry about it," he whispered. "I wish we could just keep going."

And then he tilted his head to the side, baring the puncture marks to her. And yet she hesitated because she was that unsure of her self-control. He was so good, though. He was just so damned good.

When she went to lean down again, her hips moved against his—and she was reminded that even though they had to stop the feeding, the sex could, and would, continue on. And going by the way his hands bit into her upper thighs, he didn't want to end that part of things, either.

"I wish you didn't have to stop," he repeated with a groan as he arched under her.

Nyx licked the column of his throat, sealing him up, making sure he was safe. And as soon as she did the duty, as if he had been waiting for it, he rolled her over and settled in between her legs, his tremendous size forcing her knees wide, his heavy weight pinning her down.

Looking up into his face, she threaded her hands into his hair. Breathing in deep, she knew that what was happening was special. Life-defining special. This was no one-night stand.

It never had been.

As he dropped his mouth to hers, she kissed him with everything she had, trying to communicate without speech that which she would have struggled to put into words anyway. And as if he understood what she needed from him, the rhythm he set was intense. She took every bit of what he gave her, especially as he hitched a forearm behind one of her knees and wrenched her leg high. The shift in position let him go even deeper and she scored his back with her nails.

Jack pounded into her, her head jerking as her body absorbed the dominating force of him. She didn't care about the hard rock she was on, or even whether someone would come and catch them in the middle of it. She wasn't even thinking of the inevitable separation.

All she had was the now, and she intended to live it fully.

Memories of this were going to have to last a lifetime.

The orgasm that went through her was so strong, her eyes squeezed shut and her hands clawed into him again. And as her core gripped his erection, milking him, holding on to him, he followed after her so that they both soared.

It went on for so long, even though there were so many reasons to stop . . . but eventually, their bodies halted, and he rolled them to the side. As rough as he had been, his arms were gentle now, and she felt herself slipping into a post-feeding drift as she lay, hot and steaming from exertion, against his bare chest.

Just as she was falling asleep, something registered in the back of her mind, something that her consciousness refused to release.

"Why did you wish I didn't have to stop feeding?" she murmured just before she fell asleep. "Not safe."

"Hmm?" he said in a groggy way.

"Why didn't you want me to stop?"

For the life of her, she didn't know why she was pressing the issue. What a weird thing to say.

As if he agreed with that, it was a while before he answered, and when he did, she wasn't sure whether she was dreaming or not: "If I could, I would bleed out in your arms. I can't think of anywhere else I'd rather be when I die."

Nyx's eyes flared open.

"Shh," he soothed. "We have some time. Let's just enjoy this for a little longer. Before we have to leave this all behind."

CHAPTER THIRTY

"Come into the pool with me?"

Jack wasn't sure exactly how long he let his female rest. But when the same internal clock that had always helped him keep track of the guards' schedules started to ring, he felt compelled into action.

And he really needed her to take a bath before they left here.

She already had a target on her back. If the Command scented him on her? Fuck.

Nyx stirred against him, her dark lashes lifting, her eyes unfocused and contented. Smiling down at her, he brushed her lips with his own. Then he couldn't resist. He licked his way into her mouth. Their bodies had separated, but his was quick to want a return, and given the way her hand snuck onto the nape of his neck and pulled him on top of her, the feeling was mutual.

"Come," he repeated. "Into the bath with us."

He lifted her up and carried her over to the pool. As she rested in his arms, her weight was not a burden, it was a gift, and he was content to continue to hold her as she stripped her shirt and her bra—

The sight of her bare breasts shorted out his thinking, and he let her feet down so she could

reveal herself in all her naked glory to his captivated eyes. Then there was nothing but glorious
flesh, from the cleft of her sex to the flat plane of
her abdomen to her beautiful breasts.

She smiled in an ancient way as she stepped
into the pool. First one foot. Then the other.

And as she sank down into the burbling warm
water, she removed the banding on her hair.

Jack was not so graceful. He ditched his pants
like they had insulted his moral code, and as he
straightened, his arousal was so erect, it stuck out
from his hips at a right angle. Before he joined
her, he tucked his hand behind one of the stones
that rimmed the pool and took out the bar of
herbal soap he left here.

As he jumped in and ducked under the water,
he had to ignore a grim urgency. He didn't know
how much time they had left—no, he knew that
answer and he hated it. Therefore, when he came
up out of the pool with his hair smoothed to his
skull, he refused to allow himself to waste even
a moment on remembering how he'd used this
particular bar of soap before.

The memories came anyway. Here was where
he washed himself when the Command was done
with him. Here was where he cleaned himself of
the smells and residue after he was used.

He would have preferred to put something,
anything, else on Nyx's skin. But he had to clean
her of him.

"Let me wash you," he said as he palmed the bar and called up suds from the packed lye-and-herb combination.

He was gentle with her, worshipping her with his hands, cleaning her hair, her neck, her shoulders, the familiar tangy scent of the spices rising up between them. And then he continued below her waist, reaching between her thighs, his fingers through the waves within the water—

And that was when he got sidetracked.

As he caressed her sex, his fingers entered her, and the next thing he knew, he was lifting her out of the pool and propping her up on the smooth rocks of the rim. Spreading her thighs, he nestled himself in and brought his mouth to her collarbone, her sternum . . . the side of her breast. He sucked on her while he stroked her sex with both his thumbs, and as she ran wet at her core for a reason other than the water that dripped off of her, he licked at her nipple, nibbled at it.

He did the same to the other breast.

And then he kept going with his mouth. Lower . . . lower . . .

"Jack!" she cried out.

Her fingers speared into his hair, and she pulled him tight to where he wanted to go, his lips to her sex, his tongue replacing his fingers. Plying at her, sucking at her, putting one of her legs over his shoulder, he pleasured her with his mouth

335

until she orgasmed on his face—and then he kept right on going.

Jack had not intended to take things where they were, but he was glad—

For a moment, he paused.

He hadn't realized that he'd begun thinking of himself with the name she used for him. It was a shift, like so many, that she created within him.

Something else to keep after she was gone.

Well, that happened, Nyx thought some time later as she sat alone on the sofa rock and twiddled her thumbs.

On a reflex that served no purpose, she lifted her wrist and pulled back the sleeve of the fresh tunic she'd put on. But there was no watch there. In fact, she never wore watches.

It was just one more tic she'd picked up since Jack had left her by the pool: Likewise, her left eye was twitching as if someone was flashing a strobe in it, and her foot was a metronome keeping a beat only her ankle could hear.

She wasn't sure how long Jack had been gone. It felt like ten years, but it was probably only about twenty, twenty-five minutes. In the candlelight, by herself, she was jumping at shadows, a gun in her palm and her backpack strapped on under the full set of prison clothes Jack had insisted she wear—

With a gasp, she wrenched around, heart pounding in her ears.

Except it was nothing.

Every sound was a cause for alarm. Each subtle drip of wax or groundwater, all the variations of the rushing of the waterfall, even her own breath whistling in and out of her nose, was a call to attention. And in between those spikes of high alert, she retreated into her memories of the feeding and then what happened later, in the pool.

When all of that just made her chest hurt until she could barely stand it, she switched places in her head.

To imagining Janelle dying down here, under the earth, alone.

Yeah, because that was such an improvement.

Rubbing her eyes, she recalled the last clear memory of her sister. It had been two nights before the Council had met concerning the death of that older male, but after the accusation had been formally served on Janelle by a representative of the ruling body.

Last Meal. In their little farmhouse kitchen, at the four-top where they had eaten together all their lives. Janelle had been across from her, that red hair loose and drying in curls from the shower she'd just taken. Cornflakes . . . yes, they were having cornflakes, a bowl full in front of each of them. The only sound in the room, in the house . . . in the whole world, had been spoons knocking against the cheap china.

Janelle had been very calm. Which was what you were when you were innocent of the charges against you, and had faith that justice would prevail and the truth would come out in the end. You were at ease because you believed everything would be okay—because it was crazy for anyone to think you would ever kill anybody, much less an old male you worked for and had been fond of.

Nyx could remember drawing strength from that calm.

Everything was going to be all right. No matter how scary the formal accusation was, it was all going to be okay.

That was what she'd thought at the time.

From that memory, she went further back in time, recalling Janelle laughing out by the barn, and running wild in the rain as thunder had clapped and lightning sparked the night sky.

All of that was gone now, never to happen again, even though it hadn't been happening since Janelle had been taken away, anyway. But the reality of that name listed on the Wall here in the prison was a hard stop, and as the loss truly sank in for the first time, Nyx realized that even though Janelle had been gone from the family, the fact that she had been alive somewhere had meant that there was a future. Somehow, somewhere . . . there had been a future, no matter how impossible it seemed.

Nyx's baseless hope and characteristic determination had made tangible that which she could not touch, had brought home, at least in her mind, the one who had been lost. The number of days she had lain in her bed believing she would find Janelle, *knowing* she would, had been legion. Ultimately, however, the prophecy she had spun had not been self-fulfilling. And she had the picture of Janelle's name from the Wall to prove it.

A shroud of mourning settled on Nyx's shoulders, heavy and dark, and tied up in its choking weave was the fact that she would be leaving the prison with two losses.

It was that reality that rode her hard as the males finally arrived. Jack was leading the way, with Kane behind him in a set of black robes, and Lucan, Mayhem, and Apex bringing up the rear. Getting to her feet, she did what she could to throw off her mood—and as she faced off at the group, she had a thought she was glad she wasn't meeting them in a dark alley.

Especially Apex with those obsidian eyes.

"Fancy meeting you all here," she said hoarsely.

Fancy getting my heart broken while I endangered my life to find out my sister was dead. What a BOGO, she thought.

Kane spoke up. "The Jackal told us of your bravery in evading the guards." The gentlemale bowed. "You are a female of worth."

"She's a fighter, all right," Lucan agreed. "That's for sure."

Cue a round of blushing, which in Nyx's opinion was a total waste of her time. Come on, like she was the little sister asked to play ball with the big team?

"So what's our plan?" She looked at them, and then focused on Jack. "Where are we going?"

"Kane did some investigation." Jack came over and stood by her. "The prison is still locked down, but they're calling a double shift to catch up, just like I thought, and the workers are eating. Mess should be finishing up shortly. We'll fall in line with them as they report for duty, and go into the production area."

Kane inclined his head. "From there, our best chance is to get you on a transport truck."

"Truck?"

Jack nodded. "We need to time it correctly. After the product is loaded and checked, it should be safe for you to dematerialize onto the roof of one of the cargo bays. All you need to do is keep quiet and keep down. Then as soon as they drive out from under, dematerialize free."

"It's really our only option at this point," Kane said.

Abruptly, she remembered seeing a large truck

coast over the highway as she'd gone in search of the church. Come to think of it . . . she had seen a lot of them over the last ten or fifteen years, coming and going. She'd always assumed they were passing through the valley, but maybe some of them had originated from the prison.

"Okay." Nyx took a deep breath. "I can't thank you all enough for helping me."

"Don't take it too personally," Lucan said. "Anything we can do to fuck the Command, we will run with it."

"Well, I still appreciate it. Do we wait here?"

"Yes," Jack said. "But it won't be long."

Annnnnnnd then there was nothing but awkward silence, the bunch of them standing around like they were about to be called to the counter for their order at Starbucks. Apex took out a knife—but just to whittle a piece of wood. Lucan paced around like a caged animal. Kane murmured something to Jack that was answered in a similar low tone.

"Exactly how long are we stuck here?" Nyx asked.

Kane answered. "No more than half an hour. You'll be able to tell because you'll hear the march of the guards on the other side of the wall. They need to escort the workers into the product area and will leave the Command's quarters in a group to do so."

"I'm taking a load off, then." Nyx sat down and

shucked her backpack. "Might as well conserve some energy."

In reality, her legs were sore in places that made her blush again, and her body was still logy from the feeding. She wasn't going to admit any of that to the peanut gallery, however.

Jack sat down next to her, which she appreciated. Then Kane sat across the pool from them. Eventually, Lucan and Mayhem followed the example. That Apex stayed standing was not a surprise, and out of instinct, Nyx angled her head so she could keep an eye on his position in her peripheral vision.

When she realized they'd all camped out around the pool, in a circle, she had to laugh. "This is like a group meeting."

"I'm sorry?" Jack said.

"Like for therapy. You know, a bunch of people meeting to discuss common problems or ailments." Except he didn't know, did he. "Anyway. Yeah. So . . ."

Cue the *Jeopardy!* theme.

"So how did you guys end up here?" she blurted.

On a oner, all of the males jerked to face her. Kane's aristocratic features registered shock, like she had just insulted someone at a dinner party. Lucan's yellow eyes narrowed. Even Mayhem seemed surprised.

Jack cleared his throat. "Nyx, I know that you didn't mean any offense by that because you don't know any better. But we really don't make those kinds of inquiries around here—"

"I slaughtered an entire bloodline."

As Apex spoke up from his lean against the wall, all stares went to him, and he didn't miss a beat with his sharp blade against the pale flesh of the piece of wood he was working.

"I murdered them in their sleep." He regarded the blade, turning it back and forth in the candlelight as if he were conjuring fond memories of its use. "Even the females. That's why I'm in here."

Those black eyes of his flashed to Nyx. "Any other questions? Do you want to know what I did with the bodies?"

"No," Jack bit out. "She does not."

Kane cleared his throat. "Well, if we're telling our stories, I shall share mine own. I broke an arranged mating with a female I did not love. Her sire took offense." The male's eyes went to the pool's churning water. "He arranged for the murder of the female I did love, and he blamed it upon me. I am here for life as a result of his retaliation."

"I am so sorry," Nyx whispered as unspeakable pain flared in his face.

"It matters not." Kane seemed exhausted, and not because he required sleep. "Whether I am housed here or up above, I would be suffering. I will e'er mourn my *leelan*."

343

There was another period of silence, and she glanced at Jack. He had a remote expression on his face as he studied Kane, and it seemed as though it was the first time he had heard the story—

"What of your sister?" Lucan demanded. "Why was she here?"

Nyx cleared her throat as she was addressed. "She was falsely accused of murder. She didn't kill the male. My grandfather, for reasons I don't understand, turned her in to the Council. I don't know why he did it, and I will never forgive him."

"Ne'er has more a corrupt body existed," Kane muttered. "Did they even bother with a farce of a trial?"

"Was the victim one of them?" Lucan asked. "An aristocrat, I mean. No offense, Kane."

"None taken, friend."

Nyx nodded. "He was. We're just civilians, obviously. He lived not far from our farmhouse, on a lot of property, in a big fancy house. Janelle—my sister—she would go over there and work, you know, just trying to make some money. For about a year, she mowed the meadows and tended the fences. She painted barns and the house. She took care of the gardens, too. . . . Anyway, one night, she came back to our house early and told us that the male had died of old age. Given that he had no heirs, he'd provided a little something for her as well as some of the other folks who worked there. She had some cash and a ring. It wasn't a lot of money or a piece of jewelry of much value, and I thought it was a nice gesture by an employer. And that was that, or so I thought. Except then the next night . . . we got this formal notice of accusation from the Council." She shrugged helplessly. "Why my grandfather did what he did, I'll never know, and how the Council found her guilty, I'll also never understand. She was totally innocent."

"I know why the Council blamed her." Kane shook his head. "In the Old Laws, if someone dies without issue, the estate goes to the next of kin, no matter how distant the relation. If the person is murdered under those circumstances, however, their property, real or otherwise, goes unto the Council. The intent of the law was to discourage heirs who were not first-degree offspring like sons or daughters from killing their benefactors, on the theory that direct issue have enough of an emotional connection to their blooded parents to avoid matricide or patricide no matter how large the inheritance. In fact, however, the law served as a fundraiser for the Council. If everything you say is true, they needed to find someone guilty of murder so they could split the estate."

"Those bastards."

And she included her grandfather in that. Had he been paid somehow?

"For all their dainty airs and social propriety, the *glymera* can be very cutthroat." Kane exhaled in a defeat. "Regardless of who they hurt. Or who they ruin."

"So my grandfather sacrificed her to them. Why the hell . . ."

Nyx stopped and rubbed her aching head. There were going to be no answers to all that now, but as soon as she was home, she was going to make him tell the truth.

Assuming she made it out alive.

"Was your sister dead, then?" Lucan asked. "Did you find her name on the Wall?"

"Yes." Nyx met the male in the eye. "Her name was inscribed in that lineup. She died here."

After a moment, the male nodded once in respect. "I am sorry for your loss."

"Thank you." To change the subject, she said, "What about you? What's your story?"

Lucan leaned back on his palms and crossed his legs. "I am wolven. I was put here because others of your species do not like us."

"But that's discrimination." And it explained why she had always sensed something was different about him. "They can't just throw you in here for being—"

"Can't they?" Lucan touched his collar. "And I would be out of here except for this. I can't change with this goddamn thing on my throat, though."

"I would take it off you if I could," Nyx said.

There was a moment of silence. Then he smiled a little. "In spite of the way we met, I actually believe that."

Nyx returned his smile, and then glanced over at Mayhem—who, as it turned out, was sitting forward on his butt like he was holding his hand up and waiting to get called on in school.

"And you?" she asked.

"I was bored," he announced with a kind of pride.

There was another pause. And then the whole group leaned in toward the male—like everyone was wondering if they'd heard right.

"I don't understand," Jack said.

Mayhem shrugged. "I didn't have anything I particularly wanted to do, and nowhere in particular I wanted to go, so I figured, what the hell, I'll hang in prison."

There was another pause. Just in case there was a punch line.

When Mayhem merely smiled pleasantly, there was a lot of blinking around the pool. Even from Apex the Whittler.

"Are you fucking insane?" Lucan said.

Kane shook his head. "I'm afraid that's a bit inexplicable, my friend—"

"You are *such* a twat-waffle," Jack blurted. "And no, I don't know what that means, but it is *not* good."

CHAPTER THIRTY-ONE

"It's time."

As Jack spoke, Nyx was already getting to her feet, the muffled marching reaching her keen vampire ears. Strapping her pack back on under the loose tunic and resettling her outer layer, she felt like she was moving out of a place. Which was nuts. Still, this experience had been so vivid, it was like she had been down under ground for a decade.

She took a last look around as the other males went off to make sure things were safe to step out into the prison proper. The pool was as she had first seen it, gently frothing, lightly steaming, the candles all around, offering a golden haven in the midst of hard rock and hopelessness and strife.

Then she focused on Jack. He was dressed in fresh prison togs, his hair rebraided, his face drawn, likely because of the feeding and what it had cost him to be so generous with his vein. As she worried about him, she wished she could reciprocate. She wished they had more time. She wished . . .

"I know," he murmured.

Nyx smiled even though her eyes were filling with tears. "How are you so sure what I'm thinking about?"

"I can guess." He took her hand and put her palm on the center of his chest. "Because I feel the same."

She reached up and stroked his face. "I wish . . . well, a lot of things. But I want you to know, no matter how much it hurts, that I'm not sorry I met you. I'll never be sorry."

"I will get you out of here. I promise. So you can go back to your true home."

It was a nice thing for him to say, except he really couldn't guarantee the outcome, could he. Yet she let his vow stand because she could feel the resolve he was forcing into the words: He was willing, with all the strength in his body and all the power of his intentions, for her to find freedom safely.

In a strange way, it was a declaration of love, wasn't it.

"Listen," he said urgently, "if anything happens to me, I want you to keep going. You need to save yourself. No matter how much you may want to stop and help, you must keep going. Promise me?"

"I can't do that—"

"No," he cut her off, and squeezed her hand. "You have to swear this to me, or I'll be distracted, and neither of us can afford that. You *have* to keep going. No matter what, you don't stop. Swear to it here and now, on your honor."

Nyx closed her eyes. "Okay."

"On your honor."

"Fine. I promise. Can we be done with this?"

As she stared at her hand on his sternum, the relief that rolled out of him was palpable, and that meant the lie she'd spoken was worth it.

"You know what to do, right?" he asked as he brushed the wisps around her face back.

"I know the plan." They'd run it through a couple of times after everyone had campfire'd their stories. "I'm ready."

"And you know you can trust the others."

"I do."

"Okay, let's go."

When he took her hand from his chest, she lifted her mouth for his kiss at the same moment he bent down to give her one. It was but a second of contact, however, because that was all they had, and as they parted, the candles around the pool went out one by one, willed by him.

The gathering darkness seemed a bad portent.

As they headed off together, she glanced over her shoulder at the single candle that remained alit—and felt cheated by fate. Jack was the kind of male she would have liked to go through an entire life with. Instead, all she'd had him for was this life-defining event of finding out Janelle's fate.

No offense to destiny, she'd have taken quantity over quality when it came to him. But when had providence ever cared about the opinions of the lives it ruined?

Getting out of the hidden passageway was a total blur. The next thing she knew, she was in the main tunnel and falling in with a stream of prisoners funneling toward the Hive. Mayhem was in front of her and Lucan was behind. Their cell blocks had been called in for the double shift, so the plan was for her to enter the work area with them—and they were banking on there being overruns at check-in. She was going to have to take advantage of one to slip through without being noticed.

Jack walked side by side with her for about two hundred yards, and then she felt his hand on her own. When he squeezed, she wanted to turn to him. She wanted to throw her arms around him. She wanted to . . . not lose him.

All she could do was nod subtly.

And then he was gone, paring off and disappearing down an offshoot.

Nyx's body started to shake and her feet faltered, but she kept going. Jack was never on work rotation, so he couldn't proceed into the restricted area with the others and not attract attention. So he was going to have to go through the Command's compound and meet everyone on the far side where the transport trucks were.

Wherever the hell that was.

Just keep going, she told herself. *Keep going and you'll see him one last time.*

To stay focused, she mentally ran through the plan, and realized she'd forgotten a part of it. She had to make sure she fell in with the prisoners who were assigned to transportation. That was her one job. If she fucked that up, and ended up in the production line, she was going to go to the wrong place—

When Kane appeared from out of nowhere, and fell in step beside her, she calmed a little. It didn't last.

"Change in plan," he whispered. "Follow me on my cue."

"What?" she hissed. "What are you talking about?"

"Shh. Follow me."

Glancing over her shoulder, she frowned. Lucan was gone. And when she looked ahead again, Mayhem had likewise disappeared. Warning bells started to ring.

"What about Jack?"

"Follow me."

His eyes were straight ahead, so she couldn't read them. And that face that she'd thought radiated trust? Now, she wasn't so sure.

"Where's Jack?" she whispered as she glanced around at the other prisoners. None of them were paying any attention to anyone else.

"This is the way we have to go to get to him."

Under the tunic, Nyx put her hand on her gun. "Okay."

Shit. Shit, shit . . .

They continued on another fifty yards, her nose picking up on the pungent scent of the Hive. Just before they came to its entrance, Kane tugged on the sleeve of her tunic.

As she broke off from the shuffling flow of gray figures to follow the male, all she could think was . . . this was *not* part of the plan.

As Jack entered the side corridor that would take him to the Command's restricted area, he downshifted from a walk to a wander. With the entire facility on lockdown, certain routes would be cut off, so he was having to take a round-about way to get to where he would rejoin Nyx and the others. As long as he entered the work area from the Command's entrance, no one would stop him.

He just couldn't afford to cross paths with the Command.

It was absolutely vital that he made sure Nyx got out free and clear before he was called into service again. If the Command got a hold on him? He would lose hours.

As well as his final goodbye with his female.

Disturbed by what was ahead, he took two more lefts, and as he rounded the last of the turns, he thought of Nyx entering the prison on her own and being smart enough to track her route inside by going in one direction only.

This was what was on his mind as he came up to an archway marked with white slashes.

As he stepped under the curve in the rock, he took another left and penetrated the Command's area through a steel door. On the far side, he shoved his hands into the pockets of his prison pants, as was his usual stance—but mimicking what was normal for him, playing casual, was not the purpose. He wanted his palm on the butt of the gun he'd taken from Kane. It was one of the guards', which the aristocrat had lifted when he'd bound them and stripped the males of their weapons. Jack was glad his friend was so damned thorough.

Making another corner, he slowed as he came up to the furnished cell. His heart began to pound as he stopped and looked through the steel mesh.

Empty. But it made sense given the lockdown. In fact, he was willing to bet that when he and Nyx had first come by here, the Command had already known about the infiltration, about the dead guard, about the problem, and had taken steps to control the risk—which was why the cell had been empty before.

The Command did not take chances with certain things.

And on that note, he started walking again,

but he didn't get far before his instincts prickled and he caught a pair of scents coming toward him. Moments later, two guards marched into his path. On their approach, he made like he was ignoring them, keeping his eyes softly focused on the air that was immediately before him, relying on his peripheral vision to inform him about their affect, their weaponry, their gaits.

They were hurrying, but their weapons were holstered. And though their heads turned to him, they promptly looked away.

"Evening, gentlemales," he drawled as he passed them.

Which was exactly what he would have done and said had he not been in the process of smuggling out the very female that they, and everyone else on their shift, were looking for.

Their lack of response was reassuring. He wanted everything to be uneventful.

As he came up to the bifurcation in the corridor, the one where if you took a right, you went to the Wall, he remembered Nyx putting her fingertips on her sister's name—and thought that he would have saved her female if he could have. Turning away from where they had gone, he stuck with the finished part of the tunnel, with the flooring and the sealed walls and the air that was artificially heated. The entry to the guards' bunk was closed, and the lack of chatter on the far side of the double steel doors suggested that all, or almost all, of those males had been called into service.

Continuing on, he ran through the plan again, rehearsing the stages, and by the time he approached the entry to the work area, he was ready to—

"Looking for me?"

At the sound of the low, menacing voice, Jack stopped—and hoped that his mind had played a trick on him. The scent of sandalwood denied this possibility, however.

"You missed the turn to my quarters." Footfalls approached, and when he did not look over his shoulder at them, the tone got sharper. "Aren't you going to turn around?"

The back of his neck tightened, and his upper lip twitched as his fangs descended. In his pocket, his hand tightened on the butt of the gun as he ran through calculations of distance, sound, and response. If he shot the Command here in the hall, if he killed the sadistic fucker right outside the guard bunks? The noise was going to attract too much attention, and he was just guessing there were none in there—

As if on cue, a pair of guards came in from the work area. The instant they saw him and the Command, they stopped short.

When the one on the right nodded and resumed walking, it was clear that the Command had excused them both, and they passed without looking at him.

It wasn't until their footfalls faded that he faced off at the black-draped figure—and as he did, he cleared his mind of all thoughts except for how much he detested what was before him.

The chuckle that came out from under the hood was like the hiss of a snake. "I love how you hate me." The draped arm rose and pointed to a locked steel door. "My quarters are here, as you very well know. We're going there now. I want what only you can provide me."

Jack glanced over his shoulder, in the direction he needed to go.

One minute earlier and he would have avoided this intersection. Thirty seconds might also have done it.

"Do I need to call for help," came a low snarl.

Tightening his hold on the gun, he prayed that Nyx did what she had promised to do. He prayed that she would save herself.

Because it was quite possible he'd arrived at the end of his own road.

CHAPTER THIRTY-TWO

"This way," Kane said under his breath.

Nyx gritted her teeth and tried to orientate herself. They were hurrying now, moving fast side by side, as he took her deeper into a section of the prison that she didn't recognize. The fact that the tunnel was getting smaller and smaller, and the scents of anyone else, prisoner or guard, were getting dimmer and dimmer, made her realize how far off track they were.

How far she was from Jack—

Kane stopped without warning. And as she shot by him, underneath the loose tunic, she brought up the muzzle of her gun.

Wheeling around, she pointed the weapon at him. "Where are you taking me."

One of the bald light bulbs happened to be directly over him, so it was difficult to read his face. Shadows were created beneath his brows so that his eyes were hidden, and those black robes did not help him look less menacing.

"Now, now. There's no need for that."

"I will shoot you in the face. I don't give a fuck. And you've taken us so far away from the Hive and everywhere else, no one will hear the gun go off."

Kane regarded the muzzle of the nine

millimeter calmly. "My dear female, I am trying to save you."

"I'm well aware of how the *glymera* lies. And you've taken me way off course, away from Jack. This was not the plan."

A strange rumbling vibrated up from the floor, the soles of her boots transmitting it through to her feet and into her lower legs. But she didn't look down. She kept her stare on the aristocrat's hooded eyes.

"Take me back to Jack," she demanded.

"I can't," Kane said in a low voice. "It's too late."

More rumbling, and then dust and small stones started to fall from the ceiling of the tunnel.

"Take me back to him right fucking now—"

Without warning, she was thrown against the wall by an earthquake's explosive force. As the gun her grandfather had given her swung up and over, Kane ducked and shot forward, catching her around the waist. They struggled over the weapon while the ground kept shifting underfoot, the male's superior strength winning when she couldn't get any leverage.

Just as rocks started to tumble, he wrenched her arm over her head and pinned her.

Nyx looked up at exactly the wrong moment, and caught a fragment of the cave's stone wall the size of a football helmet right on the temple. Pain exploded in her skull and the fight went out of her. As her body went loose, Kane got the gun and started dragging her back by the torso. With her vision on the fritz, the tips of her boots went in and out of focus, and she told herself to pull it together and get herself free—

The brightest light she had ever seen pegged her in the face.

It was the Fade.

It had to be the Fade.

In the midst of the pounding in her head, her thoughts were jumbled, but she knew enough that the brilliant illumination meant she was dying and the Scribe Virgin's mystical eternity was coming to get her.

Next would be a door.

There would be fog and a door. Her uncle, on her father's side, had had a near-death experience twenty-four hours before he'd actually passed. And he'd come back to consciousness enough to describe what had happened.

Bright light. Fog. A door.

Her uncle had hesitated at the door that first time—and had come back as a *wahlker*. But clearly, when the Fade had returned for him, he'd decided to open it. If you did that and stepped through? You were gone forever to the Other Side . . . where you were supposed to find your loved ones who had passed, waiting for you. Her father would be there, her *mahmen* and *granmahmen*, too. And Janelle.

God, it would be good to see her sister and her parents again, even as she worried about Posie being left behind with their liar of a grandfather . . . shit, Jack. Even though they had no future, she didn't want to die on him. That seemed like an added burden to their already packed sack of crap when it came to the future—

More rumbling now, louder, closer.

And then . . . the smell of gas? Like the earthquake had ruptured a tank of fuel used to fill up those trucks they'd been talking about?

Maybe the joke was on Kane.

Maybe they were both going to die tonight, even if he had her loaded gun.

As Jack stepped into the Command's private chamber, his eyes went to the bedding platform. Within the unadorned four walls, it dominated the barren expanse.

The steel chains that coiled on the floor at each of the four corners sparked a fury in him.

"Take your hands out of your pockets," the Command ordered.

He went over to the mattress. There was a single sheet that covered the padded plane, and as he stood over where he had been spread-eagled so many times, he thought of Nyx—and had to clear that from his consciousness quickly. Some vampires could read minds. Even if the

Command couldn't, they could certainly read his face, his affect.

There was a click. "I want to see your hands *now*."

When he looked over his shoulder, two guards were standing by the Command.

"So early with reinforcements?" Jack laughed in a low growl. "Are you sure you can spare them elsewhere."

"I'm in a rush. They'll help get you in position—after you take your hands out of those pockets."

Jack had known anger before. He had known hatred. He had been in situations with the Command where he had been degraded to levels of shame and self-loathing that he couldn't have anticipated. But never once had he felt such a roar of fury—

The dart gun went off with its characteristic *pfffht,* and as soon as he heard the sound, he wanted to curse the distraction of his emotions. There was no time to think or feel much more. The pinprick of pain in the pad of his pectoral was the calling card of the trance, and almost immediately, his body went limp and he fell to the floor.

The worst part of it was that as unresisting as his arms and legs were, his mind remained clear. And thus he was fully aware as the Command came to stand over him.

The hood turned to the guards. "Leave me. Stay by the door."

There was a click as he was shut in alone with the Command, and then he was straddled, the black draping swinging as one black boot landed on the far side of him. The hood went back and forth as they shook their head.

"You bring a gun in here. I am so disappointed in you."

As the Command leaned down, he felt his hand get lifted and tossed aside, his palm slapping into the floor as it landed as dead weight. And then the weapon was in front of his face, so close that if he were to focus on it properly, his eyes would cross.

"This. You bring *this* here to me." Another hand appeared from out of the other sleeve, and the weapon was checked. "And it's loaded—and it's one of *mine*. You brought a fucking loaded gun from one of *my* guards to *my* house?"

The nine millimeter was drawn back across the Command's shoulder, and Jack braced himself to be pistol-whipped—

Before he was struck, the Command spun off of him and stalked around, the black robes streaming out in the wake of the furious pacing. In his paralysis, Jack took satisfaction at the anger—

The Command stopped abruptly. "Did you think you were going to kill me? Did you think you were going to come here and kill me? You mother*fucker*."

The gun rose toward him, the muzzle shaking ever so slightly.

Jack stared into the black hole where the bullet was going to come out. Over the course of his life, there had been a few incidents—not many, but a few—when he had entertained briefly the idea that he was going to die: An illness when he was young. His transition. And then twice since he had come to prison.

Nothing had been like this.

The sound that came out of the Command's hood was guttural as the gun went off, not once, but many times—and Jack was utterly exposed in his paralysis. Not that anything short of a stone wall could have helped him. *Pop! Pop! Pop! Pop—*

Abruptly, the gun swung toward the door and the Command yelled, "Get the fuck out! You get the fuck out of here until I call you!"

The door was slammed, likely because those guards were afraid of being served lead as their last meal.

The Command stomped back over to Jack, double-palmed the gun, and trained it in his face. From this close, his head was going to blow up like a melon when they pulled that trigger.

And as he contemplated his death, his biggest regret was that he could not be sure whether Nyx

365

had made it out safely. That he could not save her. That—

"Open your eyes!" the Command yelled. "You will open your eyes and look at me when I kill you—"

He hadn't been aware of shutting his lids, but he reopened them because he would not be a coward. He would look his death in the face. All along, he'd know this was how it would end, and there was so much on his conscience, on his heart. Except it was too late.

The Command leaned down even farther. "You did this to yourself. You chose this—"

Jack moaned a denial.

"You bastard. You fucking bastard!" they barked.

More gunshots rang out and he didn't flinch—and not just because he'd been drugged. He stared right at the hood, at the mesh that covered the face. The irony in all this was that the Command would suffer more than he did. This flight of their anger and retaliation was temporary; his death was permanent. There would be epic regrets, and if there was indeed a Fade? For all the Command had done, they were going to *Dhunhd*. No Fade for them. Meanwhile, he would wait for Nyx. For an eternity, he would wait for his female, his fighting angel who had showed him that however trapped he was, his soul remained free.

To love who he did.

Nyx.

—*Pop!Pop!Pop!*—

The ricocheting bullets stopped, the sharp ringing ended, the echoing explosions drifted into silence.

Click, click, click—

The Command was pulling the trigger over and over again, the loose folds and sleeves of the robe swinging out as from under the hood, rasping breath beat like a drum.

Jack just stared upward, unblinking, unflinching . . . unbowed, though he was flat on his back and incapable of moving. Surely he was bleeding out and that explained why his immobile body felt nothing of all his wounds and he was unaware of his suffocation.

"I hate you," the Command growled. "I fucking *hate* you."

The Command reached up and ripped the hood off.

Red hair tumbled loose, hanging into his face, into his eyes, the female's calculating features and flashing, aggressive stare the source of his suffering these many years.

He hated when she took the hood off. It was easier for him to think of her as sexless as long as it stayed on. But now, seeing that hair, seeing that face, he was reminded that she was the opposite sex, and that she demanded to mate with him whenever she fucking wanted.

He hated that she would be the last thing he saw. But reveled in what would happen as soon as she realized that she had broken her toy, and it was never to be functional again.

"I want to kill you," the Command bit out, long fangs flashing.

And that was when Jack realized . . . for all the bullets that had been discharged, she had not hit him. She'd shot around him, into the floor.

There was no scent of his blood in the air.

Meanwhile, the Command continued to breathe heavily—until she seemed to calm herself. Straightening, she looked at the gun in her hands, and then those eyes returned to his own, suspicion narrowing them.

"Where did you get this?" The Command put the weapon in his face, so close that every breath he took was full of gunpowder residue. "Where did you fucking get this?"

He couldn't have answered even if he'd wanted to. Which he did not. He enjoyed her loss of control and what it did to her. He wanted her to suffer. After all these years, he wanted her to have a taste of what he had endured.

No control. At another's mercy.

"You're going to answer me," she spat.

Then she put her hood back into place and whistled through the mesh. When the guards opened the door, she pointed to the bed.

"Chain him up."

CHAPTER THIRTY-THREE

Nyx closed her eyes against the Fade's blinding light, and prepared herself for some kind of physical reaction to being on the Other Side. She also got ready for the appearance of the door, for the decision to open it or not—

What the hell was that rumbling? That vibration?

There was a grunt, and she felt her body get yanked to the side—just as the harsh glare of the Fade's painful illumination flared and was abruptly extinguished, a tremendous wind blowing across her face and irritating the raw wound on her head. Confused and in pain, she forced her eyes open—which was weird because she'd thought they were already open.

And then things got even more confusing.

Because she was kind of thinking . . . that she was suddenly in a tunnel. As in a road tunnel, one where vehicles came and went. And there was a truck going by her. A semitrailer truck that was the color of the gray and black walls of the cave.

Shit, she must be losing her mind. Where had the paved roadway come from? And as for the truck idea, one of them certainly seemed to be plowing past her, like she was on the side of a city street and the thing was delivering a pallet-load of something to somebody's business on a rush job.

Red brake lights flared now, reflecting off the slick walls of the cave, and there was a screeching of tires in her ears and the sharp burn of rubber in her nose. Then the back of the truck fishtailed, the rear going cockeyed to the tunnel and swinging toward her in slow motion.

Adrenaline coursed through her body. If she didn't move, she was going to be crushed—

A force from up above shoved her down and forward as the bed came at her, and as she fell into a crouch and twisted, she realized she was under the back of the truck, in between the front wheels and the rear ones, right in the middle. Doing that math, Nyx let herself go down flat on the asphalt and covered her head, rolling in the direction the vehicle's momentum was taking all that weight so she wasn't mowed over by those back wheels.

The halt took a hundred thousand yards and twelve years, and she scrambled to keep up to avoid being roadkill, boots digging in, limbs flailing, body flipping around beneath the truck's tunnel-long bed as the brakes continued to squeal and the stench of rubber got thicker, and she knew that if she hadn't seen the Fade before, she was going to now—

And then it was done.

No more movement. No more scrambling.

The truck was at a cockeyed stop, brakes hissing, that pungent rubber smell stinging her sinuses, her body flopping over one last time so that she was staring up at the undercarriage of the semi's cargo bed.

Turning her head, she wiped the grit out of her eyes and followed the axle to the set of four tires that were eighteen inches from her torso. She was so close to them, she could see their braided tread, and she coughed at the smell of hot metal and motor oil.

"Take this back."

She had no idea who was addressing her under the goddamn death truck—

"Kane?" she breathed as she focused on his dirt-smudged face.

"Take this." He pushed her gun at her. "You're going to need it. Unless you can dematerialize?"

He was speaking softly and urgently, but her brain was just not working. She was pretty sure he was using English, right?

All the confusion got cleared up real fricking quick at the sound of the cab's doors opening at the front of the semi. In the lee of the head-lights that were streaming forward down the— wait, so they really were on a road? Like a proper road? And it was a three-laner.

"Where the hell are we?" she whispered as a pair of guards walked around and met each other at the truck's front grille.

"There was nobody there," one of them said as dust swirled around their dark shadows.

"I saw somebody in the headlights."

"You're out of your fucking mind."

"You want to take the risk I'm right? After we blew the barricade into the roadway?"

"It was supposed to be removed by the prisoners. We had no fucking choice but to use explosives. The Command wants this shit out of here now, and we need two exits to get the trucks off the site—what was I supposed to do?"

Kane put his face right into Nyx's and pressed the gun into her palm. "We're going to have to fight our way out of this, and I have not discharged a gun before in all my life. You're going to have to do the shooting."

Blinking, she told her vision to get with the program as she gripped the weapon. And then she kicked her brain's ass into gear. Like a newsreel on rerun, she caught up with Kane's convo, and there was no need for a PowerPoint presentation on what he was suggesting.

She looked down toward the guards as they stood arguing with each other. She didn't require an up-close-and-personal to know they were armed and had communicators.

"Stay behind me," she ordered.

"Yes, m'lady."

Nyx went belly down, but in a quiet way—and then she tripod'd her elbows and aimed the gun. Between the cab's front tires, the guards were face-to-face, their knees and the tips of their boots close together as they talked back and forth.

She picked the one on the left and aimed. Just before she pulled the trigger, she had a passing image of herself at the farm, out by the lower paddock, picking soup cans and water jugs off the fence line at fifty yards.

This was a whole different ball game.

When she pulled the trigger, she didn't wait to see if she had hit the target of that calf. She immediately discharged the weapon at the other guard's lower leg. Then it was back to the first—but she'd always had good aim, and she'd nailed her mark: The first guard was hopping on one foot, and as he slumped against the truck's hood, she aimed again—and popped him in the other knee. As he howled and went to ground, she picked off the one who was still standing by hitting the meat of his thigh, the spray of blood a graceful sprinkle that caught the headlights in a flush of red.

As both of them writhed and hollered for help into the communicators on their shoulders, she swallowed through a dry throat. Closing her eyes, she knew what should come next.

Her . . . or them. If she let them live, they were injured and armed. A bad combination—and she and Kane had to get out of wherever they were.

"Do it," she said under her breath.

Bullet to the brain. Or the chest.

Bullet to the . . .

. . . brain. Or to the chest—

"Shit," she hissed as she sagged and let her forearms relax.

Nyx just couldn't murder two males in what felt like cold blood. It was one thing if she had a gun in her face, a direct threat to her life. But this? She wasn't a killer. She wasn't like Apex.

She wrenched around. "Where do we go from here?"

Kane looked to the guards, who were both rocking on their backs and alternating between holding one of their legs and then the other.

"Come on," he said.

When he took her hand, she scurried out from under the truck bed with him, and then they tore off as fast as they could go—

Right into a landslide.

Some twenty feet of walling had collapsed, and she didn't have time to wonder about the whys or the wherefores. Kane led the way up the mound of debris, and then they were on the other side, and tooling down the properly paved road that was lit from the ceiling. But they didn't go far.

Two or three hundred yards away, a bright light was kindling, and she could hear a big engine growling as something approached. It had to be another semi.

"In here," Kane said as he pulled on her arm.

A fissure in the rock wall presented itself at just the right time. As the next semitrailer truck rounded a corner and its headlights pierced the road right where she and Kane had stood, they jumped out of sight and squeezed into a horizontal crack the size of a shallow closet.

As he'd gone in first, she was on the outside, so she got a good look at the flank of the vehicle. Gray and black, just like the other one, with a cargo trailer that was big enough to fit two stacks of four cars. After it passed by, she caught another whiff of the sickly perfume of a diesel engine.

When she went to leap out, Kane tugged the sleeve of her tunic.

"No, wait. Those two guards will have called for—"

Multi-colored flashing lights now, down from where the second semi had come from—and then the van that streaked by them had "Ambulance" written all over it. Literally. With the red cross and a logo that looked legit on its flanks, it could have passed for an official human one—which was undoubtedly the point.

"We need to wait," Kane said. "There'll be another truck. And that'll be the one you need to get on. Right on the top of the trailer. Stay flat, stay down."

Nyx turned her head toward him and focused

her tired eyes. There was enough illumination reflecting in from the road's light fixtures that she could make out his face. He was bleeding at his hairline and pale beneath a layer of dirt and oil.

"What . . . what happened?" She sneezed into the crook of her elbow. " 'Scuse me. What happened back by the Hive? Why the change?"

Kane shuffled his arm around in the tight squeeze and then he was offering her a square of cloth. "You're bleeding."

As she stared at the kerchief, he sighed. "I wish it were of better quality. I used to have ones of hand-loomed silk. With my initials."

When he put the cloth above one of her eyebrows, she winced. "What happened?"

"The lockdown." He shook his head as if he were frustrated. "When I tried to get to the transport area, to do the risk assessment, I could not get anywhere near it. They'd blocked off the entry to where the delivery trucks were—and no one called in for the shift was allowed anywhere near them. The guards themselves were doing the loading. I realized I had to take you another way."

"What about Jack?"

"He's going to run into the same problem even if he goes through the Command's area. I don't think they're going to let even him in there. I'm so sorry."

Nyx didn't go there. Couldn't go there. She shied away from the implications of her leaving right now, without saying goodbye to Jack.

"Shit," she breathed. "I almost shot you."

Kane smiled a little. "That's the only reason I fought with you. I never would have put upon you a hand if I had not been convinced that if I did not, I would be a dead male where I stood."

"Sorry about that."

"I would have told you it all if I could have. There was no time to explain. It is I who am sorry."

Nyx exhaled. And then started talking fast. "Please. I have to see Jack one last time—"

"We cannot." Kane's face tightened. "I can't get you back there safely—and more than that, we are exactly where we need to be. I promised the Jackal, on my honor, I would get you out no matter what it took. Even if it meant you could not say goodbye. I never go back on my word."

As she closed her eyes, Kane said, "Please know, if I could do so without endangering you, I would. But where we are now is a better position than I could have hoped for. You're so close, and I gave a male I respect my word. I will not go back upon it."

"I just wanted to see him one more time," she whispered.

"I know."

When she looked at Kane again, the sorrow on

his face was so deep and heartfelt, she knew he must have been thinking of the love he had lost so cruelly. The love he had been robbed of.

"If you can't do it for yourself," Kane said, "do it for the male who loves you."

"I never told him I loved him." Her voice was so hoarse, it was barely audible. "I never said the words. That's why I want to go back."

"True love doesn't require a voice. It requires the heart. He knows how you feel."

"Will you tell him? That I love him?"

"On my honor." Even though there was very little space, Kane managed to incline his upper torso in a shallow bow. "I shall tell him, I swear. For if I could have gotten one last missive unto my love, I would have. I will not fail you. Or him."

For a moment, she searched Kane's face and the sorrow that clouded his eyes.

Then she hugged him. It was an impulsive gesture not easily accommodated in the tight space, but she couldn't not reach out. They had both lost the one they loved. Him to death's cold embrace, her to this prison Jack would not leave.

"I still don't know why," she said as they separated.

"Know what?"

Why Jack refuses to leave, she thought.

"It doesn't matter," she said.

"The next truck. When it comes by, you

378

dematerialize onto the top. You're wearing the color of the paint job, so if there's a guard monitoring things somewhere, you should be able to pass notice. Stay flat. Keep your head down."

"And my eyes down," she said roughly. "Which is the same thing."

"You can do this. I believe in you."

"The next truck." When Kane nodded, she gripped his hand. "You are a male of worth. To help me. To be there for Jack."

He squeezed her palm. "I do not know about the male of worth. But I am certain that the love the two of you have for each other is worth just about everything."

"He doesn't love me," she said.

"Of course he does. He has bonded."

"He'd be coming with me if that were true. Or he'd at least help me understand the why not. So no, he doesn't love me."

Light flared down at the far end, a truck rambling around the turn, the engine roaring as whatever guard was driving stomped on the accelerator.

"Here it is," she whispered. "I have to go."

All she had to do was picture that pool with the candlelight, the calm place she had found grace in despite being in this harsh and hopeless prison. Except now, Jack could not be part of the vision. She needed to start giving him up right away. It was not going to get any easier.

Kane reached forward and squeezed her shoulder. "You can do this. If you can face off at a squad of guards, you can dematerialize from here—"

"If you move, I kill him."

Nyx wrenched around. In the dim light, a guard stood behind Kane, having come through the fissure from its other end. The male's face and body were largely indistinct. The gun that was up to the aristocrat's head was not—

"I've got her."

Nyx whipped her head back toward the view of the road. There was a guard right in front of her, and before she could respond, he clasped a steel handcuff on her wrist and ripped the gun free of her hold.

So dematerializing was no longer an option. And neither was shooting her way free.

Out in the tunnel, the truck she had been waiting for barreled by, its diesel breath billowing in its wake, an opportunity lost.

Maybe she was going to see Jack again after all.

Too bad that was far from good news.

CHAPTER THIRTY-FOUR

A s Jack was shackled to the bed by the guards, the sounds of the chains rattling and the clicks of the steel bands locking on his ankles and his wrists were loud in the silence of the Command's chamber. Thanks to the drug dart, his unresisting flesh was alive with sensation yet totally unresponsive—and still he tried to fight, even though he got nowhere with it. He couldn't even move his head. It had lolled into a side position when he'd been carried over and laid upon the mattress, so he was stuck staring at the door across the chamber.

The guards handled him like crystal glass, nothing rushed or harsh.

The Command reserved that kind of fun and games for herself.

As the two males left, Jack's eyes went to the floor. There was a ring of bullet strikes in the tile, an outline of where his body had been.

When the Command stepped in front of his vision, the hood was down again, and that face he despised, the one that came to him in his nightmares, the one that he had endured in front of his own so many times . . . was calm. That temper had been controlled.

The gun was still in those pale hands, but it was pointing away from him.

"So where did you get this?" she demanded.

On one level, the inquiry was a waste of time. He couldn't speak. Then again, the Command didn't actually want his response. She never did.

"This came off a guard." Those hazel eyes bored into his own. "One who was killed in my quarters with three others."

Jack blinked. He knew what was coming next.

"You said you were held at gunpoint by a female in prison garb. But she isn't one of us, is she." The Command backed off and paced around, stopping to stand over the pattern of bullet holes in the floor tile. "You stated you did not know her. How true is that, I wonder."

The Command went over to a table. There was a syringe on it and two small bottles with rubber seals on their necks: The drugs that had to be used if he was to get hard, as well as the antidote to the tranquilizer. There was also the dart gun and a gathering of red-tailed darts. She put the nine millimeter down and picked up one of those projectiles.

Pivoting, she held the thing up. "If I shoot you again with this, you will die. Your respiration will cease. You will turn blue and then gray. After that, your body will stiffen for a period of time before your limbs become loose again. Blood will pool on the undersides of your arms and legs, your back and your ass, turning everything purple. You will begin to stink after that, assuming I don't choose to strip the meat from your bones and feed it to the other prisoners."

The female approached the bed and knelt down. Putting the dart right up to his face, the Command said, "I am in control of you. You're mine, and I will do with you whatever the fuck I want."

Jack stared back at those eyes.

"You are *mine*." The Command reached out and ran her hand down the side of his face. "Only mine. And if I find out you've been with another female? I'm going to make you beg for death. Are we clear? I will fucking destroy you."

He wanted to spit at her. Instead, he closed his eyes, shutting her out—

The slap was hard, her palm connecting with his cheek. "You will look at me."

She slapped him again. "Look at me!"

The Command let out an unholy sound and mounted him. Grabbing his face with her hand, he felt a fan of pain and smelled his blood as nails scored his skin.

"You will look at me, goddamn you," she spat.

When he just breathed in and out through his nose and stared at the inside of his lids, his eyes were clawed open. The Command was utterly undone, her face flushed, that red hair splaying out in tangles—

And then she stilled.

Those hazel eyes bulged. With a shaking hand, she moved his head to the side.

Trembling fingertips pulled down the high collar of his tunic. Then she took a quick, hard breath, the air sucked in between gritted teeth.

"Who . . ." That hateful voice cracked. "Who have you fed."

The Command sat back on his hips and pressed shaking hands to her mouth. "Who have you fed."

The question was repeated over and over again under her breath—and Jack had a thought that it was like storm clouds gathering on the horizon.

He was not going to live through what was going to be done to him. As soon as the Command snapped out of the trance of shock, she was going to unleash upon him all the fury in that black soul. She was going to kill him.

But it would be okay. Kane had sworn on his honor to make sure Nyx got out, and the worthy male had the three others to help him. And as for the other issue, the one that kept Jack here in the prison?

It was the one and only thing the Command and he agreed upon.

Those hazel eyes burned into his own, and he had an odd thought that she must have dropped the dart somewhere on the bed. Maybe she would find it and use it on him. Maybe she would reload the guard's gun and not shoot around him this time. Maybe she—

The tears that welled in those eyes shocked him.

They didn't last. The Command's characteristic hard aggression wiped them away, sure as if the force of her will was the back of a hand.

"You fucking bastard, you fed her. You're lying to me about everything and you *fed* her."

The door to the quarters opened wide, and the Command yanked her hood back into place. "I told you not to—"

"We have the female," the guard announced. "And the prisoner she was with."

The Command stiffened. Then she dismounted from him. As she stared down at him from behind the mesh, he knew the bite mark at his throat was a declaration of war, and Nyx was in the crosshairs of a battle that had nothing to do with her. In desperation, he tried to move his mouth, move his body—move anything.

Fuck, he thought. He needed to stop this.

The Command's hood tilted to the side. "Perfect timing. And why don't I go take care of her. How about that? Two can play at the biting game, you know."

The black robes drifted across to the door, the Command speaking over her shoulder. "I'll bring you back what's left of her. And then you and I will discuss the future. It's not going to be a pretty one."

As he was shut in by himself, he started to scream. Not that he made any noise. The only thing that changed was his rate of breathing. He started to pant.

He had to force his body to move. He had to fight to get free. He had to—

The paralysis did not yield, even to the adrenaline coursing through his system. Frozen as well as chained to the bedding platform, Jack yelled inside his skin.

His female needed him and he could not get to her.

This was the worst of all the hells he had ever known.

CHAPTER THIRTY-FIVE

Nyx was shoved into a ten-foot-square cell. As she lost her balance and pitched forward, she put out her handcuffed palms and caught herself on the rock floor. Flipping over, she jumped to her feet and brought up her fists.

All the guard did was shut her in. Then leave her.

Staying in a fighting stance, even though there was no one around and her head was pounding, she looked through the steel mesh that ran between the iron bars. She had no idea where Kane was—or where she was. From the light bulbs hanging from the ceiling, it appeared that she was in some kind of holding area, but the place looked abandoned. There was black dust on everything, and the other two cells were not only empty, they had parts of their steel mesh hanging off in sheets.

Not that the prisoners, with those explosive collars, could ever dematerialize.

With a groan, she eased up on the go-nowhere aggression and went to try the cell's opening. Locked tight. With copper.

She was stuck until someone let her out of here. "Damn it."

Before the guards had split up her and Kane,

she'd been stripped of her backpack—which meant she had no weapons, no ammo, no wind-breaker with her phone. Not that she had recep-tion in the prison anyway.

God, had they found Jack, too? Were they going to hurt Kane until the male told them everything?

The unknowns were making her crazy. And then there was—

Nyx frowned. The holding area was at the end of a dim tunnel, and off in the distance, she could hear a commotion. People were talking fast, the multilayer of voices echoing down to her. And then abruptly, everything went silent.

Marching now. Getting louder. And before she could make out how many were coming for her, a different scent, pungent and distinct, flooded into the cell and saturated the air.

What the hell was that?

Except Nyx didn't spend a lot of time trying to place the smell. A lineup of guards approached, their black uniforms and shiny weapons and coordinated movements strobing as they passed in and out of the pools of illumination thrown by the tunnel's light bulbs. As they closed in, she backed up against the cell's far wall.

Like that was going to do any good—

"Oh . . . shit," she whispered.

There was a figure behind the guards. One that was draped in black robing, with a hood over its face and head. It had to be the Command.

Well. At least she wouldn't have to wait around, wondering what was going to happen to her. Her end was right here.

As the guards filed into the holding area, they flattened against the walls, their AR-15s held across their chests, their faces up, their eyes down on the rock floor. The Command was the last to enter, the figure in black imposing and full of authority.

Nyx lifted her chin. She was not going to bow before anything or anybody on her way out the proverbial door. She had fought too long and too hard to bend. Though she was scared, she was determined not to show it—

The Command stopped abruptly. Then the hood that covered the face tilted to one side. After a moment, the figure seemed to weave on his feet, which seemed at odds with the obvious authority he wielded.

"Leave us," a low voice ordered.

As if there were any doubts in Nyx's mind as to the power of the male, the effect of the command was like someone had dropped radioactive material in the center of the open space in front of the cells: The guards flushed out of the area quick as a breath.

And then the Command . . .

Didn't do a goddamn thing.

Those robes didn't move. There were no words. No weapons being taken out, either.

After what seemed like forever, the figure took two steps forward to the cell door. A long sleeve moved up, and a hand reached for the lock. There was the sound of shifting metal, and then the section of steel mesh and iron bars swung open, the hinges creaking.

Nyx braced for a physical confrontation, moving into the middle of the cell, sinking into her thigh muscles and clasping her cuffed hands together so she could use them as a blunt force weapon.

"So you're the Command," she said roughly.

The figure went still again, and Nyx breathed deep, smelling that thick scent that seemed to coat the male as another tangible robe. Sandalwood. It was sandalwood—

Nyx.

From out of nowhere, she heard her own name in her head. Which, considering all the things she needed to be aware of at this moment, was hardly an efficient use of brain power—

"Nyx . . . ?"

Recoiling, Nyx tried to figure out what was wrong with her hearing. Maybe it wasn't her ears, though. Maybe it was her head injury from that rock falling on her temple. Because there was no way in hell the Command had just said her name like that.

The figure brought up a hand to the top of his hood, and as he stripped off the—

Nyx took an involuntary step back. And another one. The last took her right up against the back of the cell, the cold mesh and bars registering on her shoulder blades through the thin prison tunic.

She could not understand what she was looking at.

It appeared to be . . . a female with long red hair. Which was confusing, as she'd decided the Command was a male, a clear unconscious bias she was going to need to apologize to herself for later. But the sex of the figure was not the big issue.

The overriding problem was that her brain, for reasons she couldn't understand, seemed to be extrapolating from the features of what was in front of her not just a resemblance to her dead sister, Janelle . . . but an exact copy. Right down to the cowlick next to the widow's peak at her hairline. And the delicate cleft in her chin. And the arch of the brows, and the flecks of deep brown in the hazel irises, and the way the lips were slightly elevated on one side.

"You're dead," Nyx said hoarsely. "Why am I seeing—"

"Nyx?"

Hearing her name come out of that mouth was like a time machine. She instantly traveled back to before Janelle had been falsely accused and sent to prison, to when they'd lived together at the farmhouse, with Posie and their grandfather.

And then she went back even farther, to before her parents had died. And farther back still, to when Nyx had just been out of her transition.

When she hit the last memory, it was with a slam: She saw Janelle holding Posie, right after their younger sister had been born.

"You're supposed to be dead," Nyx whispered. "I saw your name on the Wall."

"You . . . were the one who came in here." Janelle—or the vision that appeared to be Janelle—shook her head. "You were the one. Who infiltrated us."

Janelle put both hands up to her face, but she didn't touch her cheeks. Her palms hovered there in midair, the fingers splayed out. Just like she had always done whenever she was stressed.

"It was you, then," she repeated. Then she shook her head, that red hair shimmering in the light. "I don't understand. Why did you come down here?"

"I was looking for you. I've been looking for you for fifty years."

"Why?"

"What do you mean, why?" Nyx frowned. "You've been incarcerated for fifty years for something you didn't do. Why wouldn't I look for you? I'm your sister."

"I didn't ask you to come after me." Janelle's voice got sharper. "Don't put this on me—"

Nyx threw some volume into her own syllables. "Put what on you? The fact that I was worried about you? That you were lost and I was trying to find you? What the hell are you talking about?"

"I never asked you to come after me."

"You didn't have to! I'm your sister—"

"Not anymore."

The dead tone to the words shut Nyx's mouth. But not for long. "I'm not your sister?"

"Janelle is dead."

"Then who the hell am I talking to right now?" Nyx went to rub her aching temple and winced when her fingers hit the place where she'd been struck. "Jesus Christ, Janelle, you're in charge here, right? You're the Command—so why don't you just leave? If you're the fucking authority, you can come home, come back to us. Why don't you come home—"

"I don't want to. That's why."

Nyx tried to breathe through the pain in her chest. "Why?" she said in a small voice. "Why wouldn't you want to return to us?"

Janelle stepped back, but she left the door wide open. As she paced around the open area in front of the cells, the black robes drifted in her wake, flowing like smoke after her body.

As if she were evil.

Except that just wasn't true.

"Janelle, come back with me—"

"Why the hell would I do that?" came the hard

retort. "I don't want to be stuck in that farm-house, going nowhere, working minimum wage for the rest of my fucking life." She stopped and looked over with a glare. "Please. What the fuck do I need that for. I'm better than that."

"We're your family."

"You are what I left behind."

Nyx shook her head. "You don't meant that—"

"You don't know me." Janelle seemed to get taller, even as she stayed the same height. "I'm where I want to be, doing what I want to do. While you've been looking for me, I haven't thought about any of you even once."

"I don't believe you."

"Like I said, you don't know me—"

"I was there when you saved that horse from the flood. I patched the roof on our house with you in that snowstorm. You used to hold Posie in your arms and rock her to sleep right after she was born because she would only settle for you. *Mahmen* always said, 'Give her to Janelle—'"

"Stop it."

" '—she'll only fall asleep for Janelle.' And after *mahmen* and dad died, you stayed up all day talking to me. You were the only reason I got through that—"

"Stop it!" Janelle put her hands over her ears. "That is not me!"

"It is!" Nyx rushed forward, to the point where she was almost out of the cell. "Let's go. Let's leave here together. You don't belong here. You're here under false pretenses. You were framed—"

"How did you find us?" Janelle dropped her arms. "How the hell did you find us?"

Nyx stopped. "Does that matter?"

"How."

"I went to that old church with the graveyard. The one that's west of our property. I found the crypt, and I went down—"

"Did you kill my guard. The one who was scorched?"

"He's not *your* guard."

Janelle's face was subtly changing, the flush leaving her cheeks, the mouth thinning. "He most certainly was mine. Did you kill him?"

"He put a gun to my head! He was going to kill me—"

"And you took his gun after you shot him."

"The gun went off when we struggled over it— and I wasn't going to leave him with the thing." Nyx slashed her hand through the air. "What the hell does that matter—"

"You're the one who stole a gun and made a prisoner take you to the Wall."

"Because I wanted to know if you were alive, if I could help you—"

"And you put that gun to the prisoner's temple, didn't you."

"I'm sorry?"

"You threatened the life of one of my prisoners, didn't you. You put a gun to his temple and forced him to carry you—"

"Janelle, why are we talking about this—"

"Because I am in charge here! This is *my* prison!" Janelle jacked forward on her hips. "Do you have any idea how long I have worked to get this far? To get this authority? Decades, you stupid idiot. I had to play my cards smart, develop allegiances, learn how to bribe guards. And as the *glymera* lost interest down here, I took my opportunity and seized control. I'm someone here, goddamn it. I matter—"

"You matter to us! I've been eaten alive by the idea that you were put away falsely—"

"Are you fucking kidding me? I killed that old motherfucker. What are you talking about?"

Nyx clamped her jaw shut and felt the world spin. "What," she whispered.

"I killed that old male. I snapped his neck because I was sick and tired of him telling me what to do."

Blinking hard, Nyx couldn't process what was being spoken. "But . . . why didn't you just quit if you were unhappy with the job?"

Janelle's chin lowered, and she stared out from under her brows. "Because I wanted to know what it was like to murder someone."

"You don't mean that."

"Oh, I do. And I've learned a lot more about

death since I took over down here. I like it. I'm good at it." As Janelle shook her head, the last of the light that had so briefly flared in her eyes faded. "I belong here. This is my world. The sister you had is dead and gone and I'll prove it."

She slammed the door to the cell shut and then stepped up to the mesh. "You put my gun to the temple of that prisoner. What else did you do with him?"

"What?"

Janelle punched at the panel between them, the mesh rattling against the iron bars. "What else did you do with him, you whore!"

As a sickening realization ran through Nyx's aching head, she took a deep breath. And that was when she made the connection. The scent on Janelle, that sandalwood, which she hadn't smelled anywhere else in the prison . . .

. . . had been in Jack's hair.

CHAPTER THIRTY-SIX

W hen the door to the Command's quarters opened, Jack shot his eyes in that direction even as his head remained where it was. He braced himself for guards. Many of them. Or maybe the Command with Nyx's body—

Apex?

The male with the dead stare and the bad past walked in with a bored expression on his face—and a severed hand . . . in his hand?

The vampire lifted the body part. "I borrowed this from one of the guards. After we're done getting you out, I'm going to slap him with it. Assuming he hasn't bled out."

As Apex tossed the appendage over his shoulder and strode across to the bed, Jack blinked quickly. It was the only way to communicate.

"What's that?" the male asked. "Why'd I cut it off? I needed a thumbprint to get in here and his worked nicely. So what do we have to do here to get you out?"

Jack cast his gaze over to the table and returned it to Apex. And then he went back to the table.

"Right." Apex walked over and picked up one of the vials of clear liquid. "This or the other guy?"

When Jack blinked twice, Apex said, "Is that

a yes on this bottle?" Jack blinked twice again. "Okay. How much."

Apex came back with the syringe, inserted the needle through the red rubber seal, and started to draw out the antidote to the tranquilizer. "Blink twice when we're good."

Jack had no clue about the proper dosage so he just blinked repeatedly when the syringe seemed fully filled.

"Where do you shoot it up? Vein or muscle?" Apex rolled his eyes. "Blink twice for vein." When Jack did not, the male said, "Blink twice for muscle." Jack blinked twice. "Leg?"

More with the blinking, and Apex moved so fast, Jack was still communicating with his eyelids when he felt a puncture on his thigh. Well aware of what was coming next, he braced himself for—

The rush of animation was like being plugged into an electrical socket, his body jerking and jumping against the shackles until the chains seethed and rattled like snakes. But instead of promptly leveling off, the burning buzz continued to build until he was shaking, great rushes of energy vibrating through his veins, his muscles, his limbs.

"Shit, I think you're exploding from the inside out," Apex said evenly. "You want me to hit you with a dart—"

The guards who ran into the chamber had

guns drawn, and before Apex could respond, one of them hauled back and nailed him on the head with a baton, knocking him out cold. As he dropped like deadweight to the floor, there was some conversation, but Jack couldn't follow it. His teeth were clapping together like a set of castanets, and then there was the raucous sound of those rattling chains. The good news? He could move his head. The bad news? He couldn't stop moving his head.

His vision was all over the place, vibrating around the chamber as his skull wobbled at the top of his earthquaking spine. He was in a tornado, but he was aware enough that he knew when the guards came over to him. They released his ankles first, and his legs danced free of the shackles with no rhythm at all, skipping, bucking—

When his arms were liberated, he flopped around the bedding platform, a fish in the bottom of a boat, the momentum carrying his body to the edge of the mattress. The guards, ever careful of his welfare, caught him before he ended up knocked out on the floor with Apex. Muscling him up to his feet, they dragged his spasming form over to the door, his feet skipping across the bullet holes the Command had put into the tile.

He wanted to fight, but he was no better off than he'd been before. On the tranquilizer, he'd had no control because he was paralyzed. Now, he had no control because his body was a lightning bolt.

From out of the chaos of his vision, he was fairly sure that the guards picked up Apex as well. And then he was out in the hall, being taken in the opposite direction from the work area, from where the transports left, from where he'd been praying Nyx would get out. When they arrived at the main tunnel, he had a passing thought that everything was very empty, and this proved especially true as he was brought into the Hive.

Just as before, when he'd come out of the fissure with Nyx, there was no one in it. Not one prisoner. And the only guards were those carrying him.

They took him down toward the dais, through the piles of trash and debris left scattered by the normal crush of inmates. There were six stone steps up to the platform, and his feet knocked into them on an ascension that ended at the middle of the three posts. As he was turned around, he heard the metal-on-metal chime of chain links while Apex was dropped like litter off to one side.

Jack's arms were bent backward, his shoulder sockets straining, his wrists burning as they were once again shackled. The seizures racking him made him kick against the greasy, stained wood, and he knew he was going to be bruised.

Not that he was going to live through this.

Dearest Virgin Scribe, he hoped Nyx had gotten free again somehow.

As Jack looked across the vast space of the Hive, he heard a rumbling off in the distance, one that rose in volume and gradually declined, like a massive vehicle was passing by somewhere close. When it happened again, his brain churned over the implications.

Double shifts called in. No prisoners in the main tunnel. No one here.

Holy shit. The Command was emptying the prison.

She was moving out everything . . . and everyone.

"What did you do with him?" Janelle demanded through the mesh and the iron bars. "The prisoner. What did you do with him."

That furnished cell, Nyx thought. The one Jack had hesitated in front of.

Maybe he'd paused there not because he missed the female who lived inside, or yearned for her . . . but because she was holding him against his will and he didn't know what to do about it?

Or how to get free, regardless of the relative autonomy he had around the prison?

"Which prisoner?" she hedged, to buy some time.

"The one my guards saw you with. The one you

threatened to kill in front of them if they didn't let you through."

"I don't know what you're talking about."

"You're lying to me."

Nyx shrugged. "I think the larger question is what you're going to do with me. Everything else is just conversation."

Janelle went silent. And then she slowly put the hood back in place, her face covered once more.

"I'll answer that right now," she said in a low, threatening voice. "Guards!"

As Nyx felt a cold rush of panic, Janelle turned away—and she did not look back as she left. The black-robed figure who used to be her sister just walked off, as if she hadn't had a conversation with a close relative. Someone who she'd grown up with. Someone who she shared parents and a sister and a grandfather with.

In the wake of the departure, Nyx remembered standing in front of the Wall and seeing the bastardized version of her sister's name carved into the slick stone.

One thing was absolutely clear.

The female she had once known as Janelle was well and truly dead.

I wanted to know what it was like to murder someone. I'm good at it.

Maybe that person had never existed.

The time for thinking ended as guards reentered the holding area and opened the cell. They were silent as they marched her out, one male at the crook of each of her arms, the three of them pivoting to shuffle through the doorway. Striding out into the tunnel, there was no wasted time. They took her directly to the Hive, and they entered through a side door—

Nyx looked up to the dais and lost her footing. Jack was chained to the center post, and there was something wrong with him. His body was trembling violently, his head jerking around on his shoulders, the chains keeping him in place chattering because of all the movement—that certainly seemed to be involuntary.

But he managed to focus on her. Even through his palsied condition, his eyes, those blue eyes, locked on her—and as she was brought closer, his shaking eased some. He couldn't seem to talk, though, his lips moving and nothing coming out. Was he sick?

No, he was drugged, she decided.

The guards dragged her up onto the dais and stood her in front of him. Off to the side, Apex was down on the ground and not moving. When there was a rustling from the shadows behind the dais wall, Nyx expected her sister to walk out— no, not her sister.

The Command.

Instead, another set of guards emerged, and they were dragging a prisoner by the male's arms, the torso and body lagging behind. They dropped the body like it was trash next to Apex, and Kane slowly flopped over onto his back.

Nyx gasped. His face was so bloody and swollen, she almost couldn't recognize him, and as he breathed through his mouth, all that came out was wheezing.

She glanced back at Jack just as one more was brought in. Mayhem was fighting against the guards who had him tied in rough rope, big body jerking and twisting, white hair ripping around as he snarled and cursed. All that fight stopped as he got a look at the empty Hive. He was so stunned that as he was chained to the post on the right, he didn't resist.

Then again, he was done for and he must have known that.

They were all done for.

The guards stepped back from them, forming a line on the left, and as Nyx's biceps were abruptly released, her balance went wonky and she had to catch herself from falling over. She steadied her balance by focusing on Jack. She wanted to ask him what they should do, how they could beat this, but she knew the impulse was the immature part of her talking, the little girl inside the grown female who was desperately looking for someone she trusted and loved to tell her it was all going to be okay: She wanted the plan that would magically free Jack and Mayhem, that would bring Apex back to life and save Kane from his injuries, that would make her sister not dead and the Command someone else . . . that would see Nyx, herself, safely back to the farmhouse, this whole nightmare never having happened.

The yearning for that fantasy was as strong as her love for the quaking male who was chained before her, stronger even than her mortal fear about the death that was surely coming.

"I wanted to see you two together."

Nyx jerked around. Down on the floor of the Hive, standing in the center of the vast, empty cave, was the black-robed figure that had briefly removed her hood and looked, catastrophically, like Nyx's long-lost sister.

The Command came forward, those billowing folds of black fabric ominous, like funeral draping about to fall on a casket. She stopped when she was five feet away from the dais, the hooding angling back as she looked up.

"Bring the basket."

Nyx looked at Jack. The trembling was subsiding in him, the unhealthy flushing in his chest and throat and face fading—to reveal a palm print on his cheek as if he'd been slapped.

"No," he mumbled. "Not her—"

"You gave up any chance to have an opinion about anything when you let her take your vein." The Command shook her head. "And your reward for being a faithless fuck is that she gets to watch everything. Then I'm going to teach her about death—"

"No!" he yelled as he strained against the chains.

"Fuck you!" the Command hollered back. "You had everything here! I took care of you—you were treated with more goddamn deference than anybody except me. And you fucked it all up—you fucked yourself when you fucked her!"

The Command grabbed the folds of her robe and marched up onto the stage. "I fucking hate you!"

Nyx started to respond, but the Command went by her like she didn't exist, getting up into Jack's face, punching at his chest. "You fucking asshole!"

"I was never yours," Jack said on a growl.

The Command ripped off her hood, that red hair glowing under the harsh lighting. "You were left to your own devices here, you were taken care of, you had everything—"

"I had *nothing*—"

"You had me!"

"I. Didn't. *Want. You!*" Jack screamed the last word, the muscles in his neck and shoulders bulging. "You drugged me and strapped me down and took what I didn't want to give you. I *didn't* fucking want you!"

The Command seemed stunned. "You lie."

"When was the last time I got on that bed willingly? It's been *decades,*" he spat.

Nyx felt the world spin on its axis again. As her brain jammed with the implications of it all, the Command, trembling with rage, hauled back with her open palm—

Nyx moved before she had a conscious thought to take action. Surging forward, she took her cuffed hands and raised them high, jacking them over the Command's head and yanking back, catching the chain between the shackles right across the front of that throat.

Blind rage gave Nyx a strength she had never had before, and she dragged the Command up against her own body, taking control, owning the situation as she wheeled around and faced the guards.

In a loud, clear voice, she spoke over the choking sounds and the thrashing of the robes. "I will fucking kill her. I will snap her *fucking* neck right now if any of you move."

CHAPTER THIRTY-SEVEN

As Jack saw Nyx jump forward, he would have yelled at her to stop, but there was no time. One moment, she was standing behind the Command, the next she had her handcuffs around the female's throat and was hauling back as if her life depended on the Command's losing hers.

Which was the truth of the situation they were all in.

His female was in a magnificent fury, her eyes glowing with retribution, her body strung like a bow as she strangled her prey. And when she ordered the guards, her voice was like something that had come from on high, from a deity of war. Meanwhile, the Command's hands clawed at the constriction, her face flushing, her eyes bulging—

Jack's awareness instantly bifurcated. Part of his brain stayed on the situation before him, his female *ahvenging* his honor like the warrior she was. The other part was looking at the two faces side by side, Nyx's right behind the Command's.

He refused to believe the conclusion he was coming to. But if one disregarded the difference in hair color . . . there was a shocking similarity between the shapes of their faces, the arches of their brows, the tilt of their eyes. They were even the same height, tall for females, and . . .

"No," he whispered as Nyx continued to bark orders. "It cannot be."

That was the last thing that came out of his mouth, the last conscious thought he had as everything went to senses and reaction rather than logic and reason: In a strange, slow-motion kind of dreamscape, he noticed from the corner of his eye that Kane was getting to his feet in a wobbly manner.

Kane looked at Jack. Then his eyes went to Nyx.

At that moment, a fresh phalanx of guards jogged onto the platform from the shadows off to the side. As they drew their guns, Nyx's forehead glowed ruby red from all the laser sights trained on her frontal lobe, but none of the males discharged their weapons.

They couldn't. The Command was too close, and the two females were moving around.

And that was when Kane, who had been badly beaten about the face and head, stumbled back toward the guards, both those lined up and frozen at attention, and the new ones who were getting up to speed on the unprecedented situation. None of the males paid any attention to him. They were all focused on Nyx and the Command—

So when Kane lifted his hands to the back of his neck, none of them noticed.

Jack opened his mouth. But there was nothing to say. He knew what the aristocrat was going to do—

There was a final moment as their stares met. The sadness in Kane's eyes was palpable, all that he had lost, all that he had had to endure, coming out of his soul. Then he nodded once, in deference and commiseration—

"No!" Jack yelled.

—as he unclipped the monitor collar.

The instant the contacts were separated, there was a shrill beeping noise that was so loud, it cut through everything. The guards with those laser sights wheeled to the sound and so did the ones standing in formation.

Their shouts of alarm were immediate, and they tried to run, but it was too late.

Jack was looking right at his dear, dear friend as the detonation occurred.

The flash of light was blinding and the energy released so great that it banged Jack against the post. And blew the guards off their boots. And blasted Nyx and the Command off the dais, into thin air. The deafening sound echoed around the Hive, and the shockwaves were so strong that there was a smoky aftermath that lasted either a split second or an entire year, Jack couldn't tell.

Then the groaning began.

At first, he thought it was the guards closest to where Kane had been, mortally wounded and begging for help. Except a fine mist floated down—no, not mist. It was dust. Dust from the—

The roof collapse started directly over Jack's head, chunks of the ceiling falling down and landing with thunder, shattering into pieces. He tried to duck—but then he was being lifted up, his feet popping free of the ground, his body falling back as the post he was on lost its verticality. As his vision swung accordingly, he knew the wood trunk was heavy as a car and capable of crushing him—or at the very least mauling his arms and hands, which were chained to its verso—when it landed.

All he could do was brace himself for broken bones—

The ten-foot-tall, three-foot-wide post landed at an angle, his upper limbs surviving, his back cracking like a bat. He had a momentary paralysis—nothing working, not his heart, his lungs, his eyelids—but then he came back to his senses, his vision clearing.

So he got to watch a boulder the size of a fully grown male break loose from the ceiling and head directly for him.

With a holler, he wrenched to the side, rolling the post out of the way—and then he planted his feet and pushed upward, lifting the heavy weight. As more debris fell, he shucked himself off the beam, pulling the chains with him down the stained expanse until they fell free off the bottom.

The pile of metal was weighty, and the shackles persistent, but it was a hell of a lot better than the whole tree trunk.

Dragging the links with him, he sought cover by leaping off the stage—

Another great groan from up on the dais announced the collapse of the post Mayhem had been chained to. But there was no helping him. No helping anyone.

Total chaos.

Where was Nyx?

Right before the explosion, Nyx had been too busy screaming at the guards to drop their weapons to notice what Kane was doing. But the instant that high-pitched beeping had gone off, both she and the Command had looked toward him.

His collar had been in his hands.

And he had looked at Nyx. Even though it had only been for a split second, his expression was engraved in her brain. He had seemed so incredibly sad and resigned . . . but there had been an affection in his eyes as well.

After which he had looked at Jack.

It was clear Kane was doing what he was to give them a chance to survive.

The blast had been so violent, she had flown back into thin air, or maybe the Command, who was in front, had pushed her—either way, Nyx had known the landing was going to be a bitch. Not only had they traveled a distance away, there also was a five-foot drop to the stone floor—and she was right. All of the breath was knocked out of her lungs as the Command landed on top of her.

Fighting to stay conscious, Nyx told her arms to continue pulling—she needed to keep the pressure on or the Command was going to escape—

The elbow went into Nyx's side like someone had stabbed her with a crowbar, the pain blooming in a new place unrelated to her shoulder blades, her ass, or her head. As the remaining oxygen pushed out of her lungs, her vision went black and white and her arms became non-responsive, falling loose. The Command took immediate advantage of this, those black robes left behind as the female wriggled out and jumped free.

From her sprawl on the rock floor, Nyx caught an indelible image of the female she had once known as her sister standing up. There was nothing but a black bodysuit and leggings under those folds of black, and with her red hair spilling down her back, she was a discordant flash of beauty as she looked up at the ceiling of the prison's largest open space.

The Command twisted around and glanced down at Nyx.

For a moment, there was a flare of recognition, a return to who they had once been to each other, the reconnection brought out by the mortal near-miss of the explosion. Or . . . perhaps Nyx saw the instant for what she wanted it to be, because part of her was stuck in the past.

And then the ceiling collapsed.

Fissures spread like tears in paper over the three posts, and the fall of rocks was not gradual, but a dam released.

Directly over Jack.

Nyx screamed and jumped up from the floor—only to rear back and cover her face with her cuffed hands. Through the lattice of her fingers, she saw bad news get worse. The post Jack was chained to began to list, and it didn't stop with a tilt. It went all the way over, crashing onto a pile of bleeding, disorientated, de-limbed guards. The fact that it didn't land flush to the ground was all that kept Jack from losing his arms.

Yelling his name, she lunged for the dais—but as more fell from the ceiling, she was forced back, rocks the size of her bouncing off the stage, rolling toward her as if they were on the side of the guards. Slipping, skipping, paddling with her pinned arms, she dodged them, lost her balance, got up again.

"Jack!" she screamed into the noise, the debris, the dust.

He must have been killed. There was no way he could have—

The second post fell, the one Mayhem was chained to.

"Jaaaaaaaaaaaaaaaaaaaack!"

Fuck it, she was going in.

Just as she rushed forward, a figure was revealed in the midst of the collapsing cave, a figure strong and true, who defied the destruction around him.

The instant Jack saw her, he took two leaping strides and went airborne like Superman, flying through the air with his arms out in front. Chains, heavy and silvered, came with him, tendrils of the prison dragging him down. And yet somehow, he landed on a roll and sprang up to his feet— and he wasted no time at all. Grabbing her hands, he pulled her away from the dais, and they ran together, down the center of the Hive's littered space.

Faster, faster . . . in spite of the chains they both wore.

When they came to the main tunnel, he took her to the right. Nyx's lungs were burning, her throat sore from the dust and the yelling, her nerves shot. But she couldn't slow down.

The next thing she knew, they were back on his cell block, and he took her past where he stayed. There was no one on any of the beds or in the shallow spaces. Gone. The prisoners were all gone—

Jack grabbed her wrists and yanked her around a corner. Then he stopped.

They were both breathing so hard, there could be no words. Not until they had panted enough to do anything other than suck in the stale, earthy air.

". . . secret . . . way . . . ," he panted, ". . . out. There's a secret way out."

"Let's go," she gasped. "Where?"

His brilliant blue eyes bored into hers. And then he brought his hand up, as if he were going to stroke her cheek. The chains, so many of them, came up with his arm.

"Goddamn it." He looked around at the tunnel. "We have to move fast. I don't know how structurally sound anything is. This whole place could come down on top of us."

Sure enough, under her boots, she felt the earth moving. At his nod, they took off again, running, running, their footfalls drowned out by the sound of the chains that bound them, their strides slowed by her pinned wrists and shuffling gait.

She lost track of where they were, but then she smelled . . . bread?

Was that bread?

He pulled her to a halt at the end of whatever passageway they were in.

"Shhh . . . ," he said as they breathed heavily.

They rounded a corner slowly, him in front.

Empty. The industrial kitchen, with its stainless

steel counters and ovens and professional-grade mixers, and dishwashers and stoves and hanging racks of saucepans, was empty—and had been left in a hurry. There were bowls with floury dough in them, and meat partially cut on wooden boards, and measuring cups still filled with liquids to be poured.

"This way—"

The rumbling in the distance brought their heads around.

"Come on," Jack said. "The collapse is spreading out from the Hive."

CHAPTER THIRTY-EIGHT

Nyx stayed on pace, keeping up with Jack as there was yet another tunnel, another passage, another straightaway, another corner. She had no idea where they were—and then . . . Jack slowed. And finally halted. He looked back and forth, and then put his hand on the wall.

"What now?" she said through sawing inhales.

Jack took her hands and pulled her in close. His eyes went around her face, and he lifted up his chains so that he could brush a strand of hair from her mouth.

And that was when she knew.

"No, you're coming with me," she said before he could speak. "We're going together. Right now—"

Lowering his arms, he put his hand back on the rock wall. When he hit something, a panel slid open. The air that was released was moldy and damp.

She sneezed and didn't give a shit. Grabbing his arm with her cuffed hands, she put her face in his. "Let's go. We're doing this together—"

"No one knows about this." He looked into the darkness that had been revealed. "It's a secret I've kept. I've been hoping to use it, but there was never the right time."

In the passageway, down thirty feet or more, a dingy bulb flared on the ceiling.

"Jack." She bent down and bundled up the chains that hung from his wrists. "I'm not going alone—"

"Follow this as far as it goes. There's only that one light bulb, so you'll have to feel your way toward the—"

"Jack! You're coming with me—"

"When you get to the end, the switch is on the right. About three feet from the ground. You'll feel it—"

"What the hell is wrong with you! She abused you! Why are you staying for her!"

Jack recoiled. "What are you talking about?"

"Are you really going to pretend I didn't hear what you said to her—to the Command? And still, after all that, you won't leave her?"

"You think this is about the Command?" The laugh that came out of him was harsh. And then his eyes narrowed and he grew remote. "Tell me. Who is she to you. And don't deny it. I saw you two side by side."

When Nyx replied, she felt as if she said the words across a vast distance—even though she and Jack were close enough that she could feel his body heat.

"She's my sister. Or she was. That was . . . Janelle."

"Dearest Virgin Scribe," he groaned. "How is it possible?"

As he closed his eyes and collapsed on the wall, he seemed so exhausted that he could barely stand, and she had a thought—a fleeting thought—that she should have fed him when she'd had the chance.

"She hurt you," Nyx said in a voice that cracked. "My sister . . . hurt you. Oh, God, Jack, why are you staying for her?"

His eyes popped open. "It's not about her. It's about . . . my young. She has my young in here. I need to go find . . . my young. That's why I couldn't leave—why I can't."

"Oh, fuck . . ." Her sister's young. Jack's young. "You had a . . ."

"I'm not in love with her. I hate her. But the young is innocent of everything she did to me."

Jack lowered his head, the shame and anger around him charging the air with emotion. And Nyx wanted to help him somehow, but there were complex emotions for her, too.

"I'm so sorry," she whispered, aware that the words covered so much about the situation. About him. About her. About what Janelle had done.

As his eyes finally focused properly on her, she was reminded of him waking out of that nightmare, back by the pool. Just as then, his stare was haunted and confused. But that changed quick.

"You need to go." When she went to speak, he put his palm up to stop her and then pointed into the passageway. "Listen to me. I dug this out with my bare hands. I kept this to myself all these years because I was going to take the one thing in this hateful place that I love out of it. It makes all the sense in my world that you would be who uses it."

Nyx grabbed at his tunic. "But I can help find—"

"Don't ask me to carry that guilt with me."

"What are you talking about? Carry what—"

He put his hands on her shoulders, the chains draping down the front of her body. "I just watched the closest thing I had to a friend kill himself. For you and me. For us. So we could survive. If you die down here? Then Kane sacrificed himself for nothing. And if I leave here without my young? I'm dead up there. So you're going now, and you're going to get out, and you're going to live—"

"We can do this together," she said desperately.

"No, we can't. If the Command finds you—"

"She could be dead." Nyx winced as she remembered Kane reaching up behind his neck. "There's a possibility she didn't get out of the Hive's collapse alive—"

"She doesn't matter to me. I don't care whether she lives or dies. But my young . . ." He shook his head. "I need to go. I can't stay any longer. You can hear what's going on where we were."

"The cell. That's whose cell it was—"

"I have to go." Jack's eyes watered. "I wish it didn't have to end like this—"

"You're choosing this."

"We've been through that before. I haven't chosen any of this."

Don't step away, she thought.

Just as he stepped away.

Nyx glanced into the passage at the soft glow of the light. In a low voice, she said, "You're killing me right now. I might as well stay here because you are killing me."

"Nyx, I'm sorry—"

"I hope you find what you're looking for."

Stumbling into the tunnel, Nyx did not look back. She was in too much pain. If she saw Jack's hollowed-out face, those blue eyes, that sorrow, she would turn around and start begging—or, worse, just follow him wherever he went.

She was about ten feet into the passageway when she heard the click of the panel shutting.

That was when the tears came. She cried as she continued forward, as she passed underneath the bald light bulb, as she started to limp. She wept so hard, it was as if she were running again, her lungs on fire, her throat raw.

Loud as her sorrow was, there was no reason

425

to stifle the sounds. What the hell did she care at this point.

As the light faded, she found herself on an ascent, and as she adjusted her weight forward, a sensation of wetness inside her right boot barged to the forefront of her awareness. She wondered what puddle she had stepped in—but then she smelled the blood.

Looking down at her leg, things were too dim to really see where the injury was.

Nyx kept going, the limping becoming worse with every step. Nausea surged. Dizzying waves of weakness battered at her. She stopped thinking and knew only her breath.

In the end, she didn't feel alive anymore, even as she kept going up the ever steeper incline. She just existed, and proof of this was that she came to the end of the passageway on a full-body bump: She walked right into the rock wall in front of her, knocking her forehead, scraping her bare arm, stubbing her boot—the good one, not the one with blood in it.

For a moment, she just stood there, her sluggish mind refusing to process what to do next. But then her hand, her right hand, the one she had killed with, reached out on its own accord in spite of the cuffs and patted at the wall. Three feet from the ground.

He had carved this, she thought as the uneven nature of the stone registered. Jack had somehow chipped away at the rock and made this exit.

She should wait here. To see if he and his young came—

The switch was hit just as that pitiful idea struck her, and the panel that rolled back seemed a condemnation on the fantasy.

Nyx weaved on her feet. And then she went forward. She wasn't sure why, though. What was she doing here?

Her feet just started walking, taking her through a portal. When she got on the other side, she looked back just as the panel started to shut itself. Three seconds. Jack had told her, back a million years ago, that the delay was three seconds.

The weak light of that bulb, far in the distance, got cut off.

As everything went pitch black, Nyx's balance shifted like gravity had forgotten about her and she was about to float off into space. She caught herself by throwing out her cuffed hands.

If she fucked around for much longer, the question of her getting out was going to be answered in the negative when she fainted from blood loss.

Blindly, she put one foot in front of the other in the pitch black. Both her arms were off to the side, touching the wall. It was the only orientation she had.

Underneath her, the ground rose some more— and then rose sharply.

Finally, she was on all fours, grabbing onto

loose, damp dirt with her tight-knit pair of hands.

The fresh air was something that crept up on her awareness. But the higher she went, the stronger the clean, bright scent became. Rain. Grass. Flowers.

Nyx was still crying, tears running down her face, when she finally emerged from the earth like an animal, covered with dirt and blood.

As the gentle rain fell upon her and the wind swirled around, nature seemed to greet her as a long-lost relation. But there was no time to think about that. Without warning—maybe the whole trip out had been the warning—her legs went loose underneath her and she landed on her knees.

Lifting her face to the heavens, she tried to see the stars. Which was dumb. Where did she think the rain drops were coming from?

It wasn't like the universe was weeping for all that she had lost.

Her sister. Her male. Her hope for anything good in the future.

For even if she made it home, she was a different person from when she'd left. She had killed. She had loved and lost. And she knew a family secret that she was going to keep from everyone else.

Sitting back on her heels, she tilted her head to the clouds above so that the rain coated her face, cool fingers tapping lightly on her flushed and overheated cheeks, and the open wound at her temple, and her hair, which she had braided and tied with one of Jack's leather thongs.

She let herself fall to the side.

The mud of the ground caught her in a sloppy embrace.

She didn't know where she was. She didn't care.

Nyx closed her eyes and let go of everything . . . and as she did, she realized that Jack was right. Freedom was so much more than being physically unrestrained. Even though she was back up here, she remained chained to where she had been, what she had seen, what she had done.

Who she had known.

And who had forced her to go.

It was a lifetime sentence.

CHAPTER THIRTY-NINE

As the escape passage's panel locked back into place, Jack laid his hand on the stone and said a prayer unto the Scribe Virgin that his love would get out safely. Then he gathered up the chain links and started running. As he raced along the empty tunnels, he thought of all the places the Command might have hidden their young.

He returned to the private quarters, retracing the roundabout way he'd had to go with Nyx because of the barricades of the lockdown. It was inefficient and a waste of time—and his only option. When he arrived at the arch marked with white slashes, he shot forward, punching through the steel door—

Blood. Fresh blood.

So much of it, and from so many different individuals, he couldn't trace all the sources.

His footfalls were loud against the tiled floor as he thundered down to the young's cell. Which was open.

Just outside of it, on the ground, was the wicker basket, the one that contained the Command's pet.

The lid was off.

"No . . . *no!*"

There was blood on the bed. Blood on the floor. Blood in a trail out of the cell—

The laughter started soft, but did not stay that way.

Jack looked down the corridor. Standing with feet planted over a still-twitching corpse, the Command was unhinged, and stained head to toe in red.

"What did you do," he demanded. Even though he knew.

And there were so many bodies to show it. Guards and prisoners alike littered the hall, their bodies tangled one into another. A dozen or more.

But there was only one that he cared about.

He'd never thought she would hurt their young. It was the one thing they had in common.

The Command smiled, her fangs flashing white in the midst of the blood that covered her face and dripped from her chin, her hands, her red hair. "I took care of things. I took care of everything. *Everything!*"

The laughter rose to the level of hysteria, and that was when he noticed what was in her hand.

"Oh, do you want to see my souvenir?" she said. "Would you like to see my souvenir?"

She screamed with maniacal mirth as she held up the heart.

"I got my souvenir from this place," she yelled at the top of her lungs. "I got my souvenir! And I'm not sharing with you!"

Her face was a distorted, ugly mask of horror, her eyes crazed and bloodshot.

"What did you do—" Jack launched himself into a run, attacking her, grabbing her by the throat and shoving her against the wall. "What— did—you—*do!*"

Bang. Bang. Bang.

In the back of his mind, he wondered what that noise was. *Bang. Bang. Bang—*

"You. Fucking. Bitch!"

Bang. Bang. BANG—

It was the Command. Her body was making the noise as he beat her against the wall, breaking through the lath and plaster with her torso, smashing the finished panels into pieces. And even as her head lolled forward and she clearly lost consciousness, he continued, over and over again, taking all of it out on her, the violations, the murder of their young, the murders of his friends, the danger to Nyx, who he loved. Matted red hair lashed his face and shoulders, and from out of the choking sandalwood spices she wore to conceal her sex, he smelled her own blood begin to flow.

And he would have continued. Until her skin was but a bag for everything he'd mangled.

Except from out of the corner of his eye, he saw something race toward him, something low to the ground, something furred—

The wicker basket. The animal therein that had been freed by its owner.

Jack looked toward the creature. The thing was part groundhog, part piranha, part rabid raccoon, with short grungy fur and feet that splayed out to the side. It ran over the bodies that littered the hallway in a wave formation, like a weasel, but it was much bigger.

And it was snarling, its red-stained muzzle peeled back from its dagger-like teeth.

Black eyes, matte and mostly blind, were trained on Jack.

He wheeled around, keeping the Command between him and the imminent attack—

"You love me . . ." The words were gurgled, and blood splattered his face as the female he hated with everything in him spoke. "You love me."

She lifted her head and those hazel eyes focused obsessively on his own. "You will always love me—"

The Command let out a high-pitched scream and her body arched in agony.

The creature had leapt up and was feasting on the back of her skull.

Jack shoved the female away from him, and as he jumped free, the Command kicked and thrashed, her hands slapping and clawing at the animal that was eating . . . chewing . . . swallowing . . . at an open wound in the back of her head.

Jack had started the process by banging,

434

banging, banging her against the wall. But that hungry little demon she kept in that wicker crate finished the job.

And Jack watched. Every time he blinked, he saw that wicker basket brought out onto the dais. He saw the underground beast released. He heard the screams of the prisoners and recalled the brutal deaths. Mostly, the creature had gone for the bellies, chewing its way inside, consuming the intestines that fell out like loose sausage in casing, slipping, sliding on the stone floor.

It appeared its palate was equally amenable to brains.

Blindly, Jack turned away, hurried away. When he tripped on a dead guard, he quickly recovered his balance and went faster.

The creature did not care for the already dead. So he needed to hurry, though he did not know where to go.

Weapons. He needed weapons.

The Command's private quarters came up to him, not the other way around, the unreality of everything making the segregated compound move, not him. He entered the chamber and looked to the table, to the tranquilizer gun and the darts. His hands were curiously steady as he reached out—

Chains. He was dripping with chains.

He hadn't even noticed them when he'd gone after the Command.

Slinging them over his shoulder, he got the tranquilizer and the darts, and when he turned away, something on the bed caught his eye.

It was a piece of clothing.

Going over, he put down the tools that had been used to subdue him and picked up the windbreaker that smelled of Nyx. He pressed the folds to his face and breathed in. For the briefest of moments, he couldn't smell blood. He only smelled . . . his female.

He tied the sleeves of the thing around his neck as if it were a scarf. Then he grabbed what he had found and left the room.

Stepping free, he looked down the corridor. The creature had left.

Nothing was moving.

He felt numb as he went to the left, jogging down the corridor toward the work area. There were fewer bodies of guards here, and then none at all, the fresh corpses like a trail extinguished.

Punching into the work area, he didn't bother to hide his presence. And there was no reason to. No one was inside the fifty-by-fifty-foot white-walled processing facility. The individual workstations were in shambles, stainless steel tables toppled, chairs pushed out of the way, plastic baggies and powder-covered scales on the floor. As he pressed on, he found nothing but diesel fumes and tire tracks where the transports had been lined up.

Gone, gone, gone.

It was all over.

But then what had he expected to find here?

Jack turned. And turned. And turned.

As he circled where he stood, he saw through the walls, past the honeycombs of tunnels, into all the spaces he had lived in for a century. He saw those who he had known as well as one could know anybody in the underground. He saw those he had endured, and those he had ignored.

He tried to imagine leaving. Going back up to the real world, with all its changes.

When his young's body was somewhere down here.

It was all his fault. If he had somehow been stronger, he wouldn't have condemned his young to this life. To this suffering. To the death at the hands of a *mahmen* who was an unholy terror.

If only he had fought harder.

If only his body had not gotten aroused against his will.

If only . . .

As the distant rumbling of the collapses registered, he went back to the Command's area, keeping the dart gun at the ready in case the creature fell upon him. But instead of returning to where he had been, he went into the rough part, where the tile beneath his feet stopped and so did the finish on the walls.

Bare tunnel now, and when he sent his will forth, candles flared.

As he approached the Wall, he held his breath.

There was nothing out of place. And no addition to what had been carved into the black rock since he had brought Nyx here—not that there would have been time for that.

As he thought of Nyx, he missed her so much that he felt as though his heart had been struck a terrible blow with a fist.

But if his young had to spend an eternity down here—alive or dead—so did he. Some debts could never be repaid, and he had been a damnation upon his progeny before the birthing had even commenced.

That needed to be righted by a sacrifice worthy of the curse.

He focused on the name Nyx had lingered over, the name of the female who had been her sister . . . the name of the scourge upon which all of Jack's suffering had been based. To paraphrase Lucan, may he rest in peace, destiny could indeed be a bitch.

How were they one and the same, Nyx's sister and his tormentor?

What did it matter.

"Where is the body," Jack growled at the Wall. "What did you do with mine dead."

CHAPTER FORTY

The light was so bright, Nyx knew that she had passed out and been found by the dawn, sure as if the sun was a predator that had closed the distance with its prey and was prepared to claim its victim.

So bright. Her eyes burned even though her lids were closed, so she dragged her arm over her face.

She should have tried harder to get home. But as with most decisions, if you didn't resolve things for yourself, the choice was made for you. She had intended to only rest and catch her breath for a moment—

Squish, squish . . . squish . . .

The sound was like a pair of kitchen sponges coming at her. And then there were a pair of soft cracks, right beside her head.

"Where are you hurt?"

That voice . . . that male voice. Nyx lifted her head—or tried to. Her whole body hurt and her neck was incredibly stiff, so she didn't get far.

"Can I move you? Or is your spine broken."

"Not broken . . ." she whispered hoarsely. Because this had to be a dream.

Her grandfather couldn't possibly be here, in the middle of nowhere, turning up just as the dawn claimed her body with its beautiful warmth.

"Is it you?" she said.

Her grandfather—or her mental manifestation of him—picked her up, one arm under her knees, the other behind her shoulders. As he carried her over muddy ground, his familiar scent—that blend of pipe tobacco and cedar boards—registered in her nose, bringing with it an awareness that this was real. *He* was real.

Forcing her eyes to focus, she took in his lined face, his white hair, his workman's shoulders and workman's shirt. Abruptly, she was overcome, tears flowing onto her cheeks.

"This is really you," she choked out.

He, on the other hand, stayed completely calm, in the way he always was, his attention fixated on something ahead of them, something he was going toward.

So yup, he truly had found her, wherever she was.

"Can you stand?" he said.

"Yes." She didn't want to disappoint him or seem weak in any way. "I can stand."

Old habits and all. She had always wanted to live up to his expectations. The trouble was going to be that limb and that boot full of blood, however. She'd been injured somehow, although she couldn't remember when. During the explosion? Or when she'd landed with the

Command on top of her as rocks had fallen everywhere.

Oh, God . . . Janelle was dead.

"Here's the car," her grandfather announced. "I have to put you down."

"Okay." Nyx sniffled and wiped her face on the sleeve of the prison tunic. "All right."

When he lowered her to the ground, she wobbled and had to lift her bad foot. Prepared to be left to fend for herself in the balance department, she was surprised as he held on to her arm while he opened the rear door . . . to the Volvo.

The sight of the station wagon got her crying. It was about everything that had gone before . . . the way things had been and never would be again.

"Get in," her grandfather said.

She couldn't move. She couldn't speak. She hopped a couple of times so she could face the front of the station wagon. The hood was uneven and held tight by bungee cords, but he'd obviously gotten the motor back to functioning.

How long had she been gone? She'd thought it was two days . . . three at the most.

"You can get in now," her grandfather said.

"You fixed it."

"Well, some of the damage is repaired. There's still a ways to go before she looks good—"

Despite her cuffs, Nyx threw out a hand and

squeezed his forearm. As she pegged him right in the eye, she wanted a hug from him, but knew that would not be coming—and not because of how things had been left.

There were other ways of connecting, though.

"You were right," she said hoarsely. "Janelle was guilty. I am so sorry—"

Her grandfather shook his head and looked away, a ruddy flush turning his wrinkled face bright red. As if he might be, underneath the surface, every bit as emotional as she was. "Lie down across the seats if you can't sit up. The sun is coming—"

"I was wrong. I'm so sorry—"

"Get in—"

"No," Nyx said sharply. "We're talking about this. Janelle was guilty. She killed that old male. She deserved . . . her sentence. I was wrong about what I thought happened with you turning her in, and I apologize. I thought . . . well, that doesn't matter anymore."

Her grandfather's old eyes drifted to the horizon, which had a subtle, soon-to-be-deadly glow kindling. "Your sister has always been who she was."

"I know that now."

After a moment, he focused on her. "Did you see her, then?"

Nyx cleared her throat. "No. She'd died long before I got there."

• • •

The trip back to the farmhouse took almost half an hour, and Nyx tried to ground herself in the familiar stretch of highway. In the low range of mountains. In the small town they passed through with its Sunoco station, and its garden center, and its diner.

But it was all a foreign country. She could barely read the signs around the gas pumps and understand what they were saying.

When her grandfather finally turned in to their farm's long driveway, she sat up from her collapse against the back seats. In the milky headlights—one of which was blinking like it was about to short out—the house looked the same. There was the familiar front porch, and the rows of windows, and the roof, and the chimney . . .

She told herself this was her home. In her heart . . . she felt nothing. As much as she recognized all the details, this was a stranger's house, her memories from inside and outside impossible to connect to.

The Volvo's brakes squeaked, and her grandfather put the gearshift into park. When he got out, she fumbled with her door handle. Her fingers refused to grasp anything.

Her grandfather opened things up for her. And he reached inside, offering her his hand. "Let me help you."

"I'm okay." Yeah, the hell she was. Her voice was so thin, she could barely hear it herself.

Her grandfather took her arm anyway, and she relied on him to get out of the back. As she weaved on her feet, she glanced to the front of the car.

"So how did you fix it so fast?"

"You've been gone three days."

Nyx turned her head to him—and cursed as a shot of pain ripped up her spine. "It felt like longer."

It felt like forever.

The screen door slapped shut, the sound making her look to the porch.

As Posie raced out of the farmhouse and down the steps, her pink flowered dress and her blond hair streamed behind her. But she didn't make it to the car.

She stopped dead halfway across the lawn.

As her eyes went wide, she dropped her hold on her skirting and clasped her mouth—and all Nyx could think of was . . . she didn't have the damn strength for this. After everything she had been through, she didn't have the energy to deal with Posie's hysteria.

Nyx exhaled and shook her head—

With resolve, Posie seemed to collect herself, regathering that dress. And as she crossed the distance to the Volvo, her eyes were blinking quick, but there were no tears.

"Come on," she said calmly, "let's get you inside."

As Nyx's fragile, hysterical sister took hold of her arm, and quietly and with purpose, led the way to the house, Nyx went along without argument or a false show of strength. It was like the pair of them had traded whole portions of their personalities.

Or at least lent them for a little bit.

The stairs seemed next to impossible, and Nyx had to rely heavily on Posie to make it up the steps at all. And getting to the front door felt like she was sprinting ten full miles.

Inside the house, she looked around and again felt no connection to any of it. Not the rustic, handmade furniture, even though she had arranged the chairs and sofa and side tables. Not the photographs on the mantel or the painting on the wall, even though they all featured family members. And the rug underfoot was a total mystery.

"Shower," she said. Mostly because she didn't want to talk to anyone and figured it would buy her some time alone.

She didn't want to speak. She didn't want to eat. She just wanted to lie down.

Posie took her to the bathroom. Opened the door. Pointed to the tub. "Bath."

"Shower."

"No, bath. You won't be able to stand up in the hot water for long."

445

When Posie forced them inside and shut the door, Nyx shook her head. "I can do it. I don't need help—"

"You must need to pee."

Nyx blinked. Looked at the toilet. Wondered if she could remember how one worked.

Strange, she didn't recall how she'd gone to the bathroom when she had been down below. She must have gone. She just couldn't remember how or where.

She couldn't remember whole parts of the experience beforehand. Just like she couldn't remember much of her time in the farmhouse. It was as if she had a drape of amnesia over everything that had ever happened to her.

"I'll start the water." Posie pointed to the toilet. "You sit there."

As her sister didn't budge, Nyx murmured, "You've changed."

"You've been gone for a lifetime, as it turns out."

As they stared at each other, Nyx thought, *Shit, the young pretrans.* Posie had not only had to deal with that death, but also with the fact that she hadn't known where Nyx was.

"Grandfather told me," Posie said. "Where you went. Did you find her?"

Nyx slowly shook her head and braced herself.

"Well." Posie turned to the tub and started the water. "There's that then."

"Are you okay?" Nyx asked.

Posie bent down and put her hand in the rush. Then she adjusted the hot side. "I'm worried about you."

"I'm fine."

"I don't think you'd tell me if you weren't." Glancing back, her sister nodded at Nyx's clothes. "Do you need help getting undressed? And sit down on that toilet now."

"I will. But I'd like a little privacy."

"I'm checking in on you in five minutes." When Nyx tried to talk, Posie put up her hand. "Just stop. I'm not going to argue with you about common sense."

Posie went to the door. "Five minutes. And if you lock this door, I'm going to get grandfather's axe and chop it into kindling."

As her sister quietly shut things behind her, Nyx stared at the panels. There were two towels hanging on a rod, and for a moment, she wondered what they were there for. Turning to the sink, the two toothbrushes in the stand caught her eye. With a shaking hand, she touched the grip of the pink one. Of Posie's.

She remembered putting her toothbrush in her backpack.

So naive. So incredibly naive.

Posie wasn't the only one who had aged a million years in such a short time.

Nyx lifted her eyes to the mirror over the

sink—and gasped. A stranger stared back at her, one with dirt and mud and blood on her face, in her hair, down her throat. Her eyes seemed like they'd changed color, and there were deep hollows in her cheeks that had not been there before. She looked as though she had been to hell and back.

With a shaking hand, she touched the wound on her temple—and then noticed her chipped nails and the raw places on her wrists.

Where had the cuffs gone, she wondered. She'd had them when she'd emerged from underground.

As her arm started to tremble, she lowered it and leaned into the basin.

Where was Jack? Had he found his young? Was he still alive?

With painful clarity, a memory of her male, with his long hair loose around his muscled shoulders, his brilliant blue eyes heavy lidded and looking at her, came to the forefront of her mind. The image lingered, tangible as a living, breathing thing, as ephemeral and heartbreaking as a ghost—

Dripping got her attention and she glanced over her shoulder.

The tub was starting to overflow. How long had she been staring at herself?

She reached to the side and cranked the faucets off.

That was when she looked down at herself. Her

tunic was covered with mud and blood, just like her face. As it was damp, the folds were cold, and as she peeled the thing off, the smell of the prison entered her nose.

The knocking on the closed door made her curse. "I'm just getting undressed. Give me a damn minute."

That's right, she told herself. Come back from the brink of death . . . to bitch at your sister like it was business as usual.

Posie's voice was strident. "Five more minutes then."

Nyx shook her head as she started to undo her pants. When her back let out a holler, she twisted around to inspect the damage. The bruising from when she'd landed after the explosion was extensive, the purple patches up at her shoulders and down on one hip.

She thought about her strangling the Command, those cuffs wrapped around the female's throat— and suddenly she remembered. Her grandfather had taken them off. In the car. He'd gotten behind the wheel, leaned into the passenger seat, and she'd heard something like change rattling in a pocket. Then he'd turned and told her to put out her hands.

He'd had a ring of tiny keys. The sixth one had worked.

Moving her shoulder into the mirror's view, she pushed at the red stripe on the outside of her biceps. And remembered getting shot. In fact, every time she blinked, more flashes of memory came back, and they were so vivid, she heard the sounds and smelled the smells that went along with them.

Screams. Moldy, damp air. Gunpowder.

Blood. So much blood.

Thrusting the recollections aside, she refocused on her pants. They came off only with effort, the wet, muddy fabric clinging to her legs—and she had a thought about how much of a mess she must have made in the back of the Volvo.

When she dropped them to the old tiled floor, the fleshy sound they made turned her stomach.

Before she got in the water, she used the toilet because Posie had said she had to. And it was the best piddle she had had in her entire life, the only thing that had felt good in what seemed like an eternity.

The bath was even better. But it came with the price of thinking of the hidden pool. Of Jack. Of them being together.

As she sank into the warm, gentle embrace of the water, she knew she was going to have to get used to the mourning. It was a part of her now, something as permanent as her arms and legs, as dispositive as the beat of her heart and the draw of her lungs.

Laying her head back on the curve of the tub, she closed her eyes and the tears that escaped were hot as they slid down her cheeks . . . and joined the now dirty brown bath water.

Knock, knock—

"I'm fucking *fine*," she snapped.

The door opened anyway. Posie leaned in. Looked in. And then retreated with a warning that there would be another five-minute check coming.

Aware that she had to get on with it, Nyx sat up and gripped the sides of the tub. Rising to her feet in the water, she couldn't believe how filthy things had gotten. She turned on the shower at the same time she took the drain plug out.

Posie was wrong. She did manage to stand on her own, although she made sure she didn't let things get too hot.

Soap was a revelation. Shampoo and conditioner as well.

Nyx reflected, as she tilted her head back and winced from the sting at her temple and the stiffness, that when you did something every day, you got used to the benefits of the service. Cleanliness. Clean water. Food that was unspoiled and prepared to taste. Rest on a soft bed in a safe place. It was a luxury to complain about inconveniences like parking tickets and coworkers who reheated cod in the company microwave and storms that took your power for a night and plumbing that leaked.

Nyx had to wash her hair through twice.

And when she got out, the dirt rim around the white porcelain was so thick, it was like a stain. She had a thought that she should get the Scrubbing Bubbles right now, but she didn't have the energy. Then, as she toweled off, she realized she hadn't brought anything in with her to change—

On the back of the door, a pink bathrobe had materialized on the towel hook.

Posie had clearly done another check-in.

Nyx wrapped herself in the softness and cranked the tie around her waist. As she went to open the door, she noted every single ache and pain. Considering what she had been through, it could have been so much worse.

She had Jack to thank for all of that. His blood, so pure and strong, had sustained her.

The bathroom door opened soundlessly. Then again, it had had plenty of Posie warm-ups.

Beneath her bare feet, the floorboards creaked softly and she smelled something coming from the kitchen that made her mouth water. Onions sautéing. Beef.

Posie was making her something to eat—

Nyx stopped in the archway. Across the shallow space, at the table with its four chairs, there were two males sitting down in front of the place settings.

The one with his back to her had thin, small shoulders and shaggy brown hair.

Just as Posie pivoted at the stove, one hand on the pan's handle, the other on a spatula, the pretrans did the same, his narrow torso twisting around in the chair.

His eyes, his brilliant, gleaming, aquamarine blue eyes, looked up at Nyx.

Someone made a strangled sound.

Herself?

Yes.

That was all she remembered as she passed out cold where she stood.

CHAPTER FORTY-ONE

The following evening, as the moon rose over the farm and the heat dropped some, Nyx stepped out onto the porch. As she looked over the property, the barn and the pasture were like something out of an artist's rendering, so perfect and homey, with the graceful, full trees, and the healthy grass, and the fences that undulated across the meadows.

It was a very all-American kind of expanse. As long as you didn't know that it was owned and built and maintained by vampires.

Her grandfather came out tamping tobacco into his pipe, the screen door clapping shut behind him. "Do you know where we're going?"

She glanced back at him, noting the fabric roll under his arm. "Yes."

"Do you have any questions?"

"No."

"Let's go out to the barn, then."

They walked side by side across the fragrant, freshly cut lawn. The maple trees seemed more beautiful than she remembered, the boughs laden with their emerald green, late-August leaves. Soon, when the weather turned, they would be red and gold, and then finally, crunchy brown upon the ground.

"Actually, I do have a question," she said. "How did you know Janelle had killed the old male? How were you so sure?"

Her grandfather put his pipe between his teeth and lit it with his old, serviceable lighter, clustering down with his palms, hunching to keep the breeze from disturbing the flame's work. And then it was *puff, puff, puff* . . . the fragrant smoke rising up.

She was becoming convinced he was going to ignore her when he finally spoke.

"He called me. Two nights before he was killed."

When she looked over sharply, her grandfather showed no signs of noticing her surprised reaction. He just took his pipe out of his mouth and peered into the belly as if checking to see it was sufficiently embered.

"He told me that she had threatened him," he said as he stopped and had to relight. When things were properly going, he resumed speaking, but not walking. "He called me as her male next of kin, in accordance with the Old Laws. At first, I thought it was disciplinary in nature. Then I realized that he was scared of her. I interceded on his behalf. I told her there was no cause to go over to the property again, that her services were no longer required."

"And what happened," Nyx prompted when he fell silent.

Her grandfather started walking again and did not respond until they were inside the barn. And even then, he waited until he was standing by a guide boat that, going by the sweet smell of varnish, he had recently put a first coat on.

He puffed on his pipe, releasing clouds of white that drifted over his head. "I am an old male now, and fifty years ago, I had already been on the planet for five hundred and seventy-three years. In all that time, I have never been looked at like that."

"How did she . . ." Nyx's voice got unreliable so she had to let the words go.

"Janelle had no soul in that moment. Behind that stare, there was . . . absolutely nothing." He put up his forefinger. "No, that isn't true. There was logic and calculation. Nothing of any humanity, however. No love or connection to me as a member of her bloodline. And that was when I saw the true nature of her. That was when I realized . . . that I had been living all of those years with a predator."

Nyx shook her head as she remembered the female's cold stare through the steel mesh of the holding cell. "I didn't know, either," she whispered.

"I fault my own reasoning. I assumed . . ." He ran his hand along the gunwale of the gleaming golden boat. "I assumed females couldn't think like that, be like that. Of course, there had been flashes of strange detachment from her, things that lingered from time to time, but I disregarded all of that because she was my granddaughter and I loved her."

"She was my sister." Nyx walked over to the lineup of orderly tools on the wall above the workstation. "I did the same."

"The next night, the old male called and told me she was welcome back on his property. Even now, I wondered what she did to get that result. I can only guess. I decided to stay out of it. I doubted myself . . . and I was, like him, scared of her. When she came home from work early the following night, with that cash and that so-called gift?" He shook his head. "I knew what had to have happened. I came out here, so she would think I was working, and dematerialized over to the house. I demanded to see the body. The butler tried to stop me, but I rushed upstairs and followed the scent of death. I saw the old male propped up in his bed, lying against the pillows. His butler informed me that it was his time. That he had been suffering the rapid descent of age. I pretended to be overcome and require a glass of water. When the *doggen* left me, I went across and inspected the male. His neck was broken, snapped free of the spinal cord. Old age does not do that."

"And how were you sure it was Janelle?"

"I could scent her soap on his nightclothes, his

458

hair, his skin. The *doggen* was too discreet to mention any of that. Too discreet to mention the broken neck, too." Her grandfather looked over, his eyes sharp. "Just so that we're clear, I have no love for the *glymera*. They are a useless drain on species resources. Except I had to protect you and Posie. Janelle was fulminating in her madness, on the cusp, but not quite there. It was my only chance. I knew the aristocrats would not hesitate to seize the assets in the event it was murder, and that they would therefore act precipitously on my information. They did so. I lied to her to get her to go unto the Council. I told her she was due a proper inheritance from the old male she had killed. That the notice of allegation had been a mistake. She was less smart than she was aggressive. She believed me."

He shook his head. "Or perhaps, as I had discounted her deviancy, she disregarded the risk to her freedom because I was her close relation. Or . . . maybe she was just overconfident. As with the posed body, which she assumed people would take at face value, she might well have thought she would be believed. I do not know. What I was sure about, however, was that I had to keep you and Posie safe. Once she had the taste of death, she was going to hunger for it, and she might well have started at home."

Nyx ran her hands over the chipped and worn surface of the workstation, at which her grandfather had spent hours. "You did the right thing."

"I couldn't bear the risk that she'd hurt either of the two of you. You both are, and always have been, all I have left to live for."

Shifting her eyes over to him, she tried not to look so shocked. "Do you really feel like that?"

Her grandfather puffed on that pipe. When his stare finally met her own, there were unshed tears in his eyes. "I have always felt this way. I lost my daughter. My *shellan*. My parents. The friends I had, the cousins I used to know. My life has long been winding down, and there has been much mourning for me. You and Posie? You have brought me such joy. Posie with her warmth, you with your brave nature. You two are everything that keeps me going."

Her grandfather cleared his throat. "And I am so proud of you, Nyxanlis. For following your destiny. And I am proud of Posie for learning her own strength these last few nights. Both of you have changed, and now I can go in peace."

"What?" Nyx gasped. "Are you ill—"

"No, no." He motioned with his hand dismissively, as if he were wiping away the words. "I am fine. But when it is my time to go unto the Fade, I now know you and Posie can take care of yourselves. You will be fine without me, and that gives me great relief."

Nyx choked up. "Oh, grandfather."

When he opened his arms, she rushed across

and threw herself against him. As he hugged her close, she grabbed on hard.

"I love you, grandpapa," she said hoarsely.

"And I, you, my Nyx. You have made me so proud. Always."

They stayed as they were, and she breathed deep, smelling the scent of fresh pine shavings and the perfume of the varnish and the smoke from the pipe. She didn't want to cry, and she didn't.

She was afraid once she opened the floodgates, there would be no stemming the course of the emotional release. And they had work to do.

Nyx was the one who stepped back, though she had waited her entire life for just this moment. In response, her grandfather nodded once, and she knew that he was going to put his emotions in the vault again and lock it all down tight. But she understood now why someone would do that. And just because you couldn't see something did not mean it didn't exist.

It was like the stars behind a cloud cover.

Like Jack beneath the earth.

"I'm ready," she said.

Her grandfather nodded and motioned her toward a table in the far corner. The surface was covered by a coarse Army blanket, and what was beneath the heavy weight of that felt made things bumpy.

"I have what we need." Drawing the blanket

back, he revealed seven handguns, two rifles, a broadsword, five holsters of clips, and—

"Are those hand grenades?" Nyx asked as she breathed in and smelled gun oil.

"Pull the pin and you have fifteen seconds to throw and run."

"Good."

As he put down the gray cloth bundle that he'd kept under his arm, and began to gather weapons himself, she picked up a nine millimeter, checked that there were bullets in the clip and the safety was on, and tucked the gun into the back of her jeans.

"Here, put this on." Her grandfather held forward an empty holster. "And pull out your shirt to hide it all."

She did as he suggested while he cross-chested a setup that included two of the three projectiles, two of the handguns, and most of the ammunition.

"Are you leaving that sword?" she asked as she picked up one of the rifles.

Her grandfather stared at the weapon with a sad longing that was more properly reserved for leaving a cherished pet home alone for five weeks.

"Yes," he said. "But I think the grenades are going to be fun."

"Fun?" Nyx had to smile. "I thought you were a craftsman."

"I am." He picked up the cloth bundle again and put it back under his arm. "But I've been other things, too."

"Mysterious."

"We all have different sides to us."

"So I'm learning." She glanced around the workshop. "Are you worried this might be the last time you see this place?"

"It will be what it will be." Her grandfather pulled a loose flannel work shirt on over his arsenal. "I learned long ago never to predict. All you can do is influence what you can and endure the rest."

Nyx nodded. "Amen to that. Let's go."

CHAPTER FORTY-TWO

Rhage reported in on time to the Audience House. Part of his prompt arrival for his shift guarding his King was his commitment to his job and to the pursuit of excellence in everything he did. There was also the unrelenting need to be there for his brothers, in whatever way they needed him.

"Good evening, Fritz," he said as he came in through the kitchen.

The butler, dressed superbly in his black-and-white formal uniform, pivoted around from the counter by the oven—and in his hands was a sight to behold: A sterling silver tray the size of a car tire bearing an assortment of homemade Danish, fresh off the baking sheet, whisked with white icing stripes.

"Sire, your timing is perfect." Fritz's wrinkly face stretched into a wide smile, like theater drapes parting to reveal a movie screen. "I have just prepared these for the waiting room. But you must help yourself."

Rhage clasped the front of his muscle shirt and wished he could bow without risking a fainting spell—on the butler's part. Which would mean all those Danish would end up on the floor.

"This means so much, Fritz. Thank you." He

took the tray. "This is just the snack I was looking for."

Fritz seemed momentarily nonplussed, but then he bent low at the waist. "Indeed, I am honored you would think so highly of my provisions. May I please get you a beverage? You will need to clear your palate."

Taking a test bite of a cherry one, Rhage knew—not that he needed the confirmation—that Fritz was a gift from heaven, sent to reaffirm for hungry, set-upon mortals everywhere that goodness did indeed exist in the world.

"This is amazing," he said as he chewed. "And I would love some orange juice."

"A liter or gallon?"

"Just a liter would be fine."

"Allow me to fresh squeeze it for you and I shall bring it into the Audience Room right away!"

Fritz seemed as excited at the prospect of halving and squeezing as you might expect somebody to jazz up over a trip to a resort. And Rhage was more than happy to be the recipient of some vitamin C benediction.

Except a quick review of the countertops revealed a copious lack of backup Danish.

"Worry not, sire." The *doggen* indicated the oven. "There is another batch as yet baking. And the appointments for the evening have been set back a half an hour. So there is plenty of time to prepare more—and they will be warm for our citizens."

"Well, if you look at it like that, I'm doing a public service."

"You are always in service unto the race, sire."

"And you are good for my ego and my expanding waistline."

Basking in his good mood, Rhage would have whistled as he made his way to the front of the formal Federal, but that was an impossibility. Especially as he tried one of the lemon jobbies.

"Mmm."

Strolling into the foyer, he nodded at the receptionist sitting at the desk in the waiting area. "How we doing tonight?"

The female smiled and sat back from her laptop. "Very well. And yourself?"

"Better now." He lifted the tray. "These will cure a multitude of ills. Care for some?"

"No, thank you."

"How about only one?"

"I'm good." She smiled. "But I appreciate the offer."

"Lemme know if you change your mind. I'm across the way."

It was with the saunter of a male secure in the number of Danish available for his imminent consumption that Rhage entered the Audience Room—or, as the space had been known back when Darius had built the mansion, the dining room. No more eating in here, though.

Present company excluded, of course.

But yeah, nope, the long mahogany table had been moved out. The eight million carved chairs as well. Gone, too, were the sideboards and the candelabra. In place of all that? A pair of arm-chairs in front of the marble fireplace that was currently, because of the heat of summer, set with unlit birch logs. There was also a desk where Saxton, the King's solicitor, sat when he was on duty, and some other chairs off to the side. The brocade drapes at the long windows were always pulled—nosy human neighbors being what they were, even in Richie Rich parts of town like this one—and the Persian carpet, which glowed like a jewel underfoot, was allowed to take center stage in a way that would never have happened if the room had been fully fur-nished and used for what it had been originally intended.

Rhage took a load off on one of the chairs that were against the far wall, so he could see through the open double doors. Then he settled his tray in his lap and picked up his second cherry Danish. He used only his right hand and only his fore-finger and thumb.

White icing, you know, could get sticky—

"Is this a private moment or can I watch as long as I don't record."

Rhage smiled at Vishous as the brother walked in—and tried to make it look like he wasn't curling himself protectively around his tray.

"Don't worry," V muttered as he lit up a hand-rolled. "I'm not hungry."

"I have literally never said that. In my life."

"I live with you, remember. I know better than to try to take your Danish."

Exhaling, V went over to where he kept his ashtray on the edge of the desk, a leather-clad hard-ass with a goatee, tattoos at his temple, and all the compassion of a sawed-off shotgun.

"I like my arms and legs right where they are, and I'm already down one testicle."

"I would never," Rhage muttered around a mouthful.

"You absolutely would. And speaking of ouchies, tall, dark, and cranky is on his way. Wrath should be here—"

A buzzing sound had V taking out his Samsung Galaxy. Putting his hand-rolled between his white teeth, he scrolled into something.

"They're early."

"Who is?"

"The special request." V put his phone away. "You can stay here with your calories, if you want."

"I hadn't had a B plan, my guy."

On that note, how was it possible he only had two left? At least he had the OJ to look forward to, Rhage thought as he heard V talk to someone out in the foyer—

Gunpowder. He was smelling gunpowder.

The tray went off to the side, and he stalked across that Persian carpet, taking out the forty he kept at the small of his back. He was halfway down the room when the butler came through the flap door in the rear with a carafe of OJ.

Rhage pinned the *doggen* with a hard stare and nodded sharply to the side.

Fritz immediately bowed and backed out. Then there was a click as the butler locked the entry into the kitchen.

Emerging into the foyer, Rhage looked through the waiting area's archway and saw an older male in a red-and-black-checked flannel shirt that was way too heavy for late summer. V, who was standing next to the guy, didn't seem worried at all, so Rhage retucked his weapon. But he remained on high alert as he entered.

Across the way, in front of the seating arrangement's coffee table, a female wearing jeans and boots was lifting a loose, white, full-sleeved shirt—to reveal a whole lot of click, click, bang, bang. Yet she was disarming, her metal joining a whole host of other shootables. Clearly, the old guy had de-leaded himself first.

"Rhage," V said, "come meet a friend of mine. This is Dredrich. He taught me how to sharpen knives."

Rhage whistled under his breath as he held out his palm. "Wow. You've done all of us a favor."

The old male had mostly white hair and a lot of wrinkles on his face, but his eyes were bright and clear.

"It is an honor." Dredrich shook what was offered to him and then bowed low. "And Vishous, please forgive me for asking for special dispensation."

V shrugged. "S'all good. Tell us, what do you need? And for fuck's sake, you could have just called me privately. You didn't need to go through official channels."

"I did not want to be a burden." The old male held out a bundle wrapped in gray. "Allow me first to return this to you."

V accepted whatever it was, unwrapping things with quick, sure hands—one of which, as always, sported a lead-lined black leather glove.

"Well, well, well," the brother said as he palmed up a black dagger. "I've been missing this."

"You left it during our last lesson. You were called away. I kept thinking you'd come back for it so I kept it hidden and safe."

V's diamond eyes shifted from the black blade to the old male. Then the brother bowed. "You're a male of worth, old friend."

Meanwhile, Rhage double-checked, just because he was like that, that the female wasn't getting any bright ideas about—

471

"Hey," he said, "are those grenades?"

The older male nodded. "Yes, they are."

Just as Rhage was going to ask where the hell the pair of civilians were going with an arsenal's worth of firepower, the female turned around. As he looked at her to get a read on things, her face drained of all color.

"Hey, hey . . ." He lunged forward to catch her in case she fainted. "Let's sit you down—"

With a shaking hand, she reached up and grabbed his shoulder.

"What?" he said. Then he noticed the healing scar at her hairline and a bruise on the side of her jaw. "Do you need a doctor?"

"I need your help." Her voice was threaded with emotion. "Oh, God, we need your help. Your brother needs your help."

It was the eyes. The incredible blue eyes, the aquamarine blue eyes that Nyx had never seen on any other people. But Jack. And Peter.

And now, this member of the Black Dagger Brotherhood.

"Please," she said, aware that she was shaking. "We need your help."

The warrior locked a gentle hold on her arm, like he expected her to pass out. "Can we get you some medical attention? You've clearly got some—"

Emotion vibrated up from the center of her

chest, making her talk too fast. "Jack, you need to help Jack—"

"—bruising on your face, and this wound on—"

"—in the prison. Jack is—"

"Who is Jack?"

"The Jackal." Even though she didn't know the Brother, she could see recognition flare behind his eyes. "Yes, him. Your blooded brother."

"I don't have any blooded brothers." The warrior shook his head slowly. "I'm really sorry, but you've got me confused with someone else."

The other Brother, the one with the goatee and the tattoos by his temple, spoke up. "Okay, okay, let's take this one drama bomb at a time. What prison are we talking about?"

Nyx looked over at the fighter. "The *glymera*'s. The one that is out west, close to where I live."

"Say what?" The Brother stabbed his cigarette out in the ashtray he'd brought in with him. "I thought that place had closed down years ago."

"The hell it's closed down." Nyx stepped free of the blond Brother's hold because she didn't want him to think she was physically weak. Which she wasn't. "I've been down in it for the last few days."

The other Brother narrowed his cold, diamond eyes on her. "Why would you, as a free citizen, choose to go there?"

"To find my sister. I've been looking for her for fifty years."

A black-gloved hand raised. "Hold up. Who did you go with?"

"I went alone. The entrances are all hidden. I found one behind an abandoned church. I thought my sister had been falsely—well, it doesn't matter. She's dead. She died there."

"And how did you meet up with the Jackal?" the Brother with the brilliant blue eyes asked.

"He was down there. And he's still down there—even though we believe they are trying to abandon the place. There are about a thousand prisoners as well as some kind of manufacturing thing. But I don't know many details about that part of it."

"How did you get out?" the goateed one asked.

"The Jackal . . ." Nyx cleared her throat and looked down at her boots, realizing for the first time that they had dried bloodstains on them. "He helped me. He got me into a hidden tunnel that he'd made himself. I followed it to the surface, and then my grandfather happened to come upon me."

"Happened" didn't really cover it. It turned out that her grandfather had spent the days fixing the Volvo and the nights scouring a fifty-mile radius on foot, on mountain bike, and finally in the station wagon, when it was operational. He had been determined to find her. Thank God.

"Why's this Jackal still down there?" the goateed Brother demanded.

Nyx glanced at the warrior with the bright blue eyes. Even though he was staying quiet, he knew something. She could just sense it.

"He wouldn't leave," she said.

"It's a prison. Not a lot of free choice when it comes to the exit."

"He was special. I mean, he was a different case down there. There were extenuating circumstances."

"Why." The goateed Brother was like a polygraph that lived and breathed, his attention fixated on her like he was reading every nuance of her facial expression as well as the pounding pulse in the jugular at the side of her neck. "And if he won't leave of his free will, why do you think he needs rescuing. Because that's what you're here for, right? You want us to rescue him."

"No," she countered sharply. "*I'm* going to rescue him. We just thought the King might want to know that a thousand prisoners are on the move, and many of them are in custody under false pretenses—"

"You and your granddad are not going into that prison, abandoned or otherwise."

Nyx lifted her chin at the goateed warrior. "You can't stop me."

"The fuck I can't, female—"

"Here you go again, V," someone interrupted, "making friends and influencing people. What

475

are you putting your foot down about now? She buying an iPhone after she leaves here or some shit?"

Nyx glanced to the archway and did a double take. The vampire standing just inside the room was bigger than even the blond Brother who had Jack's blue eyes. With long, waist-length black hair falling from a widow's peak, and wrap-around black sunglasses, he was obviously a killer. But the enormous black diamond on his middle finger meant he was . . .

"The King," she whispered.

A black brow lifted up over the top of the wrap-arounds. "Last I checked, that's right. And you are?"

CHAPTER FORTY-THREE

*W*ell, that escalated quickly.

About thirty minutes later, as Rhage re-formed in the middle of a bowling-alley-flat scrub brush meadow, the Ron Burgundy meme was going through his head. Then again, hard to think what else applied considering he had been up to his elbows in Danish, and now he was here. Wherever the fuck "here" was.

Looking around the valley and at the highway that ribboned through the low area between two pipsqueak mountains, he had a gut twist going on—but the uneasiness was not connected in the slightest to this stretch of ground that made him think of an old guy's tufted, balding head. It also wasn't about the mission they were on.

Okay, fine, not everything about the mission.

"So you did know the male," V whispered as the brother materialized right beside him. "This Jackal?"

"I haven't heard that name in a century." Rhage kept his voice down as he glanced at V. "He worked with Darius for a little bit. I met him only briefly—and my born brothers are all dead. I was the only one of my sire's male offspring to survive. So I don't know what the fuck she's talking about."

Reaching back through the years, he tried to picture the gentlemale in question. It had been a long time, a good century, but his memory was sharp enough. He remembered that asshole Jabon and the young female—what the hell had her name been?—and the *mahmen*. The peach dressing gown with the stains. The scenes in the middle of Jabon's formal receiving area in that tool's crowded meat shop of a house.

And then Rhage had an image of meeting the Jackal that first night he'd come down from that infernal guest bedroom. The guy had been in the parlor. Ready to talk with Darius.

The male had done a double take as soon as he'd looked over.

"All my born brothers are dead," Rhage repeated.

As the others arrived, one by one, he remembered another thing: the conviction that, when he'd been introduced to the Jackal, he had known the male from somewhere.

What if he hadn't seen the Jackal before in the hi-how're-ya sense, though. What if it was his own face that he recognized in the other male's? At the time, he'd been so poleaxed by recovering from his beast coming out that he'd been drained and exhausted. Mental connections that should have been made maybe hadn't been.

Like the fact that the pair of them looked a lot alike.

"Rhage? Where you gone, Hollywood?"

Shaking himself, he glanced at V. "Sorry. I'm back."

Z and Phury had materialized to the site, their guns out and down by their sides. And the female, Nyx, and her grandfather, Dredrich, were standing next to what looked like a nothing-special patch in the middle of the ugly nothing-special acreage.

"Over here," the female said, motioning to the ground.

Rhage and the brothers came across as she lowered herself onto her knees and clawed at the loose ground. Underneath, a trapdoor with a circle pull was exposed to the moonlight. When Nyx went to lift it up, the brothers interceded to help.

She was tough, Rhage had to give her credit. And she'd obviously had quite a time down underground, her limp and the fading injuries on her face and head the kind of thing that bothered him deeply because they were on a female. If she'd been male? Sure, fine, whatever. But he was never going to be comfortable with the opposite sex being all battered and fucked-up, and if that made him a throwback, fine. People could kiss his antiquated ass.

Standing over the hole in the earth, Rhage trained a flashlight into the dense darkness. There was a steep slope to the passageway, the decline disappearing out of sight.

"I'll go first," he said.

"And I'm after you." When everybody looked at Nyx, her face was set in a hard line. "I'm the only one who's been in there. You can't do this without me because you'll have no fucking clue where you are, and moreover, part of the prison has collapsed, so it's very dangerous. You need me."

Well. That just about covered it, didn't it.

Rhage sat his ass down on the lip of the trap-door hole, his shitkickers dangling into the darkness. After a resolve not to think about red balloons and clowns, he dropped himself down and landed on a scramble, his weight taking him on a slide as loose soil rained on his head and he had to use his palms to slow his roll.

When his momentum stopped, he shined his flashlight around and saw a whole lot of stone that had been chipped away. "Someone dug this out?"

The female re-formed next to him. "Yes, he did."

"Over how many years?"

"A hundred."

Phury and Z also dematerialized down, as well as V and Nyx's grandfather. The passageway was narrow, so it was a single-file situation, and he stayed in front with the female right behind him, the sounds of creaking leather and shuffling boots loud in the silence. Everyone had a gun in their hand, and he was reminded of how much he didn't like working with civilians. He had no idea what the skills of that pair were, although so far, they were calm and focused. And very comfortable with metal against their palms.

Soon enough, his flashlight became immaterial as a single bulb flared to life and then they reached a no go as they came up to solid wall.

"Let me by," Nyx said as she pushed him out of the way and patted around.

She must have hit something because a panel slid back—and the bouquet that reached Rhage's nose was a whole lot of unpleasant: Damp air, mold . . . and blood.

The latter was faint, but it was present and of complex derivation.

A lot of vampires were dead.

The tunnel they progressed through next was broader, and the female seemed to know where to go. The blood smell got thicker, and so did the faded scents of males and females. There were no obvious sounds.

No talking. No running. No screaming.

The silence in the labyrinth was what eerie'd him out the most. And shit, it was a big place. So many halls and branches of tunnels, all of this just under the surface of the earth, away from prying eyes—human and vampire. When Nyx had talked about a thousand prisoners, he'd assumed she was exaggerating.

Now? He could see it. Totally.

They ran into their first body when they came out of one of the tunnel's turns. Beneath the bald bulbs strung from wire on the ceiling, the loosely clothed female was lying facedown on the rock floor, her feet crossed, one arm outstretched with the fingers scratched into the ground.

The blood was strong, but they didn't stop to roll her over and find the wounds. She was gone.

More bodies started to show up the farther they went. Two. Three. A fourth and fifth together. All in brown/gray/black tunics and baggy pants.

Animals, he thought—and not in disrespect to the deceased. The prisoners had existed like animals down here, never seeing the moonlight or taking fresh air. This was an atrocity. How had they let this go on for so long?

"Who was in charge here?" he asked out loud.

Nyx glanced at him. Then cleared her throat. "The Command."

"Is that a warden?"

"Kind of. But from what I understand, it wasn't an official position, sanctioned by the *glymera*. It was a created authority, one that was taken by force and intimidation, as the aristocrats lost interest in the prison."

"Lost interest? Are you fucking kidding me? Like this is a toy they got bored with?" Goddamn, he hated aristocrats. "And the Command was a prisoner, you mean?"

"Yes," she answered. "A prisoner who took over, gathering power and control and using it to their own ends."

Rhage shook his head. "This is fucking awful. We should have done something—but we didn't know. Fuck, Wrath is going to lose it."

"The Command didn't want to be found."

"How the hell did they feed everyone?"

Nyx stopped. Looked around. Leaned forward so she could see around a corner. "Okay, so the barricade is gone."

"What barricade?"

The female went over to the wall and ran her free hand up a vertical stripe. "It's been retracted." She seemed to refocus. "The prison was on lockdown as I left. Most of the tunnels were blocked so that you could only go into certain areas. But that's been lifted now."

"So someone's still here?" V said.

"I don't know," the female murmured as she looked to what was ahead. "I have no idea."

In the end, although Nyx did her best to lead everyone to the Command's private quarters, she got turned around, and only figured out the miscalculation when she took the group into what had to be the work area.

Hoping to find Jack somewhere, anywhere, she pushed through a pair of steel doors that seemed like they belonged in a human hospital—and discovered a disordered work area the size of a soccer field. Long tables were out of alignment and chairs were toppled over. Stray plastic baggies littered the floor and there were scales here and there.

The kind you used for measuring food portions.

Except there was a lot of suspicious-looking white powder dusting them.

Shit. Drugs, she thought.

The goateed Brother walked over to one of the few tables still on its four legs and picked up a tiny plastic bag that was filled with something that appeared to be facial powder or flour. Licking his pinkie, he put his finger inside, then sucked off the residue.

Peeling his lips back, he licked his front teeth. "Cocaine. And maybe something else."

"Makes sense," the blond Brother murmured as he walked around, his enormous shitkickers crushing anything he happened to step on. Spoons, baggies, scales. Hell, she was pretty sure, given his size, he could ruin a table. "It's a perfect commerce system if you want to stay under the radar. Unregulated by humans with endless demand and a great profit margin."

"Plus if you're a vampire," another of the Brothers said, "and you're picked up for distributing? Take the cop's memories and you're home free."

"So that's how they fed everyone." Nyx went

over to the other side of the space where there was no debris at all. Instead, the floor was marked with tire tracks and oil stains. "And kept the prison going."

"Do the wholesale deals out of the country," someone murmured. "Import the shit here. Process it with the prisoners and get it out onto the streets. It's a money-making machine."

Nyx glanced back at her grandfather. As their eyes met, he shook his head sadly.

Guess Janelle had found her fortune, Nyx thought.

"There's a lot of blood right here," she said, pointing to the stained concrete she was standing on. "They were moving people and supplies out in big trucks. They also had an ambulance that looked really legit."

Walking forward, she sighted the road that disappeared out of the area. But she wasn't going to worry about all that. Old news, as it were. The trucks were gone, what guards and prisoners had been still alive as well.

They weren't why she was here anyway.

Doubling back into the processing area, she went down the side wall to another door. As she cranked the handle, she wouldn't have been surprised if it was locked—

The thing opened wide, and the scent of spilled blood was so strong, she recoiled, arching back.

She didn't have to call anyone over. The

fighters and her grandfather came immediately, the smell getting their attention.

Stepping through, she saw dead guards down on the floor—which was a surprise. But maybe it meant Jack was alive and had fought back?

"Jack!" she called out as her heart started to pound.

As her voice echoed, the blond-haired Brother took her arm and squeezed. "Shh. None of that. We don't know who's in here."

Except ultimately, the noise alert risk was immaterial. No one was alive. As she went down the finished hall, she had to step over limbs, torsos, and heads. When she came to a door, she opened it. Inside, there was a sparsely furnished bedroom, and as she looked to the bed, she frowned.

Hustling across, she picked her backpack up off the floor.

It was unzipped, and the weapons and ammo were gone. The toothbrush and the water bottle were still inside, though.

But it wasn't like she was ever using that Oral-B again.

She let the pack drop to the mattress. She had no desire to take it with her. Too many bad memories. And on that sad note, she stared at the messy fitted sheet and breathed in deep. Underneath the scent of spilled blood, there was a heavy undertone.

Of sandalwood. And Jack's scent.

It had happened here. Jack had been chained down . . . here.

As it became hard to breathe, she wheeled around. The Brothers were talking. Her grandfather was checking out some medical stuff left on a table.

She couldn't stand to be inside the room for one more second.

Stumbling back out into the hall, she looked to the left and quickly walked in that direction.

"Hey, wait up," the blond Brother said.

Dimly, in the recesses of her mind, she tried to remember what he'd said his name was. She couldn't recall it—or any of the others', though she knew for a fact they'd all been introduced before they'd left the Audience House. The goateed male. The one with the skull trim and the facial scar. The one with the amazing multicolored hair.

And the blond one with Jack's eyes, who was catching up to her.

Just as she arrived at the cell that was nicely furnished.

Its entry panel was wide open, the iron bars with their steel mesh having swung free of the jambs. Inside, around the hotel-homey setup of furniture, there was blood . . . everywhere.

As she breathed in, she tried to sort through and see if it was Jack's. Had the Command somehow survived the collapse? Found her way back here?

Had they fought?

Nyx's heart started to skip beats and she backed out of the cell. Blindly turning away, she started walking without really tracking where she was going—

Her body stopped before she was aware of anything registering in her mind.

And then she saw it. Down on the floor.

A tangle of long red hair.

Which was matted with blood and . . . something else. Something terrifying.

A sudden surge of paranoia made her eyes skip around at the other bodies. But they were all uniformed. None were in prison clothes. So none were Jack.

"What is it?" the Brother said.

She glanced over her shoulder and said softly to him, "Take my grandfather back out to the work area. Make an excuse."

"We're not splitting up—"

"Please." She pointed to the floor. "This is my sister, and I don't want him to have to see her. Just take him away. I'll hide the body."

The Brother shook his head. "I can't leave you. But I'll handle it."

In spite of his size, he hurried back quick, said something to the goateed fighter, and just-likethat, her grandfather was rerouted out of the Command's private area with the other two Brothers.

Taking a deep breath, Nyx glanced around. Back inside the furnished cell, there was a throw blanket of good size that had been draped over the back of a stuffed chair. Tucking her gun away, she went in and got it, and then with shaking hands, she gently wrapped Janelle's remains in the soft crimson and black folds.

She did not look at the injuries directly. Her peripheral vision told her enough.

Sitting back on her heels, she wiped her forehead with her sleeve. Then she gathered her sister in her arms and walked down the corridor, sidestepping the bodies. As she went along, she was aware of the goateed Brother and the blond one with the blue eyes following her solemnly.

Nyx went to the Wall.

As she approached the long list of inscribed names, she willed candles to light, and she was looking at the rows of symbols in the Old Language as she came to a stop.

She laid Janelle at the foot of the memorial and stepped back.

Crossing her arms, she stared at the wrapped body . . . and then she focused on her sister's name in the lineup.

After a moment, she nodded and turned away. She said nothing to either of the Brothers as she passed them by, powerful sentries who fell into her wake once more without a word.

She had a feeling they had seen a lot of death over the course of their lives.

So they knew just how to act.

As Nyx walked off, she willed the candles to extinguish their flames one by one. Until there was nothing but a shroud of darkness over her sister's final resting place.

CHAPTER FORTY-FOUR

In the end, Nyx did not find what she had come looking for.

It was kind of a theme with the prison, wasn't it. The first time she had gone underground, she'd been searching for Janelle—and ultimately been denied. The second time? No Jack, anywhere.

As she reemerged aboveground, coming out of his handmade passageway, she walked off without any direction . . . eventually making circles around one particular bush that had all the grace and beauty of a porcupine. Full of prickers and with leaves the color of dust, it seemed like the right kind of proverbial sun to orbit.

Given how she was feeling.

The Brothers and her grandfather came out as well, and the males stood together and talked, hands on hips, heavy-jawed faces nodding in the way males did when they had seen and done something serious.

She let them go.

She had different problems than they did.

While they were discussing options for clearing out the bodies, and then strategies for finding where the prison had gone, she was steaming angry.

The rage—wait, that was the blond Brother's name, wasn't it—the Rhage she was feeling was out of line, but undeniable. And it took her at least three trips around her bush to realize where it was coming from.

No body.

Jack's body hadn't been down there. Not in the Command's private area, and not when she had insisted on going farther into the partially collapsed Hive.

So he had left with the rest of the prisoners. Or he was somewhere in the tunnel system—either avoiding her or maybe dying.

Or he was out in the world. Without her.

Whatever it was, she couldn't find him—and she was pissed off. Damn it, if he had only come with her. If he had put that secret tunnel to use with her, he could have had exactly what he'd been looking for—

"Nyxanlis?"

At the sound of her formal name, she shook herself back to attention. Her grandfather had come over, and he was looking as if he wasn't sure whether her brain had broken.

"I'm fine?" She put it as a question because she wasn't sure what he had asked her. Wasn't sure that she actually was "fine."

"We're going to the farmhouse. All of us."

"Okay." As her eyes went to the trapdoor, she saw that one of the Brothers was kicking earth over the panel, keeping it hidden. "I'll come with."

Like she had any other place to go?

One by one, the Brothers dematerialized, and she had a thought about what Posie was going to do when these warriors with their black daggers strapped handles down on their huge barrel chests showed up in the side yard.

She'd better go now so she could help with the inevitable hospitality that would be offered, Nyx thought as she ghosted out . . .

. . . and yet as she traveled in a scatter of molecules, she did not head home.

She rerouted.

When she resumed her corporeal form, it was in front of the abandoned church, the place she had gone at the start of everything, the clue that the pretrans—now known as Peter—had given her.

Moonlight fell over the chipped clapboards and penetrated through the arched window cutouts where those stained glass windows had once been.

Taking out a burner phone, she texted her sister just so no one worried when she didn't show up immediately. She didn't give her location, though.

She needed a minute.

As that Brother with the blue eyes went back to meet what had to be his nephew for the first time, maybe she should have been there. But Posie had taken care of the young, and it was clear a strong

493

bond had formed between the pair of them. She would handle things.

Nyx silenced her phone and started walking. She stopped halfway down the flank of the church and remembered dematerializing up to the sill to peer down into the tangled roof collapse.

Continuing on, she went to the cemetery and pulled open the gate.

In and among the headstones, there was a scorch mark in the earth a good seven feet long and four feet wide, all the ground cover burned away, the soil black as night, the graves around it charred on their edges. She'd been right about one thing, then. The guard had gone up in smoke when the sun had come out.

The crypt's door was solidly shut, and she had a random thought that that stone panel had gotten more action in the last few days than the previous couple of decades: Peter. Herself. The guard. And there must have been other guards from the prison who had come out to check on things. That was what had led to the shut-down.

She wasn't sure why she had to go in. It wasn't like there had been anything inside the crypt except the sarcophagus. But for her peace of mind—assuming she ever found any of that ever again—she had to retrace her steps tonight.

That was the only way she was going to make it through the day, stuck indoors with nothing but her incessant thoughts, her dragging sadness, and this irrational anger that—

At first, she wasn't sure what she was looking at.

As she pulled the heavy door open, and the hinges creaked, and the interior was revealed . . . there appeared to be a pile of clothes in the far corner down on the dusty marble floor.

Clothes that were the color of shadows.

And that was when she caught the scent.

"Jack!" she screamed as she rushed in.

CHAPTER FORTY-FIVE

From out of his delirium, Jack heard his name called.

His brain told him this was significant. This was important. This . . . meant something.

But he didn't have enough energy to lift his head. Move his facedown body. Shift even an arm or a foot. He'd been bleeding for quite a while now, ever since—

"Jack, oh, God, *Jack* . . ."

Gentle hands rolled him over on his side, and that was when his eyes provided him with a vision he had been praying for. The visage above him was that of an angel, an inexplicable angel. His female. His beloved female.

Nyx was talking to him, her mouth moving, her eyes wide and scared. And though he wanted to reassure her, he couldn't seem to speak.

It was all right, though. Even if this last moment was all he had?

His prayers had been answered. All he had wanted, as he had lain here dying, was to see his female one last time. And here she was—

Nyx was putting something to her ear. A device of some sort, thin and glowing. And she was talking into it, urgently.

Then she put whatever it was away in a pocket,

pulled back her sleeve, and bared her fangs. For a moment, he was confused—and then he realized . . .

No, he thought. She didn't have to. It was enough that she was here, although he would have spared her witnessing his last moments if he could have—

Abruptly, the scent of her blood reached his nose, and it stirred something deep within him, a heat, a drive . . . something vital.

She put the puncture wounds she had bitten into her own flesh to his mouth, and he meant to say no. He intended to turn her generosity away . . . because the last thing he wanted was her trying to save him, failing, and having to live with some misplaced sense of blame.

But the instant her blood dropped onto his lips, his survival instinct took over.

Jack latched on and drank deep, swallowing what she gave him, nursing at the source of strength. As he swallowed the heavenly wine of her blood, electricity flowed through his body, animating him within moments. And her taste was so good, so overpowering, that he closed his eyes so he could concentrate on it. Savor it. Relish it.

When he opened his lids later—it could have been two minutes or twenty—there were people with them inside the crypt, big males with black daggers on their—

Jack's eyes locked on one he recognized.

Rhage. The Black Dagger Brother, who he had not seen for . . . a century? Since he had been falsely accused.

Would there be trouble, Jack wondered. Would he be treated as an escaped prisoner?

The idea of being sent back underground was enough to get him to release the vein that was saving him.

"Jack," Nyx said. "You're not finished."

He looked up at her. He wanted to tell her no, it was fine. It was enough.

Instead, Rhage came over and knelt down. The Brother's blue eyes were so intense, they seemed to glow blue.

After a long moment of staring, the warrior rubbed his face.

"Welcome back, brother mine," he said hoarsely.

Nyx wanted to give the two males time to connect. Or was it reconnect? She had a feeling they didn't know each other well—or perhaps at all.

And given the way they were staring at each other, it was clear they were both shell-shocked.

But this was still a life or death situation.

"Jack, you have to keep drinking before we can move you and get you medical attention."

His eyes swung up to her. And then a slight smile played at his lips.

"I love you," he said on a croak.

Nyx promptly forgot about everything: The males standing around inside the crypt—including her grandfather. The fact that Jack had some kind of a raw wound on the inside of his leg that had leaked out an alarming amount of blood. The reality that they were just outside one of the prison's entrances, and if there was anyone left in there who was dangerous, they were sitting ducks.

She glanced at the Brothers. They all had weapons in their hands, and it was clear they were ready to fight.

Okay, fine. Maybe she didn't have to worry about any kind of attack with them around. But still.

Refocusing on Jack, she stroked back the hair that had loosened from his braid.

"I love you," he repeated. His voice was so weak, the words barely carried. Yet given how everyone went still, it was clear they had been heard.

"I love you, too," Nyx said as she blinked back tears. "Now please, keep drinking—"

"You had the courage to go in," he interrupted. "You . . . had the courage to go in. I needed to find the courage to get out. For you, I wanted to get out."

"You did." She caressed his hair, his face, his shoulder. And as much as she wanted to hear everything he had to say, it was more important for him to feed. "We'll talk later. Just take this—"

"No." He pushed her arm away when she tried to put her wrist back to his mouth. "I am revived enough."

As if to prove the point, he went to sit up—and to his credit, his torso did make it to the vertical. But then he looked down at the wound on his leg and wobbled.

"We need to wrap that up," the goateed Brother said. "Before you even think of moving."

There was a ripping sound, and someone passed their shirt over.

"I'll go get the station wagon," her grandfather said as he went to leave. "It'll take me ten minutes."

Damn it, Jack wasn't going to drink any more from her. Licking the wounds at her wrist closed, Nyx settled for holding his hand as he hissed and groaned while his thigh was wrapped up.

And then she was his primary support as they got him up on his feet to see if he could stand.

Which was when she noticed he had something in his hand.

It was her windbreaker. He had her windbreaker somehow.

"Pass card," he said.

Nyx glanced up his drawn face. "What?"

Lifting the windbreaker, he unhooked his arm from hers and unzipped one of the pockets. The card that came out was smudged with blood. His.

"This was in the pocket." His voice got stronger with every syllable. "When the barricades retracted, I went back to where I'd first seen you, back to where you had come in through. I'd been bitten by that animal from the basket before I killed it, and I was sure that I was going to bleed out—except as I collapsed against the wall, the exit opened. I had your windbreaker around my neck and . . . this saved me. I used it twice."

"Lean on your female," the goateed Brother ordered. "You're losing color in your face again. You're about to pass out—"

Jack went lax before the Brother finished, and Nyx caught her mate, grunting as his heavy weight had to be held up.

But she refused any help from anyone.

He was hers.

She was going to get him to the car on her own.

CHAPTER FORTY-SIX

The next thing Jack was aware of . . . was softness. Softness under his body. Under his head. Along one side of him.

His lids flipped open, consciousness returning with a speed and clarity that told him exactly how far Nyx's blood had gone to revive him. And his first thought was—

"I'm right here."

Nyx leaned forward and put her face in his line of vision. She was incredibly beautiful to him, with her dark hair pulled back, and her cheeks flushed from emotion, and her eyes glowing with unshed tears.

"Hello," he said.

"Hi." She smiled tentatively. "We have a doctor coming."

"I'm okay."

"That bite wound is really nasty. We can't risk infection."

There was a pause as they both looked at each other, re-memorizing, re-affirming, re-establishing the connection that he had been sure was broken forever.

He reached up and stroked her cheek. The side of her throat. "You're alive."

"And so are you."

Jack glanced around at the homey decor. "Is this your home?"

"It is. We're in my bedroom."

Voices percolated from somewhere close by, low and calm. He recognized some of them from the crypt. "Am I really out?"

"Yes, you're really out. You're free."

Jack took a deep breath. He wanted to celebrate—he truly did. "I'm glad," he said because he didn't want her to feel anything but joy.

He, however, had left something behind. Someone. Who he had searched for and had not found, living or dead.

Abruptly, Nyx leaned back from her kneeling position by the bed. And as she started motioning with her hand, he shook his head.

"No," Jack said. "I don't need a doctor—"

As a slight figure stepped into view, Jack thought . . .

No, no. This was so unfair.

This was a nightmare clothed in the symbols of a dream, the kind of thing that stung the heart when you woke up and realized your female was not with you and your son was still dead—

"Father?"

Jack's body began to shake and he sat up slowly, as if he might wake if he moved too fast. Shifting his feet to the rug one at a time, he paused.

When nothing changed . . . when Nyx still

seemed to be beside him, and his son still seemed to be in front of him in the doorway, he stood up. If his injury hurt as his leg bore his weight, he didn't feel it.

He took a step forward. And then another.

"Son?" he said hoarsely.

Feeling as though he were taking a chance with his own life, he opened up his arms.

"Father!"

His young raced forward and grabbed on. And as the warmth of the slight body registered, and the familiar scent flooded his nose, Jack cradled the one he had sought in an embrace that took his breath away, even as it warmed his heart.

After a moment of squeezing his eyes shut, he looked over the head of that which he had been convinced he had lost . . . to the love of his life.

Who he had never expected to find.

Nyx had to cover her mouth as she regarded the sight of Jack holding Peter to his big chest. The young was impossibly small against his father's great strength, so it seemed right that the two of them were reunited at last.

The young needed his sire's protection in this world.

Especially as they both got used to living in the up-above.

Glancing through the open doorway, she nodded at Posie and her grandfather, who were holding hands. When they ducked out of sight into the kitchen, she heard the back door open and close and guessed the Brothers were departing for now. They would return. On the car ride back home, Rhage, the blond one, had said they wanted as many details as possible about the prison and how it functioned and what kind of equipment it had.

There would be time for that later, though.

And a healer was coming any minute.

Nyx refocused on Jack and the pretrans. The two had pulled back a little and were studying each other, both clearly looking for injuries.

"Are you okay, father? Your leg is—"

"I'm going to be perfectly fine." Jack patted the young's shoulder. "But how are you here? How do you know my Nyx?"

"It was an accident, father."

"What?"

Nyx spoke up. "Posie and I were driving home—"

"And I ran out into the road," Peter chimed in.

"We hit him by mistake. It was a total accident."

"But they saved me. Posie nursed me back to health."

Yeah, on that note? Nyx was convinced that her sister had willed the pretrans to pull through: Posie had been utterly determined that he wasn't going to die on her watch, and what do you know. Even the Grim Reaper had been afraid of the female's cheerful brand of not-having-it.

"Posie's my sister," Nyx explained. "My other sister. Anyway, that was how it all started. In his delirium, your son was talking about where he had come from, where he had escaped from."

Peter looked up at his father. "I wanted them to save you. I wanted her to go back and get you out because I wasn't strong enough to."

Jack cupped his son's face in his broad hand. "You did?"

As the pretrans nodded, Nyx could only shake her head. "What can I say. It was meant to be."

When Jack held out an arm, she wasn't sure what he was doing. But then she realized . . .

Nyx got up on her feet and walked over in a daze. She paused, not wanting to crowd them, not wanting to intrude if she was somehow misreading the situation—

Peter grabbed on and pulled her in, and then Jack wrapped his big, strong arms . . . around the both of them.

This time, as tears were shed, they were of joy. Not sorrow.

And would they be thus forevermore—

Jack eased back a little. With a frown, he glanced down at Peter.

"But I don't understand one thing," he said. "How did you get out? You didn't know about my secret passageway. I never told you because I was worried it would put you in danger. I'd made it for you, so that when the time was right, I could smuggle you free."

Peter swallowed hard, and as he tilted his head, the light from the lamp on the side table hit his hair. For the first time, Nyx noticed . . . the red glowing in the dark strands.

"She let me go."

"I'm sorry?" Jack said. "What?"

"The Command. She took me from my cell outside of the schedule. It was not a mealtime. I didn't know what she was going to do. I thought I was in trouble." Peter looked anxious, as if he were reliving things that had scared him. "She took me through the prison, and opened this steel door with a card. She didn't say anything. She just kept us going, until . . . I don't know, we got to this exit I'd never seen before. She gave me a leg up, through this grate."

"She freed you herself?"

"Yes. I was so confused. The only thing she said was to go north. She told me to keep walking and go north toward the mountain. She told me to look for the white farmhouse with the big tree and the red barn. She told me . . ." Peter looked at Nyx. "That there were kind people of our species there who would take me in and care for me. Then she told me to replace the grate and . . . she disappeared."

Nyx closed her eyes briefly. She hadn't heard that part yet. Had Posie? Her grandfather?

"And she was right," Peter said as he squeezed Nyx's hand.

"Yes, there are very good people under this roof," Jack murmured. "The very best."

"Can we stay here, father?"

Nyx had to wipe both her eyes. "Yes, both of you can stay. Forever."

She smiled, even though she had a pain in the center of her chest. Why had Janelle done one last good thing? Who knew. Maybe the love of a *mahmen* for her young had been enough to override the rest of her nature, in that one decision. In that one moment.

But Nyx was never going to know the full truth of it and it didn't matter anymore. She had her two males, and she was going to take care of them both: Her one true love and her nephew. For all the nights and days she had upon this earth, and all the eternity up above in the Fade, she was going to watch over them.

Indeed, Destiny had mapped this all out beforehand.

It was the only way to explain it.

CHAPTER FORTY-SEVEN

The following evening, Nyx woke up in her little bed with Jack right beside her. Rolling over in the darkened room, she discovered that he was already awake, his eyes hooded and hot as he stared at her.

"Have something on your mind, my male?" she whispered.

"Yes."

When he leaned in for a kiss, she met him more than halfway. And they were quick and silent with the undressing. Everyone else in the house was downstairs, sleeping in the cozy quarters Posie had made underground for Peter's protection, and the relative privacy of the first floor wasn't going to last.

So yes, it was fast off with the clothes, and rough with the hands, and then Jack was mounting her and she was taking him inside. He bit his lip with his sharp fangs as they were joined, and she clawed at his back as they began to move together, his long, beautiful hair silky and lush around her. Then they were kissing again and things were moving faster—and God, she hoped the bedsprings didn't creak.

It didn't take long to find a release. For either of them.

And they kept going. One more time. One more quick, intense time on both sides.

Then they had to stop.

Jack looked down into her eyes as he stroked her hair back. "I want to do this properly sometime."

"Yes, please," she murmured. "And as soon as possible."

They were laughing as they pulled apart, and she quickly disappeared into the bathroom and hit the shower. She wished Jack was with her. But there would be time for that.

And she was willing to be patient. Up to a point.

When she emerged with fresh clothes and clean hair, he was sitting at the kitchen table, looking around at the appliances. The counters. The TV that was mounted on the wall.

"I do recognize some of this," he said.

"Is it really strange?"

"Yes, it feels . . . truly bizarre."

Nyx went over and sat across from him. When his eyes eventually settled on her, she could tell he was in a bad place.

"Talk to me," she prompted.

It was a while before he spoke, and she prayed—*prayed*—that whatever it was had time to get expressed before anyone came up from the basement.

"It's about the Command," he said. "Your sister."

Nyx dropped her head. Shook it from side to side. "I am so sorry. I feel like I have to apologize for everything she did. She was a monster."

"I want you to understand . . ." He cleared his throat. "How it started between us. When she, ah, when she came into the prison, she was looking for a mentor. She had a manipulative way about her, and I'll admit that, for a time, there was an attraction for me. But that faded fast as I learned who she really was. As I pulled back, she got more attached until I became an obsession for her. Peter—by the way, I love that name—came about when I was forced to service her needing. It was right after that that she began to take control. I'd often wondered . . . well, I don't know what the hell was going through her brain a lot of the time, but it was almost like she had to make it safe for him. She mostly took control for her own reasons, of course, but young in that environment? Almost none survive. Again, though, with her, ascribing any altruistic motivation may well be a mistake."

Nyx nodded. Then she reached across the table and held Jack's hand. "Any time you want to talk about anything, I'm always here."

"Thank you." He rubbed his face. "I also need you to know how she died."

"I found her body."

"You did?"

"I disposed of it properly and with respect. Even though . . . I don't know, it's complicated."

"You did the right thing. For Peter's *mahmen*." Jack went quiet again for a moment. Then he cleared his throat. "She told me she'd killed him. Peter, that is. I don't know why. Probably to make me suffer."

When he couldn't seem to go on, Nyx had a feeling what had happened.

"It's okay if you killed her," she said softly.

"How can you say that?" He cursed. "You should hate me for killing a member of your bloodline. And Peter . . . Peter can never know."

"She hurt you. On purpose. She hurt a lot of people—killed them, tortured them. I have to be honest. I don't feel anything about her being dead except for relief. Well, and confusion. But as you said, who knows what was going on inside of her."

Jack stared off into space. "She was covered with blood. She had a heart she had ripped out of someone's chest in her hand. She was screaming at me about killing him. I just . . . I snapped. I grabbed her around the throat and just banged her into the wall over and over again. And then that animal—the one who bit me—ended up attacking her. I got free because she was . . ."

"It's okay. It's all okay, I promise. You didn't do anything wrong."

Jack stared into her eyes. "I love you."

Nyx squeezed his hand again. "Right back at you, my love."

As he leaned in to kiss her, she leaned in as well. And just as their lips met, footsteps began to ascend from the cellar.

Nyx stroked the side of her male's face and then let herself fall back into her seat. As Posie and Peter and her grandfather emerged from down below, she reflected that among all the phrases in all the languages in all the world, there was one that never lost its luster, no matter how many times it was spoken.

"I love you" never got worn out.

Whether it was between parents and children, sisters and brothers, or people who had a romantic connection, those three little words were as strong, as vital, as steadfast and enduring . . . as the powerful emotion they described.

"I love you" was immortal.

Even death couldn't fade those words. And for vampires, who existed in the darkness, they were the golden sunlight that kept the species warm and alive.

CHAPTER FORTY-EIGHT

Exactly one hour after Jack enjoyed a delicious First Meal of eggs, bacon, and toast with his family, the sixteen-seat bus that had been sent to collect them arrived. The Black Dagger Brotherhood's vehicle had blacked-out windows, comfortable leather seating, and a traditionally dressed butler behind the wheel.

The trip to their destination took a while. And in the roomy back area, behind the partition that had been raised, they passed the four hours talking about everything and nothing at all. Posie, Nyx's sister, had a sweet disposition, and there was true fondness between her and Peter, a brother/sister connection that had been born out of the healing she had helped him through. The grandfather was a hoot. Dry as the desert, quiet as a library, smart as an encyclopedia. You couldn't not like him.

And then there was his Nyx. Who was perfect in all ways as far as Jack was concerned.

Time flew, and suddenly, they were on some kind of ascent. Jack squeezed Nyx's hand and tugged her closer to him on the bench seat.

He had spent a lot of time stealing glances at her, and he knew he was not ever going to get tired of the sight of her. The sound of her. Her scent and her laugh, her smile and her secret little flushes—which cropped up whenever he went to naked places in his mind. It was as if she knew exactly what he was thinking of.

Which was often, but always discreetly.

When the bus stopped, the butler put down the partition and smiled at them all, his elderly face radiating warmth and good nature. "We have arrived! Please do depart the vehicle at your leisure."

Jack was content to let the others go first— because it allowed him to sneak a kiss from his female. And then she was shuffling out and he was in her wake, the pair of them going down the center aisle and descending some short steps onto cobblestones that—

Jack tightened his hold on his female's hand.

As he looked up . . . up . . . way up . . .

"He built it," Jack breathed as he took in the breadth and height of the magnificent stone mansion that he himself had designed and labored over in his mind. "He *built* the house."

The great gray manse was exactly as Jack had envisioned it, from the complicated roofline, to the two wings, to the enormous center core that rose up to the heavens—

The grand double doors opened wide, and Rhage, the Brother with the bright blue eyes, came out. With him was a brunette female and a pretrans young who had to be their daughter.

Jack felt his throat close up with emotion.

Walking forward with Nyx and Peter, Posie and Grandpapa, as Peter called the older male, Jack felt as though he was bringing his family . . . to meet the Brother's.

His brother's.

"Have a good ride?" Rhage said.

"Yes. We did."

As Jack surmounted the stone steps, he kept staring at the Brother while the Brother stared back at him, both of them frozen.

The females did the intros, Nyx and Mary, Rhage's *shellan*, stepping forward, hugging each other, hugging everyone, the melding happening.

Even as Rhage and Jack stayed where they were.

"I'm just going to take the kids inside?" Mary said to her *hellren*. "We'll let you two have a minute out here, 'kay?"

Rhage seemed to shake himself. "Hey, would you mind taking the kids inside so that Jack and I can have a moment?"

The female smiled at him. "I'd love to. What a good idea. Come on, Nyx. Have you all had anything to eat? We have food here like you wouldn't believe."

Nyx hesitated. When Jack squeezed her hand, she nodded, kissed him quick, and followed the others inside.

And then he was alone with the Brother.

"So . . ." Rhage cleared his throat. "You feeling

better? You know, after a good day's sleep?"

"Oh, yes. Much. Thank you for asking."

And then . . . nothing.

Until they both spoke at the same time.

"I'm sorry, I know this is weird—"

"Please forgive me, I don't mean to—"

They both laughed. And then Jack said, "Who was your father? When I first saw you at Jabon's, I had a thought in the back of my mind that perhaps we were related. I wanted to follow up on it, but I didn't know who to trust, and I was a stranger to you."

"My sire was the Black Dagger Brother Tohrture. He was a brave and proud warrior."

Jack shook his head. "I've never heard the name. My *mahmen* never told me who my father was, but there were rumors he might have been a Brother. When I pressed her on the issue, she forbade me to ever go to Caldwell. That was why . . . well, she had her reasons, I guess."

"My sire was not formally mated unto my *mahmen*. And yes, I got my eye color from him." Rhage shrugged helplessly. "I was told all of my blooded brothers had died, but when I look in your face? Anyway, I had that flash of recognition when I met you as well, but I didn't make the connection, because I didn't think it was possible. Not with what I knew of my family."

"My *mahmen* . . . on her deathbed, she made me promise I would never go in search of my father. I have had a century to ponder it, and I believe . . . well, I think she felt as though she had had an affair with my sire. She did not want to ruin a family."

"Our sire was not mated unto my *mahmen*, as I said. So there was nothing to break up. And in any event, that is all in the past. We have now, though. We have the present. Let's start as we mean to go on, shall we?" Rhage put his palm out. "Oh, and by the way, nice to properly meet you."

Jack clasped the dagger hand that was extended to him. And then he was pulled into a hard embrace.

"Welcome to the family," Rhage announced before stepping back.

"How can you accept me so readily? Do you not want some kind of proof?"

"How many people do you know with eyes like ours? Yours, mine, and your son's?"

"Not many." Jack thought about it. "None, actually."

"There you go. We can do a Maury if you'd like, though."

"What's a Maury?"

Rhage blinked. And then clapped a hand on Jack's shoulder. "Oh, the things that are waiting for you here in this age of TV and the Internet. Now, you ready to come inside and check out what you planned with all those drawings?"

Clearing his throat, to keep the emotions down, Jack looked up again at the mansion's exterior. The leaded glass windows were glowing with light, a beautiful sight.

"It's just as I constructed it," he said. "I can't wait to speak to Darius about——"

"I'm really sorry."

Jack glanced over to ask what the low-voiced, grim apology was for. But instantly, he knew by the expression on Rhage's face what it was about.

Jack hung his head for a moment. "When did Darius die? Please tell me he got a chance to see this? It was his dream."

"He saw the house. But he was called unto the Fade before he saw it full."

"Your loss must be so great."

"Yeah. It is. And it happened not so long ago." Rhage indicated the entry. "Come on, you've got to want to see everything."

Nodding, Jack followed the Brother into a vestibule. "When did construction start?"

"Right after you . . ." Rhage stopped and pivoted around. "Look, I gotta clear this up. I didn't know what happened to you. Where you ended up, that is. Jabon was a weak piece of shit, and I was just done with him after that night. You've got to know that I had no idea he was turning you in to the Council. If I had known, I would have told them what I knew to be fact. That you did not dishonor that young female.

That you are a male of worth who would never do such a thing."

Jack bowed. "I appreciate you saying this. But I took for granted all that was true. Jabon was the bad one in it all. I don't even blame that daughter and the *mahmen*."

"If the aristocrat weren't dead already, I'd kill the fucker. In fact, I'm considering digging him up just so I can murder him all over again?"

"Did he die by violent means?"

"Two females killed him about twenty-five years after the incident involving you." Rhage leaned in. "When they found the body, they couldn't locate his courting tackle, if you know what I mean."

Jack winced. "Wow."

At that moment, there was a buzzing and the sound of a lock freeing. And then the vestibule doors were opened wide by the butler who'd driven the bus to Caldwell.

"Greetings!" the *doggen* said. As if he had not seen Jack for twelve years and Jack was the most honored guest who had ever been invited over the threshold.

"Thank you," Jack murmured as he stepped into—

He stopped dead just inside the door. The foyer, with its marble columns and its grand staircase, its three-story-high ceiling and its mosaic floor, was every bit as majestic as Jack had envisioned it. And the spaces on either side . . . the grand dining room with its carved archway and the billiards room over to the left.

Just as he had hoped.

Abruptly, the fact that people were all around registered—in fact, it was a very large crowd of people, including males and females along with young of all ages, and they were all standing by a huge dining table, sharing greetings and introductions with Peter, Nyx, Posie, and Grandpapa. There was such joy among them, smiles and hugs given freely, the chatter and laughter and bubbling welcome filling the huge formal room, indeed all the square footage under the slate roof, with life . . . and love.

Jack looked at Rhage. At his brother who was a Brother.

"This is just what Darius wanted."

Rhage's handsome face grew sad. "I know. His dream is our reality."

"He told me that he was building this to house everyone he loved. To give them a safe haven to raise their families in. He told me he felt like it was his legacy to leave the world."

Rhage rubbed his eyes as if they were stinging. "Yeah. Much as I doubted him at the time. . . it did come true. Just too late for him to enjoy it."

As the Brother seemed overcome with emotion, Jack put an arm around the male's thick shoulders. "Come. Let's go join them, shall we?"

"Good plan." Rhage took a deep breath. "Great plan, actually."

Together, they walked toward the dining room.

"Say," the Brother intoned, "I have a craving for some ice cream. You want to join me?"

"I happen to love ice cream, as it turns out. I had my first taste of it last evening."

"Isn't it the best?" Rhage made *mmmmm* noises. "And I'm happy to share my stash with my newfound brother. No more Rocky Road for me, though. I'm sticking with vanilla."

Entering the dining room, there was an instantaneous cheer, and the two of them were promptly overwhelmed by their mates, their family—and on Jack's side, so many new friends.

And soon thereafter . . . much dessert.

ACKNOWLEDGMENTS

With so many thanks to the readers of the Black Dagger Brotherhood books! This has been a long, marvelous, exciting journey, and I can't wait to see what happens next in this world we all love. I'd also like to thank Meg Ruley, Rebecca Scherer, and everyone at JRA, and Hannah Braaten, Andrew Nguyen, Jennifer Bergstrom, Jennifer Long, and the entire family at Gallery Books and Simon & Schuster.

To Team Waud, I love you all. Truly. And as always, everything I do is with love to, and adoration for, both my family of origin and of adoption.

Oh, and thank you to Naamah, my Writer Dog II, who works as hard as I do on my books—and the Archieball!

Center Point Large Print
600 Brooks Road / PO Box 1
Thorndike, ME 04986-0001 USA

(207) 568-3717

US & Canada:
1 800 929-9108
www.centerpointlargeprint.com